THE TAF

The final book in the *Hu*
paced, gritty thriller of (

Scores to settle. Devastation. Revenge. Suffering. Pain.
Who is in the crossfire?

Neil Sparks has a score to settle. In fact, he has several…

His first port of call when returning from France after a five year exile
is to catch up with his estranged wife. Secondly, Neil wants to even a
score with the people instrumental in his departure and thirdly, he
wants an explanation from the man who promised his marriage would
be free from hassle. The trouble is, he's not the only one with an
agenda…

Reeling after the recent devastation in her life, Tori wants an end to all
the revenge, suffering and pain. When Hunter makes the decision to
return to the Reapers it seems his decision has only brought more grief
just as she feared it would, but that is only one of her problems.
Her life, and of those around her are still blighted with Richard
Stevens' deceit, but his deeds are catching up with him and the net is
closing in from all angles – including from places he hadn't expected.

Everybody could be a target…

What readers are saying about *The Target of Lies*:

- *"…Love this author, she never disappoints…"*
- *"…Gripping from beginning to end…"*
- *"…OMG what a fantastic story…"*
- *"…Violence, gangsters and sex make for a fantastic book…"*
- *"…Another blinding read…"*
- *"…Real characters you love to hate…"*

THE TARGET OF LIES

HUNTED SERIES #3

EDIE BAYLIS

AᵗHAME
press
· LONDON ·

First published in Great Britain in 2020 by Athame Press.
This paperback edition published in 2022 by Athame Press.

Front cover design Copyright © Athame Press/Edie Baylis 2022
Front cover photography: heckmannoleg/envato.com,
twenty20photos/envato.com
Back cover photography: Steve Halama/Unsplash

ISBN 978-1-9161627-2-3
e-ISBN 978-1-9161627-1-6

Athame Press
Unit 13230 - PO Box 6945 – London – W1A 6US

1992

IT WAS AWKWARD when Hunter walked into the White Hart for the first time since leaving. The silence descending upon the room with his appearance was so thick it could have been cut with a knife.

People glanced at one another in shock and disbelief, then with amazement when Noel walked in behind, but it didn't take long before things settled back into old times.

Almost.

There was a lot of explaining to do, which Hunter had been more than ready for, but much to his surprise, Noel volunteered the information of his own part in the plans to betray the Reapers and half the town in the process. Understandably, there was hostility, but after lengthy discussion they managed to smooth things over.

Hunter expected it would take some time before the underlying unrest fully resolved, if it ever did, but much to his astonishment, it was unanimously agreed he should resume his role as the Reaper's President.

He couldn't pretend he wasn't chuffed. He was. It felt like

he'd come home, but it wasn't like he could forget why this had all come about and Noel and the Reapers were the only ones who could help in his quest for revenge.

Walking up to the bar, he deposited his empty pint glass on the beer towel. 'I'm off now, Sarah,' he smiled. 'Tori will be wondering where I am.'

Sarah nodded towards the newly attached President patch on Hunter's leather jacket. 'How do you think she'll take that?'

Hunter shrugged. 'Not too well, I don't expect, but it's what I need to do.'

Sarah swallowed uncomfortably. Tori had barely been out in the week since the funeral, preferring the little bubble she'd created where if she remained in her own little world, then perhaps everything would be ok, but it wasn't ok and never would be. It wouldn't bring her son back, neither would it help anything and Hunter stepping back into his rightful place as the Reapers' President was not something that she'd like at all.

Sarah had spent as much time with Tori as possible since the funeral last week and she, like everyone else, had been on tenterhooks when Noel had turned up that day. To kick off at a child's funeral would have been unforgiveable, but for once in his life, Noel had surprised her. In fact, he'd surprised everyone. It seemed the death of Hunter's child and the knowledge that he'd been hell bent on discovering who had really attacked Noel's mother had forced all the resentment and hidden hatred for Hunter to run out of Noel like water from a sieve.

What bothered Sarah more was what it all meant. She knew Tori was desperate for the revenge and hurt to stop. And, Jesus, the poor girl had had more than her fair share of it, but Sarah knew Hunter of old. She knew that whatever was said he'd have no intention of letting it go unpunished. Hunter may not be able to get revenge on Matt for murdering his son, but aside from Carmen, Matt's family were all involved in the pain and suffering Tori had endured and by proxy they would pay.

And then there was Jeanie - the woman who tried so hard to look after Hunter as a boy, then moved Heaven and earth to help him as a man. Although the police were still no nearer to formally identifying the remains found in the hospital incinerator, it was very much leaning towards them being hers. *Someone* in this town was responsible for her disappearance.

What a bloody mess the last few weeks had been and things would definitely now ramp up again because Hunter would be unable to let anything rest until he'd avenged these wrongs.

Watching him leave the bar, Sarah felt a strong sense of foreboding.

ONE

NEIL SPARKS LOOKED AROUND the dark room situated at the back of the club for what seemed the thousandth time since he'd returned. It was strange being back in his old office.

He'd had the niggling worry that after almost five long years away, someone else would be sitting in his office or at the very least, moved things, but it wasn't like that at all. It was *exactly* as he'd left it.

Pulling out a sheaf of paperwork from the top drawer of his large desk, he leafed through it. He didn't know where to bloody start. Well, he knew where he *wanted* to start.

From what he could see, things had been looked after well in his absence, but it was strange. After all that time masquerading as somebody else in that garish bloody French chateau it was weird getting his head around everything. He'd kept as close tabs on the firm as possible from over the pond via a telephone, but it wasn't the same as physically being somewhere, was it?

Neil smiled to himself, picturing everyone's faces when he'd casually strolled into the club last night. No one had been expecting him.

He pulled down the starched white cuffs of his expensive

shirt, making sure the gold cufflinks were facing the correct way. He hated it when things didn't line up properly.

Hearing a sharp rap at the thick wooden door of his office, Neil glanced up. 'Come,' he said, swivelling his leather desk chair around.

Neil smiled watching John Turner step into the room and wedge his big frame into the chair opposite. Both now in their fifties, John had been a great asset to him over the years, but they thought in very different ways. To ensure his plans played out in the required way, Neil knew that given the situation and the lie of the land, he must play things differently, rather than steaming straight in with all guns blazing, like he *wanted* to do. But that was ok – he liked a challenge.

John smoothed his large hand over his dark brown hair and studied Neil. It was good to have him back, but he knew the man well enough that he'd want to dive straight in where his wife and those Reaper bastards were concerned. The issue that had set off the domino effect of Neil's forced departure in the first place was down to the deal made with the then president of the Reapers, Rafe - and that was to never return. Rafe may be long dead however, it still wouldn't pay to cause another war.

What the bloody hell did it really matter if one of them was knobbing Neil's old lady, anyway? It wasn't like he'd ever wanted the woman. Hell, no. Although stunningly attractive, John knew that Carmen bird did absolutely *nothing* for Neil whatsoever. Women never did. Not that it was any of his business, but given the history with that bunch of greasy northern wankers, he fully understood what Neil's wife doing a runner on him and then screwing a Reaper *represented*. Oh yes, he got that alright. Even if Neil hated his fake marriage, it was how things looked to everyone that was important to him.

Out of all the possible people in the universe, Carmen would have to pick a bloody Reaper to bang, therefore he needed to keep a very close eye on how Neil would deal with this.

'How are you settling back in?' John asked, breaking the

silence.

'I'm taking another trip,' Neil said calmly.

John's head whipped up. 'What? You've only just got back. Where are you going?'

Neil clasped his hands and smiled slowly. 'I'm sure you can work that out?'

John sighed deeply, his worst fears realised. 'You're going after those Reapers, aren't you?'

'Relax!' Neil smiled. 'I'm not quite as impetuous as you remember. Pretending to be a fucking garlic muncher for the last five years has smoothed my edges somewhat.' *It hadn't. Not at all, but he'd make it out to be the case. For now.*

Since receiving the phone call from that Matthew ponce, he'd spent weeks vividly dreaming of all things he would do to that bitch and her bit on the side. But he wasn't lying when he said he'd be doing things differently. 'Listen, all I'm doing is checking how the land lies and get my bearings. I'm not going to start anything just yet, so you needn't worry.'

John stared at Neil. He *was* worrying. Worse - whether he worried or not wouldn't change that Neil would go regardless, which brought him to the next issue. 'We have some new staff,' he said quickly.

Neil glanced over the takings and the last couple of rosters. 'New staff? Things look like they've been running well from what I've seen so far.'

John frowned. He'd put off telling Neil the news and hoped he wouldn't find out about it. He hadn't thought a return was on the cards, let alone after such a relatively short space of time. At the end of the day *he'd* made decisions and Neil may not like what he was about to hear, but where John came from, family was important.

· · · ·

TORI MADE THE dinner and laid the little dining table in the kitchen of their small terraced house ready for when Hunter returned. She knew he'd gone to the White Hart with Noel, who he'd spent a lot of time with since Andrew's funeral.

She admitted to thinking the worst when Noel had emerged between the trees as they'd walked away from their son's graveside. She'd truly believed he'd come to cause trouble, but she'd been wrong.

When Hunter assured her Noel had come to make amends, Tori had been immediately suspicious. There had been so much bad blood between them. If it hadn't been for Noel blackmailing Hunter, then she may never have found out the truth about her father's murder.

Tori swallowed hard, unsure which was worse. Knowing or not knowing. It didn't matter, because she *knew* and regardless of whether she wished she didn't know that the man she loved had wrongly murdered her father, she did. And she was trying her best to deal with it.

Tori knew Hunter felt cheated out of revenge on the true target for his initiation hit, but despite his constant searching to rectify his mistake in the only way now available, that had been thwarted discovering the real culprit had died six months ago.

Tori had been glad. Hurting someone else wouldn't bring her father or son back, would it?

Her life had hit rock bottom when Andrew died. Her husband murdering her baby when he discovered Hunter was the father was the last straw and not a second went past when she didn't think about it. She didn't think she'd *ever* get over it.

Tori opened the cupboard, retrieved two glasses and placed them on the table with shaking hands. Her nerves were shot to pieces. Well and truly shot, not helped by Hunter's incessant rage of also being unable to take vengeance on Matt for killing their new-born because the hateful man had beat him to it by killing himself.

That left Richard, her father-in-law and the man who had orchestrated her forced marriage to Matt in the first place. Richard had been fundamental in *all* of her problems from the off and she despised him, but she just wanted to get on with her life now – what there was of it. Hunter didn't though - he wanted to make people *pay* and she didn't quite believe him when he'd said he wouldn't go looking for trouble.

The most important thing now was no more pain. Enough people had suffered and she couldn't deal with any more. Hunter's promise of no further repercussions was the only thing holding her upright at the moment.

Tori sighed. Hunter was far from levelling with her when he said he'd leave things be, but she needed him to. She didn't want to be governed by hatred, malice and revenge anymore.

Tori stared at the wall, drifting off into space. She'd spent a lot of time like that recently, despite knowing she needed to carry on. She admitted she was just going through the motions. *Everything was meaningless.*

People kept promising her that things would improve, saying she'd start to feel better eventually and it had only been a few weeks.

Except she didn't. She felt every bit as hollow and desolate as the day she found out her son was dead.

She'd tried to pull herself together and had even managed it for a while. That was until Hunter had begun associating with the Reapers again. And along with everything else, the question kept resurfacing whether she'd *ever* be able to reconcile in her own mind what he'd done to her father.

She *wanted* to reconcile it. She wanted to somehow make this work. She had to, otherwise all of this would be even more pointless than it already felt.

Sweat beaded at the back of Tori's neck and her heart raced uncontrollably. Taking deep breaths to control the familiar panic, she leant against the cool kitchen wall, reminding herself that Hunter was only *talking* to the Reapers. It wasn't like he was *part* of it again.

If she concentrated on that and remembered how she'd felt without him, then maybe they could somehow come to terms with and move past the last few months' awful chain of events. It wouldn't change anything, but it might make living with these things more bearable.

Hearing the sudden roar of Hunter's motorbike, Tori swiped her hair away from her face and busied herself with getting the dinner she'd plated up out of the oven.

Things would get better. Hunter had said so, hadn't he? *Everyone* had said so. She just had to be patient with herself and refrain from falling apart in the interim.

With her hands in oven gloves, Tori pulled one of the plates out and laid it on the table as Hunter strode into their kitchen. Regardless of anything else, she'd never tire of looking at this beautiful man even if she was sometimes unsure how she felt about him – or *anything* any longer.

'Dinner smells nice.' Hunter kissed Tori and placed his crash helmet on the table.

Forcing a smile, Tori pulled the second plate from the oven, but turning to place it on the table, her eyes locked on the back of Hunter's leather jacket hung over a chair.

The President Patch.

She was unable to stop the plate slipping from her hands and smashing on the tiled floor.

TWO

LILLIAN SLAMMED THE PAPER down on the coffee table, her magenta lips twitching in suppressed fury. 'I cannot believe they've published this!' she spat.

She'd wondered why she'd got the cold shoulder when she'd waved to Isobel Gristhorpe in Waitrose this morning, but now it made sense. 'It's supposed to be drinks evening tonight. How can I go when we're clearly the talk of the town?' Lillian wailed.

Susan's bouffant hair quivered. Did Lillian really think coming round here, moaning about how horrified she was over some small talk possibly compared to what *she* was going through? But that was Lillian all over, wasn't it? Self-obsessed. At least Lillian still had a daughter, whereas *she'd* lost her son for *ever*. Finding Matthew dead had been the worst day of Susan's life. Even worse, dare she say it, than the day her darling grandson died.

'It involves you too, Susan,' Lillian sniped. 'What my treacherous daughter has done also brings shame on your family.' If what the newspaper said was true, then Victoria was living with a biker. *A biker.* And one from that club the whole town was terrified of. She could barely believe it. How the hell could Victoria do this? And so soon after losing dearest Matthew and their child. *Despicable, that's what it was.*

She would never forgive Victoria. Never in a million years. The girl couldn't have cared a jot for her child, otherwise how could she have moved on so quickly from the boy's father? Poor Matthew; so successful, so handsome... He had everything to look forward to and her daughter – her evil daughter had driven him to his death. *Oh Matthew, Victoria wasn't worth it. You could have done so much better.*

Lillian seethed. Her daughter's actions had all but cancelled out everything she'd worked for since Jack's death and now she stood to lose everything. *Again.* 'What does Richard think about what Victoria's done?' she spat, staring at Susan. Was the woman so half-soaked that her daughter-in-law betraying all of them had not sunk into her brain? Did it not even bother her?

Susan continued staring blankly ahead. She hadn't given much thought to what Victoria had done. She was still struggling to take the whole chain of events in. None of it seemed real. Sometimes, for a split second when she first awoke, her brain cruelly tricked her into believing that everything was merely a bad dream. That was until reality seeped into her consciousness. As for Richard – well, she had no idea about him. He'd barely spoken to her the last few weeks and had completely refused to discuss Matthew.

'Are you even listening?' Lillian waved her hand in front of Susan's face. 'I said, what does Ri...'

'I heard what you said,' Susan snapped, trying not to shout. She wished Lillian would go away. All she did was cause problems. All of this was *her* fault. If Richard hadn't helped the woman out in the first place all those years ago then they wouldn't be in this position and their son would still be alive.

'Richard must be beside himself. How embarrassing this all is!' Lillian continued, oblivious to the expression on Susan's face. She reached for the newspaper and opened it back to the article. 'I mean, listen to this...'

Squinting at the small type, unable to see clearly without

her glasses, Lillian spat out the words: ' *"Victoria Stevens, after tragically losing all four of her new-born children and then dealing with the untimely suicide of her successful husband, Mr Matthew Stevens, has shocked her friends and family by disappearing, allegedly with a local biker..."* And that's only *part* of the article. My God, Susan have you not read it? People must be laughing at us. It's so humiliating. I would love to know how they got this story. I mean, who ev...'

'Just be *quiet!*' Susan barked. She'd had enough. Lillian had no issue feeding stories to the press when it benefited *her* – like the lies about the quads for a start. As for this story, she didn't know if it was true or not, but either way it didn't change anything.

'W-What?'

'For Christ's sake. My son is *dead*, Lillian. Your daughter isn't. Whatever she's done or hasn't done, Victoria's *alive!*' Susan rose from the chair, her legs wobbly. She didn't think she'd ever shouted at Lillian in all the years she'd known her and it felt good to tell her to shut up.

'B-But... I...'

Susan walked to the door and opened it. 'I won't listen to any more of your bleating. Now please *leave.*'

• • • •

RICHARD FLINCHED hearing the door slam. Why did Susan have to do that? She must realise he'd got a headache. Didn't she think about anyone but herself?

The answer to that was no.

Getting up from his chair, Richard walked over to the cabinet and reached for the decanter, noticing it was almost empty. Shrugging, he poured a large measure of whisky into a crystal tumbler and wandered over to the study's large sash window overlooking the meticulously landscaped garden. His eyes wandered along the topiary hedges, coming to rest on the summerhouse. He studied it carefully. *No one there.*

He'd been *convinced* he'd seen someone there yesterday.

Well, not *someone*, but a movement. A figure? Perhaps it *had* been someone, perhaps not...? A trick of the light or his overtired mind playing tricks?

It could have been an animal? As long as it wasn't a tramp living in his summerhouse...

Richard sipped at the whisky, refraining from downing it in one, like he'd got into the habit of doing more often than not lately.

Matthew's death had rocked him to the core. He'd admit that. He'd had no hint that his son would do something like that. Granted, he knew Matthew was angry over Victoria, but the kid was out of the way, so it was just a case of tying up loose ends. But to kill himself and all but hint that he'd had something to do with the death of the child was beyond logic. It had just caused more problems. Susan for one couldn't understand what Matthew's note referred to and kept badgering him as to what he thought.

Richard took another gulp of whisky. He hadn't been sure either, but the last thing he wanted was for Susan, or anyone else for that matter, to suspect that Matthew had anything to do with the child's death. He was happy with the general consensus that the child had died from natural causes. He didn't want his son being posthumously labelled as a child murderer.

He'd suggested to Susan that Matthew's suicide must have been over guilt about not being able to make Victoria happy, not that anything would have made that ungrateful little bitch pleased. Besides, Victoria's happiness had been the least of Matthew's concerns - his son knew how things worked, so maybe it was just a stunt that went too far?

Richard sighed. He didn't know and never would, but his initial devastation had rapidly turned to irritation when everything else had started mounting up.

Like who would take over the manager position at the bank? He'd be damned if he was coming out of retirement. He'd only just bloody left! But if headquarters replaced Matthew with someone who dug into the discrepancies with the various portfolios he'd hacked around with, then that was a *huge* risk. However, on the surface things tallied, so in reality there was no reason why anyone should be looking anyway. He ran his hand across his chin. *He must keep things in perspective.*

But then there was Victoria. He'd seen this morning's paper and had a good mind to sue them for defamation. Was any of their twaddle even factual? Worryingly, from what Matthew had said about the girl and that thug, it was possible.

Shrugging, Richard downed the last of the whisky. He'd had enough of this. Dealing with the article about Victoria was easy. He'd just put it about that she was mentally ill. He could prove she'd been sectioned, so that one was solvable. Whatever happened, that girl was out of their family now for good. And not a moment too soon.

He smiled. Lillian could take a bloody hike as well. He'd make sure that scheming old hag never set foot through his door ever again. In fact, he might start letting things slip about her past that she'd been desperately hiding all of these years.

See. There was always a silver lining.

Walking back to his desk, Richard pulled at one of the drawers and stuck his hand in to grab his Filofax. He needed to get back in the swing of things. There were some functions pencilled in some time ago, long before any of this had happened that he'd never confirmed. He'd presumed he'd be swamped with invitations and important events to attend once Matthew began his new role that he hadn't wanted to commit to less important engagements.

But then everything screwed up; first playing the devasted grandparent after the usurper kid incident and then by Matthew selfishly killing himself. Those two things alone had *completely* ballsed up his social calendar, but not to worry. He would rectify that now by calling up a few of these pencilled entries and tell them he was now available to attend.

Frowning, Richard felt around, unable to lay his hand on his Filofax. Where the bloody hell was it? It was one of his most important items. It held all of his diary dates, not to mention all of his contacts' numbers and addresses and he'd kept it in the same place for *years*.

This was Susan. How many times had he told her not to meddle in his study or touch his things? What the hell was she playing at?

Pulling open the drawer fully, Richard peered inside. It was definitely missing. His eyebrows furrowed deeply, his anger escalating. 'Susan?' he yelled. 'SUSAN!'

Susan rushed into the study. 'Whatever's the matter? Are you alright?'

'No, I'm bloody well not!' Richard barked. 'Where the hell have you put my damn Filofax? How *dare* you move it! How many times have I told you not to rummage around my personal items?'

Susan stared at the flecks of spittle on Richard's cleanly shaved chin. He'd told her thousands of times not to touch his stuff and so she hadn't. This was mainly because she never wanted to find out for sure just how many lies he'd told her throughout the *long* years of their marriage. The marriage that she was now seriously questioning why she bothered with. Matthew's death had underlined just how hollow her life had become and how one-sided and miserable her life actually was.

'I haven't moved anything, Richard,' Susan said quietly, almost beginning to hate him.

'You *must* have! Why else would my Filofax not be where I've put it without fail for the last twenty years? Tell me that?' Richard roared.

Susan glanced around the study and sighed. Walking over to the cabinet she picked up a large A4 leather-bound organiser. 'Is this it?'

Richard glared at Susan, quickly snatching the Filofax from her hands. '*I* didn't put it there! Don't treat me like an idiot! *You* moved it, didn't you?'

Susan sighed again – this time loudly. 'No, I did not! You tell me not to, so I never touch your things.' *Like everything else you tell me what I can and can't do.*

'Why would I have suddenly decided to put it there? Stop talking drivel, woman!'

'Oh, Richard. You haven't been yourself since Matthew… You've been drinking an awful lot too… Maybe yo…'

'You don't know anything! How *dare* you try insinuate that I'm going crazy!' Richard's voice got higher as his rage increased. 'Does doing that make you feel better just because you're the one who's mad?'

'I-I didn't say yo…'

'Get out of my sight!' Richard roared, glowering as Susan hurried from the study.

THREE

JORGE CASTELLO EYED the woman's shapely backside encased in tight jeans standing in the queue in front of him and did a quick mental calculation as to how long it would take him to chat her up and get her into his bed.

Not long, but still too long considering Mr Turner had instructed him to come to the club for 8pm even though it was his evening off and he'd been up to his neck all day doing collections. He was knackered, but as he'd been summoned, there wasn't room for arguments.

Besides, he had a lot of respect for John Turner. The man had given him a job, which was a lot more than most people would do. The man had also accepted what he'd said about Neil Sparks and promised to look into it, so Jorge wanted to make a good impression. Furthermore, he needed to try extra-hard being as he hadn't been entirely honest when asked his about his enforcement experience.

As the girl with the shapely behind paid for her items and turned to leave, Jorge gave her one of his trademark smiles. Grinning inwardly, he stepped forward to place a bag of crisps and a Mars bar on the newsagent counter. He was bloody starving and probably wouldn't get time to eat anything else tonight.

'Hello Jorge,' the man behind the counter smiled. 'Having a good day?'

Jorge fished some money from his pocket and handed it over. 'Not too bad, thanks. Yourself?'

The man continued speaking, but Jorge's mind was elsewhere. Since starting his job at the Sparks' firm a couple of weeks ago his local status had risen dramatically. People now fell over themselves to acknowledge him. Ok, so he'd done a bit of collection work in the past and was pretty fly with his fists when the need arose, but it was an accolade to be working for the Sparks' firm.

Neil Sparks – his father.

His father that, up until recently, he'd believed to be dead. That's what his ma had always said. He hadn't even known the man's name and still wouldn't if he hadn't been present at the Nags Head that night when his ma and Vera were trolleyed, got maudlin and blurted everything out. She'd tried to backtrack, but it was too late. He'd heard and couldn't, nor wouldn't pretend that he hadn't.

His mother refused to go into further details about how Jorge came to be in existence, saying it wasn't important, but it was to him. It always had been, even if he'd done a good job of pretending it wasn't.

He'd always presumed his mother just couldn't remember. She was a fucking mess and only interested in how much booze she could lay her hands on, so it had been feasible that she might never have been sure *who* his father was at all. He'd usually have felt sorry for someone in her position, but in this instance he didn't. His mother was crap.

Jorge's childhood memories consisted of random men wandering through their little council flat, some staying longer than others, but all having no problem raising their hand to him whilst his mother looked the other way. Sometimes when he got punched for having the audacity to exist, he wasn't sure which one of them had clobbered him because they all acted the same.

22

That was until he got to around twelve and had learnt to use his fists himself. Not that it mattered because as the drink and whatever else his mother frequently ingested caught up with her looks, so the steady stream of men diminished.

Jorge took his change from the shopkeeper, nodded his thanks and walked out of the newsagents, inwardly smiling at the way the queue immediately parted to let him pass unhindered.

After a quick glance at his watch, he continued down the road towards the Sparks' firm whose headquarters operated from the back of the Diamonds club. It had taken a few weeks after discovering the truth before plucking up the courage to go there.

He'd always wondered what went on inside those kind of firms, but up until recently he hadn't had the first clue that his own *father* was in charge of one and was none other than the infamous Neil Sparks. It was common knowledge Neil Sparks had disappeared several years ago, but being as the man had been absent from Jorge's life for the last twenty-five years, it hardly mattered if he'd been there or not.

Jorge frowned. For all he'd known his father could have really been dead, but he'd been determined to try and find something out from the firm and he'd succeeded.

When he'd turned up unannounced, John Turner had been the one to give him the time of day, ushering him into an office at the rear of the club. Jorge had had a lot of questions, but namely he'd wanted a job – like a *proper* job at a *proper* firm. This had been the part when he'd been asked what previous experience he'd had and so he'd ramped it up a bit. Well, a *lot* actually.

The Sparks' firm would never have taken him seriously if they knew the real extent of his experience was a bit of loan shark collection for a two-bit firm the other side of the river. That and several fights down the pub – usually over some daft tart, but he couldn't tell John Turner that, which was why it was even *more* important to learn fast, not screw up and do the job well.

But then had come the bit where he had to drop into the conversation that Neil Sparks was his father. He'd fully expected to be accused of being a liar, but that hadn't happened. In fact, John hadn't even raised an eyebrow.

'You're the spit of your mother, you know?' John had said, looking Jorge up and down. 'I fully expected you to turn up one day. I was there the night Marianne told Neil she was pregnant.'

Jorge thought perhaps he should have felt miffed hearing how Neil had abandoned his mother, but he hadn't. Not really. His mother had lied to him his entire life, so he could hardly blame this Neil guy for doing a runner, but he wanted a father and he also wanted a job.

Learning that Neil was still very much alive, living in France, but unlikely to return was disappointing, but at least John had promised him work – saying it was the *least* he could do in his father's absence. And this John had done, so therefore Jorge was determined to make a good impression.

. . . .

REACHING THE SIDE DOOR of the club that all the staff and "associates" used, Jorge rapped on it loudly. The front, with its gleaming façade and posh gold lettering outlined it as the upmarket Gentlemen's club that it was, attracting a high class of clientele.

The door was opened by one of the many security, a huge bull-headed man with a grizzled face and no neck, who waved him through. 'Mr Turner said to go straight in.'

'Thanks Jimmy,' Jorge smiled, hoping John would be pleased with what he'd achieved today. Several reluctant payers had had a change of heart and he was getting the hang of how things needed to be done to get results.

Knocking on the office door, Jorge walked in. 'Evening, Mr Turner. I've g…' Stopping mid-sentence seeing a man standing next to John wearing a finely-tailored grey suit, he studied the handsome face, somehow immediately knowing that this tall, well-built brown-haired stranger was his father.

'Jorge? Good to meet you.' The man's voice dripped with authority. He extended his hand. 'Neil Sparks.'

Jorge froze. What exactly was he supposed to do? Pulling himself together, he shook Neil's hand firmly.

Neil walked around the other side of the desk and motioned for Jorge to take a seat.

Jorge sat down, irritated that his legs felt unsteady and covertly studied Neil Sparks. He didn't want to give anything away and wanted this person who was his father to like him, but didn't want to start babbling questions.

It was Neil who broke the silence. 'Drink?' he asked, reaching for the large, exquisitely cut crystal decanter on his large, polished desk.

Jorge shook his head. 'No thank you,' he said, glad his voice displayed no waver as Neil slowly poured a measure of what smelt like fine bourbon.

'How's your mother?' Neil's asked. 'Marianne, isn't it?'

Jorge swallowed his immediate irritation. This man had fathered him, yet he had to double check the name of the woman he'd made pregnant? Christ, he was unprepared for this. In his mind he'd always thought of what he'd ask his father, given the opportunity. But he hadn't expected to *get* the opportunity. He willed the sweat to disappear from the back of his neck and rearranged himself in the chair. What the hell was the matter with him? He was acting like a bloody scared schoolboy.

'Yes, my mother's name is Marianne,' Jorge said, a slight caustic edge to his voice. 'And she's fine.' *No, she wasn't. She never had been, but he wasn't about to tell him that.*

'You look just like her,' Neil continued, exposing a row of straight white teeth. 'It's good to meet you, son.'

Jorge flinched. *Son? He was calling him son?* It sounded odd, but nice all the same.

Neil watched Jorge closely. He'd been more than surprised when John said his son had pitched up. He'd got enough to sort out as it was, without *that* inconvenience. But when John said he'd done a bit of homework on the boy; he was handy with his fists and clever to boot, his initial reticence to want anything to do with the kid had softened. The boy might come in *more* than useful with his plan, so once he'd returned from his short visit up north, he'd given John the nod to bring the lad in.

'I appreciate this is awkward for you and I must admit, it is for me too, but John tells me that you've been working well for the past couple of weeks, which I'm pleased to hear.'

Unsure of what else to do, Jorge nodded and brushed away the tingle of pride he felt by getting unfamiliar praise.

Neil clasped his hands on the shiny surface of the desk. 'I have some things I'm dealing with at the moment, hence my unexpected return from France.'

'I was under the impression you weren't returning,' Jorge answered.

'Although I didn't expect to be back, I am and you're here, so what I'm proposing is that we get to know each other.'

Jorge saw John glance at Neil. It was a discernible look that had he blinked, he'd have missed it, but it was there all the same.

'I thought the best way to do that, apart from spend some time together of course, is for you to help me out with what I need to do,' Neil continued.

Jorge frowned. 'What is it?'

Neil took another sip of whisky. 'It's complicated and may take some time, but would that be something you might be interested in?'

John frowned as he watched the proceedings unfold. Neil hadn't mentioned pulling Jorge into this and it bothered him. He'd seen from the off that the kid had nowhere near the collateral he'd made out. The most he'd probably previously done was shout at a couple of old dears late with their payment for a cooker, but he'd wanted to give the kid a chance so had vastly embellished his opinion of the kid's ability to Neil. He knew with help from his team of enforcers that Jorge would learn the deal quickly enough and he'd been right, but he wasn't ready for heavy or complex shit like Neil had planned and if Jorge took Neil up on his offer it complicated matters.

FOUR

CARMEN DROVE TOWARDS Tori's house, grateful when she'd seen Hunter at the Factory earlier that he'd asked her to drop in. She was glad of the change of scenery.

She did however, feel horribly responsible. Apparently, Tori hadn't taken Hunter's return to the Reapers well and she felt partly to blame. It had been *her* blurting out everything to Noel that she'd promised not to, so Tori must hold her *partially* accountable, if not completely. It had only been weeks since Tori had lost Andrew and she was desperate for no more retaliation, yet must know this was on the cards, as did everyone else.

Pulling into Tori's street, Carmen glanced around for a parking space. She drove up and down the narrow terraced road twice, hovering on seeing a car with someone in it just down from Tori's house, but seeing no hint of movement, drove round for the third time before nipping into another space that had just become vacant further up the road.

Walking towards Tori's house, getting the distinct sense of being watched, Carmen glanced over her shoulder. She was becoming paranoid. Hardly surprising. Too much had gone on to be anything but.

Thankfully, despite expecting it, she'd heard no word from Luca and hoped with all her heart that her fake French husband was happy to let her walk away. After all, it wasn't like their marriage had ever been full of love or passion.

Sighing, Carmen pulled out the spare key Tori had given her and with a final glance behind her for good measure, slipped it into the lock and went inside.

Listening for noise or movement and finding none, she made her way into the kitchen, only to find Tori sitting motionless at the table. She hadn't seen her friend look like this since Andrew's death and although it was still early days, she seemed to be holding it together. At least that's how it had looked – until now.

Carmen's eyes flitted over to the sink piled with a mound of unwashed plates, spotting remnants of broken crockery scattered over the floor and a deep sense of unease radiated through her. When Hunter asked her to visit, he'd given no hint that Tori was in this sort of state. What was he thinking of leaving her like this?

Slowly, Carmen moved closer. 'Tori?' she said quietly. 'What's happened?'

Tori slowly tilted her tear-stained face up to Carmen. 'As if you don't know,' she spat. 'You *knew* he was back with the Reapers, didn't you? You knew and you didn't warn me?'

'I-I didn't find out myself until last night,' Carmen spluttered. She'd been surprised enough when Noel returned, telling her he'd offered the presidency back up to Hunter, considering the past bad blood between them. By his own admission, Noel had gained the Presidency through underhand means and she was proud that he was big enough to do something to put it right. It might have been the decent thing to do from a Reaper's perspective, but by the looks of *this*, it wasn't the best thing for Tori by any stretch of the imagination.

'You know what this means?' Tori cried, her voice high-pitched. 'It means that it's *never* going to be over. I can't deal with this anymore. Too much has happened. Too much has been lost.' She shook her head sadly. 'I just can't do it…'

Carmen frowned. She knew Hunter had promised Tori there would be no reprisals, but she couldn't say she'd believed him. She nodded toward the pieces of broken crockery. 'What happened there?'

Tori sniffed sadly, wiping tears from her face. 'I threw them at him.'

'You threw a plate at Hunter?' Carmen almost laughed, imagining a dinner plate breaking over Hunter's head, but refrained. None of this was remotely funny.

Tori nodded. 'I can't believe he's taken back the presidency. He promised me. *Promised*!'

Carmen remained silent. She, herself had questioned why Hunter had agreed. Considering what had gone on, along with the problems Sarah had told her the Reapers had caused, she'd thought he would prefer that part of his life to remain closed. Even more so knowing how Tori felt about it.

Her lips set in a tight line. 'When did all this happen with the plates? This morning, I take it?' she asked.

Tori shook her head. 'No. Last night. I saw the patch on Hunter's jacket and lost my temper. I haven't seen him since…'

Carmen was shocked. 'You mean you've been here on your own, like this, all night?' She glanced once more at her friend. What the hell was Hunter playing at? She'd call the Factory herself right now and tell him to come home. She'd got problems of her own. The worry lodged firmly in the back of her mind about Luca was bad enough, but coupled with not being able to see her mother was weighing heavily. Her brother was dead, for Christ's sake. Was it not bad enough that he'd killed Tori and Hunter's child, but hiding that from her mother, letting her mistakenly believe Matt killed himself over Tori was even *worse*. And now *this*?

Getting up, Carmen helped herself to a bottle of wine from the fridge. 'Drink?'

Carmen took the slight shake of Tori's head to mean "no" and so set about pouring herself a glass before walking to the telephone to call Hunter.

FIVE

RICHARD SLAMMED THE front door and stomped down the steps to his car. His frown felt welded into position across his forehead. *Damn Susan.*

He'd got up at the crack of dawn to make sure he wasn't lumbered with looking at her miserable face during breakfast, but his plan to go out before she'd got up had failed. All that had happened was they'd argued yet again.

Well, not exactly *argued.* Susan had sat like a dummy, turning on the waterworks all because he'd told her to clear Matthew's bedroom out. The bloody woman was going insane, he was sure of it. For a start, refusing to go in that room was bad enough - it wasn't like Matthew would suddenly jump out on her, the stupid woman. And if that bizarre attitude wasn't ridiculous enough, she refused to clear out his things. "It's wrong to invade his space", she'd said.

What a load of rot.

'Matthew's dead, you stupid bitch,' Richard muttered, swearing under his breath as he dropped his car keys on the gravel. 'He won't care *what* you do with his stuff now!'

Susan didn't have any problems moving *his* stuff or invading *his* privacy though, did she? Like that Filofax for a start. Plus, other things had gone missing too. One of which he was especially concerned about. The notebook with the list of amounts he'd moved from various portfolios at the bank; an entire record of everything he'd fudged in the past recorded in black and white. He'd always meticulously written things down and this habit aided his organisational excellence, but the notebook was important and he damn well needed it.

Richard grated his teeth. Susan must have taken it, snooping around looking for an extra account to get her hands on more of his money. By God, hadn't he given her enough over the years and she had the cheek to insinuate he forgot what he was doing? He forgot *nothing*.

He needed that book and he needed it *now*, but he could hardly ask Susan for it back or accuse her of moving it outright on the off chance that she *hadn't* taken it. That would only guarantee an interrogation.

Richard shook his head angrily. As for all this business with Matthew's room, he'd had enough. It wasn't healthy keeping a room as a blasted shrine. Having Matthews memory hanging around like that wasn't nice for anyone.

He irritably unlocked his car door. Susan had to sort it now because he'd told her that if the room wasn't cleared within the next few days, he'd get someone in to do it; one of those house clearance firms would get rid of everything.

He huffed loudly. Susan had looked at him sadly as he'd stormed away. Did she really think her fake crying and acting wronged would incite him to stay or back track on his instruction?

It hadn't.

All it had achieved was to put him in a bad mood and she wondered why he was never around?

About to get into the car, Richard stopped. Who the hell was that parked over the end of the drive? He squinted against the low morning sun and anger surged. The damned cheek! They were parked across the gateway! He squinted further, seeing it was just one person. A man – but he couldn't see much more than that because they were too far away.

What the hell was someone doing just sitting there? Was he being *watched*?

Richard slammed the car door, all set to stomp down the drive to find out exactly what was going on when the car drove away.

. . . .

JORGE FIDGETED in the drivers' seat; his legs cramped from being in the same position for so long. Despite an incredibly early start, he'd made an error of judgement by taking the decision to have a quick look at where the bank manager on Neil's list lived.

His plan was to see where all these people he needed to deal with were located so that he could weigh up the most efficient way of playing it, but he hadn't factored in that the route from there to the target house was inundated with temporary bloody traffic lights which had taken an eon to get through. This hindrance had added far too much time onto his meticulously organised schedule and completely scuppered his chances of getting here as quickly as planned. Because of this, he hadn't arrived at the target house until just gone 10.

The impromptu visit to the rather impressive house of the bank manager had however, afforded him an unexpected sighting. In his opinion, the man who left the place was extremely jumpy – almost like he was *looking* for someone. Either that, or he was one of those people who scrutinised anyone in the near vicinity.

Jorge shrugged. *Not his problem*. The bloke was clearly paranoid and when the man made movements to come down the drive, he'd had no choice but to drive off.

That was bank managers all over though, wasn't it? Terminally suspicious. But in this one's case, from what Neil had said, he had every right to be!

Thankfully, the most important thing was that his lateness to the target house hadn't made any difference. The biker was absent, but he'd half expected that. In fact, he'd thought the house was empty and had been all set to give it up until the following day when he'd clocked a woman walking down the road towards the house.

He'd noticed a car cruising past a few times, but it was only when that woman got out had his senses gone on full alert recognising her as the person in the photograph - *Neil's wife*.

Shunting himself down in the seat, trusting the tinted windows were doing their job, Jorge watched the woman glance nervously over her shoulder and then enter the target house. She certainly was a looker, there was no doubt about that and she must live here, so Neil's digging on her possible whereabouts had come up trumps.

Jorge frowned. Neil had given this address as the location of the biker – Hunter, but he had no proof that Carmen was living with the man, or even that she was having an affair. From what he'd grasped this suspicion stemmed from something Neil's brother-in-law had said. However, the possibility that Carmen was having an affair looked plausible if this was Hunter's house and she had a key, but he was reluctant to jump to conclusions. He had to make sure he'd marked the correct target. He'd definitely identified the correct woman - it would be difficult to mistake her, but he *did* need to corroborate that she was indeed the biker's lover.

Jorge glanced back to the house. Still no sign of movement. He hoped something would happen sooner rather than later because he'd all but seized up and his backside felt welded to the bloody car seat!

He rummaged through a carrier bag in the footwell and fished out a squashy Twix bar, wishing he'd left it a bit longer before eating the sandwiches he'd bought on the way up. Not that they were particularly edible, but he was starving again and this stake out could go on for hours. He daren't leave now that the wife was on the scene. He must stay put and see if the man showed up, however long it took.

As he munched on the chocolate, Jorge wondered, not for

the first time, exactly why he'd agreed to get involved in this business for Neil Sparks. He'd been told very little about the situation surrounding this whole issue or what was going on with the wife and got the distinct impression he'd only been given a very basic account. And what he had been told had only been due to John Turner's insistence.

Jorge frowned and ran his hand over his cleanly shaven jaw. *Had he agreed to this just because he wanted to get to know his father?*

Even though it pained him to admit it, that was partly true but on that front he was already disappointed. Short of an hour of Neil listing what he expected from this job was all he'd received from the man.

How long would he be stuck in this godforsaken place for anyway? It could be some time if things didn't go to plan. And these sorts of things *rarely* went to plan. Not that he'd know because he'd never done anything like this before.

Despite the reservations, Jorge felt a sense of exhilaration. Was this his chance to make a *really* big name for himself? Neil Sparks, by anyone's opinion was the business and he was experiencing a rush of excitement working for a *real* firm, rather than the peripherals he'd worked for on and off the last couple of years.

His mouth curled into a sneer. He'd show all those people who'd ever looked down their noses at him. He'd instil the fear of God into every low-life his mother had brought into their flat and he'd show *her* that all the years of lying, treating him with indifference and hiding the fucking truth had come back to bite her on the arse when he'd made a name for himself and had the readies to prove it.

Jorge grinned. He could see it now... He'd end up getting on with his father really well. They'd be like two peas in a pod. Neil would be exceptionally proud of him and would introduce him to important, influential faces. *"Here's my son..."* he'd say.

Of course, he'd inherit the whole Sparks firm in the end. In fact, he'd probably be promoted to a high-up position straight away if he did a cracking job on this case.

His mother and Vera had done him a favour the day they'd spilt their guts down the Nag's Head and it was all working out very nicely.

. . . .

HUNTER SETTLED BACK INTO the familiar surroundings of the ramshackle space utilised by the Reapers in the old Victorian factory building he owned. He hadn't yet been back up to his living quarters in the attic, but it felt good just to be within the Factory's four walls again, even if it had been this very place to spawn the long list of problems and cause the unlikely association of Tori, Matt, the Reapers and everyone else involved in the ensuing collection of nightmares.

He took another long swig from his beer and contemplated what Joe had told him earlier. After receiving a cast-iron promise to keep him informed over any developments about Jeanie, the man had finally agreed to leave and return to Polperro.

Hunter was relieved about this because he was determined to make at least *one* thing right. Joe's life had been turned upside down since agreeing to his request to bring Jeanie up here. Joe was a decent man; he'd already done enough and he didn't want him around when things began to move here. He didn't want another innocent person getting caught up in the crossfire.

Joe hadn't been comfortable in coming to the Factory, but they could hardly have discussed the topic of Jeanie at the White Hart and taking him to the house was a no-no. His continuance to dig around in everything had to be kept as far away from Tori as possible.

Hunter signalled to a grizzled biker with a long ginger beard for another beer and let his thoughts return to the immediate matter in hand.

Joe had returned to the psych unit where Jeanie had last

been seen. He'd spoken to the receptionist working the day of the disappearance who had a clear memory of Jeanie, mainly because of her strange behaviour.

Hunter nodded his thanks as his replacement beer was deposited in front of him.

Being as at the time Colin had previously mentioned the receptionist saying Jeanie had been muttering about a man, Joe had quizzed her about that, but the woman remained adamant there had been no one about.

Hunter had thought he'd well and truly reached a dead end, but then Joe added that the woman had said that if Jeanie had come out of the toilet a minute before then she'd have seen *Mr Stevens*.

His blood had run cold with the immediate assumption that Matt had been there, but it was the father, *Richard Stevens* that Joe was referring to.

Hunter frowned. Now, Jeanie couldn't have *seen* Stevens, but she could have *heard* him. Had he been looking for Tori or what? It was the day Andrew died so had Stevens been there to tell Tori what had happened only to find she'd been discharged?

Now, he'd never met the man, but judging by what Tori had told him and the mere fact he'd fathered that heinous bastard Matt, spoke volumes. Maybe it was time Stevens was paid a visit? He had no connection with Jeanie, but he might have seen something or someone who *had*. As much as he resented asking for information or favours from anyone belonging to *that* family, there was no other way. *Something else Tori wouldn't like.*

Hunter's teeth grated remembering how she'd launched herself at him last night. He'd known she wouldn't be happy about the Reapers' presidency, but he hadn't expected her to lose it like that. The way she'd screamed, pummelling her fists against his chest had taken him by surprise, but not as much as when she'd thrown his dinner at him. Luckily, he'd dodged the plate otherwise at the very least he'd be sporting a black eye this morning.

He shouldn't have stormed out of the house and returned to the Factory though. He also shouldn't have stayed out all night, but he was too tired and angry to fight. He was trying to do right by her and make things better, not worse. He wanted everything to be as it had been before all of this had happened. Before his son had been killed and before Tori knew about what he'd done to her father. But nothing could ever be as it was. *Even being the President.*

At least being back in the Reapers' fold gave him normality. Normality in *his* world anyway. Tori couldn't understand that. She'd *never* understand it. All she associated it with was misery, pain and grief. Yes, the Reapers may have brought him untold problems, but they were also his family, his *life*. They had both saved and destroyed him.

It didn't make sense to outsiders what the loyalty and sense of belonging meant, but Hunter knew it was the only thing holding him together right now. And the only thing that could help him wreak revenge for Tori *and* for himself.

Tonight, he'd talk to her again and try and get her to see sense. He didn't want to lose her. With a sad resignation, Hunter allowed the possibility that he might already be losing her gain momentum. Maybe it could never work between them now? Not now she knew he'd killed her father and they'd lost their beautiful child. Maybe despite their best efforts, the gulf was too large to bridge and the damage too deep to ever properly heal?

Grin approached the table, knocking Hunter from his deep turmoil. 'Phone call for you,' he said.

Six

NEIL SIPPED HIS WHISKY and put on a show of admiring the scantily-clad women on the stage from the best table in the house. He flashed his award-winning smile at the blonde seductively gyrating in front of him, allowing her to continue vying for his attention with the hope of him promoting her, or perhaps taking her as a mistress. That was what all these women did.

Neil grinned inwardly. Not much chance of that, but he had to be careful. It wasn't like he could disappear off to "parties" or discreet clubs like in France. No one knew him over there. All they knew was that he was rich, but *here* it was a different story.

His face contorted into a scowl. In the industry he'd fought so hard to get to the top of, having a relationship with a *man* was the cardinal sin and one not to be tolerated.

His resentment for this caveman attitude of the people he'd been surrounded by for years flared once again. Because of *them* he'd been forced to parade around pretending to find these plastic women attractive and it was exactly because of *this* that he'd ended up with that stupid bitch, Marianne.

From the off, publicly pretending he was besotted with her

had been a pain in the arse. Even though she'd served his purpose it had still made him feel positively sick. And he certainly hadn't wanted a kid – with her or *anyone*, but that night she'd walked in on him in a compromising position with a guy had forced him into a corner, giving him no choice but to get rid of her. What she'd witnessed had given her something she could have used against him and bring his world crashing down.

Neil smiled nastily. He'd made it quite clear to her at the time what would happen if he *ever* heard her speak of it, but she hadn't and thankfully, had only come knocking once since. He should have taken that opportunity to offload the silly mare as well as the brat that had appeared by then, but John had been present and Neil knew how he felt about family.

Now the kid was no longer a kid and was here on the scene. *Here.* It was a shock, but thankfully it seemed the boy had inherited some of his abilities. How good he was exactly, the next few weeks would show. And if he wasn't good, then he would be promptly exiting stage left. Either way, he was useful for this leg of the plan.

Neil forced himself to smile and nodded as a beaming waitress ingratiatingly deposited a fresh bourbon on his table, then he moved his eyes back to the dancefloor.

And then there was Carmen... Because of the bloody Reapers and his new "proposed identity" her father offered as a shield, he'd had little choice but to marry her. At least she'd looked good in photos and that was the point, wasn't it?

He gritted his teeth. Carmen had been stupid too. That was why women didn't interest him. They were fundamentally stupid. Being stupid equalled dangerous. Stupidity caused things to go wrong. Stupidity caused problems.

Plus, she'd insulted him. *Publicly.* Leaving him and shagging a *Reaper*? Was she having a fucking laugh?

Neil tipped the remains of his drink into his mouth. He had not forgotten the problems that bunch of wanker bikers had caused and neither would he. Not in a million years. Especially *now.*

Even though the firm was based in London, they'd expanded well, muscling their way into a great patch up north supplying coke and guns. That was until the Reapers got wind of their trespassing, not taking kindly to it.

Neil knocked back his refill and placed his glass back down on the table, catching the waitress' eye for another.

After a couple of their own men were caught up in a fracas, much as he'd hated it, he'd been forced to enter into negotiations with their gorilla of a president, Rafe.

Eager to avoid any more of his worthy men being taken out, he'd made a reluctant agreement. The firm and the Reapers had worked together on a decent earner involving a couple of post offices, but it had gone pear-shaped. Rafe blamed him for some of his last minute changes to the schedule, leaving everyone under scrutiny.

Neil glowered. His firm had a *lot* more to lose than the Reapers and they knew it. John had gone batshit when he'd found out. He hadn't wanted any involvement in the first place, but Neil had gone ahead regardless, and suddenly they were in a position where they risked losing everything, so he'd had no choice but to acquiesce to Rafe's demands. Several hand-picked Reapers would take the rap and go down for the foreseeable future in return for Neil's firm walking clean away from any involvement.

But it had cost him. Cost him *dearly*; both financially and in every other way. To get his firm off the hook, Rafe's deal meant Neil was forced to hand over the *entire* northern patch, plus several hard-earned other patches and then fuck off out of the country, never to return.

He'd had no choice – not if he wanted his firm to stay afloat. Hence Luca LeVere was born with a fully-built history, bank account and credentials, as well as a beautiful fiancée, courtesy of a contact's contact, Richard-fucking-Stevens.

Between them, the Reapers and Stevens had ballsed his life right up. Having to fuck around pretending to be a frog called

Luca had pissed him off irreparably. He'd even had to learn fluent French, for fuck's sake. It wasn't good.

Neither had it been good to be saddled with another bloody woman and after all of that – after all of his sacrifices, the final bloody insult was Carmen taking the bloody piss by buggering off with a Reaper!

Well, it wasn't funny and *none* of them would be laughing soon - including Richard Stevens, the supercilious bastard. He'd assured him Carmen would never cause issues. Well, she had and now the old bastard would pay, along with those fuckhead bikers.

SEVEN

'OH, IT'S COMPLETE RUBBISH, Mercer,' Richard exclaimed pompously. He sipped his whisky and casually crossed his ankles. There was no way on God's earth he would let Andrew bloody Mercer, the fat git, realise his questioning over the article had rattled him. It was bad enough playing golf and bridge with the pig of a man, without him thinking he'd got something to gloat about. *No bloody way.*

'I'm sure it is, Stevens,' Andrew Mercer replied. 'It's just that everyone's talking about it. Surely you expected that?'

Richard made a conscious effort to look angry. 'Has it not crossed your mind that we've had enough to deal with, what with our son dying?' he spat. That would throw a spanner in Mercer's attempt to have one over, the puffed-out old fool.

Andrew Mercer had the decency to look slightly contrite. 'I know that, old chap. You could do without this on top of everything else.'

'Isn't that so,' Richard said, pleased to get the upper hand. He'd had plenty of sympathy from everyone at the Conservative Club over the past few months. Firstly, for the pseudo-quads death and then losing his son on top of it. But he did need to quash this speculation over Victoria.

Whether the papers' surmising about her was true or not, it was imperative he put a stop to the fast-spreading consensus that there was any grain of truth in it. The *last* thing he wanted, after public embarrassment, was mention of bikers involved with his family – even more so if the bikers were the bloody Reapers.

Now was a good a time as any to sow the seeds in his favour and by doing so, finally getting his own back on Lillian. After everything that grasping bitch had taken over the years and the endless problems her family had caused, it was about time he got his payback, whilst enjoying sentencing her to public ridicule at the same time. He'd waited *years* for this. The best thing was she had *nothing* on him anymore. It was only *her* who could lose now and lose she would. Now she'd receive her comeuppance for all the years she'd had him over a barrel.

'I still think the papers print complete twaddle. You know what they're like,' Richard snorted. 'I've refused to lower myself to even comment on their latest libellous article. They've tried to get a response from me of course, but I won't give them the time of day. If anyone is so deluded to believe it, then that speaks volumes about them on a personal level. You see, I'd prefer to give people *we* know more credit!'

'Oh, absolutely!' Andrew nodded, not wishing to admit both he and his wife and just about all of their joint acquaintances thought it *could* be feasible for Lillian Morgan's daughter to behave in such a manner. His wife had said only yesterday that the Gristhorpes were having nothing to do with Lillian until they heard something to the contrary. He wouldn't tell Richard Stevens that though.

'It still baffles me how they dreamt this story up,' Richard mused. 'I mean, we all know Victoria must have lost her mind again, poor dear, but that's only to be expected - especially with her history and her family.'

Mercer's ears pricked up and he adopted a concerned expression. 'I know, the poor darling girl. Her children and then her husband.'

THE TARGET OF LIES

Richard feigned sadness. 'I'll admit we have no idea where she's gone.' The difference was that now it was nothing to do with him or Matthew, he didn't much care. He hoped to never set eyes on the horrid devious little slut again in his entire life.

'It's so sad,' Mercer nodded. 'But what did you mean by lost her mind *again*?'

Richard leant closer, trying not to inhale his companion's offensive breath which smelt like a cross between cabbage and rotting flesh. 'I don't mind telling you, in fact, it would be good to get it off my chest and, seeing as it's you, I know what I'm about to say won't go any further.'

Did he hell! He knew Andrew Mercer couldn't be trusted to keep anything to himself even if his life depended on it, but that was *exactly* the point.

Richard continued, his voice low, 'I presume you know Victoria was in hospital for quite a while after having the baby, I mean, babies?' *Damn, he almost slipped up there. Concentrate, Richard, concentrate.*

Richard watched Mercer nod, his eyes greedy for information. 'It wasn't down to complications from the birth like we made out.' He paused for effect. *Oh, he was enjoying this.* 'It was because Matthew had no choice but to have her sectioned…'

'Sectioned?' Mercer spluttered. 'You mean like "mental hospital" sectioned? Christ! Was it the shock of the death of the children?'

Richard shook his head. 'No, it was nothing to do with that. To be honest, she'd always shown signs of being unstable, but as a family – and, I suppose for Matthew's sake, we'd always tried to see past that.'

Mercer took a sip of his drink, then signalled to the bar for refills. 'Go on.'

'Victoria went completely berserk and because she was too irrational to voluntarily accept help, the hospital gave Matthew as her husband, the unenviable choice of sectioning her for her own and the children's safety. It was either that or they would have forced a mandatory section on her.'

Mercer whistled between his teeth. 'Phew, I had no idea of any of this.'

Richard shook his head sadly. 'Why would you? No one did. We made the decision as a family to keep it to ourselves. With Matthew's new position at the bank, his wife having a mental illness didn't look good, did it?'

'No. No, it wouldn't. Not at all. I completely understand,' Mercer agreed.

'But being as Matthew's no longer with us it doesn't matter now, although he was devastated, of course,' Richard continued. His son had done exceptionally well by engineering Victoria's section the way he had. Actually, he'd go as far as to say he couldn't have masterminded it better himself.

Mercer moved closer still. 'I hate to ask this, but Victoria wasn't responsible for the deaths of the children, was she?'

'No.' Richard paused. 'At least, I don't think so. That was just unfortunate.' *Let Mercer think that too if it got suspicion away from Matthew or more importantly, himself.*

Richard smiled as the barman brought two fresh whiskies over to their table and waited until he had left before continuing. 'I can't say I'm too surprised at Victoria's downfall, what with everything she's endured with her family.'

Mercer remained silent. Although desperate to know what Richard was alluding to, he didn't want to make it obvious.

Richard sighed, inwardly ecstatic that Mercer was swallowing this and committing it to memory for the not-too-distant retelling. 'I don't think she ever really got over what happened with her father.'

'Oh yes,' Mercer nodded. 'We heard Lillian's husband was tragically killed in a car accident when Victoria was young. Thank God you and Susan had the decency to take them under your wing and include Lillian in your circles. It was exceptionally good of you.'

Richard nodded. 'I thought I was doing the right thing – the *only* thing under the circumstances. I knew Lillian from school days and if the same thing had happened to me, then I'd like to think someone would have done the same for Susan and the children.'

'You're a good man, Richard,' Mercer acknowledged.

'But imagine my shock when I found out that it was lies!' Richard said. *This was what he'd been waiting for.*

'What? You mean Lillian's husband isn't dead?'

'No, he's dead, alright, but she fabricated everything about it. Her husband was *murdered*. He was a drug dealer and killed because of that.'

'*WHAT*?' Mercer shrieked.

'I know,' Richard hissed. 'Can you believe it? I certainly couldn't, but it's true. Victoria told me when she was in the hospital. All of these years Lillian lied. It turns out she married beneath her... Well, you know... she had no choice... a shotgun wedding.'

Mercer's mouth hung open. 'You mean...?'

'Yes, pregnant with Victoria and her parents disowned her... That's why she had to marry. Lillian is upper class by birth and she went and did that, shaming herself and her family.'

'No wonder she wanted to keep it under wraps!' Mercer snorted.

'Exactly, but can you wonder why Victoria's not quite the ticket? Lillian forced the poor girl never to breathe a word of the truth. She needed to keep up the cock and bull about a car accident. Couple that with half Victoria's blood being from a dreg of society and you can't wonder the way it's turned out.'

'I'm completely astounded!' Mercer gasped. 'Dear God. Does Lillian know you have discovered this?'

Richard nodded. 'She does now. Why do you think I've banned her from having anything to do with our family?'

'I didn't know you had?'

'Yes, even though I knew of her lies for a while, dealing with it took a back seat because of the deaths... But last week I couldn't bear the hypocrisy of putting up with her any longer, so I cut all ties with Lillian for good. I'm hurt, if you must know.

It's all been lies… from the start…'

'I don't mean to be heartless, but in a way it's a blessing in disguise about the children…'

'I know what you mean, but I would never say that to Susan. On top of everything else, this has just about floored her.'

'I can't say I'm surprised,' Mercer said. He couldn't wait to go home and recount this conversation with Sandra. She'd never believe it.

'Of course, I'm not making this public knowledge – for Susan's sake.'

Mercer blew out a long sigh. 'I don't think I'll ever be able to look at Lillian the same way ever again.'

Richard nodded. 'I for one, will not go anywhere near that awful woman and will refuse to attend anywhere she's present. I never want to see her again in my entire life.'

'You can rest assured that we certainly will not be inviting her to anything from now on,' Mercer said, his face twisted with contempt.

Richard nodded solemnly. 'I appreciate that, Mercer.'
Phase one of Lillian's ostracization complete.

EIGHT

CARMEN FELT A MIXTURE of both anger and relief hearing Hunter's bike roar up outside. Rushing to the door, she yanked it open, tripping into his arms.

'Carmen? You phoned? What on earth's going on?' Hunter said, his rugged face etched with concern.

'I'm so glad you're here.' Carmen leant against Hunter's chest, pulling the door closed behind her so Tori wouldn't overhear anything.

Hunter wrapped his arms tightly around Carmen's shaking body trying not to let his worry escalate. Grabbing her gently by the shoulders he held her away from him to study her face. 'What's happened? Is Tori alright?'

'Keep your voice down,' Carmen hissed, her eyes wet with tears. 'She's like she was the day Andrew died and I can't bear seeing her like this again. You've got to do something. You're out of order.'

Hunter was gobsmacked. *He* was out of order? 'Wha…'

Carmen placed her hands on Hunter's face, pulling him close and stared into his steely grey eyes. 'Your return to the Reapers is making her ill. Don't you understand? It's finishing her. You knew it would distress her, yet you accepted it without even discussing it?' Her hands increased the grip on the sides of Hunter's face. '*Please* reconsider this presidency?'

Hunter stood immobile, shocked. He knew Tori was angry, but was she in that much of a state? He pulled Carmen back against his chest and stroked her hair. Tori was fortunate to have found such a good friend in such an unlikely place as Matt's sister, but this put him in one hell of a quandary. If what Carmen was saying was right, how could he risk Tori's state of mind and happiness by remaining in the Reapers? On the flip side, how could he walk away from the group he needed to exact his revenge?

'Don't worry,' he muttered. 'I'll think of something. I'll sort it out somehow, I promise.'

As Hunter released Carmen and rushed through the door into the house, Carmen hastily wiped her eyes. She had no choice but to hope he could sort it. She didn't know what else to do. What else *could* she do? It was out of her hands.

She walked back into the house after Hunter and shut the door behind her.

· · · ·

NEIL SPARKS GLOWERED listening to Jorge's report. As soon as the phone call came through, interrupting the set at the club, he knew it would be about this. 'I presume you had the sense not to call from a local telephone box?'

'Of course not. I've driven over ten miles from the target house before calling!' Jorge said, slightly put out that anyone would think him so stupid.

He was also annoyed, beginning to wonder whether his inclusion on this job was some form of test? This was only the third time he'd spoken to Neil in his life. Neil - the father who purported to want to get to know him, but only seemed interested in what he was doing regarding the job. He didn't like it, however he had to remember that he needed to impress the man if he wanted to get anywhere.

'Good, good,' Neil muttered. *So that ponce, Matt, was right*

and his whore of a wife, was indeed having it off with a Reaper?
'And what does this son of a bitch look like?'

'Big bloke – massive, in fact. Long, scruffy blond hair. That's about as much as I can tell you. I wasn't close. I think he may have a beard, but I didn't get much of a look of him from the front.'

'Hmm…' The boy had done well. He hadn't expected such cast iron results so fast and from what Jorge had said, publicly snogging on the doorstep didn't leave much denying that they were at it. It was all very well him promising John he wouldn't go steaming into the Reapers all guns blazing, but if Jorge was producing decent results as quickly as this, then reaching the end might not be quite as slow-going as he'd feared.

Neil raked his fingers through his hair, spoiling its usual immaculate appearance. Bloody Carmen. This was *exactly* the sort of thing a woman would do purely to spite him. She didn't know the history between him and the Reapers, yet she'd still selected a person to screw that would cause the biggest insult. 'You still there?' he barked, his anger grating, aware Jorge hadn't said anything further.

'Yes, I'm still here. I guess I'll make my way back now. I've got quite a lot of things coming up that I ne…'

'You won't be going anywhere until I get the shit I need on all these people!' Neil snapped, before remembering that on the surface, he was supposed to be nurturing a father and son relationship with this boy. He took a deep breath and forced his voice to sound more amicable. 'Sorry, son. I don't mean to take things out on you. It's just hard having my suspicions confirmed. Carmen's my wife…' *That sounded relatively convincing, even to himself.*

Placated, Jorge almost felt sorry for Neil. He clearly loved the woman. He also admitted, more than what he first cared to, that he *did* want a relationship with his father as well as a piece of what the man had and he didn't want anything to spoil that. 'What else would you like me to do?'

Neil thought hard. He knew what he *wanted* to do to both

his wife and the Reaper, but he would save that for a later date. He needed to test this boy out a bit more first. 'I need you to build a rapport and get to know them. Do it whatever way you like, then fuck with their heads. By the time we're finished they won't know what's hit them!'

Jorge remained silent, noticing the mention of "we". As far as he could see, it was *him* doing it all for the foreseeable future, but if that's what it took to get what was long owed to him, then so be it.

From Jorge's silence, Neil realised his error. 'I will, of course, come and join you on a regular basis for proper catch ups so we can properly get to know each other. Please believe me when I say that despite all of this, you're very important to me. I'm well aware I've been out of your life from the start and I intend to make up for that.' *Lies. Utter lies, but it sounded impressive.*

Neil could sense the smile forming on Jorge's face even down the telephone line, but back to what was *really* important. 'Going back to the job in hand, a good place to start is a gaff called The White Hart. The Reapers frequent the dump as an informal meeting place.'

Jorge frowned. 'The Reapers? You want me to concentrate on all of them? I thought you meant just Carmen and th…'

'I want you to concentrate on *everything*!' Neil didn't like this "having to be nice to people" thing. He wasn't very good at it. 'Just get in with them. I don't care how. Become a biker if you have to, but just do it.'

'I don't think it will be quite as easy as that.'

'*Make* it as easy as that!' Neil barked, his false patience running out. 'First things first though, wait until Hunter and my wife go out and then go and smash their house up. That will piss on Carmen's chips. Take a few things – whatever, but make it look like a burglary. Shit on the bed, if you like.'

Jorge scowled. Short of nicking sweets from Woolworths as a kid, he wasn't a burglar and he didn't make a habit of shitting on people's beds whilst robbing their TV either.

Furthermore, he didn't particularly want to start now.

Sensing Jorge's hesitation, Neil swallowed the fast-rising urge to roar at this lad and remind him that what he requested from people was *never* up for discussion, but he kept it together. *Play the game, Neil. Play the game.*

'It's just my way of releasing a bit of frustration,' Neil said softly. 'It's pathetic really, but I want to cause my wife some extra hassle. It might make me feel a bit better.'

'I understand,' Jorge said, feeling sorry for Neil once again. The man had just found out his wife was doing the dirty on him and that was bad – especially for someone of his standing.

'Then concentrate on infiltrating the Reapers and once that's done, I'll be up for a catch up.' *Don't rush though*, Neil thought, having no real wish to spend any time whatsoever with this boy – son or not. 'Oh, and I almost forgot – don't forget about that old bank manager bastard, or should I say – *retired* bank manager. I've told you what I want you on that score.'

'Don't worry. I've got all that. I swung past there earlier and spotted the old duffer leaving his house. His eyes were everywhere. It's like he knows he's being watched,' Jorge said.

Neil smiled. 'That's exactly how I *want* him to feel. I made a start with him myself when I came for a look around the other week. I also got some info from his place that could come in useful. Be careful though. He's a snide bastard, that one.'

Jorge silently took in everything Neil said. This was one hell of a big job for one person and he had no idea how he would pull any of it off, but he'd better think of something. If it got him what he wanted, then he'd work 24/7 to achieve it.

Neil wanted to wrap this conversation up. He'd said what was needed and was uninterested in talking to this loser. 'You have full use of that flat, ok? You still got that address I gave you? It's not a great place, being slap bang in the middle of a bunch of deserted shops, but it's a great base for not attracting attention.'

Jorge felt his pocket. 'Yep. I'll go there once I've done the house and then work out my next move.'

'Good. I don't need to tell you not to give anything away, do I?'

Jorge grimaced. 'No, you don't. I'll call you once I've g…'

'You don't need to constantly update me,' Neil interrupted. The *last* thing he wanted was this idiot calling every five damn minutes. 'Only get in contact if something's really important, otherwise I'll leave you to get on with things as you see fit. I trust your judgement, son,' he added, knowing the occasional interjection of the word "son" would have a positive effect on a fatherless loner with a shit-for-brains foreign mother, such as Jorge. 'If I haven't heard from you in two weeks, call me and I'll see when I can come up to see you, ok?'

'Ok.' Jorge was about to end the call when he realised Neil had already hung up.

NINE

TORI WASN'T HUNGRY but felt too empty to argue the point. She looked around the kitchen feeling for once calmed by the silence. Hunter insisted she should eat something, so she'd nodded blindly and after a lot of hesitation over leaving her on her own whilst he went to the chip shop, she'd finally been left in peace.

The silence usually unnerved her. Their home should be full of the cries and gurgles of their baby, but it wasn't. It was silent. Then there was the type of silence when people scrutinised her expressions or mannerisms – everything she bloody did. Waiting for her to lose it and end up back in the madhouse.

When Hunter had rushed in earlier, his face awash with worry, Tori knew immediately that Carmen had asked him to return. She wasn't stupid – it was obvious, but she hadn't *wanted* Hunter to come back unless it was to tell her that everything had been a hideous mistake and he wasn't returning to the Reapers after all. And *mean* it this time.

She wrung her trembling hands together. Hunter had promised *yet again* that he'd do something to make this better and hadn't realised quite how much his return to the Reapers would bother her. Did he really think she'd buy that? Did he honestly not remember she'd begged, yes, *begged* him to have nothing more to do with them?

Tori had silently listened as Hunter continued with further assurances – like that *she* was the most important thing in his life and he would do whatever necessary to ensure she was ok and happy.

Happy? Would she ever be happy again?

There was little point in saying or doing anything apart from nod occasionally. She was too tired and empty to do anything else. Forming physical words about the subjects that haunted her caused familiar balls of panic to form in her gut and she'd been almost relieved when Carmen said she had to go.

Hunter, meanwhile, had continued apologising. Apologising for leaving last night and again for not returning, but apologies didn't matter. She just wanted it all to stop. She didn't want a life of being let down. She'd had enough of that, but from the darkness a tiny glimmer of hope formed. Perhaps he *would* make this better? He said she was to tell him everything she needed and then they'd discuss how it could be achieved.

Was that possible?

Swallowing hard, Tori realised that she had to believe it was otherwise she would go completely insane.

• • • •

AS SOON AS THE taillights of the bike faded from his rear-view mirror, Jorge reached under the passenger seat and retrieved a black balaclava. Glad that he'd had the foresight to remove it from the bag stashed in the secret compartment within the boot earlier, he smiled.

Doing a double check that no one was about, he jumped from the car and made his way down the street, pulling the collar of his jacket high around his ears. He'd put the balaclava on soon, but not until he was off the road. Even though it was dark and the streetlamps were hardly giving off a dazzling illumination he didn't want to chance an encounter with someone appearing to put their bin out or catch them on their way to the pub.

Zipping his jacket up and making sure the balaclava was safely in his pocket he continued walking, looking for an alleyway further down the row of seemingly never-ending terraced houses.

He'd been beginning to think Hunter was in for the night so would have another day on his hands tomorrow watching the house, when the door opened, the big man jumped on his bike and roared off. Probably going to that White Hart place Neil had mentioned and where he was planning on going himself either later tonight or tomorrow.

Carmen had left around half an hour before and Jorge had initially been tempted to follow her to see if she led him anywhere that could prove interesting, but instead forced himself to remain where he was and wait.

In all honesty, he'd been glad when it looked like he wouldn't be able to pull off the pseudo-burglary. It wasn't his thing and although at a push, he understood Neil's reasoning for wanting to cause his estranged wife and her lover some extra hassle, he still couldn't help but feel that on the scale of things, it rendered rather pointless – not to mention risky. It was hardly worth the chance of getting a tug purely to piss someone off – especially not when there was a whole host of other things Neil wanted to achieve.

Jorge shrugged his shoulders. If that was what Neil wanted, then that was what he'd do.

Coming level with the arched opening of an alleyway between two terraces, he took a quick glance around to check the coast was still clear before quickly moving into the darkness.

Pulling his balaclava from his pocket, he yanked it over his face, already resenting the itchy material and waited a moment before moving, doing a quick mental calculation of how many courtyards or back gardens he needed to cross before reaching the back of the target house. *Ten, if he wasn't mistaken and he was pretty sure he wasn't.*

Jorge was well versed with the setup of terraces and the sporadic alleyways periodically placed between the wedged buildings. He just hoped the walls between the back gardens weren't too high and there were no random savage dogs lurking ready to rip his leg off.

Taking a deep breath, he stepped through the alley and effortlessly scaled the first wall. As he loped from backyard to backyard, thanks to a decent fitness regime, he barely broke a sweat and it all ran surprisingly smoothly, apart from once when he landed on a full bin bag which, as luck would have it, happened to be directly beneath the part of the wall he'd scaled. Satisfied that no one would notice until the morning that their weeks' rubbish had exploded over the backyard, Jorge continued. Counting under his breath, he stopped on reaching the tenth backyard and looked up at the back of the house. There was a light on. *Was this the right one?*

Creeping up to a sash window, he peered through the slightly open blind into a tiny utility room. From what he could see, no sign of life in there, but he expected most people wouldn't spend their evenings clustered around a utility room – although up in this neck of the woods it wouldn't have surprised him.

Why was he questioning himself? He'd counted the houses and this was the tenth. The target house was the tenth and both the occupants were out. *Easy.*

Grabbing a small piece of tarpaulin by the dustbin, Jorge held it over the small window and broke the single-glazed pane with his elbow. He then swiped the tarpaulin around the frame to dislodge any remaining shards and not wishing to hang around longer than necessary, pushed himself through the frame and dropped quietly to the utility floor.

He hadn't thought about what to do once inside, apart from smash the place up a bit like Neil suggested, but pushing open the kitchen door he froze seeing a woman staring at him wide-eyed, her back against the other door. *Shit! Who was that?*

'Who the hell are you?' the woman shrieked.

Jorge stared, unable to stop his eyes from roaming over the woman's shapely body. On any other occasion he'd be tempted to ask if she fancied a drink, but remembering himself, he narrowed his eyes. She must be a lodger. *Damn. He should have made sure no one else lived here. Stupid, stupid.*

'W-What do you want?' the woman cried, her voice getting shriller by the second.

Gritting his teeth, Jorge moved forwards, grabbing the woman's top and pushed her to one side. 'Get out of my way and you won't get hurt,' he growled.

He swiped at a pile of recently washed crockery, neatly washed and stacked at the side of the sink, sending it crashing to the floor. The woman screamed in fear and he cringed. *Christ, if she kept on like this, someone would hear.* She might be a pretty one, but he wasn't getting nicked because of a stupid bint with a big gob. All he had to do was smash the gaff up and then he'd be gone.

He stepped forward, hoping he looked intimidating in his balaclava, which was now itching him incessantly. 'Shut the fuck up,' he snarled. 'Otherwise I'll shut you up myself!'

The woman cowered against the wall in terror, her big blue eyes filling with tears as Jorge stormed into the small sitting room leading off from the kitchen. Spying the small television, he picked it up and launched it against the wall where it loudly imploded.

'P-Please leave. My boyfriend will be back soon,' the woman said.

Jorge turned, surprised this woman was stupid enough to follow him. He clearly didn't look menacing enough. *He'd have to work on that.*

'Your boyfriend?' Jorge tried not to smile. This silly cow was definitely not the girlfriend. From what he'd seen earlier it was clear who that Hunter bloke spent his time buried in and it wasn't *her.*

'He's only popped out.'

Jorge laughed. He had to give this tiny slip of a girl credit for playing the defiant card, even though she was terrified. He continued swiping at anything that wasn't nailed to the floor. 'Nice try, sweetheart. If that blond bloke that I saw snogging someone on this very doorstep earlier is your fella, then he's certainly not just shagging you!'

He watched the woman pale and stagger backwards. *That shut her up. Trying the "boyfriend will be back soon" chestnut.* It didn't change that he needed to get out of here pretty damn smartish though.

'What the fuck is this piece of shit?' he roared, grabbing something woolly remaining on the mantlepiece.

The woman's eyes widened and she flung herself forward. 'No! You can't take that!'

Surprised at her quick movement and obvious need for whatever rubbish was in his hand, Jorge tossed the woolly object into the fire. Screaming, the woman clawed at his balaclava, yelling at the top of her voice. Not knowing what else to do, he backhanded her, causing her to fly across the sitting room, smash into an armchair and land in a heap on the floor.

Dismayed he'd been forced to strike a woman, Jorge stood over her. 'Don't mess, lady. Tell Hunter his card's marked. He has an enemy - one he *doesn't* want.'

Quickly retracing his steps, he leapt from the utility window and back across the gardens, his heart hammering. *Fuck. That had not gone well.* It wasn't part of the plan to find a strange woman in there and neither was it the plan to whack her. He also knew he'd ballsed up by mentioning Hunter. It was supposed to be an anonymous "burglary". *Damn.*

Once safely in the alleyway between the terraces, Jorge ripped off his balaclava and adopted a leisurely pace back to his parked car. Should he call Neil and update him?

Jorge shrugged. He wouldn't. Something like this was hardly the impression he wanted to give. It made him look incompetent. Besides, Neil made it clear that he didn't want to be contacted unless it was an emergency and as far as he was concerned, this did *not* constitute as one.

Sod it, the job was done. He'd go and find this flat he'd been given the use of and make a start at the White Hart tomorrow.

TEN

'HOPE YOU'RE OK with sausages?' Hunter called cheerfully as he walked in the door.

Carmen was right. He'd been selfish accepting the Reapers' presidency without taking Tori's feelings on board or at the very least, discussing it with her. He knew she was struggling with everything, as was he, but his way of coping was like it had always been – revenge. Payback. *Retribution.* It was the way he'd always worked – the way he lived. But if he wanted Tori in his life, which he did, then whether he liked it or not he'd swallow the burning urge for justice and put it to one side.

He knew what he had to do. If it was the only way to keep Tori with him and give him a chance of her full forgiveness for what he'd done, as well as enabling her to get past the death of their son, then he'd walk away from the only family he'd ever known and go it alone with the woman he loved. It would be difficult, but she was more important and he'd just have to find a way to let the rest go.

'Tori?' Hunter called again as he walked down the hallway. 'Did you hear me? I'm back. I couldn't get fish, so I got saus…'

Tori was slumped on the sofa, blood spilling from the cut on her lip and her eyes puffy from crying, Hunter froze. He took in the state of the sitting room; the television was lying face down on the floor and there was stuff everywhere. *No...*

'What the fuck?' he shouted, rushing towards her. 'Are you alright? Who's done this?'

Tori burst into a fresh round of sobs. 'H-He threw Andrew's booties on the fire!' she cried, her voice choked.

'Threw his...? What? *Who?*'

'Andrew's booties. They were on the mantlepiece. H-He wouldn't listen. I tried to stop him...'

Hunter glanced at the bare mantlepiece. Everything which had been on it was now on the floor. He knew what Tori was referring to - those tiny knitted booties were the only thing remaining of their son. His temper spiked and he grabbed Tori by the shoulders. 'Who did this?'

'I-I don't know. I... A man... I was washing up and then the next thing I knew a man was in the kitchen.'

Hunter's eyes narrowed and adrenalin pounded in his veins. He ran his finger gently across Tori's split and bruised mouth. 'He did this?'

'I tried to stop him.' Tori burst into a fresh round of sobs. 'Those booties were the only things left of Andrew...'

Hunter pulled Tori's shaking body against his. 'Hey, come on,' he soothed. 'You're ok.'

But she wasn't ok. And neither was he. *None* of this was ok. How *dare* someone break into their house and touch her. This was his fault. The area was hardly the best, but it wasn't just him now. He had Tori to take care of. And what if Andrew had been here? The thought sickened him. It also sickened him that the one memento of Andrew's short life had now gone too because of some low-life.

'Bloody scum of a petty burglar,' he muttered, peering into the kitchen, growling at the pile of smashed crockery. His rage heightened but he knew for Tori's sake he must keep his temper.

Petty burglar or not, the prick had picked the wrong house and when he got his hands on whoever had done this and laid their hands on his missus, he'd wish he'd never been born.

'I-I'm not sure, Hunter,' Tori said quietly.

Hunter gently lifted Tori's head and looked into her frightened eyes questioningly. 'What do you mean?

'He said he'd seen you kissing someone... this afternoon... on the doorstep.'

'He said *what*?' Hunter could have laughed with the utter ludicrousness if it hadn't been so wrong. This scumbag who had smashed his house up and whacked Tori was accusing him of kissing another woman? 'What a load of bollocks! He was messing with your head. Probably a druggie.'

'I don't know...' Tori continued. 'He said your card is marked. He said, "tell Hunter he's made an enemy".'

Hunter's frown deepened. 'He knew my name?'

Seeing Tori nod, Hunter growled deep in the back of his throat. 'Are you sure?'

'Who was it?'

Hunter sat back on his haunches. That was the point – he had no idea. If this piece of shit knew his name, then it wasn't a chance break-in. It was a clear message, but from whom? He'd hugged Carmen on the doorstep this afternoon, but certainly nothing else. Regardless of that, it meant he'd been watched... 'Did you see anyone hanging around?'

'I haven't been out. I...'

Hunter rose to his feet, pulling Tori with him. If someone was watching them, knew his name and had sent a warning, then this wasn't something he could brush under the carpet. Tori had already been hurt, which meant she would continue to be at risk until he wiped the floor with whoever was behind this.

'Come on.' He dragged Tori towards the stairs. 'Throw some stuff in a bag. You're not staying here.'

'But we can't just leave!' Tori wailed.

'Oh yes we can. You can't remain here. Not until I know who's behind this.' Whatever his intentions were about walking away from the Reapers, he now had no choice but to backtrack on that.

'But where will we go?' Tori gasped as Hunter pulled her

up the stairs.

Hunter stopped and faced her. 'We're going to the Factory. We'll stay there.' Turning, he quickly walked up the rest of the stairs, not needing to see the expression on Tori's face.

· · · ·

GETTING UP FROM the armchair in the large living room, Susan wandered aimlessly around the huge expanse. She felt like a tiny pawn in a chessboard where she was the only piece.

The house felt empty, barren and huge. It felt cold and devoid of character. She'd never felt like this about her home in all the years she'd lived here, but now just how pointless everything seemed was weighing heavily.

She glanced up at the large chandelier dripping with crystals suspended from the middle of the high ceiling and felt like screaming at its obscene opulence. How she'd loved how her home oozed wealth, class and grandeur. How very important it had been. It proved that her marriage was successful and that she'd done well. It held her in good stead socially, making her feel that she'd achieved a lot. Now it all felt bland. Fake. *Empty.*

Richard was never anywhere to be seen – lost in his new social calendar of events that he'd suddenly decided were imperative. There was no Matthew, no Carmen. Not even Victoria. And to think she'd spent so long looking down her nose at the girl. It had only been when Victoria became pregnant had she felt her less of a usurper. Due to the nature of Victoria's initial admittance to the family, what with the arrangement Richard had made with that stupid woman, Lillian, Susan had never really approved, but by the end, she'd become quite fond of the girl.

And Susan had doted on little Andrew. Now there would be no more family dinners or a house full of children's chatter again, like it had been when Matthew and Carmen had been young, that's when Richard had allowed it, of course.

She sighed. She'd been expecting Matthew and Victoria to

add to their family quickly after Andrew was born. She knew Matthew was eager for several children and she'd been looking forward to it. She'd been looking forward to having her days filled with something more rewarding than lunch dates or bridge evenings with people she didn't like.

Even Lillian was no longer welcome and at first Susan had been glad of that, but now Richard had officially washed his hands of the entire Morgan family her loneliness meant that she was even starting to miss Lillian's bitchy comments.

Sighing once more she moved towards the staircase. *Should she do it? Should she go in and look?*

It had been several weeks since Matthew's funeral and she hadn't been able to face going into his room. Even though he'd had his own place for several years, he'd always spent a good deal of time here, staying half the week rather than at his own apartment. Susan smiled weakly. Matthew was her baby and always would be.

She'd cried so hard at Richard's suggestion to clear out their son's things, he'd stomped off to the Conservative Club to drown his sorrows. *Again.*

In fact, she was worried about him. Even though there was no way he'd admit it, she believed Matthew's death and ostracising their daughter had hit him harder than he'd ever say. She'd never seen him behave quite so erratically, acting paranoid - accusing her of moving and hiding things... Only the other week he'd been convinced he'd seen people in the garden...

Susan's bottom lip wobbled. Was he developing dementia? If he was, then she had no idea how she'd cope. Maybe it was the effect of retirement? If Matthew was here to take over the role at the bank as planned, then Richard would still be involved to some extent. But now he had nothing to do with the place. Maybe that was it? Everything had happened almost at the same time.

His behaviour was adding to her misery and she'd even begun to doubt whether there was anything between them anymore. But she couldn't possibly consider a divorce at her age. What would she do? She'd put up with a lot of things during her marriage, but the wealth and status Richard had kept her in had made up for it. Now it was wearing thin and felt unimportant.

Susan frowned. Whatever happened, for her own sanity she needed to do something. Something to shift her from the forlorn state she'd become entrenched in. Matthew wouldn't want her moping around for ever, would he?

She smiled, imagining the cocked eyebrow on her son's handsome face whilst he asked her what she was playing at.

Reaching the top of the stairs she padded along the upper hallway. Reaching the closed door of Matthew's room, she faltered, remembering the last time she'd stood in this very same spot, what had been the next thing she'd seen.

Shaking away the memory, Susan took a deep breath and opened the door. *It was time to move on.*

ELEVEN

'I UNDERSTAND what you're saying.' Sarah topped up Tori's glass of wine, 'but you've got to see it from his side too.'

She understood Tori's reluctance in relocating to the Factory and knew it was the last place she wanted to be – especially as from what Hunter had said, he'd made the decision to step away from the Reapers after all. But what had occurred last night put a different slant on things.

For someone to smash up Hunter's place and give that message, left no doubt that it was not a random thing. It was the start of retaliation from *someone*, but as to who...

Tori was still green over a lot of things, but Sarah appreciated Hunter's urge to remove her from where she could be a target. If someone was out for retaliation, Tori would be the first person to centre on to cause him the utmost pain.

She studied Tori's cut lip and bruised face and scowled. The poor girl had had enough of that from Matt and although he wasn't in the picture anymore, she didn't need that sort of shit from anyone else. For once, Sarah wholeheartedly backed Hunter's decision. It was the right thing to do. No, it was the *only* thing to do.

Tori gulped at her wine. 'What about what he said about

Hunter cheating? On my own doorstep? The only person that it could be is Carmen. Do you think it could be true?'

Sarah raised her eyebrows. 'Hunter would *never* cheat on you! That arsehole was looking for something to upset you. Ignore it – it's ridiculous!' She folded her arms across her chest. 'And Carmen? Come on, Tori. For a start, she thinks the world of you and even if she didn't, for some crazy reason she's too loved up with psycho Noel to even *look* at anyone else!'

Sarah frowned. Tori was the only one who'd seen Carmen for the last few days - she hadn't been in here – and, come to mention it, neither had Noel.

'You're right, I know.' Tori stared into her drink, flinching when someone dropped a glass behind her.

Sarah peered over Tori and glared at the perpetrator. The White Hart didn't get many new faces, however, this one was easy on the eye, with his tanned complexion and neat dark hair. Yep, he was nice-looking, but that wasn't too difficult based on half the folks who frequented her pub. But they were *her* people and she didn't know this guy from Adam. Clearly not from around here, she thought, clocking his clothing. A bit overdressed for a joint such as this, but still – that was his prerogative. Whoever he was she'd still tell him to sling his hook if he bust any more of her jars.

'He'd best not do that again or I'll be charging him for a new set of fucking pint glasses!' Sarah hissed, continuing to eye the stranger.

Despite everything Tori smiled, silently wishing she could be more like Sarah - hot-headed, but strong, taking everything on the chin, no matter what. She always looked at the logical or realistic side of things, so maybe she had a point about the Factory?

Tori had been both surprised and warmed when Hunter admitted he'd been planning to relinquish the presidency. Her lips pursed into a line. If only last night hadn't happened, she might have been free from the vicious circle the Reapers brought with them.

She shuddered. It had been horrible stepping back into the Factory last night, but the reception had been more welcoming than she'd expected. Despite this, she was grateful to Hunter for taking her straight upstairs, even though he was itching to discuss the nights' events with Noel, Grin and the others.

Tori glanced across the tap room to the alcove area where Hunter was deep in conversation with the other Reapers. They were clearly discussing the subject right now. Should she accept this was the way it would be? Was she being unfair expecting him to walk away from his life and how he knew to protect her?

Probably - a little, but that he was willing to meant a lot.

Sarah was right. She couldn't expect anything different now this had happened. If it was retaliation, then she'd still be in the same position – living in a state of fear. A cold chill ran up her spine and she trembled. *Hunter was a marked man.* That was what was said. *What happened if he was attacked? Murdered, even? What would she do? She couldn't bear to lose him.*

This epiphany made Tori realise that despite everything and her worry whether she could move past what had happened, one thing remained the same: she loved Hunter.

She took a deep breath. She would try her utmost to support what he needed, even if it was the polar opposite of what she'd hoped for. And if that meant embracing his return to the Reapers, then so be it.

• • • •

JORGE WAITED a few moments before making his way to the bar. He'd seen the death stare the bird behind the bar gave him when his glass slipped from his hand. The last thing he wanted was to draw attention. Infiltrating the club looked like it would be every bit as difficult as he'd presumed and he needed to think of a viable reason how to become involved, but all he could think of was how it seemed he'd royally fucked up.

He'd been minding his own business at a table against the far wall for about an hour, casually watching the group of bikers at the back of the pub when the man had come in – that Hunter bloke. With his senses on high alert, Jorge watched him stride over to the bar with a woman in tow, astounded to see it wasn't Carmen, but the woman he'd belted last night.

His stomach lurched, but reminded himself this didn't necessarily mean he was wrong over what he'd decided was going on. Unfortunately, he was left in no doubt seeing the way Hunter rested his hand protectively at the base of the woman's back, the way he touched her face and gently pressed his lips to hers. What she'd said was true – *she* was Hunter's missus…

But he'd seen Hunter kissing Carmen, hadn't he? And she'd been letting herself into the house too. Was the man having an affair literally on his own doorstep? Jorge wasn't sure, but what was obvious was that he'd jumped the gun. And if he'd jumped the gun, then he had no proof that Carmen was screwing a Reaper.

His neck prickled. Neil would not be happy if he'd got this wrong.

Jorge pursed his lips. He wouldn't inform Neil about this either – not yet. Besides, he may still be right. The big bloke might well be so arrogant to have an affair under his other half's nose. Whatever happened, he had to find out and get a move on about it. Firstly though, it was time to get his feet under the table around here.

Reaching the bar, Jorge flashed a dazzling smile, whilst purposefully not yet looking at the woman he'd cuffed. He still felt very uncomfortable about that, but the stupid cow had flown at him like a wildcat leaving him little choice.

Oh, who was he trying to kid? He'd given her a slap because it made it easier to do what was needed to impress Neil. And he didn't feel all that good about it.

Keeping his grin firmly in place, but not receiving a smile in return, Jorge instead mustered his best contrite, yet cheeky expression. 'Sorry about the glass. I've got holes in my hands tonight,' he laughed. 'Another pint please and a dustpan. I'll sweep the mess up.'

'Don't make a habit of launching my glasses, mate,

otherwise you'll get the bill!'

Jorge held his hands up in submission. 'Understood. I'll try my best not to do it again.' *Snotty bitch.* 'Now where's that dustpan?'

'Did you hear that, Tori? A man offering to clean something up! You can tell he's not from round here, can't you?'

'Oh dear,' Jorge smiled. 'Is it that obvious?' *So, the woman he'd whacked was called Tori?*

'That and your voice. I'm guessing you're from down south?'

Jorge's smiled remained. He'd expected to get grilled over that. His London accent stuck out like a sore thumb anywhere north of Watford bloody Gap, but it was ok because he'd already concocted a story. 'I'm actually from Bermondsey.'

Frowning, Sarah handed him the dustpan. 'What brings you to this neck of the woods then?'

Jorge's face fell. *This would get them. Women were always the sympathetic ones.* 'Bit of a long story. My sister was killed by a hit and run six months ago. It devastated me. We'd been very close since our parents died.' He sighed deeply. 'Thought a change of scenery would do me good, getting away from the memories, you know?'

'Sorry to hear that. That's tough.' Sarah glanced at Tori.

Jorge smiled. *He could feel the sympathy coming off them in waves.* He made a point of looking down sadly. 'Not sure if I'll settle here. Depends if I like it and of course, if I can find work.'

'What do you do?'

'I'm a mechanic,' Jorge said. *Well, almost.* Until his collection work became regular a couple of years ago, he'd done a few months of an engineering course for want of nothing better to do, so that counted, surely?

Sarah frowned, eyeing the stranger suspiciously. 'Bit overdressed for a mechanic!'

Jorge grinned, hiding the realisation that he probably shouldn't have worn such smart jeans and a shirt to a dump like this. 'Can't a man make an effort?' He glanced at Tori. 'What do you think? Am I dressed too smartly?'

'Hey, don't start hitting on her!' Sarah interjected. 'She's more than taken. As I am, in case you're wondering.'

Jorge wasn't wondering at all. Not about the barmaid anyhow and "hitting" on the pretty dark-haired girl was a very unfortunate phrase considering he'd been doing just that this time last night.

He turned to Tori, hoping the balaclava he'd worn had been enough to stop her recognising him and plastered on a look of concern as he pretended to notice her cut and bruised mouth. 'What happened?'

Tori looked down, embarrassed. 'Oh, erm nothing.'

Jorge frowned. 'I hope this boyfriend of yours isn't responsible for that!'

'I wouldn't let him catch you saying that! He'll have your guts for garters,' Sarah cried. 'If you must know, some bastard broke into her house last night. Fucking scum. Smashed the place up as well as her.'

Jorge raised his eyebrows. 'That's awful! Does that sort of thing happen a lot around here?"

'I can't see it being any worse here than Bermondsey, mate, so you should be alright,' Sarah snapped.

Jorge held his hands up. 'My, you're spiky! I didn't mean any offence.' *He hadn't expected an opportunity so soon, but here it was.* 'Come to think of it, last night I saw a dodgy guy hanging around myself. It looked like he was casing places...'

Sarah's ears pricked up. 'What? Around here?'

Jorge smiled. 'I doubt whether he was anything to do with the scum that broke into your place.' He looked at Tori. 'There were a lot of dodgy looking guys around last night, but that may just be how it is here. I've only been here a couple of days, so I've no idea of the lay of the land, what's normal, what isn't etc.'

Now, if he could only make this sound realistic. 'Anyway, it wasn't around here,' Jorge continued. 'I'm staying a couple of streets away, but, don't laugh – I got lost whilst coming back from the supermarket and I ended up driving all over the place. Haven't a clue how I managed it, but I remember where I saw this guy because there was a hairdressers with a cracking name at the end of the road: *"Hair Today Gone Tomorrow"*, it was called. Bloody good that,' he pretended to laugh at the memory.

Sarah stiffened and glanced at Tori. That was the name of the hairdressers by where Tori and Hunter lived. Could it be possible this man had seen the guy? 'What did the bloke look like?'

'About so high.' Jorge motioned to just over his shoulder. 'Five-eight at a guess? Standard trampy gear – trackie bottoms and zip up top. Blond scruffy shoulder-length hair. Looked a bit of a dope-head. Oh, and he was carrying a large holdall. Can't tell you more than that – it was dark, but he was right suspicious looking.'

Tori gauged how tall the man was when he'd stood menacingly in front of her last night. She'd thought him taller – more like six feet, but she couldn't be sure. It had happened so quickly she wasn't sure of anything, apart from that she'd been terrified. He had been wearing a tracksuit though, that she *did* know.

'I hope you got a good look at the bastard?' Jorge asked, scowling at Tori's cut lip. He needed to know if there was any recognition – even if it was just from his voice.

'No, his face was covered,' she muttered. Just thinking about it made her feel unsafe.

'Typical coward!' Jorge spat, glad he'd worn the balaclava. *She didn't have a clue, meaning he was home and dry.*

'Do you think it could be the same man, Sarah?' Tori asked, her heart racing. 'If Hunter can find out who it was then he'll be able to discover what it's all about. Maybe then he won't need to return to the Reapers after all?'

'Could *who* be the same man?' Hunter growled as he approached, placing his arm protectively around Tori's shoulder. 'This guy bothering you?'

'No, we were just talking about last night.'

Hunter bristled. *He'd told them not to discuss that. Not whilst he didn't know who was behind it.*

Tori clocked Hunter's expression. 'This man was just describing someone who was hanging about last night.' She lowered her voice. 'On *our* road…'

Jorge smiled. 'I'm Jorge, by the way. I've just been chatting to these two lovely ladies and trying to make up for smashing my glass.'

Hunter didn't return the smile. He wasn't in the mood for pleasantries. 'Then Jorge, you'd best fill me in with what you know on the off chance it's of use.'

TWELVE

SUSAN WAS PROUD OF HERSELF. Keeping it in her mind that she was just tidying up Matthew's room, like she'd done on countless occasions when he was a teenager, she'd managed to bag up all of his clothes without bursting into tears.

But it was no use kidding herself. Nothing could distract from the glaringly obvious truth that she was *clearing* his room. If she was merely "tidying" then she wouldn't be boxing things up, would she?

Matthew wasn't coming back – she knew that, but the act of emptying his room just seemed so… so *final*.

She wouldn't throw anything away even though Richard wanted her to. *"No point in keeping it, Susan"*, he'd barked. Susan pursed her lips. He could say what he liked; she wasn't doing it. Richard would get what he wanted with the room being cleared, but she wasn't getting rid of Matthew's things. She'd store them in boxes in the attic; they wouldn't bother Richard up there. In fact, she wouldn't even tell him. He never went up there, so he'd never know.

Finding one last shirt, Susan pressed it against her face and inhaled, detecting a faint hint of her son's aftershave. Her eyes filled up, but she quickly blinked the tears away.

Next was the desk and bedside table. This was the bit she'd been dreading. She felt awful, like she was trespassing or violating Matthew's privacy even, but it had to be done.

Holding back a sob, Susan emptied the desk, placing correspondence, unused notepaper and envelopes into a shoebox. *Matthew would never use these now.*

Sighing, she stared forlornly out of the window, resisting the urge to look up at the beam where her son had taken his life. If only she and Carmen had come home sooner. If only they hadn't gone out. If only Matthew had spoken of his pain, then she would have told him his marriage to Victoria wasn't ruined and that she was certain they could work it out – even after the devastation of losing their child.

Susan swallowed the lump in her throat and groaned audibly. 'Oh Matthew,' she whispered in the hope that he would somehow hear, wherever he was. 'Everyone goes through bad patches. There was nothing for you to feel guilty about. Victoria didn't blame you for Andrew's death, I know she didn't. She just needed time to get her head around it. You didn't have to do this, sweetheart. Victoria loved you just as much as I know you loved her...'

Finally giving in to her emotions, Susan staggered to the bed and sat down, her legs shaking. It was no good. She couldn't cope doing any more of this today. Richard might turn up for dinner tonight and if he did, then he'd know she'd been crying and would start on her again. Lately, he'd been nothing but horrible. Snappy, dismissive and generally suspicious.

Loneliness cascaded over her once again. Right now, she could do with his support rather than him adding to her problems, but each day looked like that was less likely.

Susan sighed. She yearned to see Carmen. It could be days or even *weeks* before the opportunity to spend time with her daughter without Richard's knowledge presented itself. She didn't dare risk it if there was a chance he might find out. That would push him even further away and she couldn't bear the thought of being even more alone than she already was.

Standing up, Susan smoothed down the bedspread. She must strip and wash those bedclothes, but that could wait for another time.

Suddenly her eyes caught something. Something on the floor under the bed. Just a small part of it was sticking out. *What was it?* Matthew had always been fastidious with tidiness. He must have dropped something without realising.

Tutting, Susan stooped down and put her hand under the bed, retrieving an envelope. She was about to put it in the shoebox with the other correspondence when the address caught her eye. *Matthew's solicitor.*

Surely this angst with Victoria hadn't gone as far as legal separation or divorce, had it? Oh God, no! Was that what had pushed him to take his own life?

Susan stared at the sealed envelope. Should she open it? It was wrong to read other people's personal things, but what if it was important?

She had to know, she just *had* to.

Quickly tearing open the envelope before she had chance to change her mind, Susan looked at Matthew's handwriting on the enclosed letter and with shaking hands, began to read.

· · · ·

LILLIAN HAD MORE than had enough of the enforced hiding she'd subjected herself to. Today, she was getting back out there and if anyone had anything to say about the newspaper article then they could do it to her face.

Sitting on the toilet in the Marlborough Hotel where the weekly luncheons were held, Lillian sniffed in derision. For several weeks running she'd bypassed these gatherings purely because she'd allowed everything to bother her. But no more.

After the incident with Isobel Gristhorpe in Waitrose following the publication of that article, she'd believed she was being publicly blanked everywhere she went. It was, of course, a ridiculous notion. She'd let one incident and the way Susan had all but thrown her out of the house, get to her and she was angry for allowing it to fester and affect her in the way it had.

Lillian fumed silently, still finding Susan, the candyfloss-haired has-been, audacity hard to believe. She'd specifically made the effort to warn her about that bloody article on Victoria and instead of gratitude, she'd been treated disgustingly? The mealy-mouthed woman had never so much as raised her voice before. *Never.*

Lillian pulled angrily at the embossed toilet tissue sitting in its gold-engraved holder. She'd fully expected Susan to call the next day apologising profusely about her unexpected outburst, but she hadn't. In fact, she'd heard nothing from the woman since. Neither had she heard from Richard and he should *definitely* know better.

Well, she wasn't having it anymore. If Susan wanted to play things that way, then she was on her own and she wouldn't let it impede her association with the social circles they shared anymore.

Standing up, Lillian rearranged her tights and dress suit, eager to get into the terrace restaurant when the external door to the powder room opened, along with a voice she recognised.

'I can assure you, hand on heart, that's what Richard said.'

Lillian remained motionless. *That was Sandra Mercer's voice. Was she talking about Richard Stevens?*

'Are you *sure*?' another voice asked.

Lillian hardly dared breathe. That was Isobel Gristhorpe! What was this about? It sounded interesting. God knows how much gossip she'd missed during her absence. She had loads to catch up with and just hoped they weren't still prattling on about the article. That would have surely been done and dusted by now, but she refrained from opening the cubicle door just in case.

'Look,' Sandra continued. 'Richard was at the club with Andrew and he said – no word of a lie – that Victoria was known for mental illness. Like I said, she'd been institutionalised earlier this year, apparently.'

'But that's astounding! And to think Lillian expected her

daughter to keep those secrets about her father for all of these years! Fancy marrying a drug addict or dealer, whatever he was!'

Lillian almost choked from within the small space of the cubicle. *Was she hearing correctly?*

Sandra tittered. 'Well, she had no choice, being as she was already with child! Fancy that! I'd never have guessed, you know?'

Isobel laughed loudly. 'The next time Lillian berates someone's morals, I don't know how I'll keep a straight face!'

'I for one won't be seen associating with her anymore. Her husband was a cheap criminal! One of the lower class too, by all accounts,' Sandra sniffed.

'No wonder she just appeared out of the blue all those years ago with her daughter. We all questioned where she'd come from at the time, remember? Why on earth Richard introduced her in the first place, *that's* what I want to know.'

'Apparently, she's of good blood - Richard knew her from long back, but when she married a thug, they lost contact. I still can't get over it. I feel terribly sorry for the Stevens for being lied to all of these years. Richard told Andrew he's banned the woman from having anything to do with his family from now on.'

Lillian's face burned with humiliation and resentment. Richard had said all that? And to Andrew Mercer? Between him and Sandra, *everyone* would know about this. Feeling her legs shaking she leant against the cubicle walls to steady herself. What was she going to do?

'No wonder the girl turned funny!' Isobel said. 'And, I hate to say it, but it's a good job what happened with those kiddies otherwise the Stevens would forever be burdened with not only that sort in their family, but also in their bloodline.'

'What a horrific thought! Anyway, let's get back in there before everyone presumes we've gone missing as well,' Sandra laughed.

Hearing the external door close, Lillian fumbled with the

catch on the cubicle door, anger pounding through her body. She walked out to the mirrored vanity unit and stared at her reflection. Her life was over. Everything she'd worked so hard to ensure didn't happen, just had. She shook her head, still unable to quite believe Richard had done this to her.

Groping in her handbag, Lillian somehow kept her hand steady enough to apply another coat of her favourite magenta lipstick. She'd call a taxi. She couldn't go in there now. And when she got home, she knew exactly what she was going to do.

THIRTEEN

'JESUS CHRIST, I never realised it was *that* bad!' Carmen exclaimed.

Noel scowled, anger radiating. 'I resented Hunter for years. And I mean *years*. I thought he'd covered things up to save his own skin, but he hadn't. He'd been trying to right his mistake.'

Carmen nodded, although she wasn't altogether sure how anyone could ever put right killing someone, let alone the wrong person? And that person was Tori's father? A mistaken identity? Jeez. No wonder Tori felt screwed up. And Matt had told her this when she was heavily pregnant? What was the matter with people? Damn her brother for making things worse.

She studied Noel, her eyes running over the deep crease lines on his forehead. There was a lot of things she couldn't and never would understand about how the Reapers worked. How must Noel feel being a product of rape? His poor mother.

Carmen swallowed dryly. It made her own issues with Luca and her anger over the marriage arranged by her father pale into insignificance.

Lots of things began to fall into place and a further rush of tenderness for the big, yet very dangerous man she'd fallen in love with flooded over her, but she wasn't quite ready to question how she felt knowing the things she now knew or by being surrounded by the people who did them. All she knew was after her loveless marriage, Noel had shown her that real love and hot passion really *did* exist.

Carmen smiled to herself. She and Noel had spent a lot of time together the last couple of days. Just *them*. She'd been astounded at Noel's suggestion that since stepping down as President, he wanted a short break from the Factory *and* the White Hart. This was unprecedented. He'd always been at either one place or the other and the only time they'd ever spent alone, up until now, was in bed. And even then there was usually someone banging on the door! But she wasn't complaining. As well as spending a most enjoyable amount of extra time between the sheets, they'd also talked. And talked a *lot*. They'd had some great conversations and she'd learnt a massive amount about this man of hers. Regardless of being rough and ready, Noel was more intelligent than people surmised – herself included and despite everyone's initial reservations about her involvement with him, she wasn't in the remotest bit sorry.

Noel had opened up these past few days – more than she'd ever expected and against all odds, their relationship had moved further than she'd ever thought possible. Although her feelings for this brute of a man had always surprised her, she now knew without any shadow of a doubt, that they had connected deeply and her love for him was without question.

Putting her hands either side of Noel's face, Carmen kissed him gently. 'Thank you for being so honest,' she whispered.

Noel looked away, embarrassed. He was unsure what this woman had done to his brain, but with her... with her, it was different. She'd released something he hadn't thought he possessed and for the first time in his life, felt there was more the world could offer besides rage, resentment and violence.

'I wonder how Tori will take the lesson Hunter's planning for her?' he said, steering the conversation away from his personal circumstances. He'd already spoken more about those lately than he'd ever done.

Carmen stroked Noel's thigh teasingly. 'What lesson?'

'Hunter's teaching Tori to shoot.' Despite his initial resentment of Tori, Noel had developed a new-found respect for the woman. She was good for Hunter and furthermore, she'd stuck by him and he had to give her kudos for that.

'To *shoot*?' Carmen shrieked. 'What? A gun? Are you serious? Why?'

Noel pulled Carmen onto his lap. 'Why do you think? Given the current situation, he needs to know she can protect herself and I get that. I'd do the same if it were you.'

Carmen wrapped her arms around Noel's neck. 'Would you now...?' she smiled. 'I'm not sure how Tori will feel about shooting though.'

Noel's face adopted its usual harsh stance. 'She needs to learn. She's a target as long as Hunter is and will remain so until we find out who's behind this shit.'

Carmen nodded. She was worried too. It didn't take a scientist to work out that the Reapers had made plenty of enemies over the years. She shuddered slightly, wondering if she should broach the subject with Noel about Luca. Both of them could be at risk of reprisals if Luca decided he wouldn't let her go, but then he was too busy making money and swanning around in his flash car to bother fighting for her.

Noel wasn't though. Noel would fight for her.

'Do you want me to teach you to shoot?' Noel murmured, his thick fingers making their way under the waistband of Carmen's skirt.

Carmen pushed Noel backwards on the sofa and unzipped his flies. 'Not right now, I don't...'

Noel groaned as Carmen straddled him, his mouth searching for hers. Whether he liked it or not, he was in love with this woman and he'd made his decision. *He wanted her for keeps.*

· · · ·

UNABLE TO SLEEP the entire night, Susan had the most excruciating headache. She massaged her temples to achieve a tiny bit of respite from the pain, but it didn't work. She didn't think anything would.

She fumbled for her glass of water whilst Richard's contemptuous glare burnt into her from the opposite side of the table. On any other day she'd have been grateful of his company, even if lately he'd had nothing nice to say to her, but now his presence made her want to be *anywhere* but in the same room. The same house. Even the same *world*.

She had to talk to someone about what she'd found, but who?

Susan sipped at her water, making sure her eyes remained averted from her husband. She couldn't bear to even look at him.

'What's the problem?' Richard growled. 'You're more morose than usual and look a complete mess. Don't you even have the self-respect to do your hair, Susan?'

'I don't feel well,' Susan muttered, the words lodging in her throat. She didn't think she'd ever feel well again if what she'd read was true.

'You should go to the doctors,' Richard sneered.

'I don't need a doctor. It's only a headache.'

That's a matter of opinion, Richard thought, his eyes narrowing. If Susan had taken his notebook she'd no doubt put two and two together and worked out he'd been filtering the bank's money for years. Maybe *that's* why she was acting weird?

A flutter of panic stirred and he rapidly pushed it away. What was he worrying about? Susan wouldn't say anything because no one would believe she hadn't been party to it and there was no way she'd want people thinking she was involved. It also meant that, by association, Matthew would have known about it too – which he had, well, some of it and Susan definitely wouldn't want *his* memory sullied.

On top of that, not only would she lose the way she was

accustomed to living – it was the way she'd *expected* to live. His wife had only ever been interested in how she was perceived and how much she was worth financially. He'd always delivered what she'd wanted, but it wasn't up to her to question *how* he'd done it.

Richard almost laughed out loud. He was safe. Susan wouldn't breathe a word about the suspect financial decisions he'd made - she had too much to lose. The worst she could do is nag him, but he wouldn't put up with that either.

Talking of greedy interfering women, his plan to oust Lillian was paying off. Andrew Mercer must have done the rounds because Susan was receiving phone calls from a selection of her busy-body "friends". She may not be happy about the constant stream of questions, but he was because it meant Lillian would by now be more than aware that her dirty laundry had been publicly aired.

He hadn't yet heard a word from her about it, presuming she'd gone into enforced hiding and would remain there for some time before showing her face again – if she ever did... Not that there was much chance of her being invited to anything anymore, at least by anyone he knew.

Richard couldn't help but smirk. Lillian's time was up. The best she could do now was to pack up and disappear to pastures new. Yes, his plan to rid of her had unfolded perfectly and so quickly too.

'Are you going out today?' Susan asked, hoping for once the answer would be yes.

'I might hang around and give one of those house clearance firms a call like I said I would if Matthew's room wasn't cleared. From what I can see, it hasn't been.'

Susan paled. 'You don't need to do that. I've already made a start.' But she doubted whether she'd be able to finish. Not now. Not until she'd decided what to do. She needed time to think.

If she called the police, then Richard would be arrested. He'd probably go to jail and everyone would find out. Sweat formed across Susan's chest and trickled between her breasts. Then she'd have no one. *No one*. And she was unsure if she could bear that. But could she stand being around him now?

What was she to do? Should she talk to Carmen? Was it fair to burden her daughter with this? That was of course, assuming it was true? She knew what she *wanted* to believe, but the niggling suspicion was there all the same.

'Are you even on this bloody planet?' Richard barked, jolting Susan from her torturous thoughts.

'What? I...'

Richard shook his head in derision. 'This is ridiculous! I'm going out.'

'Out?' Susan parroted, concealing her relief.

'Yes, *out*. I'll be back at some point later.' Grabbing his jacket, Richard walked out of the front door, slamming it loudly behind him.

He looked down the drive, making sure that car wasn't parked there again. He'd been convinced he'd seen the very same one drive past as he'd gone into the Conservative Club last night, but he was being stupid. All of this stuff with Susan must clearly be getting him down.

FOURTEEN

JOHN TURNER LISTENED stony-faced as his best enforcer brought him up to date with the state of play. And what he heard wasn't good.

Shaun was the best and most experienced collector and John trusted his word. He knew for a fact that Shaun's team were already up to their necks with the bigger, more complex debtors because he'd allotted these jobs himself. If Shaun was saying he and his team were getting overrun and caught up with the stupid little collections that Jorge had been dealing with, then that was exactly what was happening.

'I'm having to use Tony for the small jobs. Being one man down is causing havoc with our schedule,' Shaun said, hating to be the bearer of bad news.

John frowned as he looked at the team roster evidently showing collections had not been followed up in the expected window of time. It was obvious losing the muscle and time dealing with Jorge's workload in addition to everything else was causing problems. To have someone like Tony wasted on piddling jobs was a complete waste of manpower, but *one* of them had to take care of it. It was a pain in the arse and a lot of hassle purely to pull in a few quid, but it was a vicious circle.

People couldn't be allowed to take the piss. If they let one off the hook – even a nobody, then it was only a matter of time before word spread that the firm was getting slack.

John's lips formed a tight line as he glanced at Neil, more interested in the newspaper than what was being discussed and seemingly oblivious his demands had caused a backlog. Neil's decision to use Jorge for his own gain was not working. This was *his* side of the business, not Neil's and there was a very good reason for that.

'How much longer do you require Jorge up north?' John asked, keeping his irritation under wraps.

'Not sure yet. What's the issue?' Neil said, glancing up.

'One of our team's having to step into Jorge's place in his absence and we could do with him back.'

Neil frowned and stared at Shaun. 'You'll get him back soon enough, but you need to juggle your workload better in the interim. Whether these people own a tenner or ten grand, *no one* takes liberties - you know the score. I won't have tossers encroach on our business.'

John bristled and glared at Neil, not appreciating the insinuated incompetence on his men's part. 'Shaun knows what he's doing, Neil. Taking one of these men to spend all week chasing the toenail debtors isn't a good use of their time.'

'I'm managing the schedule in the only way possible, but we can't let the lower debtors slide because they'll start talking,' Shaun said, aware of John's growing anger towards Neil. 'But it's causing delays with the follow ups for the larger debtors.'

Neil's eyes glinted. 'There's an easy way around that!' Pulling a machete from his waistband, he enjoyed the look of shock of the other men's faces. 'Hack a hand off one of them,' he smiled. 'Word will rapidly spread that *no one's* getting slack!'

He was sick of excuses and people taking liberties. His intention of playing things differently with his slag of a wife, the Reaper twat and Richard-bloody-Stevens was getting right on his tits and every day sitting on his hands not doing what he *really* wanted was getting more frustrating. Although initially impressed with how quickly Jorge had got cast iron info that Carmen was playing away and who with, the rest of what he wanted achieving would take *ages* to pull off. Laboriously slow games weren't his cup of tea. Quite frankly, they irritated him.

'If Jorge being off the scene is causing so much of a fucking problem, give me some names of these dregs. I'll visit them myself and get the message across!' Neil glanced at the massive glinting blade and felt the familiar rush of adrenalin. *God, he'd missed this.* Doling out some well-deserved warnings would be just what the doctor ordered to take his mind off everything else as well as an opportunity to release some pent up frustration.

John stepped forward, his face a mask of rage. He looked at Shaun and nodded towards the door. 'Get yourself out of here for a while. There's some things I need to discuss with Neil.'

Shaun glanced at Neil uncomfortably. He'd always taken orders from John Turner, but Neil Sparks was also the boss and he felt like a pawn stuck between them. Eyeing the machete in Neil's hand and the fury on John's face, being in the middle of these two wasn't somewhere he wanted to be, so nodding, he quickly left through the office door, shutting it heavily behind him.

John remained impassive as Shaun left the office, watching Neil casually clean his blade. Having it out with him in front of one of the boys wasn't good for the firm. Privately, yes, but nowhere else.

What was Neil thinking of suggesting this sort of shit? They were equals in this firm, even if lots of people assumed Neil was the head honcho. Staying out of the limelight was fine as far as John was concerned, but he would not have Neil rocking back up and treading on his toes. *He* dealt with the enforcement side of things and that had always been the arrangement.

Satisfied Shaun was no longer in earshot, John snatched up the decanter and poured himself a large bourbon, his hands shaking with rage. 'Are you going to tell me what the fuck that was about?'

Neil held his hands up. 'Just trying to get the point across. If you can't get your men to keep up with demand, then I...'

John slammed his glass down. 'Cut the crap! Telling my boys to hack a man's hand off over a late payment isn't the way we do things!' Well, it wasn't the way *he* did things. *He* did things the *right* way and if Neil thought he could waltz back in here and start that lark, then he could fuck off back to France.

Neil opened his mouth to speak, but John was far from finished. He paced around the other side of the desk. '*I* deal with enforcement Neil, not *you* and I'll only sanction heavy-handed tactics under warranted circumstances. We're not fucking *Yardies*!'

Neil folded his arms across his chest. 'People need reminding! There should be *no* late payers. End of!'

'What the hell is the matter with you?' John roared.

Neil's eyes narrowed and he snatched up the decanter, pouring himself a large measure. 'I'm sick of people taking the piss.'

John studied Neil. He could almost see the frustration seeping out of his pores. 'Is this to do with Carmen?' Detecting the tiny twitch below Neil's eye, he knew he'd hit the nail on the head. 'What's the problem? Jorge's dealing with what you're asking of him, isn't he?'

Neil downed his bourbon and slammed the empty glass on the desk so hard it was a miracle it didn't shatter. 'Things are too fucking *slow*! I want to go up there and deal with it myself.

John sighed. He'd wondered how long it would take Neil to get impatient, despite what he'd previously said. 'You know that can't happen. You'd be the first in the line of suspects if you go in heavy-handed with anything concerning the Reapers. We can't risk coming under scrutiny again. That stuff with them last time all but wrecked everything, remember? This is *my* life and business too, Neil. You're not even supposed to be back in the country! The deal you made was to never return.'

'The Reapers set that condition, not me,' Neil spat. 'And

the person I agreed that with died yonks ago. A different generation's in charge now.'

'And you really think Rafe wouldn't have informed the rest of them? We handed over our Northern patch to save the business and get you off the hook. The Reapers weren't going to take the flack for nothing!'

Neil poured another drink. 'That's irrelevant. The bastard was an underhand fucker.'

'A deal's a deal,' John continued. He didn't want a war with the Reapers or anyone else, for that matter. He certainly didn't want a war purely because Neil was a stubborn, cantankerous nut-job.

'That as maybe, but the deal became null and void once their President started knobbing my wife!' Neil roared. 'They've done this to wind me up and I'm *not* having it! Neither am I having it that the ponce who arranged my identity papers and promised me a wife who could stay the distance, lied. I paid that twat thousands for Carmen and I mean *thousands*!'

John nodded. He knew only too well because the money had come from the business, almost breaking it. 'Does she know?'

'Does *who* know?'

'Carmen. Does she know about you? I mean, *you*, rather than Luca?'

'Why the hell would she? And don't mention that name again. I'm not Luca and will never be!'

'Why did she leave then?'

'How the fuck do I know? As far as I knew she was visiting family. It wasn't like she wrote *"Oh, by the way, I'm not coming back and I thought I'd go looking for a Reaper to fuck instead"*, was it? The first I knew of this Reaper bollocks was when her brother phoned.'

John perched on the edge of the desk. 'Getting back to the issue in hand, how long will Jorge be up north for?'

'For however long I need him,' Neil muttered.

'The things you're asking of him take time.'

'I'm not waiting for ever. It's not the way I work.' Neil sighed. 'Look, I'm trying to do things the way I said, but I've sped things up a bit now, so hopef...'

Alarm bells clanged in John's head. 'What do you mean you've sped things up?'

'Keep your hair on. Just sent a little note to Stevens for amusement value and also put things in motion to get that Hunter prick taken out. Jorge confirmed the man's shagging my wife, so he's good to go!'

He'd wait a bit before signing off the hit on Hunter though. He wanted to piss Stevens off first and would enjoy knowing, if the man had one ounce of sense in his big fat stuck-up head, then once he received the note he'd put two and two together and realise, he, Neil Sparks, wanted compensation for the shite wife he'd been saddled with.

'Have you updated Jorge about this?'

Neil glowered. 'Why the fuck would I? He takes orders from *me*, not the other way around!'

'But you may have interfered with his plans?'

'Well, he should have moved fucking quicker on whatever he's doing.'

John slammed his fist on the desk. 'For God's sake, Neil! You could put him at risk by adding this into the mix.'

Neil shrugged. 'In that case it will give him the hint that I expect faster results.'

John's concern bubbled, fast wishing he hadn't stuck his neck out giving the inexperienced lad a job in the first place. If he'd known this was part of the equation rather than info gathering, he'd have found a way of talking Neil out of sending Jorge, or at least insisting Shaun accompanied him. Most experienced men would struggle single-handedly with what was expected, let alone under such unrealistic timescales.

John glared at Neil. 'You need to think about this. He's your *son*!'

Neil shrugged. He couldn't give a rat's arse *whose* son Jorge was.

. . . .

JORGE WAS BACK in the White Hart after a fruitless day watching the target house. He'd sat outside in his car for hours and had seen nothing - no comings or goings or anything. *Again.*

He took a long slug of his pint, refraining from wrinkling his nose up at the strong smell of disinfectant emanating from the glass. He needed to see Carmen with Hunter again like he'd witnessed on the doorstep, but she was nowhere to be seen. He'd also been stupid mentioning anything to Tori about it. If she *wasn't* party to it then she'd have confronted Hunter, so he'd have cooled things with Carmen. Either that or be more conspicuous about their lust and take it elsewhere.

What a bloody stupid thing he'd done and with the *worst* possible timing to boot. Now he was stuck between a rock and a hard place. If Carmen *hadn't* got a thing going with Hunter then he'd have to inform Neil, but firstly he needed to find out if it wasn't Hunter, then exactly who the source of her affections was with. The way things were going, he was no closer to finding out either.

Jorge glanced around. There were several Reapers here, including Hunter, but he was getting nowhere with infiltrating the group, despite hanging around in this fleapit every night.

Watching Hunter make his way over to the bar, Jorge decided it might be time for another drink himself. He glanced at his half-full glass and rather than forcing himself to put his mouth back on the detergent-scented pint, he surreptitiously tipped the remains onto the garish carpet.

Getting up, he slipped into the space between Hunter and another man who looked worryingly like he should be wandering around with a chainsaw. Standing awkwardly, he willed himself to relax. He didn't usually have problems making conversation, but this lot unnerved him.

Waiting to catch Sarah's eye, Jorge glanced at Hunter and nudged him gently. 'Alright, mate?' Seeing the unbridled ferocity in the man's unusual grey eyes as Hunter spun around, he quickly stepped back.

'Oh, it's you,' Hunter muttered.

Jorge smiled. 'I was just wondering if you'd had any luck finding that bloke, you know th...'

'Too many fitting that description around here for your info to be worth looking into,' Hunter shrugged.

'Oh.' Jorge looked crestfallen. 'I was hoping my description would have helped.'

'Yes, Hunter?' Sarah said brightly, picking up a fresh pint glass in readiness.

'Same again please,' Hunter grunted.

Jorge remained silent. He'd get *nowhere* at this rate.

'Bad day?' Sarah asked Hunter. 'You've got a face like a slapped arse!'

Jorge bit back a smile. This woman must be on *really* good terms with this lot to get away with comments like that!

Hunter ran his thick fingers through his shaggy blond hair. 'Billy's bike's playing up. I think it's the carb. I'd look myself, but I haven't got my tools and of course, Grin isn't about when I need him.'

Jorge had no idea who Billy or Grin were and didn't really care. What he wanted to know was why Hunter wasn't at his house, but he could hardly sneak that question into the conversation.

'Billy's on an early job tomorrow and Grin won't be back until tomorrow night, so it's a total pain in the arse,' Hunter continued.

Sarah glanced at Jorge. 'Maybe *you* could take a look? Don't suppose you've got your tools with you, have you?' She turned to Hunter. 'Jorge is a mechanic.'

Hunter stared at Jorge quizzically. 'Know anything about bikes?'

Jorge grinned, hoping he looked convincing. 'Not as much as I know about cars, but I'll take a look. I've got some tools in the back of my motor and might have the ones I'd need.' *Fuck.*

Fuck. FUCK. What could he remember from the stuff he'd learnt during the short period at college? Why had he told Sarah he was a mechanic?

Hunter nodded. 'Ok, better than nothing, I guess?'

Jorge remained smiling. *Better than nothing? The ungrateful bastard!*

'See!' Sarah winked at Jorge. 'You may well get some work yet! Oh, hang on, there's the phone. I won't be a tick.'

Jorge watched Sarah answer the phone. 'I'll go and get my tools,' he muttered, planning to rummage around in the boot for anything which would suffice in dealing with a carburettor.

'Hunter, do you know where Carmen is?' Sarah asked, returning to the bar.

Jorge's ears pricked up. He remained where he was, pretending to search his pocket for his car keys.

Hunter shook his head. 'Haven't seen her for a couple of days. Guess she must be at the flat. Why? What's up?'

Jorge listened. *Flat? What flat?*

'That was her mother. It's urgent she sees Carmen,' Sarah said. 'I'll go and tell her. Colin will have to run the bar – he's doing paperwork upstairs.'

Hunter tipped the dregs of his pint down his throat. 'No need. I'll tell Carmen. Let Colin get on with his stuff.'

Sarah grinned. 'Oh, thanks so much! Are you sure?'

'It's not a problem. I should be going anyhow. Give the drink you've poured to him.' He nodded towards Jorge.

Jorge signalled his thanks. *This was excellent.* He'd give Hunter a couple of minutes to get on his bike, then he'd tail him. Now he'd discover where Carmen was. It was hardly surprising that Hunter should offer to give her the message – it was a good excuse for a quick shag.

Jorge's elation at his good fortune was fast reduced to rubble when Hunter shouted across the bar. 'Bill? This bloke's going to take a look at your bike.' Nodding in Jorge's direction, Hunter strode from the White Hart.

Jorge's chances of tailing Hunter were well and truly

scuppered when a mountain of a man with no neck and arms like tree trunks lumbered across.

'You the mechanic?' Billy growled, slapping Jorge on the back just that little bit too hard.

FIFTEEN

CARMEN WAS BOTH SURPRISED and concerned to receive a message from her mother. She'd only handed her the White Hart's number in case of emergencies. She was already worried about her mother's well-being. The last time she'd seen her she hadn't been in the best state of mind, but Hunter had said her mother hadn't given Sarah any impression of being unwell, just that it was urgent to see her.

Carmen turned into the familiar long driveway of the house she'd grown up in, glad to see her father's car wasn't there, but her heart still pounded with nerves.

The door opened before she even reached the top of the steps. 'Hi Mum,' Carmen said, hiding her shock at her mother's tiny, shrunken appearance and pulled her into a hug, not dwelling on the bony frame beneath her hands.

'I'm so glad you're here,' Susan whispered on the verge of tears. She was unsure whether she'd made the right decision calling, but she had to do something before she went crazy. Depending on Richard's movements, this could be the only opportunity she might get to see Carmen for a while.

'What's going on?' Carmen asked, following into the hallway, frowning at her mother's hollow, grey face. 'Are you alright?' That was a stupid question. It was obvious she was *far* from that.

Susan turned to Carmen, her eyes red and watery. 'It's Matthew... he...'

Seeing her mother's bottom lip tremble, Carmen steered her into the sitting room and sat her down on the sofa. 'What is it?' she asked warily.

'I went into Matthew's room to clear his things away... Your father... he wants the room emptied. He's been on at me for a while now, saying it's not normal to keep it like a shrine.'

Carmen's lips pursed. Her father really was a thoughtless bastard. Could he not see how hard this was for her mother? But what if being in Matt's room had brought everything back? What if she'd been going over in her head about the suicide note and what it meant? Had her mother come to the same conclusion that she, herself had? That Matt couldn't live with what he'd done? Did she now suspect Matt had killed Andrew too?

Susan grabbed Carmen's hand. 'I found a letter under Matthew's bed. He must have dropped it. It was sealed and addressed to the solicitor ready to be posted.'

Carmen frowned. 'Matt's solicitor?'

Susan nodded. 'I thought Victoria might have asked for a divorce and then started thinking if it was that, did it push Matthew over the edge? Was it that which made him...?'

'Did you open it?' Carmen pushed, wishing her mother would get to the point. 'Was it about a divorce?' Surely Tori would have mentioned it to her if she'd begun divorce proceedings against Matt before he died?

'Oh God,' Susan flapped her hand in front of her face. 'I didn't know whether to call you. I've been up all night... I...'

'Mum! Are you going to tell me what's going on, or not?'

Susan swallowed nervously and reached for her handbag. Unzipping one of the internal compartments, she pulled out a folded envelope and with shaking hands, handed it to Carmen.

Hardly able to control her haste, yet weirdly reticent to

discover what had upset her mother so greatly, Carmen fumbled to get the letter out of its envelope, immediately recognising Matt's writing. A lump formed in her throat as her brother's face flashed vividly in her mind.

Carmen unfolded the rest of the letter and began to read:

Jake,

As I've explained before, here's the letter to open in the event something happens to me. Being as you've opened it, you'll know that something HAS.

My father, Richard Stevens, has admitted to killing the kid because I wasn't handling not being the boy's father. He was worried people would find out.
He also was unhappy that I'd called Luca (that's Carmen's husband) to tell him she's been sleeping with a Reaper. He's had an issue with those bikers for ages – I don't know all the reasons, but one is because they know he stole money from the bank to pay them off. He also paid Lillian. Probably others too.

I don't trust him. If he sets me up for killing the kid, the money or something else and I go to jail, I want you to use this info any way you need to get me out.

Yours

Matt

Carmen stared at the words swimming in front of her eyes. *No, this couldn't be right.*

'What should I do?' Susan wailed. 'I'm so worried. I didn't know whether to even tell you. He's your father and…'

'You *believe* this?' Carmen asked, reading the letter again, struggling to take in the contents.

'I-I don't know what to think,' Susan whispered. 'Your father... He's acting very strangely. I'm beginning to think he could have dementia... I...'

'*Dementia*?'

'He keeps forgetting things and accuses me of moving stuff. He's also paranoid and he...'

'He hasn't got dementia, Mum. Far from that!' Carmen's mind swirled. Matt wrote their father had admitted killing Andrew, but Matt had admitted to that, hadn't he? And what was this about phoning Luca? Why would he do that?

Her eyes narrowed. Because he was like that, that's why. A cold rush passed through her. If he *had*, Luca would not agree to an amicable divorce. She knew him well enough to know that although he'd been uninterested in her throughout their marriage, he'd take this as a personal affront.

But she *didn't* know him. That was the whole point. She didn't have a clue *who* Luca was... But her father? Killing a baby? He might be an obnoxious controlling twat, but *that*? Matt on the other hand...

'Is any of this true?' Susan said, her voice tiny.

'I-I don't know... I...'

Susan gripped Carmen's arm. 'Tell me, was Andrew Matthew's child?'

Carmen hesitated. She'd hoped never to be asked that question. She saw the desperation in her mother's eyes and would love to give her the answer she wanted, but it was no good. There had been too many lies.

'C-Carmen?' Susan whispered, not liking her daughter's hesitation.

Carmen sighed. 'No, Matt wasn't Andrew's father.'

Susan put her hands to her mouth, her face pained. 'Oh my God! Who... who...?'

'Ashley Hunter,' Carmen sighed. 'He's the president of the Reapers.'

Susan retched, her face a ghastly white. 'The *Reapers*? That dreadful motorbike group? Oh no, oh Carmen, how could she?

How could Victoria…'

'You don't understand. Matt forced Tori's relationship with the man. It was part of a deal he was working on at the bank.'

Susan looked like she might pass out. 'W-What?'

Carmen nodded. 'It's true. Except Hunter and Tori fell in love for real. Hunter's a good man.'

'A good man?' Susan spat. 'How can people like *that* be good?' She folded her arms. 'You *knew* all of this? And Victoria let Matthew think th…'

Carmen understood her mother's indignation. This, combined with the shock of finding out she'd never been a grandmother would make it difficult to be rational. 'Mum, however much you don't want to hear it, Matt was *horrible*. He was my brother and I loved him, but I despised him too. He, thanks to Dad, messed with Tori's contraception and Matt was too stupid to figure, after what he'd asked of her, that the child might not be his.'

Carmen couldn't gloss over her mother's rose-tinted view of Matt any longer. If her mother wanted the truth, then she would get it. *All* of it. 'He hit her too. Did you realise that?'

Susan's eye twitched, as she struggled to take the information in. 'Matthew would have never do…'

'I saw him hit Tori with my own eyes! Why do you think I made her go to Lillian's? There was so much stuff Matt did. He arranged to get her sectioned too.'

Susan felt sick. 'And your father knew all of this?'

'Of course! He engineered half of it. He arranged my marriage as well. Did you know that?'

'I had no idea…' Susan said quietly, her mind spinning. She had never been happy about Richard arranging Matthew's marriage, but at least he'd been aware of it, but to do this to Carmen without her knowledge? And Matthew – the way he'd treated Victoria? Even though her children had always cultivated a dreadful sibling rivalry, she could see just by Carmen's face that her daughter was not being untruthful.

'I don't even know who Luca is!' Carmen cried. 'I heard

him on the phone – that's how I found out about Dad's part in it. Luca's not even French, for God's sake!'

Susan's mouth dropped open. '*What*? Who is he then?'

Carmen shrugged sadly. 'No idea and now I find out Matt told him abo…'

'That part's not true though?' Susan interrupted, forcing herself to crack a smile. 'What Matt said? You're not… not… with one of those biker people too?'

Nodding, Carmen tingled with the thought of the man that made her heart soar. 'His name's Noel.'

Susan's heart sank further. What had happened to her family? She wasn't a grandmother and never had been, her dead son had been beating his wife and her husband… well…

She took a deep breath. 'Do you think… do you think that…' She couldn't bring herself to voice the words. It was hard enough comprehending Richard could have been involved in any of the things Carmen said, but killing that baby, that beautiful little boy…?

Carmen could guess her mother's thoughts, but she had to level with her despite all but destroying her mother's belief over her only son. 'Dad didn't kill that child,' she said, staring her mother in the eye. 'He might be a pompous bastard, but…'

'Carmen!'

'Well he is, but regardless of that, Dad had no motive, but *Matt* did. That letter to the solicitor was Matt's attempt to protect himself should the truth come out. It was *him* who killed Andrew, I know it. The night Andrew died I saw him…'

'What do you mean, *saw* him?'

'In Andrew's room. Matt was standing over the cot, just staring. I thought it was strange at the time, but I didn't suspect him of having anything to do with what happened until I saw his suicide note. Remember what it said?'

Susan covered her mouth with her hands, suffocating the building scream. 'You really believe Matthew killed the child?'

Carmen nodded. 'I do, yes.'

'Y-You didn't say anyth…'

'How could I make things worse for you than they already were? Besides, it wouldn't have brought him back, would it?'

'But why would Matthew say it was his father?'

Carmen's mouth set in a straight line. 'Because Matt's a wanker? Excuse my language, but it's true. Like I said, he was protecting himself. He wrote this because he rightly believed people were sussing out it was him, so he devised a backup of blaming Dad if he ended up getting arrested.' She folded her arms. 'But the guilt of what he'd done finally got the better of him. *That's* why he killed himself.'

Susan remained silent. Had her son killed that baby because he wasn't the father? There was something that just didn't sit right, but as much as she loathed to believe it was possible, she had to take on board that it might be. Everything Carmen said made sense, but her gut told her it wasn't right. *It wasn't Matthew.*

But did that then mean it was Richard? Everything else Matthew had written Carmen confirmed to be true. She looked at her daughter and took the letter. 'Should I go to the police?'

'To do what? They'll only draw the same conclusion I have. It was Matt! Then it will come out that you suspected Dad! Come on, Mum, for all his faults? And on top of that, your friends will find out the truth about Matt.'

Susan nodded, but that didn't make any difference – she hadn't got any friends – not *real* ones. Even if she had, she didn't care what they thought, but she wouldn't go to the police. At least, not yet.

Whether Richard was capable of murdering that child should be an easy question to answer and she should immediately feel it impossible, but the harsh reality was she wasn't sure. She was beginning to think that it really must have been Richard – and where did *that* leave her?

Sixteen

RICHARD COULD BARELY believe his eyes, but there it was in black and white. He forced a neutral expression on his face rather than give any of the people intent on watching him, especially Andrew Mercer, any hint of what he was *really* feeling. And what he was feeling was panic. *Pure unadulterated panic.*

He willed his heart to slow down and hoped the perspiration running steadily down his neck remained there rather than manifesting on his forehead which would be a lot harder to disguise.

Richard rapidly stuffed the note back into the envelope before anyone sneaked a glimpse. He could see they were itching to know its contents because it was unusual for members to receive personal mail at the Conservative Club. In fact, he didn't think he'd *ever* seen anyone get a letter before.

Andrew Mercer's bulk lumbered into Richard's personal space as he sidled nearer with a view to catching a glimpse of the note. 'Anything interesting, Stevens?'

'Nope, just a stupid invitation to become a member of another club,' Richard said hastily. 'What a cheek, eh? Trying to poach members from one club for another.' He tutted loudly.

'Some people!'

'It's not really poaching if it's from a London club, is it?'

Richard frowned. 'A London club?' *What was he talking about now?* Mercer's head was most likely addled after all the gossip he'd kindly spread about Lillian, saving him the job.

'Oh, was it not a London club? I only presumed that from the post mark,' Mercer said pompously.

Richard hid his scowl. Trust Mercer to be the one who'd offered to pass on the letter. He might have known the nosy bastard would scrutinise it. 'I didn't take much notice once I realised what it was. I'm happy with the clubs I'm already a member of.'

'Membership of a London club might be good though, would it not?' Mercer continued. 'Which one was it?'

Richard shoved the letter deep in his pocket. 'Oh, damn! I promised Susan I'd be back by 4. We've got an engagement tonight, so must dash.'

Turning away before he got interrogated further, Richard collected his coat and hurried to his car. He wasn't really going home. He had no prior engagement at all, but he did need to think. Glancing around to check no one was hanging around the car park, he fished the note from his pocket and stared at the typed words once again:

Richard,

I'm polite, so I wanted to advise that you're being watched. Watched ALL the time.
I've been in your house and I know everything about you and what you have done. It's only a matter of time before you will pay for everything and I will be the one to decide when that should happen.

Be warned.

Richard brushed off the shiver, refusing to give in to the

temptation of glancing over his shoulder to check no one had concealed themselves in the back of his car. *This was somebody's idea of a joke, surely?*

He drummed his fingers on the steering wheel. Was this to do with Lillian? Was the old witch trying to scare him because he'd exposed her? She must know he'd been the one behind it.

Richard gritted his teeth. It couldn't be her - this wasn't something she'd do. Besides, she'd be far too busy licking her wounds; raging and rattling around her house drinking wine by the caseload, whilst simmering over what she could do to get back at him, but the harsh truth was there was nothing she could do. Nothing at all. She had no leverage left.

So, if it wasn't her…

Wait. It was them again. Threatening kidnap-style notes were just up their street. This was just the type of thing they'd do to intimidate – short of using mindless violence, of course.

This was the bloody Reapers.

If Tori had run off with that ape, like Matthew had said and like the papers speculated, then it made sense.

Richard felt a horrid creeping sensation running down his spine as he looked at the note once again. *"I know what you've done…"*

Had the Reapers discovered about that woman at the hospital? That gypsy, Leila's friend? But even if the bitch had been identified, why would they think her sudden disappearance was linked to him? He had nothing to do with the woman – not one that anyone knew about, anyway.

Richard frowned forming thick grooves along his forehead. Could it be about the kid? Had the Reapers discovered the truth about that?

Come on, Richard you're being irrational, he thought, angrily scolding himself. The only person who knew about that was Matthew and he couldn't exactly tell them.

What about Luca? Was he angry because Carmen had run off on him? They'd had an agreement after all. But Luca was in France and even though Matthew had been stupid enough to stir things up, Luca had better things to do than run around based on the word of someone he barely knew.

Richard turned the envelope over. Mercer was right. This was posted in London. It *had* to be the Reapers. They'd have sent someone down there purely to pop it in a letterbox just to confuse him.

He shivered again with the thought of that filth poking around in his house and realisation dawned. He *knew* he'd seen someone lurking in the garden. He'd seen someone down by the summerhouse a couple of times, maybe more, from the corner of his eye. It *must* be them. They were dab hands at breaking and entering without leaving a trace, so had the Reapers taken his notepad and the things he was missing? Was it them who had moved his stuff about, rather than Susan? They had plenty of motive as well as the knowledge to cause him a great deal of problems. Thanks to Matthew those low lives knew what he'd pulled at the bank to pay them off after that botched property contract.

Richard gritted his teeth, his jaw aching as his fear combined with anger. Or had Tori put them up to it? Was she using the Reapers to get her own back? He wouldn't put it past her, the conniving little bitch.

Richard shoved his key in the ignition. He was going home. If he was right about his suspicions, then he was making sure he was protecting himself.

• • • •

TORI'S HANDS TREMBLED even though it had been a good hour since she'd put the gun down.

She looked around the village pub Hunter had brought her to for a bite to eat following her "lesson". She'd surprised herself by agreeing to go anywhere other than the safety of the four walls of her home, but then she didn't have the safety of her house anymore.

Swallowing the urge to dwell on being forced to move to the Factory she instead reminded herself that she'd accepted

Hunter's way of doing things. He was doing what was needed to protect her and she had to keep that forefront in her mind.

Glancing up, Hunter's gun-metal eyes met with Tori's and his face broke into a smile. 'You're staring,' he said, his hand reaching for hers. 'Decided what you're having?'

Tori melted at his smile. She studied his face, his strong jaw and sculptured cheekbones. Hunter was an extraordinarily attractive man and part of his charm was because he didn't realise it. 'I was just reminding myself why I fell in love with you.'

Hunter squeezed her hand. 'I know it's been difficult and I know we've got a load of stuff to work through – most of it my doing…'

He couldn't explain the relief he felt that Tori seemed to be turning a corner. He'd promised to tell her *everything* he planned from now on – even if she didn't like it. He wouldn't shield her from things anymore and her attitude was thawing, with more and more glimpses of the "old" Tori returning - the Tori that hadn't been all but destroyed. 'I know the Factory is the last place you want to be and I realise it's not the way you wanted things.'

Tori shrugged. 'You have to do what's needed, I get that. I just find it difficult.' *Difficult was an understatement.* She couldn't dress it down to herself or anyone that she'd spent the last two hours learning to fire a gun in a secluded wood for her own protection. And she was terrified. Would her whole life be like this from now on? She didn't know, but the harsh reality was if she wanted Hunter, then she had to accept this was how things were right now.

Hunter frowned, as if reading her mind. 'I meant what I said, Tori. Once all this is over, we'll have more of a normal life.'

Tori smiled, unsure whether that would ever be feasible but appreciated the sentiment all the same. She glanced down at her menu. 'I'll have a Ploughman's.'

Hunter beckoned the waitress over. 'Two Ploughman's,

please.'

Once the waitress had taken the order and scuttled off, he stroked Tori's fingers softly. 'You did well today. I'm proud of you.' *He was.* He knew she was terrified of guns, but he wouldn't rest until he knew she'd be safe on the rare occasions he or one of the other Reapers weren't around.

Tori smiled, unconvinced. Hunter had the patience of a saint, showing her how to load, aim and fire over and over, but it had gone in one ear and out the other. She'd been too frightened of the heavy piece of metal in her hands to concentrate. 'I was hopeless! I think I'm in more danger with one of those, than without!'

Hunter grinned. 'You weren't too bad. A couple more lessons and you'll be grand.' *Maybe not.* She *was* atrocious at aiming despite his standing behind her, holding her shaking body in position and constantly reassuring her, but she'd improve - at least he hoped so...

'Have you got any further with... you know... the house?' Tori whispered.

'No. The description that bloke gave fits half the people in the area. Besides, whoever did it isn't necessarily the person we want.' He looked thoughtful. 'This might sound odd, but do you think it could be anything to do with your mother? After than article in the paper?'

Tori's eyes widened. 'My *mother*?' She hadn't seen her mother since Andrew was born and wanted nothing more to do with the woman, but did her mother really despise her enough to arrange a break-in? 'She might well hate me, but she wouldn't know where to start to arrange something like that. Do you seriously think she had something to do with it?'

'No, I don't. I'm just thinking out loud.'

Tori smiled as the waitress brought over their lunch, but the woman barely noticed anything but Hunter and surprised herself having to suppress a giggle. 'I think you've got a fan,' she whispered.

Hunter rolled his eyes. 'Have a day off!'

Tori laughed, this time openly. *He really didn't see what anyone else saw.* With a jolt, she realised for the first time in a *very* long time she was enjoying herself. Guilt immediately replaced her happiness. Should she even be smiling when her son was dead? Was that wrong? And things were hardly great, being as they were virtually in hiding and someone was out to get them. *Hang on a minute...*

'What?' Hunter questioned seeing Tori's sudden frown.

'What about Richard Stevens? *He's* the sort to arrange something like that.'

Hunter raised his eyebrows. *Richard Stevens?* Anger pulsed like it always did when anyone from *that* family were mentioned. 'I'm paying him a visit soon, so I'll weigh it up then.'

Tori all but dropped her fork. 'You're doing *what*?'

Hunter leant forward. 'Keep your voice down,' he hissed. 'I told you I'd keep you in the loop, so I am.'

'But wh...'

'Remember Joe? The man who brought Jeanie up here when you were in hospital?'

Tori nodded. *How could she forget*? 'What does that have to do with Richard?'

'Before I sent Joe back to Polperro he told me Stevens was at the hospital the day Jeanie disappeared.'

Tori's fork remained poised mid-air. 'But Richard wouldn't know Jeanie from Adam! He wouldn't have ever met her, so how could you th...'

'I'm not saying he had anything to do with her disappearance, but he might have seen someone - someone who *did*. So, as much as I resent it, I need his help.'

Tori's eyes widened. 'You're asking him?'

Hunter shrugged. 'I don't have a lot of choice. I'm not mentioning this to the others though. It's my fault Jeanie was here in the first place, so I owe it to her to find out what happened. I also need to rule out whoever attacked Jeanie isn't behind what's going on with us.'

Alarm flickered across Tori's face. 'Why would it be? Jeanie was to do with Noel's mother and what happened with... with my...'

Hunter didn't want to get into the subject of Noel's mother or Tori's father, but everything was inextricably linked.

'You said the real attacker died months ago, didn't you?' Tori pressed.

Hunter nodded. 'That's right. That photo – the one with your father and Leila. The one taken in the wood?' He looked down guiltily. 'I pinched it from your stuff... A long story... I showed it to Jeanie and she pointed out the real attacker – the guy on the far right. She didn't know his name, but I tracked down another man on the picture. I paid him a visit and he also pointed out the man on the far right. The name was Ed - Edward Barratt.'

Tori frowned. She hadn't seen that picture for so long she had no idea who was on the far right. When had Hunter taken it? Not that it mattered now in the big scale of things.

'Further digging uncovered this Ed bloke died from a heart attack a while ago.'

Tori swallowed nervously. She'd had in her possession a photograph of the real attacker? She'd seen his face and not thought anything of it? The man who her father died for? That Hunter had...

No. She wouldn't go down the road again. It didn't change anything, but none of this made sense. 'If he's dead, why would what happened to Jeanie and us have something to do with him?'

Hunter shook his head. 'I'm not saying it does. I'm stabbing in the dark. It's unlikely, but I need to rule everything out – even things that don't seem plausible.'

'You should take one of the others when you visit Richard. What if he calls the police?'

Hunter laughed. 'He's more likely to call the police if a group of bikers rock up! Anyway, I won't be there to make trouble even though I'd love to smash his fat head down his neck. All I want to know is whether he saw anyone that day at the hospital.' He frowned. 'And, like I said, I don't want this mentioned to the others, especially Noel. Talking about Jeanie brings it back about his mother. He's a lot calmer lately and I want it to stay that way.'

'I think that's down to Carmen's influence,' Tori joked.

'At least one good thing came out of that family,' Hunter muttered.

'When are you planning seeing Richard?'

'Sometime over the next couple of days. The quicker I find out what I need, the quicker I can rule one thing out and then the closer we are with finding out who the hell's messing with us.' Hunter grasped Tori's hand once again. 'We mustn't forget that at this point in time we don't know what's going on, so I want you to promise me one thing...' He looked deeply into her eyes. 'If I ever ask you to carry, then do so.'

Tori blinked, Hunter's penetrating stare making her nervous. 'Carry?'

'The gun. The one I'm giving to you.' Hunter kept his voice low. 'I'm not saying you should walk around with it or wave it about, but what I *am* saying is that if I ever ask you to, then you're to do exactly that, no questions asked. If I ask you, there will be a very good reason for doing so.'

His eyes continued to search Tori's face, reading her reluctance. 'Tori, it's important. You'll know if you ever need to use it. Can you promise me?'

Tori nodded. Very slightly, but nodded all the same. What choice did she have? She trusted him, but that didn't mean she was comfortable with what he asked.

She pretended to resume her lunch although she'd lost her appetite. Just the mention of Richard Stevens made her teeth on edge.

SEVENTEEN

SUSAN HAD TRIED not to act strangely when Richard unexpectedly returned. He'd walked straight past without uttering a word. That was fine with her – she wasn't sure she could even look at him, but she realised if she didn't force herself to act "normal" it would make him even more bad-tempered.

Carmen hadn't been gone long and she'd been hoping for time to think – not that it would do any good. She was in the most dreadful quandary, her mind whirring and struggling to process *any* of the avalanche of information her daughter had confirmed.

Was her entire life a lie? Did she know any of her family at all? She was more uncertain than she'd ever been and the foundation of everything she'd believed felt more unstable than a child's bouncy castle.

Susan listened to Richard clattering about in the study. It sounded like he was moving furniture. Why had he chosen today of all days to venture back so early? It would have been preferable if he hadn't come back *at all*. At least that way she'd have been able to quieten her mind down a little, but now she had to act like nothing was amiss, when *everything* was.

Susan's nerves jangled incessantly. Her first reaction was to question Richard why he hadn't told her about Carmen's wedding? And if Luca wasn't really Luca, then who was he? And what about Richard's involvement with Matthew and Victoria? Had he really been aware or part of what Matthew had done to the girl?

Her eyes wandered over to a framed photograph placed face down on the sideboard of Andrew when he was two days old. No wonder Richard had insisted on turning it over. She hadn't wanted him to, but she hadn't dared argue. Now she realised why.

He knew that baby wasn't their grandchild all along. Or was it because he'd snuffed out Andrew's little life?

Sitting forward in the armchair, Susan massaged her temples to still the crashing thoughts chaotically tumbling around inside and relieve the throbbing not being helped by the noise Richard was making.

Forcing herself to her feet she made her way along the hallway, grabbing the post which had arrived after Richard had left earlier this morning.

Pushing open the door, Susan walked into the study. 'Richard, I...'

She watched Richard hastily shut a tall walnut cabinet and her heart raced. That was what all the noise was about. He'd been moving furniture to get to that cabinet hiding behind a row of filing cabinets. That thing hadn't been opened in *years* and she was glad because she hated what it contained.

Richard swung around. 'What is it with you?' he barked. 'Why are you creeping up on me?'

'I-I wasn't creeping up on you, I...'

'Yes you were!' Richard snapped. 'Come to see what I'm doing, are you?'

Susan felt sick. Richard's behaviour made everything Carmen said sound even *more* feasible. 'Why are you going in that cabinet?'

Richard knew how she felt about what was in there. It had

only been her insistence what had made him lock his guns away years ago, promising not to use them again. 'Why do you think?' he barked. He'd half expected her to be snooping around as usual, so he had it covered. 'If you must know, I've been invited shooting for the first time in donkey's years.'

'But you know th...'

'I know you don't like it but for God's sake, Susan, they're only pheasants - almost paramount to vermin. You're too soft. It's a sport!'

Richard forced himself to crack a half-smile. He had to cool it from taking things out on his wife. Letting her believe he was planning to shoot pheasants was the best thing all round. He could hardly say he would threaten the next idiot who thought it a good idea to come into his house. He would *not* allow low-life tramp bikers to belittle him. They'd got away with far too much in the past and he would not let them blackmail or frighten him anymore. If he had to wave an old shotgun in their general direction to achieve that, then so be it!

Susan's aim of maintaining a normal façade faltered. The urge to get away from being in an enclosed space with the man she'd been married to for three decades multiplied at a rate of knots. Her breath caught in her throat. *Don't panic*, she silently repeated. *You don't know anything. It's all mere speculation.*

Matthew hadn't been himself for several days before making the dreadful decision to end his life, so it stood to reason that he could have written rubbish. Maybe he'd believed those things in his own head?

The horrible prospect that her son might have been having a breakdown entered Susan's thoughts. If he'd really done all of those awful things to Victoria like Carmen had said, then he couldn't have been well. He was a good boy, Matthew.

Susan dared to raise her eyes, only to find Richard studying her.

'Are you alright?' Richard made a special effort to keep his voice calm, when really all he wanted to do was scream.

Richard's voice knocked Susan from her reeling mind.

'What? Oh, erm.. yes... I...'

Richard took a step towards Susan and frowned as she backed up against the door. 'Whatever's the matter?' *Christ, why was she so nervy*? Had he got it wrong? Was it her who'd taken his things after all? Was he barking up the wrong tree with his theory about the Reapers?

He bit back the urge to tell Susan to get out of his damn study and leave him be if all she was going to do was stand there shaking like a bloody wraith and stare at him like he was possessed.

'Have you heard anything from Luca?' Susan blurted, immediately wishing she'd stopped the words leaving her mouth.

Richard blinked in surprise. 'Why would you ask me that? If something's happened, you need to tell me.'

Susan shook her head. 'It's just me being silly. I'm all over the place with everything. With Matthew, with Victoria...' She watched Richard's face closely for a flicker of anything pointing to guilt on his alleged part, but found nothing. 'It's been on my mind how much of a mess Carmen's marriage is in. I was hoping they could work it out, but I don't think that will happen, do you?'

Richard inwardly sighed with relief. He'd thought for a minute that something had occurred to add to his list of issues. 'We can't presume that.'

Susan swallowed. From what Carmen had said there was no chance of reconciliation, especially with this other guy – Noel, on the scene, but the urge to ask Richard why he'd arranged their daughter's marriage grew fiercer and she wanted to ask who Luca really was, but she couldn't. She just *couldn't.* 'Luca hasn't been in contact for ages and you'd have thought he would, being as Carmen's been gone for months.'

Richard kept his gaze trained on Susan without faltering. He'd lied enough through work and life in general to be convincing and his ability hadn't let him down so far. 'He hasn't called me if that's what you're asking in a strange roundabout fashion. What's brought this all on? Has this palaver with Lillian got to you? Are those meddling women still putting silly thoughts into your head?'

Susan shook her head. 'I just don't know...' She hadn't paid any notice to anything any of the women phoning her had said. She was, quite frankly, sick of the lot of them and had far more important things to worry about other than Lillian's damaged reputation and what those women thought of her. And why was Richard suddenly being so pleasant? That was more unnerving than anything else.

Turning, she moved towards the door needing some air. 'I'll leave you to it, then. Oh, I almost forgot. This came for you.' She placed the envelope on Richard's desk before leaving his study.

• • • •

STEPPING OUT OF THE TAXI, Lillian took a deep breath. She'd thought about cancelling her hair appointment but then decided against it. She'd been coming to this salon on a weekly basis for twelve years and wouldn't let what Richard had spread about change that. Just because he'd gone back on his word never to discuss her past business didn't mean that anyone would *believe* it and felt she may have overreacted over what she'd heard Sandra and Isobel discussing.

Lillian pushed open the heavy door, hearing the tinkling of the bell. Smiling brightly, she walked to the reception desk. 'Good morning, Poppy. I'm here for my usual style and blow dry.'

Poppy glanced up. 'I'll let Bridget know. Take a seat, Lillian.'

Lillian frowned. Poppy usually chatted ten to the dozen, but today she looked awkward. Embarrassed, even. 'Are you alright, Poppy, my dear?'

Poppy rose from her seat, not quite able to meet Lillian's eyes. 'Yes, yes, I'm fine,' she answered, hastily walking into the main salon leaving Lillian standing at the desk.

Frowning once again, Lillian took a seat on a sumptuous velvet occasional chair in the waiting area and picked up a copy of *Home and Antiques*, rather than analyse why the chatting from the salon had reduced to nothing short of hushed whispers. Refusing to allow herself to entertain the notion that it could be anything to do with her, she thumbed through the glossy pages of the magazine, stopping with interest at an article on Ming vases.

'Hello, Lillian.'

Lillian looked up startled, then relaxed seeing the top stylist standing in front of her. 'Hello Bridget,' she smiled. 'Busy today?'

Picking up her handbag, Lillian went to move through to the main salon, but Bridget put a hand on her arm.

'Can I have a word?'

Stopping, Lillian turned. 'Of course. What seems to be th…'

'If we can just go in here?' Bridget pushed open the door to a small office off the main salon.

Lillian breezed in confidently, successfully ignoring the looks burning into her from the other customers.

Shutting the door behind them, Bridget wasted no time getting to the point. 'I'm afraid we can't do your hair at this salon any longer.'

Lillian's magenta mouth fell open. 'I beg your pardon?'

'I don't have to explain my reasons, but being as you've been a customer for so long, I will.' Bridget's face exhibited both hostility and embarrassment. 'I'm sure you're aware things about your past have recently become, shall we say, a talking point? Due to the nature of this we don't feel it's appropriate for us to con…'

'My *past*?' Lillian cried. 'What on earth are you talking about? If you're referring to what that drunken fool, Richards Stevens, has been broadcasting, then I can assure you that it's nothing but co…'

'Lillian,' Bridget interrupted. 'Whether I, or any of the staff believe what has been said is irrelevant, but…'

'But you *do* believe it, don't you?' Lillian spat, her cheeks crimson. She could tell by Bridget's eyes that she believed every single word. 'Well, you have no ri…'

'Like I said, it's irrelevant what I think, but some of our customers have threatened to go elsewhere if you continue to come here.'

'Like who?' Lillian raged. *Sandra for one. She came every week, as did Isobel Gristhorpe. It must be them.* 'You expect me to glibly accept that you are considering "banning" me or whatever you want to call it, based on a couple of busybodies' opinions? That's ludicrous, Bridget and you know it!'

Bridget's lips formed into a thin line. 'Actually, it's not a couple of "busybodies", it's the general consensus of *all* the customers and the staff. We've had countless complaints.'

Lillian froze. So, *everyone* believed it? And if they'd reacted like this here, then would it not be the same everywhere?

Bridget opened the door. 'I'd like you to leave now.'

Usually, Lillian would launch into a scathing rant but right now she was too mortified. *Completely and utterly mortified.*

Knowing her face must match the colour of her lipstick she dashed from the salon, the many pairs of eyes following her in hushed silence and the burning shame staying with her long after she reached the sanctuary of the pavement.

By the time Lillian arrived home, her humiliation and embarrassment had morphed into self-righteous resentment. Opening the glass-fronted door of her display cabinet, she reached for one of her bone china teacups before grabbing a bottle of Harveys Bristol Cream, along with a glass instead.

Pouring her favourite sherry, Lillian placed the glass on an occasional table in front of the large patio windows and gazed into the garden. Was this what she was reduced to from now on? Sitting alone watching the birds, unable to leave the house unless she didn't mind being ridiculed and looked upon with disdain? *That's if she hadn't been banned from everywhere?*

Lillian sipped at her sherry, her nose wrinkling at the magenta smudge her lipstick left on the crystal of the glass.

Richard Stevens had really done it this time. She had been ostracised and everyone believed what had been said about her without a second thought. It might be true, but that wasn't the point.

Lillian's lips twisted into a sneer. Susan must be enjoying this. Well, she and her moronic husband may be laughing now, but they wouldn't be for long. The bank had been very interested in hearing what she'd had to say.

She glanced in her diary, now woefully empty of engagements and checked the date, but still smiled. By now the bank should also have received the paperwork she had forwarded to back up her claims and so it wouldn't be long now before Richard was hung out to dry and exposed for what he was for all to see.

She was glad she'd had the foresight to think ahead and provide herself with leverage in the event of needing it. The night Susan had the audacity to ask her to leave, she'd done well by swiping that notebook off Richard's desk that he'd been stupid enough to leave lying around. She presumed, being such an obsessively organised person, he'd undoubtedly keep a record of all his past "transactions" and she'd also had the inkling they would come in handy. And they most certainly had.

Now she had finally done what Richard had most dreaded and it was his own bloody fault.

EIGHTEEN

'I DON'T KNOW WHY you feel the need to be so nice to him?' Colin muttered, topping up the optics.

Sarah glanced across the tap room at Jorge sitting on his own, quietly thumbing through a copy of the local paper. 'I'm not being "so nice" at all, just friendly. Isn't that what we're supposed to do as bloody landlords?'

Colin stifled his retort. There was something about that man he couldn't quite put his finger on.

Sarah shrugged. 'He seems nice enough to me. I feel sorry for the bloke. I told you what happened to his sister and he was helpful telling us about that man he'd seen. You know, the one who broke into Hun...'

'Yes, I know. You said,' Colin interrupted. 'Just be careful. You don't know him and...'

'Ah, get away with you!' Sarah laughed, flicking Colin's rear end with a beer towel. 'You're just touchy cos he's nice-looking and younger than you!'

Colin pulled a face and grinned, not wanting bad words between him and Sarah. Seeing the man in question rise from his chair and head towards them, he frowned. 'Talk of the devil...'

'Hi, handsome,' Sarah smiled as Jorge deposited his empty pint glass on the bar and winked at Colin before he got his knickers in a bigger twist. 'Same again?'

'Yes please, Sarah,' Jorge said, nodding and smiling at Colin at the same time. He needed to get things moving with getting himself into the fold, otherwise Neil would have his guts for garters. Concentrating on the White Hart and the Reapers was about all he could do at the moment because he'd drawn a complete blank with Carmen, not having seen hide nor hair of her for days.

It was frustrating. He'd have got somewhere if he hadn't been stuck with fixing that knucklehead's bike the other night, but at least it should have earnt him some brownie points with the Reapers. Having nothing else to go on, he'd continued his vigil of the target house, but there was still no movement. He hadn't set eyes on anyone going to or from the place at all and he'd been beginning to think they'd buggered off on holiday, until he'd caught a glimpse of Tori leaving the White Hart the other night.

'Any more news on that tosser who broke into your friend's place?' Jorge asked as Sarah poured his pint. 'I wish I could have been of more help.'

'Not your fault. There's a lot of folks meeting that description around here, so it was a bit of a needle in a haystack, but appreciated you speaking up,' Sarah said.

'How's your friend now? I only saw her briefly the other day,' Jorge asked. 'She looked a lot happier.' *Much happier than he'd expected for someone who had been recently threatened.*

Sarah deposited Jorge's pint on the beer towel. 'She's a lot better now they've moved to the Factory.'

'The *where*?' Jorge frowned, acting dumb. He knew the Factory was where the Reapers gathered because Neil had said, but he had to pretend otherwise. And furthermore, where was Carmen? He could hardly ask that, could he?

'I keep forgetting you're not from around here,' Sarah

smiled. 'The Factory's the official Reaper Chapter House.'

Jorge cracked a smile. 'Starting to blend in now, am I?' *He had to eke out some info on Carmen somehow. Maybe this would work?* 'I'm sure I saw Tori yesterday up in the town. Has she got a friend with long blonde hair – tall and...'

'Ah, that sounds like Carmen,' Sarah interjected. 'I doubt whether you'd have seen them out though because no one's seen Carmen for days an...'

'Nosy, aren't you?' Colin butted in, his eyes scrutinising Jorge suspiciously.

'Sorry,' Jorge said quickly. 'I didn't mean to bombard you with questions. Only making conversation.'

Sarah shot a look at Colin, surprised by his abruptness before turning back to Jorge. 'Any luck on the job front? I heard you fixed Bill's bike.'

Jorge grinned. 'The Reapers haven't offered me a full-time mechanic job yet, if that's what you mean, but I have a couple of potentials knocking around, so we'll see, but,' he smiled at Colin, 'if you ever need your car fixed, mate, look no further.'

'Jorge is a mechanic,' Sarah said, glancing at Colin.

'Yeah, I gathered that,' Colin muttered. 'Anyway, this barrel needs changing.'

Sarah watched Colin disappear down the steps to the cellar before smiling apologetically. 'Sorry about him. He's a bit grumpy tonight.'

'No worries. I think we all get like that from time to time.' Jorge picked up his pint and headed back to the table, pretending to look back through the paper when really his mind was working overtime. So, Tori and Hunter had moved into the protective nest of Reapers? There was no point watching the target house now and no one had seen Carmen.

Jorge inwardly scowled. There was no question about it. He had to get into the Reapers' inner circle or the Factory. *But how?*

He'd already attempted to get on side with Hunter, but it was clear the man wasn't the sort to easily make friends. That would take a huge amount of time to pull off, if at all. *A huge amount of time he didn't have.*

What about Tori? She was pleasant enough, but being overfriendly to her would probably only achieve the loss of his teeth in the process.

A small smirk slid across his face. What if she were to have an accident? Imagine if he was there to help just when it was needed? Hunter and the Reapers would be grateful to him and more likely to cut him some slack.

Yes, that was a good idea. Well, it was actually the *only* feasible idea he'd had so far. All he had to do now was work out exactly what sort of accident Tori would need; how severe it should be and where it should take place?

• • • •

'HOW'S THINGS GOING TODAY, JOHN?' Neil asked, his tone relaxed. He'd been practising this for a good hour to ensure he would come across as chilled and rational, when he felt anything but.

'Busy,' John said, flicking through a binder of figures.

Neil watched John avidly, knowing he'd stepped on the man's toes the other night, which was a gross oversight from his side and one he should have known better than to make. Things would be difficult if John didn't believe he was on the level, plus for some reason John seemed overly concerned about Jorge, so that was something else he'd have to grit his teeth and work at – at least in front of everyone. As long as he got things right then he would be left alone to do what was required. Only afterwards would it become apparent that he was nowhere near rational and calm, but it would make no difference because John would be busy limiting the damage to the firm, whilst *he'd* achieve what he wanted on all sides. *Voila!*

The question was, how much did John need to know to keep him sweet?

Neil sat down and crossed his ankles. When John placed the binder on the desk and looked at him questioningly, he took that as a good starting point to say what he'd rehearsed.

'I've been thinking about what you said and I can assure you that despite what it looked like, I'm not about to go on a rampage.' *God, this was painful, but it if put things on an even keel, then it was worth it.* 'You were right about Jorge too,' Neil continued. 'To be honest, him turning up like that came as a bit of a shock and I guess it brought back a part of my life I'd rather forget.'

John nodded, tapping his fingers on the desk as he listened. 'I can appreciate that, but none of what happened was Jorge's fault. He didn't ask to be born. So, are you going to get to know the boy or is he involved purely as being useful for your job?'

'No, I want to get to know him, although it's probably come across otherwise,' Neil lied. 'It's bad timing, that's all.' He made a forced effort to look contrite. 'I'm going up north to spend some time with him.'

John frowned. 'Is that a good idea? You can't afford to get recognised.'

Neil opened his hands submissively. 'You were right about me loading a lot of stuff on Jorge's back and perhaps putting him at risk. I'm more than aware I owe the lad some of my time, being as I've been absent for twenty-five years.'

John studied Neil. He seemed on the level, but he could never be quite sure.

'I won't get recognised. I'll stay somewhere out of town and won't get involved. Besides, I don't think there's anyone left to recognise me, short of Carmen and her bloody father of course, but Jorge is keeping tabs on them, so I can keep well clear.' *Was John buying any of this, or not?*

John folded his arms across his massive chest. 'You said you'd put things in motion to take out this Hunter bloke? I want to know exactly what those things are.'

Neil nodded, eyeing John carefully. 'Ok, well… that's the plan, but I don't want Jorge or any of our firm involved in that, which is why I'm in discussions with someone unlinked to us to undertake that side of things.'

John raised his eyebrows. This was a turn up for the books. He'd been sure that if Neil wasn't roping Jorge into doing it, it was because he was planning on doing it himself. In fact, he'd have even have bet money on it.

'I can read your mind, John. I promised I wouldn't jeopardise anything and I meant it. Hunter will be taken out but by a third party and not one of us.' *He hadn't promised he wouldn't take out Richard Stevens and his own fucking wife himself though, had he?*

Neil smiled showcasing his perfectly straight, over-white teeth. 'My first priority is to get to know my son, but I'll admit going up there means I can kill two birds with one stone, metaphorically speaking of course.'

Or not, he thought, but it sounded so plausible, he could almost convince himself.

'Who are you using?' John asked.

'Liam McFadden,' Neil answered. 'You know as well as I do that he's reliable and not traceable to us.'

John nodded. 'True. McFadden's a good choice, but make sure you look after Jorge – he's a good lad,' he said, silently pleased. Neil seemed sincere and it would be good for Jorge too. Besides, it was easy enough to check to see if Neil had been in touch with McFadden.

'I intend to,' Neil lied. And then when Jorge had done everything required, he could fuck right back off to wherever he'd come from.

NINETEEN

TORI LAY BACK ON the bed and gazed around her. Despite Hunter's place being on the top floor of the old factory and more of a garret than an apartment, it was a really nice space.

Amazingly light and roomy, thanks to the high ceilings mostly covered with skylights, the front wall was floor to ceiling glass too, giving a fantastic view over the city. Ok, so the vista wasn't Manhattan or London's St Pauls' and instead a panorama across the industrial area, its accompanying surroundings of dilapidated terraces, canals and shops, but it still afforded a bird's eye view of the distant city centre which was a lot better than staring at a brick wall.

Tori sighed contentedly, feeling more at ease than she had in a long time. Last night, for the first time since just before Andrew's birth and again this morning, she and Hunter had made love. It had been wonderful, reminding her yet again that she owed it to herself and to him to ride through all the bad things which haunted her more than she liked.

Hunter had been patient over her recent reticence for intimacy and hadn't pushed it regardless of how much he must have wanted to. Many men wouldn't be quite so understanding.

An involuntary shiver passed through her as she imagined

how Matt would have reacted to the same situation, before pushing his image to the recesses of her mind. He was gone, thank God. *That was over.*

Tori sighed happily and stretching, she tingled in anticipation of Hunter's return later. Slowly but surely, she was getting back to her old self.

She glanced at the large clock on the wall, realising she'd been lying here daydreaming most of the morning and hadn't moved since Hunter had left for the day to visit the handful of businesses that hadn't taken the news that he was back in the helm especially well. She may not like that the Reapers made the majority of their money by protection rackets and security, but she did have every faith that he'd smooth things over, feeling proud that he took an active hands-on role without passing the buck to one of the other Reapers.

The only fly in the ointment was that once Hunter had finished doing the rounds, he was paying Richard Stevens the visit that he'd mentioned yesterday. She understood why he wanted to do this, but would have preferred him to have nothing to do with that man. The sooner she could completely put that part of her life away, the better. She didn't want Hunter in the same vicinity as Richard Stevens. He'd need a shower to wash away the miasma, but if it had to be done, then so be it. Besides, it wasn't all that bad.

Last night, before falling into bed, they'd spent a long time talking – a conversation long overdue and Hunter promised that once this latest problem was sorted he'd concentrate on his initial plan for the Reapers; property and perhaps a pub or two? The light at the end of the tunnel was again visible and she felt more optimistic than she'd believed possible compared to how she'd felt this time last week.

· · · ·

FOR DAYS CARMEN HAD put what she'd read in that letter her mother had found to the back of her mind, but it still niggled. She hadn't breathed a word of its contents to a soul –

not even Noel even though they were closer than ever, but maybe that was wrong? Maybe she should tell Tori and Hunter?

She frowned. What would that achieve? Whatever her mother thought, *she* stuck by Matt being the perpetrator. The letter may have confirmed her father was an underhand manipulator and a thief, but she didn't believe he was a killer.

Feeling nausea rise, she wondered how much Luca had paid for her hand in marriage. Being sold like a piece of meat by her own father made her feel dirty, *unclean.*

Her father was indeed a money-grasping selfish man and Matt, a chip off the old block, had inherited their father's greedy and manipulative attitude, along with even worse attributes. Although she still hated the thought that her baby brother was capable of murdering a child, it was feasible whether she liked it or not.

It hurt. The whole thing cut her to the quick, but at least she had Noel. Without him in her life she didn't know what she'd do.

Carmen looked over to Noel sitting with his muscular legs stretched out in front of him, his steel toe capped boots resting on a small table as he perused the racing section at the back of *The Sun.* Even his slovenliness and lack of social grace didn't faze her. Neither did swapping an eight-bedroomed chateau and weekends spent on a yacht with the French elite for a one-bedroomed flat situated over a line of shops, bother her. She, for the first in her life, was happy and was determined to move on from what her blighted family and false husband had done.

She continued to study Noel's cragged, but handsome face, feeling the familiar twinges of arousal. With a jolt of surprise, she realised she'd begun entertaining the possibility of being with this guy for the long haul. A family, even.

Carmen smiled. *Was she starting to feel broody? Dear God, she'd got it bad.*

Noel looked up from his moth-eaten armchair. 'Fancy a drink?'

'A drink?' Carmen laughed. 'Isn't it a bit early?'

'It's never too early,' Noel smiled, pulling two warm beers from a carrier bag at his feet.

Nerves fluttered in his belly. He'd done nothing but think about what he was about to do. He'd made his decision, but did he have to do all the claptrap that accompanied it? Or rather, what he *heard* accompanied it? He didn't know. It was hardly something he made a habit of. In fact, this was the first time he'd ever remotely *thought* about doing it, let alone doing it for real.

Noel ignored the nerves. Why the hell was he nervous, for God's sake? If Carmen didn't agree, then it was no skin off his nose.

He frowned inwardly. *Get real, man.* It was everything to him and he just hoped Carmen felt the same, but he'd never know unless he did it...

Noel looked at Carmen again. Maybe he should wait for a better time? She didn't look in a great mood. Maybe she was going off him? She'd been quiet the last couple of days... *No, he was doing it.*

Pulling Carmen towards him, he handed her a can of lager. 'Are you alright?'

'I was going to ask you the same thing. You're sitting there all shifty-looking...' Carmen hoped Noel wasn't going back down the cloak and dagger route – not when he'd been so open with her lately. She hesitantly opened her can. *Maybe she could use a drink after all?*

'Shifty? Me?' Noel said, getting to his feet.

Carmen eyed him suspiciously. 'Are you planning something you haven't told me about? I thought th...'

'You're right,' Noel said. 'I am.' *It was now or never.*

Seeing Carmen's crestfallen face, Noel knew he had to do this quickly before she thought the worst or before he lost his nerve. Taking a long swig of beer for good measure he clumsily dropped to one knee and pulled the ring box from his leather jacket.

'W-What are you doing?' Carmen cried, not sure she

believed her eyes. *Was he... Was he going to...?*

Noel opened the ring box, irritated to detect slight trembling of his hands and held the sparkling diamond out. 'Fancy getting married?'

'W-What?' Carmen shrieked. 'Are you serious?'

Noel bypassed the immediate knee-jerk reaction to scramble off the floor and pretend he'd been joking. *Was it such a stupid proposition?*

Of course it was. Look at her - drop-dead gorgeous and well out of his league. He must have been insane to entertain the thought.

Carmen watched Noel; saw him faltering. 'You haven't answered my question. I asked if you were serious?' *Because if he was serious...*

'And you didn't answer *mine*. And yes, I *am* fucking serious. I want to marry you.'

'Yes,' Carmen whispered.

Noel froze. *Did she just say "yes"?*

'I said, I'll marry you,' Carmen cried, her smile wide as she stuck her hand out. 'Put the ring on.'

With fumbling fingers, Noel slipped the ring he'd bought on to her finger. It fitted perfectly. *She'd said YES.* Pulling himself to his feet, he yanked Carmen against him and crashed his mouth onto hers.

· · · ·

HUNTER PULLED UP AT the gated entrance to Richard Stevens' house and yanked his bike onto the centre stand. Surprised to see the gates open, he began walking up the long gravel drive to the imposing house looming out of the twilight.

He'd been aiming to arrive earlier, but some of the businesses had proven trickier to placate than others. There were several bridges he'd had to mend as well as dole out plenty of reassurances, but despite this he was confident he'd succeeded in smoothing things out. After all, it had been necessary and overdue.

To be honest, the day had been exhausting and he could do without having to deal with this Stevens prick. Still, he had no plans to hang around longer than necessary and the sooner he could get back to Tori, the better.

It felt an age since he'd last been in front of this house. A lot of things had happened since he'd first knocked on that door with the excuse of looking for Matt just to see Tori. His lips curled into a half-smile, remembering the first time they'd made love here, in this very house. He'd been blown away – *lost* that night. That night he'd known that Tori was the woman he wanted to spend his life with and if last night and this morning were anything to go by, then things were getting back on track.

Maybe one day in the not too distant future there would be children running around their feet? *One day*. Certainly nothing he'd broach any time soon – it was still far too raw - for *both* of them. Still, if there was a next time, he'd make sure he was there from the off. Wild horses wouldn't keep him away.

Pulling his concentration back to the here and now, Hunter clenched his jaw, reminding himself exactly why he was walking towards Richard Stevens' faux mansion. This bastard who had been instrumental in making Tori's life a misery.

The *last* thing he wanted was ask the tosser for information, but needs must. He might get some more info about Jeanie and hopefully at the same time, rule out a connection with who had threatened him. There had been no developments on that score, so it could have been a chancer? The loser who broke into his home may have known who he was and thought in a drug-addled state it was a good crack to try and put the fear into the Reaper president, but he wasn't taking any chances. He'd rather give some muppet a laugh than risk another hair on Tori's head.

Hunter looked up at the house. Three lights were on, meaning someone was home. He just hoped he'd get this bastard to speak to him without threatening the twat, but he'd do whatever was needed.

TWENTY

JORGE WAS IN his usual position reading the paper at a table in the White Hart. The local rag was as dull as ditch water, but he had to keep up the pretence of being involved in the area and his search for work.

He returned the nod a Reaper passing his table threw his way. He was getting acknowledged now – a small step forward, but one in the right direction. Fixing that bonehead's bike the other night had achieved something, even if it meant losing the chance of discovering where Carmen was hibernating.

Looking around the pub, Jorge returned Sarah's smile before concentrating back on the paper. So far, no Hunter or Tori tonight either. He'd been thinking more about that too – about what he could do to Tori to put him in a favourable light. What he could do that would make the Reapers *grateful*?

Could he mug her whilst she was walking back from somewhere? Give her a good kicking and then somehow, a couple of minutes later, rescue her? He'd have to be mega quick with a clothes change and not speak in case she recognised his voice. He could punch her to the ground and rob her bag? But what if someone else stepped in to help before he turned back up, or worse, whilst he was doing it? And if his balaclava was dragged off...

Oh, it was stupid! A silly idea.

Jorge's face screwed into a frown. What was he thinking? Was he really so desperate to impress his father? Ok, so he may have been dragged up by a useless mother, but he still had his own line of what was acceptable. *And this wasn't.*

Jorge took a swig of his pint. There had to be something better? Did Tori drive? Could he tamper with her car? That might work if it happened not too far from here; say he'd driven past and recognised the crashed car? But then it might be discovered that the car had been tampered with...

Wait! If that was the case, Hunter would undoubtedly connect it to the previous threats – the ones no one suspected *him* of...

Jorge frowned, scouring his brains yet again through the scant memories of his mechanics course for hints of how he could do this, but hearing a commotion looked up, startled to see Carmen.

'If it's not the intrepid wanderers!' Sarah shouted. 'Where have you two been hiding. We thought you'd emigrated!'

Jorge watched Carmen strut across the bar wearing a big smile. *And she had a man with her.*

He studied the tall, stocky man sporting a Reapers' patch, his dark hair pulled into a ponytail. Even though he too was smiling, the tell-tale gleam of danger shone brightly behind his eyes. And the question as to who this biker was in relation to Carmen was answered when the man effortlessly picked her up with one hand, deposited her non too gently on the bar top and kissed her savagely.

'Argh! Give it a rest!' Sarah cried, batting at Noel with a rolled-up newspaper.

Noel grinned. 'Our usual please, Sarah. Plus, a bottle of champers if you've got any?'

Sarah pulled a dusty bottle of Moet from one of the fridges. 'So, where have you been?'

Carmen smiled shyly. 'We've been having a break from

things.'

'Everything ok with your mother?' Sarah asked. 'I haven't seen you since she phoned.'

Carmen nodded. 'Yes, she's ok.' Well, she wasn't, but she didn't want to talk about that. Rather she *couldn't* talk about it even if she wanted to, which she didn't. Besides, she was too happy to think about that right now. Both her and Noel had been unsure whether to break their chosen absence, but they were too excited to keep their news to themselves.

'So,' Sarah said, eyeing Carmen curiously. 'For the *third* time, where have you been hiding?'

'For fuck's sake, Sarah! Can't people do anything around here without having to explain themselves to you? Noel's big meaty hand trailed the length of Carmen's spine. 'Do you want to know how many times I've made Carmen squeal today too?'

'Noel!' Carmen cried, slapping him playfully with a beer mat.

'Hang on!' Sarah grabbed Carmen's hand and eyed the large diamond ring. 'What's *this*?'

Noel grinned widely. 'It's a *ring*, Sarah. Yep, a ring.' He turned and faced the tap room. 'Hey up, everyone – listen here! Me and Carmen – we're only getting married!'

A stunned silence ensued, followed seconds later by a raucous cheer. Reapers piled out of their seats to slap Noel on the back, shake his hand and kiss Carmen on the cheek.

Jorge remained sitting. *Shit.* He'd definitely been wrong in his assumption. Carmen wasn't with Hunter, she was with this bloke – *Noel*.

And how could she be getting married when she was already married?

Jorge scowled. Now he really would have to call and tell Neil he'd got it wrong. *For fuck's sake.*

• • • •

'YES, THAT'S CORRECT,' Lillian said. 'Check in tomorrow night and I'll be staying for a week initially.'

She tapped her finger on her address book. She knew the taxi firm's number off by heart what with all the business she'd put their way over the last God knows how long, but *this* time she'd use a completely different firm. She'd look for one she'd never used before in the Yellow Pages. That way there was no chance any of those two-faced bitches would discover her whereabouts. She wouldn't give them anything else to gossip about.

'Will there be an option to extend my stay if I so wish?' Lillian asked as she continued with the booking. 'Good, good… No, that's fine.'

Giving out her name and address, she wondered whether she should have used fake details, but decided against it. This wasn't Cagney and Lacey and she wouldn't hide from everyone. Her face screwed up. *Wasn't this exactly what she was doing? Hiding?*

No. No, it damn well wasn't. She was taking a well-deserved break to relax and decide what to do next. Her time may be over here, but it didn't mean *everything* was over. And she didn't want to be too far off the radar when Richard's face was splashed across the front of the paper, exposing him for the fake and thief he was. The story might even make the Nationals? That would be even more pleasing, but to see his life crash down around him would be gratifying wherever it was reported.

Lillian turned her attention back to the telephone. 'I meant to ask, can you ensure I have full access to the spa facilities for my stay? Oh, that comes as part of the rate for a suite, does it? That's fine then, thank you… No, that's it… I'll look forward to coming tomorrow… Many thanks….'

Putting the receiver down, Lillian smiled. That was sorted. Now all she needed to do was book a taxi for tomorrow, go and pack a suitcase and then she was ready.

· · · ·

RICHARD FUMBLED WITH the decanter as he shakily

poured himself yet another whisky.

He didn't want to read the letter again. None of the words would have changed between now and when he'd read it less than five minutes ago.

The letter Susan had innocently placed on his desk was from Steven Turnbull – a good friend of his from the start of his banking career. They'd joined the branch at the same time, both as Senior Loan Managers and while Richard had quickly progressed to becoming the overall branch manager, Steven had, thanks to his better connections, gone one better by being promoted to Finance Director at the bank's headquarters in London.

Richard had been miffed, feeling more qualified for that coveted role than Steven, but he couldn't do anything about it. The only good thing to come out of it was Steven putting in a good word for him about bonuses and inviting him to the best corporate events reserved for elite members of the corporation. Any correspondence from Steven was usually gratefully received. *Not this time though.*

Raising his glass to his mouth and slopping whisky down his shirt on the way, Richard took a large gulp and forced himself to read the letter again:

Dear Richard,

I hope retirement is suiting you well? I've still got a few more years before they'll consider letting me escape!
I'm afraid the reason for my getting in touch this time is a little awkward, but we go back a long way, so I wanted to give you a heads-up.

Headquarters have received information from a woman – can't tell you who because they won't even release that information to me! She's made serious allegations about you (not sexual harassment - we all know how common THAT is against us men these days and am still

astounded women get jobs the way they play that card!)
– anyway, I digress! It's alleged that you've been
siphoning money from portfolios over a period of many
years. This woman's provided a list of people who
received money and when (you're also on the list as a
recipient!) The total is substantial – we're talking £4
million plus over the last 25 years!

Waldron, (your replacement at branch), was asked by
HQ to look into it and indeed found discrepancies, but
I'm thinking these must be clerical errors? I've had some
useless secretaries and clerks over the years, so did you
sack anyone who may have a grudge?

The long and short of it is that they're investigating you
for theft and fraud. Ridiculous, I know and I've told them
as much, but they have to go through the motions, as I
know you understand.

You'll be glad to know they're not involving the police at
this stage and will be in touch with you over the next
couple of days.

Anyhow, I'm sure it can be easily sorted out and you'll
soon able to put their minds at rest.

All the best

Steve
P.S. Destroy this letter otherwise I'll get it in the neck
too!

Richard wiped the back of his hand across his sweaty brow,
then wiped the moisture down his trousers. *Fuck, fuck, FUCK!*

If Matthew had replaced him as planned, he'd have found a
way to gloss over this, saying there were no discrepancies.
Blast.

His eyes narrowed. This wasn't a disgruntled customer or

someone he'd sacked... Oh no, *this* was Lillian-fucking-Morgan. *Or Susan…*

No. It was Lillian. This was her style and she certainly had the motive now, the wizened, interfering old bitch.

Richard's teeth grated as he clenched his jaw. *Don't panic. Do. Not. Panic. Think and think HARD.*

What reason could he come up with to explain this? Who could he blame and pass the buck to?

Matthew. He'd blame Matthew – it was perfect. He'd been in charge of the property portfolio so that one was a done deal, but what about the others? Matthew wasn't around when he'd paid Lillian off or when he'd filched that chunk for his house. Or the extended cruise they'd had for a second anniversary celebration. Or for Carmen's wedding... And then there was the landscaping… *Shit!*

Richard's teeth dug into his bottom lip. Ok, so at the time he'd needed the help where Lillian's payoff and purchasing his house were concerned but not since then. But why should he have used his own money when he could take the bank's anyway? He'd worked hard enough for them, damn it.

He raked his hands through his hair. He'd thought being retired he'd be home and dry, but now he'd got to deal with *this* on top of these new threats from the bloody Reapers.

Richard knocked the remainder of his drink across the letter splayed over his desk. Wiping whisky off with his shirt sleeve, he folded the letter in two and angrily stuffed it into the bottom drawer of his desk. He'd get rid of that tomorrow, but right now he needed to think.

Hearing the crunch of gravel, Richard froze. The bank wouldn't pay him a visit at this time in the evening, would they? He glanced at his desk clock. 5.45. They could be trying to catch him off guard?

Sweat tricked down his temples. *What if they'd changed their minds and it was the police?*

Slowly rising from the chair, Richard crept forward. Being twilight, he didn't want to be visible at the window and if it was the police, he'd have to pretend to be out.

Oh, Christ! Susan was downstairs and she'd let them in straight away! And she'd go crazy if she found out what he'd done with the money. Furthermore, if he didn't get out of this he'd go to jail.

Edging up to the window frame, Richard gingerly peered around the side of the open curtains, wishing more than anything that he'd shut them in the first place. He adjusted his vision to the gloom outside, focusing with one eye and centred on something on the driveway. It was one person. It wasn't the police if there was just one of them? Didn't they usually send two?

Wait a minute... That was...

He squinted harder. Yes, it was. Goddamn, it was a Reaper. And not just *a* Reaper, it was *that* Reaper. The one in the hospital when Victoria was giving birth. *The fucker coming up the drive was the kid's father!*

For the second time this evening, and for separate reasons, Richard felt fear twist his insides, his bowels behaving like they might liquify. How did this man get through the gates without calling the intercom?

He scowled. *Susan.* She'd pressed the wrong bloody button again, hadn't she? She'd pressed the "open gates" button instead of the one for the round gatepost lights. *Damn the woman.*

Richard watched the big blond man stride further up his driveway with a look of steely determination on his face. Jesus wept! Had this bruiser found out what he'd done to the kid? *Oh no, no, NO!*

Jumping back into the safety of his study and pressing himself up against the wall well away from the window, Richard scrabbled for the lock on his cabinet. He wasn't having this bonehead come to his house and do God knows what to him!

Glad he'd had the foresight to dust off and grease up his old shotgun he unlatched it from its fixings. He'd show this ape that he didn't take kindly to threats.

. . . .

HEARING RICHARD STAMPEDE down the hallway, Susan jumped at the sudden noise. She'd been dropping off - a welcome respite from the constant jangling in her head.

Getting up quickly from the armchair, Susan rushed to the sitting room door and yanked it open. 'Richard, what on earth are yo…' Stopping mid-sentence, she froze seeing her husband brandishing the shotgun from the cabinet he'd been fiddling with earlier.

'Get back in there *now*, Susan!' Richard hissed. 'We've got an intruder. You left the gates open again!'

'T-The gates?' Susan spluttered. *Had she? Oh no, she could never remember which button was which. But an intruder?* 'W-Who is it?'

'I mean it! Stay out of the way. I'll scare them off,' Richard hissed, pushing Susan back into the sitting room. 'Hurry!'

As the door closed in her face, Susan hardly dared breathe, hearing Richard move further up the hallway towards the front door. Her mind raced. Was it coincidence that he'd got his gun out after all this time? Had he been expecting someone? Or was it like he said – an intruder?

With her heart crashing, Susan heard the front door open and Richard's voice shouting. *"Get away from my house, you filth!"*

Trembling with fear, Susan heard a man shout something in response, but couldn't make out the words. She edged towards the phone, feeling faint. If she couldn't make out what the intruder shouted, then he wouldn't hear her call the police.

Her hand hovered over the receiver. If she called the police, would Richard get into trouble for brandishing a shotgun and threatening someone with it, even if they were about to break in? Impossible. Richard had every right to defend the house. Besides, he had a shotgun licence. But what if he got overpowered and the intruder got in? He'd catch her calling the police and might kill her!

She picked up the receiver. No, she *had* to call the police. Richard could be in real danger. The intruder might have a gun or a knife and use them!

Susan got as far as dialling "9" before a gunshot rang out with a deafening bang. Screaming in terror, she dropped the phone and before she could question her logic, raced into the hallway, relief washing over her to see Richard standing on the doorstep like a statue.

Rushing up behind him she placed her hand on his arm. 'Thank God! I thought something had happened to you! You scared them off then?'

Receiving no reply, Susan followed Richard's gaze across to the crumpled figure lying on the drive. 'Oh my God!' she screamed. 'What have you done? You've shot him, haven't you!'

Susan's shrieking jerked Richard from his stupor. 'Shut up!' he hissed, shaking her hand from his arm.

Tentatively he moved down the steps towards the man as steadily as his shaking legs could carry him and looked around furtively. At least the gunshot hadn't brought any attention from nearby. *Yet.* One great advantage of having neighbours a good distance away, but they would have heard *something* and that meant there was a chance someone could come to check. Or worse – call the police. Most likely that old sod, Greaves, from down the road. So far this year, he'd called the police several times over a back-firing bloody car.

Edging nearer the body, Richard saw blood seeping profusely from a wound, possibly in the stomach. *But the man was still alive...*

He could finish it. This was the perfect opportunity to get the Reapers out of his life for good. The man said he'd come to talk, but people like that didn't have conversations - he'd been here to kill over the kid, Richard just knew it.

His eyes narrowed. He *had* to finish this off and quickly.

'Oh, my life, he's bleeding heavily,' Susan wailed, joining

Richard on the driveway.

'Get away from him, you idiot!' Richard roared, aiming the gun when Susan crouched at Hunter's side.

Susan stared at her husband in horror. 'What are you doing? You were going to shoot him again, weren't you? What on *earth* are you thinking?'

Richard scowled. He *was* about to shoot again – although he wouldn't have needed to try hard, considering he was pretty much at point blank range, but Christ, why did Susan have to be here? Fuck. He couldn't do it now. He couldn't shoot this bastard with her looking. *Damn, damn and DAMN!*

He felt like clubbing her with the butt of the rifle and then shooting the bastard anyway, but he couldn't. Not now. *Think, Richard, THINK!*

'We have to call an ambulance,' Susan sobbed.

Pulling Susan up by the back of her blouse, ignoring the sound of the ripping fabric, Richard yanked her towards him. 'Don't be ridiculous! I'll go to prison! Besides, I didn't mean to shoot him. I only wanted to frighten him. The gun misfired!'

He gritted his teeth. That, for once was the truth. He'd had his finger on the trigger, granted, but hadn't pulled it. The mechanism must be faulty due to age, or perhaps he'd dislodged something when he'd cleaned the thing. He wasn't sorry though. All he was sorry about was that the man was still breathing.

'Richard, we need to get him help and quickly otherwise he'll die,' Susan wailed, hearing the man groan. 'I'm calling an ambulance.'

When Susan began moving away, Richard grabbed her by the shoulder, pulling her backwards so quickly she all but lost her footing. 'You're *not* calling anyone!' Spittle flew from his mouth and landed on Susan's cheek. 'We need to get him away from here. Help me drag him into the car.'

'You want me to dr…'

'You want to get him help, don't you?' Richard barked, rabid with panic and frustration. *He'd just about had enough. If*

Susan didn't pull her head in and help him sort this, she'd be joining this bastard.

'You're going to take him to hospital? What will you say?' Susan blathered, still unable to comprehend what had just occurred.

'Don't be stupid! We'll dump him somewhere.'

'W-What?'

'If you think I'm going to prison for this piece of shit, then you're mistaken. If you're so hell bent on getting help – fine, but it will be anonymously. We'll leave him somewhere that he'll be found.'

Susan's panicked eyes looked down at the man, blood trickling steadily from the gaping wound in his mid-section and stood immobile whilst Richard reversed the Jaguar. This man would bleed to death if they weren't quick and that was the only thing stopping her from thinking rationally about Richard's actions.

Twenty One

IT WAS ALMOST 11pm when the call came through. Colin snatched up the incessantly ringing telephone. 'The White Hart.'

He'd been hoping whoever was on the other end would have given up by now. Thanks to everyone hell-bent on drinking as much as possible to celebrate the unexpected news of Noel and Carmen's engagement, the pub was chaos and now the lager was about to run out. He glanced at Sarah, also up to her neck serving pints to the steady throng of people clamouring at the bar. The last thing he needed was a bloody phone call and if it was one of those cold-callers again...

Colin's concentration suddenly sharpened. 'Yes, we know an Ashley Hunter. What's happened? Is he ok?'

Ignoring the heckles of the waiting customers, Sarah stopped serving and rushed to Colin's side.

Colin flapped Sarah away and placed a finger in his ear to drown out the pub's background noise. 'No, we're friends.' He nodded. 'Yes, I understand... No... Ok, well that will be Tori Morgan.'

Sarah paced agitatedly but Colin ignored her attempts to discover what was going on. 'No, but we'll get the message to her as soon as possible. Thank you for letting us know.'

'What's going on?' Sarah searched Colin's face as he placed the receiver down.

'You need to get Tori,' he muttered.

'What's happened?'

'It's Hunter… They called here because his only identification was his driving licence and a leaflet for this place.'

A creeping sense of dread crept along Sarah's neck. 'Who? Identification?'

'Hunter's in hospital. He's been hurt,' Colin said quietly.

'*Hospital*?' Sarah screeched, causing the entire pub to fall silent.

Colin glared at the sea of faces. He'd been trying to keep things down and now she'd yelled it out.

'I need to go and see him!' Sarah blathered.

'Wait,' Colin cried. 'It's next of kin only and Tori should be that.'

Sarah's eyes filled up. 'Oh fuck! Next of kin? How bad is it? I told him his luck would run out on that bloody bike, I *told* him, but he never fucking listened. Is he…?'

Colin placed his hand on Sarah's arm. 'It's not the bike… Some fucker's shot him and he's not in a good way…'

Sarah gasped, nausea rising. *Someone had shot Hunter? No!* 'W-Who?'

Colin shook his head. 'I don't know any more than you. They just asked me to get in touch with Hunter's next of kin.'

Sarah glanced around blindly. 'Tori must be at the Factory. I'll get over there straight away.' She reached for her car keys. 'Oh shit! My car's in the garage until tomorrow. I'll have to call a cab and hope they get here quickly.'

Waiting for another drink, Jorge listened intently. Seems like Hunter had more than Neil Sparks as an enemy. Maybe this unexpected change of circumstances meant he wouldn't need to set Tori up after all? Someone had very kindly helped him with his plan and if Hunter was out of the picture, then he could be of assistance. A perfect opportunity.

He leant across the bar. 'I couldn't help overhearing. My car's outside. I'll take you wherever you need to go, if that will help?'

Sarah looked at Jorge and then at Colin. She knew Colin had reservations about this guy, but now wasn't the time to be finicky. She needed to reach Tori and get her to the hospital. 'Thanks, that would be great,' she said, forcing a smile.

Jorge nodded at Colin and followed Sarah as she rushed out of the pub.

Grim-faced, Colin reluctantly turned back towards the now silent bar. This was all anyone needed. When the Reapers discovered who had done this, there would be an all-out war.

· · · ·

JORGE SAT PATIENTLY in the driver's seat with his engine running. He would have preferred to go inside with Sarah, but she hadn't given him the option. Before he'd even pulled on the handbrake, she'd shot out of the passenger door with a barked *"wait here"* in his general direction, so he hadn't had a lot of choice but to do exactly that.

Unaccompanied, he stood little chance of being granted admittance without a thorough grilling, judging by the heavy reinforced door he could see.

So, this was the "Factory", or whatever they called it? The nerve centre of the Reapers and the place he needed access to?

His eyes roamed over the massive old red brick building and along the row of gleaming motorbikes lined up outside. There had to be at least twenty machines there, meaning there must be a good few bikers inside and as decent as he was with his fists, Jorge didn't relish taking on that lot. There was *no way* he could casually slip past them, so he'd have to ensure there was a good reason to get in – preferably via invitation. Hopefully whatever had befallen Hunter would provide that.

He'd tried extracting snippets of useful information on the journey over, but Sarah was unresponsive, her whole focus elsewhere, clearly troubled by the turn of events.

Jorge glanced at the temperature gauge on his dashboard, hoping Sarah wouldn't be long. His car didn't cope well with running idle and he didn't want it to overheat.

The sudden noise of the metal door opening got Jorge's attention and he watched Sarah rush out, closely followed by a pale-faced Tori. While the two women hurried towards his car, his focus moved to four bikers busy firing their motorbikes into life.

Instead of getting into the passenger seat, Sarah flung open the back door, quickly following Tori in. 'I'll sit in the back with you,' she said, clasping Tori's hand.

Jorge looked in his rear view mirror, meeting Sarah's eyes. 'Ready?'

Sarah nodded towards the revving bikes. 'They'll make sure we get no hold ups.'

· · · ·

TORI FORCED HER LEGS to robotically propel her into the hospital, the familiar but unwelcome smell of antiseptic and misery hitting her in the face the second she entered the double doors.

'This way,' Sarah said, leading Tori towards the reception desk.

Tori stood numbly in front of the rickety-looking counter whilst a woman shuffled paper, finding herself unable to formulate coherent words. She didn't want to be here. Hospitals represented misery. Misery, pain, suffering and *death*.

Her heart pounded. She was scared of discovering what had happened to Hunter. To *her* Hunter – the man she loved.

At the apartment earlier, she'd half-expected him back long before and had been just about to get into bed, not wishing to waste any time once he *did* return, when banging on the apartment door had knocked her from her eagerness. And what that knock brought had thrown her straight into the pits of hell.

Sarah nudged her and Tori realised she was still standing

mutely in front of the hospital reception.

'You need to say... Don't worry...' Sarah turned to the woman at the desk. 'We received a phone call asking to come urgently. Ashley Hunter?'

Frowning, the woman tapped something into her keyboard and perused her screen for an excruciatingly long time. 'We need to see him,' Sarah said impatiently.

The receptionist lifted her hand. 'Please, just take a seat for a moment.' She gestured to a group of plastic chairs. 'I need to make a call to let them know you've arrived.'

'I-Is he alright?' Tori's voice was barely more than a whisper. *If he wasn't, then... then she couldn't bear to think about it.*

The receptionist smiled kindly. 'Someone will be down to see you shortly.'

Sarah steered Tori over to the group of plastic chairs, not wishing to voice that so far none of this looked good. She'd seen how the receptionist looked at them, giving them one of those smiles reserved for people about to get bad news.

She stared at the sea of worried-looking faces around her. God, these places were depressing. She was about to get drinks for them both from a rather ill-looking coffee machine in the far corner when a tall man entered through another set of double doors and Sarah knew straight away that he'd come for them.

'Miss Morgan?' The doctor looked between Sarah and Tori.

'I-I'm Tori Morgan,' Tori muttered, her voice cracking.

'Please come this way.' The doctor turned on his heels, his open white coat flapping.

Hesitatingly, Tori followed the doctor through the double doors with Sarah close behind.

'I'm Sarah Mathers. I'm a friend of...'

Without breaking pace, the doctor spoke over his shoulder. 'I can only discuss details with next of kin, I'm afraid, but you can accompany Miss Morgan and wait for her outside if you wish.'

Swallowing her frustration, Sarah continued following

along the never-ending corridor. She wanted to see Hunter too. He'd been her friend for years.

Dread churned deep in Tori's stomach as she concentrated on putting one foot in front of the other, blindly following the maze of corridors, trying hard to blank out the wall signs on the route all pointing to "Intensive Care".

Stopping outside a door, the doctor opened it and ushered Tori inside, motioning to yet another row of plastic chairs shoved tightly up against the corridor wall. 'Please take a seat out here, Miss Mathers.'

Tori hadn't time to catch her breath and prepare herself for a sight she was dreading before she found herself inside the small room alone with the doctor. She stared around in confusion at the two chairs and a low table. She'd been expecting a hospital bed. She'd been expecting Hunter. *Did this mean... did this mean that he was...?*

'Please, Miss Morgan, take a seat. I'm Doctor Frost. Ashley has sustained a gunshot wound to his abdomen, as I'm sure you're already aware.'

Tori blinked. *Did that mean he was still alive?* 'I-Is he... is he...?'

'He's in a critical condition, having lost a large amount of blood,' the doctor continued. 'If he'd been found even slightly later, then it's doubtful he would still be with us.'

Tori's heart pounded with relief. 'So, he'll be ok?' *Oh, thank God!*

The doctor's face remained grim. 'It's difficult to say at this stage. We've had to put him into a coma whilst we st...'

'A *coma*?' Tori shrieked, her newfound relief evaporating. Tears poured down her cheeks. *Was he brain-damaged? Would he ever come round?*

'Miss Morgan, allow me to finish. It's an *induced* coma, meaning we medicate to put the body to sleep. This allows the best chance of healing in situations such as these. Ashley has already had surgery to repair the wound, but stomach injuries are difficult to treat and it has been hard to stabilise the blood loss. We're hoping the bleeding will now stop, giving him a greater chance of a full recovery.'

Tori nodded. She wanted to ask what happened if the bleeding didn't stop, but didn't dare.

'Now you know the situation, I suggest you go home and put some of his things together and return tomorrow. There's nothing more you can do tonight.'

'I-I think I'll just stay with him for a while,' Tori whispered.

'I'm afraid there is no admittance to anyone at the moment. Not while he's in such a critical state.'

Tori looked up wide-eyed. 'You mean I can't even *see* him?'

The doctor sighed. 'I suppose I can allow you to look through the window, but I can't allow you into the room.'

TWENTY TWO

TORI WALKED INTO the Factory, bracing herself for the onslaught of questions, but it was eerily still – just a sea of expectant faces. Taking a deep breath, she leant against the bar for support, unsure whether she would even make it up to Hunter's apartment.

Carmen rushed to Tori's side and placed an arm around her. 'How is he?'

Tori blinked away the rapidly forming tears and swallowed the lump in her throat. *A good question.* She didn't know. Neither did the doctors, but time would tell. 'He's not in a good way,' she croaked, her voice hoarse from crying the entire journey back. 'Can Sarah fill you in? She's just thanking Jorge and then she'll tell everyone everything I've told her. I-I really need to be on my own right now.'

Carmen nodded and hugged Tori. 'Of course. I understand.' She wouldn't bother saying anything blasé such as *"I'm sure he'll be ok"*. Neither would she ask Tori who on earth Jorge was.

Watching Tori walk unsteadily towards the stairs, Carmen glanced at Noel and the other bikers and raised her eyebrows. After being unable to tell Hunter and Tori the news of their engagement due to their absence at the White Hart earlier, Carmen had been itching to break it to them when they returned. The celebrations had been in full swing at the pub and the plan was to carry it on back at the Factory even though they'd been offered a lock-in. That was until everyone got wind of the telephone call.

Colin relayed as much information as he could, which was very little, so everyone was on tenterhooks. Understandably, the celebratory atmosphere had died quicker than a plague victim, but Carmen was glad that was the only thing which *had* died. At least so far... From what Tori had said, Hunter was still alive, but things didn't sound good.

All the Reapers were distraught and angry, but especially Noel. It had been a breath of fresh air for him to finally realise after all those years that Hunter wasn't the enemy and now this had happened. Carmen glanced at Noel sadly, his face set in a harsh grimace, his veins pumping with adrenalin-fuelled anger and watched Tori leave the silent room.

· · · ·

SHUTTING THE DOOR behind her, Tori sank to her knees. Being within the confines of the apartment, away from everyone, she could release the guttural howl festering inside her that had been building.

Shuffling back against the wall she hugged her knees to her chest, her howl now reduced to quiet hiccupping sobs. Nothing had prepared her for seeing Hunter lying motionless and the image had burnt itself into her brain.

Peering through the window of the intensive care room, she'd stared horrified at Hunter's huge frame dwarfing the hospital bed. The arms that had held her and the hands that had teased her to so much pleasure only this morning lay still and limp by his sides. Wires snaking up from his wrists joined to tubes leading to bags of liquid suspended from stands to the side of him and dried blood covered his hands and forearms.

His chest had risen and fallen rhythmically, governed by the

THE TARGET OF LIES

machine pumping artificial air into his lungs from the tube taped into his mouth, but apart from the dried blood there was no sign of damage. Wherever the wound was, it had been covered by the bedsheets. Her beautiful handsome man looked asleep. Except he wasn't asleep – she knew that. It was far, far different from being asleep. A whole *galaxy* away from that.

Tori had stood suspended in time and space, listening through the glass to the muffled beeps and whirrs of the equipment that was keeping the love of her life in suspended animation for only a few minutes before the doctor had gently reminded her that she must leave. She couldn't even remember walking back to where Sarah had been waiting or how she got back to that man's car. She also had no idea whether anyone spoke to her during the journey home or what she'd said in reply if they had. Her mind was blank – totally devoid of everything, short of the picture of Hunter lying helpless, covered in tubes.

Was that the last time she'd see him? Would he die?

She vaguely recalled the doctor telling her that Hunter had been found on Sawyer Street by a passer-by who had thankfully called an ambulance, but so far no one had any further information. The police would interview him if and when he was able.

She'd noticed the doctor had used the word "if" before quickly changing it to "when".

Further tears welled, recalling how good she'd felt this morning, which now seemed a lifetime ago. She'd felt a fresh page had been turned and renewed hope for the future glimmered. *And now this had happened.*

The age old feeling of a curse following her resurfaced in the depths of Tori's mind. Was she doomed? Was she the magnet or the totem causing bad situations? Was she the instigator?

Who had done this? Was one of the businesses Hunter had seen today responsible? He'd said some had a deep-seated resentment to his reinstatement, holding him personally responsible for the steady decline of their businesses after he left. They believed his absence allowed underhand dealing, an influx of drugs and unsavoury characters to descend and flood the area.

She wracked her brain to remember what firms Hunter had mentioned he would be seeing, but to her disappointment found she couldn't. In fact, she was certain he hadn't named any at all. There was no point asking the other Reapers because he'd already said he wasn't telling them that he was seeing anyone, so they wouldn't have a clue who he'd seen.

Tori put her head in her hands. *What was she to do?*

If it wasn't the businesses, could it be something to do with that break in? The balaclava-wearing man had given a warning, so that would make more sense than a local firm taking it upon themselves to take out the Reaper's president.

A shiver ran through her. Hunter had been warned and the threat had been delivered.

Taking a deep breath, Tori pushed herself to her feet and glanced at the clock. It was late – almost 2am, but there was little point going to bed. She knew she'd never get a wink of sleep. If Hunter made it through the night, there was a decent chance of him recovering. *And if not...*

Not wanting to dwell on the "what if", she decided to use the time to put some things together for him like the doctor suggested. She had to remain optimistic – do things as if there was no question about it – *Hunter would be fine...*

If she kept putting that out there, perhaps it would manifest in reality.

Tori pulled a small holdall out from under the bed. Now, what would he need? A toothbrush? Toothpaste? Some soap? Maybe something to read?

Frowning, she looked around for inspiration. Hunter would be bored beyond belief lying in a hospital bed. He wasn't one for books and definitely wouldn't appreciate a wordsearch or crossword to while away the time, but she had seen him thumbing through a motorbike magazine not long ago.

With a renewed sense of purpose, she shoved the toiletries

into the holdall and pulled open the chest of drawers looking for the magazine. It wasn't in there, but he'd need *these*, she thought, folding fresh underwear, two T-shirts and a pair of clean jeans into the bag. But what about the biker mag?

Ah! Was that it? Pulling out a magazine from under a bunch of paperwork in the bedside table, Tori saw that it was what she was looking for and smiling, placed it into the bag on top of the other things.

Reaching to shut the bedside table, Tori paused, spotting a familiar face. *Her father.* That was the photo Hunter had taken from her things. The urge to study her father's face was intense but what had been said about this very photograph made her uneasy. It bothered her to think that for all that time she'd had in her possession a photograph which included the face of a brutal attacker. *That rapist.*

She shuddered. There was no way she could destroy a photograph of her father, but she *could* cut the other person out of it - the man on the far right.

Gingerly, she pulled the picture from the drawer. Even though she was loathe to rest her eyes on such a man's face, her eyes moved involuntarily to the far end of the picture. She blinked and then blinked again.

No. It couldn't be.

Like a bolt of lightning, Tori recalled previously recognising Richard Stevens on this photograph but what with everything that had gone on it had bypassed her memory. She certainly hadn't paid any attention to where Richard was positioned, but there was no mistaking it. It was *definitely* Richard Stevens, not someone called Ed Barratt.

Nausea rose and she retched violently.

· · · ·

'THIS HAD BETTER BE IMPORTANT!' Neil spat, snatching up the receiver, not appreciating being called on his private number unless it was a matter of life or bloody death. Especially when it was gone two in the morning.

158

'I called as soon as I could,' Jorge said, his voice breathless.

Once leaving Sarah and Tori at the Factory he'd driven as quickly as possible to locate a phone box suitably far enough away, only to discover the handset was missing. He'd found a similar state of vandalism within the next two phone boxes and only after finally locating a *fourth* had it been in working order – though stinking of tramps' piss. *Bloody British Telecom.*

'I've got a busy day tomorrow and need at least *some* sleep!' Neil ranted.

He'd arranged for the final meet with the man hired to carry out the hit on that Hunter wanker. It was costing him a pretty penny, but if it meant speeding things up, then that's how it would be. It was partly down to Jorge's slowness that he'd been forced to make this decision in the first place and on top of that, he was planning on making tracks up north too. Not that he'd tell Jorge that just yet. He'd spend a day or two watching what was being done, enabling him to gauge exactly what else the boy would be useful for. *If anything.*

Neil gritted his teeth. Jorge Castello wasn't his flavour of the month right now and this call in the middle of the night was enough to break the camel's fucking back. 'You were supposed to be doing this well, Jorge, but I'm really fucking disappointed.'

Neil swallowed a smirk. This tactic always provoked a better response. By treating these monkeys like failures, they worked extra hard - almost breaking their backs in the hope he'd change his opinion. In all due fairness, nothing any of these men did would ever make him see them as anything other than a means to an end and cannon fodder. They were all the same, regardless of who they were or what they achieved.

'That's why I'm calling,' Jorge interrupted. 'I need to tell you th…'

'It doesn't really matter *what* you're going to tell me because I got so sick of waiting for results, I've set up stuff myself.'

Jorge hesitated, irritated, before reminding himself what

was in it for him. 'Your wife isn't connected to that Hunter man,' he blurted.

'What are you talking about?' Neil barked. 'You said th…'

'Yes, I know what I said, but it wasn't what it looked like.'

'What do you mean it wasn't what it looked like! You confirmed Carmen was having it off with him, didn't you?' Neil raged. *Was this idiot telling him that he hadn't seen what he'd told him?*

Jorge paused, sensing Neil's wrath loud and clear. 'I… erm… It looks like I got it wrong…'

'Got it *wrong*?' Neil raged. 'How could you get it the fuck wrong? Are you telling me that Hunter isn't sleeping with my wife?'

'That's about the long and short of it, yes,' Jorge said.

'You fucking idiot!' Neil roared. *Oh, this was bloody brilliant, this was.* He'd already given McFadden the down payment for the hit and now it was a hit on an incorrect target!

He paused. What did it matter *which* Reaper was taken out? He had beef in general with every single one of those fuckers, but this was not something he'd divulge. Jorge believing himself at fault was imperative to getting results. 'You stupid, *stupid* bloody moron!' he shouted for good measure.

Jorge cringed, his ears ringing from the screaming reverberating through the receiver. 'It's not as bad as you think. I've been working hard infiltrating the Reapers and now I know who sh…'

'Working hard?' Neil laughed sarcastically. 'At what? Have you any idea how much I've forked out to get what was supposed to be *your* case moved along?'

Jorge remained silent, a horrible thought creeping into his mind. That was twice now Neil had mentioned moving things along. Was he behind Hunter's shooting? Because if he was, that meant that he, himself, was responsible for that by the intel he had passed on. *Oh shit.*

'You're a bloody waste of space!' Neil yelled. 'Now I've g…'

'*You* arranged to have Hunter shot?' Jorge yelped, glibly ignoring the torrent of scathing abuse.

Neil paused. Did this idiot – his alleged *son* – even have one brain cell in his head? Matters like that were never discussed over the telephone. 'What's wrong with you?' he hissed. 'I don't know what you're talking about.'

'But you said that you paid fo…'

'Walls have ears, son. Walls have ears…' Neil gritted his teeth. 'Be at the flat in three days. I will come and see you and work out how I can rectify your fucking mess.'

He was glad he hadn't mentioned he was coming up north anyway. This would add to the boy's need to please and he had even more to prove being so desperate for a father, the sad, deluded shit. Yeah, he'd drag out making Jorge feel bad about his mistake for as long as possible, but what he'd inadvertently done could end up working in his favour.

Jorge swallowed, painfully aware he had royally ballsed up and his chances of being handed the reins of the firm after this were scant. 'Ok,' he muttered. 'I'll carry on with the other stuff in the meantime.'

Neil sighed. 'You might as well, that's if you can without getting anything else wrong! By the way, I presume you now know who the correct man is?'

Jorge's jaw tightened. *That's what he'd been trying to say.* 'Yes, it's N…'

'Keep it for when I see you,' Neil interrupted. Yes, this would work well. He'd get McFadden to take Hunter out as planned. Being in hospital may prove a bit trickier, but the man was a professional, so undoubtedly he'd find a way. Even so it was probably best not to bother passing that bit of info until last knockings. Either way, the tosser who thought it acceptable to knob Carmen, whatever his name was, was *his*.

He cracked his knuckles in anticipation. He'd get the details off Jorge when he saw him and then take the man out with his own bare hands as originally planned. This meant he could get what he wanted on both counts; the Reapers' president would be dead by the hands of McFadden, just like he'd promised John, but when Carmen's fancy man just "happened" to attack him when he's there getting to know Jorge, then he had absolutely *no choice* but to retaliate. John couldn't argue with that one.

Neil smiled widely, glad Jorge was on the other end of the line so he couldn't see just how happy he was.

Plus, he'd be the one to take Carmen out of the picture too, the lying whore. And her idiotic father. No one would stop him doing that. *No one.* John could moan all he liked, but once it was done there was no turning back and he'd have to swallow it whilst picking up the pieces like he usually did.

Jorge listened to the silence. He may have made a mistake, but he wasn't an idiot and when Neil showed up, he'd make sure he'd reached a place which he'd be grateful for. He wasn't losing his credentials because of this, no way. It had been an easy enough mistake. *Anyone* would have come to the same conclusion as him had they seen Hunter and Carmen on the doorstep of that house, wouldn't they?

'Concentrate on the bank manager for a while. Send him a message regarding his daughter, you know, my slag of a wife? Do you think you manage that? Put a note in with it, ok?' Neil said.

With gritted teeth, Jorge jotted on the back of a fag packet what Neil wanted the note to say.

'Right then. I'll be up in a couple of days and *don't* balls anything else up,' Neil said, before slamming the phone down.

Lying back against the pillow, he exhaled slowly. This was good. He'd get on the road first thing in the morning after the meet with McFadden and find somewhere to lie low for a while, whilst keeping an eye on Jorge. And then once the time was right… *BOOM*!

TWENTY THREE

SUSAN'S HAND SHOOK as she passed the paper across the table. 'Have you seen this?'

Richard glanced uninterestedly at the headline; **_"Man Found Shot In Street"_**, before concentrating back on his breakfast. 'What else do you want it to say? It's a fact, isn't it? What's the problem? Nothing to do with us.'

Susan's mouth fell open. 'Nothing to do with us? How can you say that? It must be the same man that yo…'

'Shut up,' Richard hissed, his eyes boring into Susan's. 'Like I said, nothing to do with us…'

'We need to talk about this, Richard,' Susan pleaded. 'We can't just pretend last night didn't happen. We need to th…'

Richard slammed his croissant down on the plate. 'I won't tell you again, Susan. There's nothing to say! Leave this alone and forget anything you _think_ you may have seen. We all know you haven't been yourself lately.' He didn't need her bleating on top of everything else. He'd got to get his story straight for when the bank summoned him to head office, or worse – turned up on the doorstep. That could be any day now and he couldn't think straight with Susan whining in his ear.

Susan stared at the floor, unable to hold Richard's harsh

glare. Was he insinuating that she'd imagined everything? That he hadn't forced her to help him get that young man in the back of his car last night? That she didn't know the man had been shot by her own husband, who if she hadn't been there, would have done it again?

She'd seen Richard pointing the gun inches away from that man's head and was sure he would have pulled the trigger – purposefully this time. *That's if it had been an accident in the first place?*

Susan wrung her trembling hands. At least the man was alive. *At the moment, anyway.*

Sweat formed on her brow. How could Richard make her an accomplice to something such as this? She'd never hurt a fly in her entire life!

Speeding panic picked up pace thinking of the man's features twisting as he lay groaning in agony on the ground. How would she feel if that poor young man died? Did he have a family? A mother? Such a handsome man too, she thought wistfully, her eyes filling with tears.

'What's the matter now?' Richard snapped, eyeing Susan's expression with contempt.

'W-What? Nothing... I was ju...'

'Well, don't!' Richard glanced out of the window, pleased to see the company he'd called first thing had wasted no time arriving. He suspected there would be little hesitation to pick up a less than a year old Jaguar, especially at the price he'd offered it up for.

He grinned inwardly. It was a shame he'd had to bother giving the inside a whip-round after they'd got back last night, but he didn't want any stains warranting awkward questions. Thanks to his foresight of laying that greenhouse cover over the back seat there was no sign of anything, save a bit of mud and that had come off easily enough with leather upholstery cleaner. Besides, the car firm would give it a thorough valet before selling it on. It was all a bit of a nuisance and had quite liked that car, but it was sensible not to take risks.

Hearing the noise of the Jag being chained into place on the back of the pickup, Susan craned her neck to see out of the window. 'Richard! Someone's taking the car!' she exclaimed. 'Oh my God! Is it the police?'

Richard waved his hand dismissively. 'Don't be absurd, woman! Police? No, of course not. Why would it be the bloody police? I've sold it, that's all.'

'*Sold* it?' Susan cried. 'You mean you've sold it because y…'

'I sold it because it's a year old next month and you *know* I never have my main car being older than that.' Richard gritted his teeth. *She was determined to keep on, wasn't she?* Ok, so he'd have preferred to wait another couple of weeks before trading it in for when the brand new plates were released and certainly wouldn't have let it go quite so cheaply, but what was a couple of weeks anyhow? Besides, he still had all the other collection of classic motors he'd amassed over the years in the garages and he'd just use one of those in the interim.

He glanced back out of the window. 'Right, it looks like they're ready to do the paperwork. I'll go and deal with them and sign what they need.' He forced himself to pat his wife on the shoulder as he walked past. 'You don't need to worry. I've done nothing wrong, remember?'

Susan slightly recoiled at Richard's touch and held her breath as he left the room. *Done nothing wrong? Oh, he'd very much done wrong.*

She watched him walk down the steps to converse with the men. She wasn't stupid. She knew exactly why he was selling the car. She'd watched all six series of Juliet Bravo on BBC1 in the 80s and saw people got rid of evidence that way.

Heart clamouring, Susan forced herself to stare at the front page of the paper again. She may not have pulled the damned trigger, but she may as well have done the way she felt. It *must* be the same man. He hadn't yet been named, but it said he'd been found by a passer-by who had called an ambulance.

She dabbed at the tears now flowing freely down her cheeks

which burnt with shame. *She* should have called the ambulance and never should have allowed Richard to coerce her into being an accessory. Why was she so weak and pathetic? Why had she allowed him to make her part of this?

If Richard was capable of this and had dealt with it so... so *coldly*, then what else was he capable of?

Capable of what Matthew wrote, perhaps?

• • • •

TORI EXPECTED TO have no sleep with her worry for Hunter at the forefront, but she hadn't expected additional layers to take on board too. She stared at the packed holdall and fidgeted pointlessly.

The constant pacing had done nothing to calm her mind – all it had achieved was sore feet and her whole body ached from sheer exhaustion. She'd even spent half of what remained of the night cleaning to take her mind off the never ending spin of thoughts, but it was fruitless. Nothing she'd done had helped and it was doubtful anything would. Although there hadn't been much left of the night, the remaining hours until dawn dragged with painful slowness. Now every minute until Sarah's arrival was taking centuries.

Tori glanced at the clock. Almost 8. *Thank God*. Nothing could shield her from what she would learn at the hospital today, neither would it change what she'd discovered last night, but having someone with her might interrupt the endless roundabout in her head.

Walking over to the huge expanse of glass, Tori looked down onto the line of motorbikes below. She could go downstairs, but it wasn't company she craved. It was an answer. An answer whether Hunter had made it through the night. *Or not...*

A small glimmer of hope flickered. She'd left the Factory's number with the hospital and they'd said they'd call if anything changed. There had been no phone call, so that was a positive sign, wasn't it?

She placed her hands against the glass, the cold cooling her hot palms and forced air into her tight lungs.

And what about the rest? *How would she tell Carmen? How would Carmen take being told her father was a rapist?*

A long shudder enveloped Tori's body. She wished above anything that she could speak to Hunter, but she couldn't. Even if she could it was unreasonable to dump that on him because he wouldn't be able to react to it – not for a while at least.

And he would react.

Tori felt sick with fear. This would undoubtedly cause more misery. God knows what Hunter would do to Richard if she told him what she knew. Well, she knew what he'd do – and Carmen would lose her father. There was no way Hunter would let Richard walk away. It was because of Richard that her own father had died, but she didn't want to be responsible for Carmen going through that same heartbreak.

Tori's speeding mind gained momentum and she leant further against the window, wondering if the glass might fall out sending her plummeting to the ground several storeys below. At least that way she wouldn't be the one to ruin Carmen's life.

Wait - as far as Hunter was concerned the perpetrator was already dead and he'd eventually accepted that. If she told him otherwise that would change. It would cause him more stress, cause Carmen undeterminable pain and cause herself anguish. As much as she despised Richard Stevens, now even more than ever, *she'd* be responsible for his death.

More death. More pain. More suffering. *For everyone.*

Would it be so bad to keep what she'd discovered to herself rather than ruin more lives?

Tori removed her hands from the window and stared at the sweaty imprints left on the glass.

Hunter was the most important thing right now. Only he mattered at this point in time. Once, yes, *once* he'd recovered – because he *had* to, then she'd make the decision whether to tell him. How she would deal with keeping this knowledge to herself in the interim wasn't something she wanted to dwell on, but she had to do what was best for everyone, rather than what was or wasn't best or easier for her.

Spotting a car turn into the Factory's drive, Tori focused on it pulling up behind the row of motorbikes and watched Sarah get out of the passenger seat. With relief, she grabbed the holdall from the bed and quickly left the apartment, hoping that Carmen wasn't downstairs. She knew she wouldn't be able to look the woman in the eye knowing what her bastard of a father had done and knowing that she was the one keeping it to herself.

• • • •

LILLIAN STRETCHED OUT ON the massage table, a warm towel covering her from the waist down. She sighed in contentment as the masseur kneaded her shoulders and back, magically loosening all the pent-up stress and worry. She'd only checked into the Palm Court Hotel and Spa just under an hour ago, but hadn't wasted any time lining up a whole list of relaxing treatments. Luckily, there was a spot free with a masseur straight away which she'd eagerly snapped up.

What a good start to the break she so desperately needed to get her head straight, Lillian thought smugly, already feeling better, both physically and mentally, encouraged by the thought that in these comfortable surroundings she could make rational sense of her options. She had total faith she'd reach the right conclusion and by the time she left the hotel she'd have decided *exactly* which direction to head, whether that be in a week or in a month.

It wasn't like she couldn't afford it and besides, not being around the people and the situations causing her stress was worth its weight in gold. Neither would she think about Victoria. Not that she usually wasted much time on that subject anymore. Her daughter was *officially* nothing to do with her now and was no longer any use. Victoria had nothing to bring to the table, so as far as she was concerned, it was a case of good riddance. Besides, she'd never wanted the child in the first place.

Lillian smiled. The best thing about being at the Palm Court was not having the worry about bumping into anyone. The hotel might only be fifteen miles away, but no one she knew *ever* ventured here, thanks to a situation which, at the time had been absolutely ghastly, was now useful.

She remembered it well. Derek and Brenda Knowle-Sutton's daughter, Fenella, held her reception here several years ago. *Everyone* was impressed with the grand palatial hotel with its balustrades and wonderful grounds – the perfect backdrop for the wedding photographs. But the place had ruined what should have been the perfect day.

Lillian felt almost faint with the memory. It had been unbelievable. Instead of being served lamb for the main course of the two-hundred guest wedding breakfast as ordered, the hotel had somehow disastrously got it wrong and had served *chicken.*

Imagine it?

She felt cold just thinking about it. Fenella had been inconsolable. Every aspect of the wedding had been planned right down to the most intricate detail and for a hotel of this calibre to get something so unforgivably wrong had been just awful. Of course, everyone pretended it hadn't mattered, but it had. Attention to detail was important - *everyone* knew that and Lillian had completely understood why Fenella had disappeared in tears to the bridal suite, refusing to come out for the rest of the evening. The hotel, of course, had apologised, but that didn't change the mistake had *completely* ruined Fenella's day.

After that, everyone agreed never to use The Palm Court for any further bookings. Weddings, social engagements, *nothing.*

Lillian deeply inhaled the relaxing scent of the lavender essential oils being expertly massaged into her back. Fenella's misfortune meant that *she* could relax, knowing she would be unmolested by anyone she knew and that was exactly what was needed.

TWENTY FOUR

JORGE KNEW HE'D GOT a least a couple of hours to play with before Tori and Sarah needed a lift back from the hospital, which would give him more than enough time to get what was needed. He stretched his neck out, stiff with stress. Having to adopt a caring demeanour driving the two women to hospital had taken all his concentration. He wasn't in the mood for playing Mr Nice Guy, but couldn't afford to forget what he wanted to achieve.

Still smarting from the offhand way Neil had spoken to him during last night's conversation, he hadn't had much sleep, but his fuming thoughts and resulting insomnia had at least given rise to another idea. He'd show Neil that he was in no way stupid. He'd get him results and would chuck the proverbial cat among the pigeons with bloody bells on!

Jorge glowered as he drove up and down roads keeping his eyes peeled. He couldn't go too far afield, but neither could he shop anywhere he might be recognised.

He wiped his hand across his brow. Christ, this was too much for a one-man-band. Anyone with brains could see that, but fuck it, he'd do it. He had to. He wanted what Neil had. The man *owed* him and would be thanking him by the end of this, he'd make sure of it.

Pulling up swiftly against the kerb and scuffing the tyres, Jorge swore to himself as he got out of the car. He walked into the butchers, his eyes scanning the meat a man placed in metal trays in the counter cabinet. Another man, his back turned, busily hacked away with a meat cleaver at something on the work surface.

'Morning, Elsie,' one butcher said cheerfully as an old lady with a string shopping bag entered the shop behind him, her brown coat buttoned up tight against her double chin, before turning his attention to Jorge. 'What can I get you, mate?'

Jorge smiled. 'Got any tripe?'

'Tripe? Aye, we've got some out back. How much do you want?'

Jorge paused. *He* didn't actually want tripe, he wanted a heart. *Concentrate, man.* 'Erm, half a pound?'

'Ooh, I loves tripe!' the old lady piped up as the butcher moved to the back room. 'What are you making? Tripe and onions?'

Pretending he hadn't heard, Jorge felt slightly sick when the butcher returned with two handfuls of something slimy which he dumped in the metal dish of the scales. *He would rather die that eat that.* 'Oh, erm… it's for my dog.'

'Your *dog?*' the old lady squeaked.

Jorge quickly caught the butcher's eye. 'I'll have a pig's heart too, if you've got one?'

'Don't tell me that's for the bloody dog too?' the old woman cried.

Refraining from shoving the woman into the mincer just to stop her from putting him off, Jorge slid on a smile. *Be pleasant.* 'It's my dog's birthday today, so I'm treating him.'

The old woman's face creased into even more wrinkles and her jowls wobbled precariously. 'Spoilt dog, if you ask me! That's good food, that is. Far too good to waste on a mutt!'

I didn't ask you, Jorge thought, willing his smile to remain in place whilst the butcher bagged up the tripe and heart in a paper bag.

'You young 'uns haven't a clue,' the old woman droned. 'When I was a girl, we'd be lucky to get something that nice in a bloody blue moon and you lot give it to a dog?'

The butcher gave Jorge a covert grin and a slight roll of the eyes and grinning, he handed over the money and hurriedly left the shop.

Getting back in the car, he ignored the blood and other suspect juices already seeping through the brown paper bag and wound down his window a crack before he puked from the smell. Jesus, he'd have to launch it in the boot, but he'd do that once he got away from here in case that mad old bag came out and set upon him with her handbag for being so offensively wasteful.

. . . .

'I BET THERE'S A few in here you've got your eye on,' Tori said brightly, thumbing through the motorbike magazine. 'I reckon you wouldn't swap yours for any of these though!'

She glanced at Hunter. *Still no flicker of life.* It wasn't surprising. Her unrealistic hopes of finding him sitting on the edge of the bed, dressed and impatient to leave were immediately dashed when on her arrival, the doctor informed her that Hunter was still being kept in the coma. The good news was that the bleeding had stabilised, though it was still very early days.

Flooded with a strange mixture of relief, gratitude, disappointment and worry she was at least able to spend some time with Hunter, even if it was one-sided. She'd decided to act as if everything was normal, having read somewhere that people in comas were aware of everything, but couldn't respond, so it was important to talk to them.

She showed him a page of the magazine. 'Here, look. What do you think?'

Blinking back a tear at the expected lack of response, Tori put the magazine down and sat for a moment in silence. Silence, apart from the consistent hissing, whirring and bleeping of the machines.

Reaching out, she placed her small hand over Hunter's large one, careful not to catch any of the cannulas feeding fluids into his veins. His skin was warm and his hand felt the same, yet different – like something was missing... The life force – the strength, the power was absent, despite the hulking presence of his body dwarfing the small metal bed.

'You'll get through this,' Tori whispered, her eyes travelling over Hunter's rugged face to his full lips that she loved feeling on hers, now accommodating the tube pumping air into his lungs. She scanned for any slight twitch, movement or flicker behind his closed eyelids but there was nothing, just his dark blond lashing resting on his cheeks.

Tenderly, she smoothed his hair off his brow. 'Can you hear me?' she asked quietly. 'I said, you'll get through this. You'll mend and then we'll carry on with our lives. We'll be ok, me and you.'

Tori smiled sadly. If she had the chance after this, then they *would* be ok. Whatever Hunter needed she'd be right beside him. 'When you get out of here, we'll get married just like we planned before, ok?'

Sarah quietly let herself back into the room, not wishing to disturb Tori. She'd been desperate to see Hunter, overjoyed to hear he was through the worst, but still hadn't been quite prepared to see him lying there like that. Unable to take in her own feelings without breaking down, she'd left to compose herself with a cup of machine-stewed coffee and a packet of crisps.

She'd caught the end of Tori's words and hoped more than anything that Hunter would get through this. She couldn't imagine things without him. She didn't *want* to imagine things without him, so could only guess at the depths of Tori's despair. 'Alright?' Sarah asked pointlessly.

'Yes, we're ok,' Tori smiled weakly, unsure who she was trying to keep the act up for – herself or Hunter.

The door opened again and Doctor Frost entered the small private room. 'Hello Miss Morgan,' he said kindly and nodded towards Sarah. 'Miss Mathers.' Walking to the end of the bed he picked up the clipboard and ran his eyes over the latest observations. 'If I could ask you to leave the room now please? The nurses need to do their next set of checks.'

Tori looked at the doctor nervously. 'Is there anyth…'

'We'll talk elsewhere. It's best not to disturb Ashley for long periods.'

Tori rose from the plastic chair at the side of the bed and leant over, pressing her lips to Hunter's cheek. 'I love you and I'll see you later.'

Moving into a small consulting room, Tori sat down with Sarah opposite the doctor, her heart beating erratically. 'Is there a problem?'

Doctor Frost smiled. 'Not at all. We're very pleased with Ashley's progress. It might not appear outwardly great, but his internal bleeding stabilising is a very good sign.'

'Does that mean he'll be fine? Sarah asked hastily.

The doctor's lips pursed and he pushed a strand of dark brown hair away from his eyes. 'I'm afraid I can't say for definite, but it's looking better than it was yesterday. Of course, we have to remain vigilant for signs of infection, but like I said, the bleeding stabilising is a step in the right direction.'

'How long will it be before he… you know…' Tori could barely bring herself to utter the word.

'Before we bring him out of the coma, you mean?' Dr Frost frowned. 'A lot depends on how the rest of the day goes. We don't want to bring him around too soon because patients frequently become distressed as they regain consciousness. Being confused and in pain they can become agitated. Similarly, we don't want to leave him longer than necessary as that may increase the risk of infection.'

'Knowing Hunter, when he comes around he'll end up smashing the place up, he'll be that frustrated and eager to go home,' Sarah joked.

The doctor didn't laugh. 'That's partly the problem. Because Ashley's such a big man, we don't want him overexerting himself. If he makes any sudden or strong movements there's a risk it could start the internal bleeding off again and then we'll be in an even worse position.'

Seeing the expressions of horror on the women's faces, Doctor Frost smiled. 'Don't worry. It won't be for too long. Best case scenario is twenty-four to forty-eight hours more. The other end of the scale would be no more than four days, providing of course that nothing worsens.'

'So, there's still a chance that something could?' Sarah asked worriedly.

'There's always a chance. I won't make things out to be better than they are. Like I said, the main problem now, short of the bleeding reinstating, is the risk of infection.'

'Infection from what?' Sarah snapped. 'Aren't hospitals supposed to be clean places?'

'It could be from a lot of things, Miss Mathers. There are always germs, especially whilst wounds are deep and open. There are a thousand and one ways a bullet wound like Ashley's could become infected.'

'But isn't there something you should be giving him to prevent that?' Sarah's frustration grew. Why were they waiting to see if it happened rather than stopping it in the first place?

'He has and is still being pumped full of antibiotics as we speak, so yes – we're trying our best to prevent infection.' Doctor Frost calmly folded his hands on the desk in front of him. 'Unfortunately, some bacteria are more resilient than others and despite the antibiotics as a preventative measure, they find their way in regardless.'

'What would happen then?' Tori whispered.

'Septicaemia - blood poisoning. And that can cause all manner of serious issues.'

'Like what?' Tori asked pale-faced, still nauseous from the word "bullet" – imagining how that hateful piece of metal had ripped through Hunter's insides, tearing them up. *Hurting him.*

Doctor Frost frowned, not wishing to add to the worry by the long unsavoury list of what sepsis could lead to. 'Let's hope it doesn't come to that. You've got to keep in mind that so far it's looking good and that's what we need to concentrate on.'

'And afterwards? Will he be back to normal afterwards?' Sarah pushed.

'Again, too early to say. We are presently unsure to what extent Ashley's stomach and digestive tract has been damaged from the bullet.'

'Can we go back in to see him now?' Tori asked, her voice hollow. She'd really thought Hunter was out of the woods, but it seemed there was a whole forest to pass through first.

'We'll be running additional tests on Ashley over the next few hours to ascertain the induced coma length, as we've already discussed, so plan on coming back tomorrow. That way you'll have had chance for a good rest and hopefully I'll be in a position to give you more definite answers to some of the things we've talked about today.'

The doctor rose from the chair, signifying his leave. 'Please keep it forefront in your minds that at the moment everything is going well. It's important to remain positive.'

TWENTY FIVE

JORGE COULD BARELY CONTAIN his excitement. 'Well, if you're sure I won't be in the way?'

Tori nodded. 'It's the least we can do. You've been kind enough to ferry us around the past two days and I'm sure you could use a drink?'

'Thanks,' Jorge smiled. 'I must admit I'm a bit parched, but how are *you*? I mean, are you ok?' Tori had been quiet on the drive back from hospital, despite Sarah's reassurance that what the doctor had said was on the whole, good news. He didn't know the ins and outs, but he had deduced the man had not yet regained consciousness, which was good – for him at least, because it afforded him a bit more time.

'I'm clinging on to remaining positive. It's all I can do, even though my brain keeps telling me otherwise,' Tori said sadly.

Feeling a sudden and unexpected surge of empathy for Tori's situation, Jorge risked putting his hand on hers. 'I think that's only to be expected. We all tend to focus on the worst possible scenario even when we don't want to.'

Tori nodded. 'I'm glad Sarah's giving everybody the update so that I don't have to. You don't know what they're like in there. They'll all jump on me, wanting to know the details, and oh... I don't know... I don't blame them of course, they're worried too, but it's difficult going over and over it.'

Jorge glanced at the large metal door on the front of the Factory that he'd had his eye on for the past two days. 'She's a good sort, Sarah, isn't she?'

'She is. I'm very lucky to have her as a friend. She's done so much for me.'

Reminding himself what he was actually trying to do here and sensing an inroad for more information, Jorge squeezed Tori's hand. 'It sounds like you've been through a lot in the past.'

Tori glanced at Jorge before looking away. She couldn't discuss her past. It was too painful. She pulled her hand away. 'Come on, let's go in. Sarah should have filled them in by now.'

Jorge followed Tori up the steps. He clocked the numbers Tori inputted on the door's keypad and rapidly stored them in his brain. He smiled widely. He was getting in here – *invited* and now he also had the entry code. *This was good.*

Following Tori into a vast square entrance area, Jorge tried not to look as eager as he felt or make it obvious he was committing as much as physically possible about the layout to memory. He didn't yet know when or if he would need it.

Entering a huge cavernous room off to the right, he stared at the collection of battered old leather sofas, armchairs and pub tables and chairs. A makeshift bar stood to one side and at the far end of the huge room, although it was very dark and dim, he could just about make out a whole load of old furniture stacked against the wall. *Jeez, this place was massive and this was only the one room!*

His demeanour had clearly morphed from being unobtrusive to gawping like a freak as heavy silence and many pairs of accusing eyes bore heavily into his psyche.

'Who the fuck's this?' Noel growled, stepping towards Jorge menacingly.

'Chill out, Noel. This is Jorge, the one I told you about,' Sarah said.

Jorge extended his hand towards the man he now knew to be involved with Carmen. 'Hi.' His gesture sank like a brick in water and he received no response apart from a glare harsh enough to burn a hole in his brain.

Sensing the atmosphere, Tori put her hand lightly on Noel's arm. 'Jorge has been very kindly ferrying me to and from hospital for the last two days, so I'm sure Hunter wouldn't have an issue with him being here.'

Nodding in acquiescence, Noel turned to the biker behind the bar. 'Get the man a drink,' he grunted.

'Thanks,' Jorge muttered. He really must remember not to get side-tracked. He'd come too far now to fuck it up. He was *inside* the Factory and at close quarters with the new target, *plus* he had access to Tori and with any luck, Carmen.

'I really do appreciate what you've done, Jorge,' Tori smiled, feeling slightly more relaxed and was determined to stay positive about Hunter's recovery, like the doctor suggested. She couldn't let panic escalate again. 'I'm sure you must have other things you should be doing.'

'Not really,' Jorge smiled, nodding his thanks when a beer was heavily deposited in his hand. 'I'm glad to be able to help out in such a shitty situation.' He placed his hand on Tori's shoulder. 'Anything you need, I'll be happy to do.'

Noticing Noel's piercing glare aimed in his direction, Jorge quickly removed his hand. 'I mean it. Anything you, Sarah, Hunter or *any* of you need, I'm happy to d...'

'What's in it for you?' Noel snarled, stepping closer.

Jorge stepped back, plastering offence over his face. *This could backfire, but it was worth a try.* 'Look, mate, we may not have previously been introduced, but I can assure you I've no ulterior motives, ok? I'm just trying to build a new life for myself. From where I come from, that means getting involved with the community. Folk do stuff for one another and help each other out if they can. That's how I was brought up and if you don't like it th...'

'He's been drinking in the Hart for a while,' Sarah added,

attempting to diffuse the situation.

'And he fixed my bike,' Billy said from a table behind the group.

Jorge smiled at Billy. *The silly fat cunt. At least he'd come in useful for something.*

'You a mechanic?' Noel said, the statement alone an unspoken truce.

'Yep – for my sins!' Jorge lied.

'Might have some extra work on the bikes we could sling your way then,' Noel said sourly.

'That would be great,' Jorge smiled, knowing Noel would watch him like a hawk, regardless. He had the creeping feeling this man with the piercing eyes had sussed him out, which didn't fill him with a great deal of confidence. Still, it was unlikely that Noel would be around for very long if Neil had his way.

Jorge covertly studied Noel so he could describe him down to a tee. That man was definitely a loose cannon if he'd ever seen one. He turned the chuckle bubbling in his throat into a cough as he imagined whipping out a camera, saying, *'Just wanted a quick pic to show the guy who wants to kill you exactly what you look like…'.*

It wasn't funny. If it was uncovered what he was *really* doing, then several years from now he'd be found propping up the foundations of a motorway gantry. This lot were dangerous. *A lot more dangerous than he was.*

It was a sobering thought and one that had been sneaking into his mind more and more the longer he spent in this town. As much as he'd been skilfully ignoring this niggling fact demanding his attention, he'd finally swallowed the truth and it was an unpleasant kick to the teeth. He knew he'd become a bit of a cocky bastard and perhaps had a slightly over-inflated sense of his of own ability. Back home, people treated him with respect because of who he now worked for, but compared to this lot… well, maybe he needed to up his game.

Christ, London was supposed to be the kingpin of hardnuts,

wasn't it? Either way, he was no match for this lot, should the tables turn. And what he'd said about people doing things for one another was a blatant lie and it prickled at him painfully. Where *he* came from people walked over you if you were on fire! No one gave a shit and whether he liked it or not, this lot genuinely cared about each other. It was strange. Maybe there was something in the water, or perhaps they were all inbred? Maybe it was because deep down he was a tad envious. No one had ever been nice to him, unless they wanted something. Not even his own bloody mother!

The sudden realisation that this bothered him deeply and no amount of money would stop his hurt slapped him hard in the face.

Standing awkwardly, Jorge risked glancing around the room again, only to see Carmen strut through the doors, her long legs making quick work of crossing the large room. He watched her hug Tori, grasping both of her hands.

'Sarah's just told me the news,' Carmen smiled. 'I'm so pleased to hear Hunter's moving in the right direction.'

Tori returned Carmen's smile. 'He's not out of the woods yet, but the doctor said it's looking positive.'

'That's great!' Carmen beamed. 'I have no doubt Hunter will be fighting fit before you know it, you'll see.' Suddenly noticing a stranger standing behind Tori, she looked at her friend questioningly. 'And who's this?'

'This is Jorge. He's been driving us to the hospital.' Seeing Carmen's confusion, Tori felt she should explain further. 'He'd been drinking in the White Hart and me and Sarah got chatting.'

'Pleased to meet you.' Jorge extended his hand in Carmen's direction.

Shaking Jorge's hand, Carmen smiled. 'I'm sure Hunter will thank you personally when he's out, which,' she winked in Tori's direction, 'shouldn't be too long, by the sounds of it.'

Not too soon though, Jorge thought. He could do with a bit more time to ingratiate himself. 'No need for that. Just glad to help.'

Before the conversation drifted off to something else or Carmen wandered away, Jorge tried to think of something to keep her talking. 'By the way, congratulations on your news! Do you know when the wedding is yet?' *You know, the one you can't have until you get divorced from my father?*

Carmen glanced at Noel awkwardly. 'Well, erm…'

'What's this?' Tori frowned. 'What wedding?'

Carmen shot Jorge a look. 'We haven't mentioned it before because it didn't seem right, what with Hunter, but…'

Noel stepped forward and hooked his arm around Carmen's neck, his other hand firmly on her hip. 'Yep, me and Carmen… We're getting married!'

Tori blinked, hesitatingly wondering whether she'd heard correctly. 'You're getting married? Oh wow! Congratulations!'

She wanted to be happy, but the memory of what she was keeping from Carmen returned fourfold. Hunter had taken sole precedence today and she hadn't thought about Richard Stevens and the predicament – until now. This was another reason not to tell Carmen. How could she spoil her happiness now?

Carmen frowned, hoping for a better reaction to her news. 'We didn't want to upset you.' She cut Jorge another filthy look.

Tori forced a smile. 'No, it's great news, really. It's just been a long day and I'm exhausted.' She hugged Carmen tightly and then kissed Noel on the cheek. 'Seriously, I'm pleased for you both, but I really do have to take a shower. I'll catch you a bit later on, yes?'

'Sorry,' Jorge muttered as Tori stumbled from the room.

'You weren't to know,' Sarah said, patting Jorge's arm. 'On the whole Tori's had good news today, so a bit more never goes amiss.'

'She wasn't very happy about it,' Carmen said miserably.

'I don't think it's that at all,' Sarah said, seeing Carmen's disappointment. 'She said she didn't sleep a wink last night. She'll be more chipper later on, you'll see.'

• • • •

MOVING UP THE STAIRCASE to the apartment, Tori steadied her breathing. That incident was a stark reminder of what she still had to deal with.

Shutting the door behind her she sunk gratefully onto the bed, before almost immediately jerking bolt upright.

Holy shit! How had she missed it? How had what was staring her in the face all along bypassed her brain?

She covered her mouth to stop the scream from escaping and the room span as the truth hit her squarely between the eyes.

If what Hunter had said about that photograph was correct, then Richard Stevens was the rapist... That she now knew, but it meant he'd raped Noel's mother – Leila. Leila Cooper, right? And Noel was the product of that rape...

Which meant... which meant that Noel was Richard Stevens' son...

Nausea rose rapidly into Tori's throat and her hand flew to her mouth. Carmen was Noel's *sister*... Half-sister, but sister all the same.

Oh, dear Jesus.

Sweat trickled down Tori's neck. This was a lot worse than telling Carmen her father was a rapist. Finding out the man she wanted to marry was her own brother would destroy her.

Tori knew that now she had absolutely no choice whatsoever but to be the one to break this news.

TWENTY SIX

JORGE WAS CROSS for putting his foot in it. He'd seen the looks Carmen gave him and he'd also upset Tori at the same time. How was he supposed to know that they hadn't told her? The whole bloody pub and probably half the city knew but of course, *he* had opened his gob when everyone else in the entire world knew better.

Pulling over at the side of the road, Jorge got out of the car and yanked the boot open, retrieving the paper bag holding the purchase from the butchers. Taking a deep breath, he opened the cardboard box he'd brought along in preparation and, trying not to gag, held the bag by the tips of his fingers, gently shaking it. The gelatinous, slimy gloop of the half pound of offal, as well as the heart slithered into the box and Jorge scowled. The very *opposite* of what he wanted to happen.

Knowing there was nothing else for it he closed his eyes and stuck his hand into the box, cringing as his fingers closed around the sinewy slop of the tripe and steeled himself to scoop it back into the bag.

Unfortunately, he'd never been great at holding his breath and retched from the combined smell and texture as the tripe slipped and slid through his fingers. After what felt like an indeterminable age, he got it all out, leaving only the heart in the box and rued the day he'd ever thought this a good idea. He hadn't even needed the tripe, only asking for it because he hadn't thought through what to say.

Jorge stared in dismay at the gloop covering his hands and looked down at his jeans. *He wasn't wiping them on those. No. No way!*

Bending down, he dragged his hands across a patch of grass, keeping a watchful eye out for any sneaky hidden dog turds, then looked at his hands again. Not even a puddle where he could wet them. *How typical.*

Sighing, Jorge yanked a T-shirt left in the boot and dejectedly wiped his hands on it, making sure he'd got between his fingers before getting back in the car.

Driving further along he stopped on seeing trade bins at the side of a corner shop and quickly retrieving the bag and T-shirt from the boot, tossed them in. No doubt some lucky fox's luck was in tonight, he thought as he jumped back in the car and headed towards Richard Stevens' house.

Coasting past the gated driveway of the bank manager's abode, Jorge saw no cars on the drive which was a good start. From what he'd seen, there was no one about in the vicinity either; no direct neighbours overlooking the imposing property, so all was quiet on the Western Front.

Turning the car around, Jorge drew to a halt outside the house and after another quick check up and down the road, slipped the package into the wall-mounted mailbox. It was a bit risky delivering it himself, but sod it, he hadn't got time to mess about.

Clambering back into the car he sped off. His next port of call was the flat to give his hands a bloody good wash!

· · · ·

HAVING TAKEN THE Aston Martin out for a run to break up the day and more importantly, give him something to do other than pace around the house listening to Susan, Richard had decided a quick lunchtime drink at the Conservative Club was in order. There was a man from the bank who drank in there and he managed to drop a couple of subtle questions into the conversation in the hope of gleaning info about any on-going investigations currently running, but nothing was forthcoming. The majority of the talk centred around the "dreadful shooting".

'Absolute shower, isn't it, Stevens?' Andrew Mercer flopped down in the next chair, stabbing his finger at the newspaper. 'Have you seen this?'

Richard scowled. *Of course he'd seen it. He'd heard nothing but that.* 'Yes, awful,' he muttered.

'What is this town coming to? It's like the bloody Wild West! First bodies in hospital incinerators and now people getting shot in the street?'

Richard grunted in mock agreement and signalled to the bar steward for another whisky. He'd only planned on the one, but now Mercer had felt the urge to join him he was in need of more alcohol. His fingers twitched against his trousers. He still hadn't heard anything from the bank and the waiting was playing havoc with his nerves, plus Susan's flapping over this shooting debacle didn't help.

Mercer's squinty eyes focused on Richard. 'Did I see you arrive in your Aston Martin, Stevens? Why's that come out of mothballs? What happened to the Jag?'

Trust Mercer to notice that, he really was a nosy bastard, Richard thought. 'Oh, I fancied giving it a run. I'm getting a new car shortly. It's the new plates any day now, remember?' he winked, sure Mercer would have had *his* on order since last year or even the year before if it were at all feasible.

'Oh, right you are,' Mercer agreed enthusiastically. 'Most definitely.'

An awkward silence ensued and Richard wished Mercer would go away. The man was always digging around for something and he didn't want anyone digging around at the moment. Or *ever*, come to think of it.

'Did you take up that club's offer?' Mercer asked.

'Club? What club?' Richard glanced over to the bar. *Where the hell was his bloody drink?*

Andrew Mercer's eyes narrowed. 'The London Club. Your invitation? It came here, don't you remember? I ga…'

'Oh yes, of course,' Richard said, hastily. *Damn, he'd forgotten he'd said that.* 'No, I didn't bother.'

'They must be desperate for you to join them.' Mercer pulled a crumpled envelope from his blazer pocket. 'This came for you the other day. Sorry it's a bit creased. I presumed you'd be in on Sunday, you usually are. I'd have left it behind the bar if I'd known you weren't coming in for a couple of days.'

Richard snatched the envelope from Mercer's pudgy hand, a wash of dread flooding him. He eyed it to see if Mercer had made an attempt to steam it open, then checked the postmark but it was smudged and couldn't make it out. 'When did this arrive?'

'I saw it Sunday, meaning it must have arrived on Saturday.' Andrew Mercer frowned. 'No, wait a minute… or was it yesterday? One or the other.'

Richard scowled. *It was important when it was sent if it was from the people who'd sent the last one.*

'Is it from that London club again?' Mercer pushed.

'How do I know?' Richard snapped.

'Aren't you going to open it?'

Richard shrugged nonchalantly. 'What's the point? You're right, it's probably that club again. They'll give up eventually.' Standing up, he signalled for the bar steward to cancel his drink. The useless boy had most likely forgotten he'd even requested one.

'Leaving already?' Mercer asked, watching Richard do up his sports jacket.

'Yep, got a lot on today,' Richard lied, stuffing the envelope into his pocket. He had to get out of here and read what was in this letter. And he was dreading it.

• • • •

NEIL FOUND A SPACE in the corner of the car park. He'd done one circuit already and didn't want to draw attention. He shouldn't even be here, but the temptation was too great as he'd driven past. However, it didn't look like anyone was about because he hadn't spotted the Jaguar.

He'd taken note of Richard's car and where he frequented during his recce a few weeks ago so it didn't hurt to have a breather for five minutes and check to see if the loser was here before carrying on, did it? Besides, he'd only got another twenty miles to go before reaching the hotel.

Pulling down the sun visor, Neil glanced at himself in the small vanity mirror, doubting whether anyone would recognise him in this ridiculous get up anyway. He eyed the faded baseball cap and the scruffy collar of the blue Adidas tracksuit top scathingly. Christ, he looked a right prick; a teenager crossed with one of those sad, middle-aged skanks who hung around park benches drinking two-litre bottles of cheap cider.

It was ok though. He'd only don this get up whilst venturing inside city limits. The rest of the time he'd wear his usual clobber. It was hardly likely he'd bump into anyone where he was staying. And as for this motor. Bloody hell, he'd get more poke out of a cow pat, but the knackered old VW Golf was the only car the rental place had available at short notice for an open-ended return. Neil's nose screwed up in derision, genuinely surprised he'd made it up here at all.

Right, he'd best make tracks. He'd wet himself if he didn't get a move on and that would not help his overall look. It was bad enough checking into a hotel dressed like a scrubber, let alone sporting a large suspect stain over his crotch. Furthermore, he had no idea where the hotel was. There hadn't been a huge selection of places out of town that weren't just a pub with a couple of rooms and he dare not risk somewhere like that. He needed somewhere that he'd be anonymous whilst still remaining close enough to keep tabs on Jorge and the hotel he'd booked sounded like a decent gaff - somewhere to keep his head down whilst McFadden did the business.

Neil smiled as he coaxed the engine of the Golf back into life. This morning's meeting went ahead without a hitch. He'd confirmed the date of the job, making sure it coincided with when he'd arranged to meet Jorge, but he still hadn't yet mentioned that the target was in hospital. He'd drop that in when he made his final phone call the night before. It wouldn't cause any issues – McFadden knew what he was doing.

He'd also given the man the go ahead to remove anyone getting in the way of accomplishing the task. He winced. If that was needed then it would up his bill dramatically, but needs must…

Putting the Golf into gear, Neil cringed at the unpleasant crunch as the gearbox engaged and was about to pull out of the space, when someone leaving the large building at the other end of the car park caught his eye.

He squinted against the low sun. *He thought so. Fucking Bingo! Richard Stevens was here after all!*

Baring his teeth, a quiet growl escaped from the back of Neil's throat watching Richard move across the car park, glancing left to right, exhibiting all the signs of a scared animal. 'Yeah, you should be scared, you bastard,' he muttered, his adrenalin pounding.

How he'd love to run him over here and now, the lying, two-faced, stuck-up ponce that he was, but he'd have to wait.

Neil followed Richard's progress across the car park. It was unmistakeably Richard-bloody-Stevens. A little thicker around the middle, but still as smarmy as ever since he'd last set eyes on him.

Stopping at the side of a dark green Aston Martin, Richard glanced around once more while he fumbled for his keys and Neil smirked. That would explain why he hadn't spotted the Jaguar. *Probably trying to go incognito.*

Stevens should have received the final letter over the weekend and Neil wondered whether he'd had the balls to show up. It would have been fun watching him shitting himself with fear outside the Corn Exchange, but that wasn't feasible.

Actually, Stevens probably hadn't even shown, but at least it would have given his fat head something else to worry over and that was the point.

Before he acted on the temptation to cave Richard's head in, Neil pulled out of the Conservative Club car park without a backwards glance. He couldn't sit here any longer. Apart from the need to use the toilet, the exhaust from this thing was choking him out.

'Don't worry, Richard. You're on the list,' Neil spat under his breath.

· · · ·

IN THE DRIVER'S SEAT, Richard's hands shook as he ripped at the crumpled white envelope.

Richard,

You couldn't have taken my last letter seriously because from what I can see you're acting like you haven't a care in the world.

What sort of person doesn't care about their own wife or daughter? I would say son too, but you've already lost him. Shame about that.

Be at the Corn Exchange at 7pm Monday 10th. If you don't show or do not come alone, then you'll lose someone else.

Fear coursed through Richard's veins. *The Corn Exchange? That was in the city centre? And on Monday 10th?*

Hang on... what day is it? Oh shit, it's Tuesday - Tuesday the 11th...

He gripped the creased paper harder between his clammy fingers. The Reapers had wanted to meet him last night and he hadn't showed? That's what it was all about. Last night that man he'd shot had come to take him out because he hadn't turned up for the requested meet. Or maybe he'd been gunning for Susan? *He'd come for one of them.*

Relief coursed through him with the revelation. He'd been right all along. These threats were from the Reapers and now he'd shot the perpetrator, it was over. At least it would be providing the man didn't make it and remember who had shot him in the interim.

He glanced at the clock inlaid beautifully in the Aston Martin's walnut dashboard. He'd go home and make a couple of calls to see if he could find out what the state of the casualty was. With any luck he'd have died by now, although maybe he should go to the hospital and find out himself? It shouldn't be difficult to get an update on the state of that thug's health from some thick receptionist bint.

As he started the car a wide grin spread across Richard's face. This was good news. Once he'd put this to bed, all he had to deal with was the bank. The list was becoming smaller and more manageable.

• • • •

JORGE DIDN'T REALISE he looked quite so openly miserable. The crud on his hands was the last in a long line of straws which had mounted up and it was grinding him down.

After having a nice hot shower and getting that revolting gak off him, he'd arrived for his usual liquid dinner at the White Hart, hoping to glean further info like he'd been doing for what seemed *months*. He thought he'd perfected the art of masking his underlying feelings but seemingly he wasn't quite as good as he thought. A bit like a lot of things. Either that or Sarah was an amazingly perceptive judge of emotions. Probably a bit of both.

There was a lot he'd learnt about himself over the last couple of days. The main one being he was nowhere near as hard-faced as he'd believed. He didn't like what he'd done this afternoon with the heart. Giving someone the impression their kid had been butchered wasn't on and he couldn't say he felt good about it. Neither did he feel good over upsetting the apple cart with Tori about Noel and Carmen's wedding. The poor cow had enough on her plate.

He scowled, not thinking he'd be bothered about stuff like that, but even though he was loathe to admit it, he actually quite liked this lot. And that was the *last* thing he should be feeling – especially now.

That was another thing – the meeting with Neil was looming and although he'd previously been determined to impress the man, he was now questioning his involvement with the whole thing. Neil was expecting results and Jorge had nothing to give him, short of Noel's death warrant on a plate and as much as he didn't particularly like the guy, Noel and Carmen seemed genuinely happy. *He didn't want to be the one to ruin that.*

Jorge frowned. Here he was pretending to be everyone's knight in shining armour when really he was their worst enemy. *The proverbial snake in the grass.*

He felt a total heel, a fake and a phony and this admission both surprised and upset him. *He didn't like it. Neither did he like himself.*

Sarah prodded Jorge. 'Are you on this planet? I've been talking to you and you're off with the fairies.'

Jorge pushed a smile of sorts on to his face. He'd always found it easy to turn his smile on, but now – especially today, it was hard. Harder than ever. 'Sorry, I'm a bit down at the moment. I don't know why. I haven't really got a reason, especially compared with some folks around here.' *Of which if I carry on with what I've been doing, their lives will get a whole lot worse*, he thought bitterly.

'Hey, come on. I'm sure after what you've done, Hunter will chuck some decent work your way once he's up and about again.'

Jorge shrugged, feeling even worse. 'I didn't do anything really.' *Apart from hit her and smash their place up.*

Frowning, Sarah rested her elbows on the bar and placed her chin in her hands. 'Are you *sure* you're alright?'

Jorge felt a worrying burn of tears at the back of his eyes and turned away in case he couldn't contain them. 'Yeah, I'm fine.'

Sarah straightened up. 'You don't look fine to me.' Grabbing his hand, she pulled him through the bar hatch. 'Come on. You could do with a decent bit of grub and a chat. It's not busy down here, so I'm sure Colin can manage while I make you something.'

Not knowing what else to do and further humbled and guilt-ridden from Sarah's kindness, Jorge followed her through the door leading to upstairs.

Twenty Seven

RICHARD SNEERED as he paced along the corridors signposted to the Intensive Care Unit. He wasn't wasting time questioning that goofy-faced thick cow on reception. He'd seen just by looking at her that she had difficulty working out which way was up. More sense in a paving slab, that one.

He didn't need to ask anyway. If the thug was still in the land of the living it was more likely he was still trussed up in intensive care, like the papers reported. It was all but impossible for him to have improved so dramatically to be moved to a general ward within the space of twenty-four hours.

However, the other option and the one he was hoping for, was that the bastard lay in a cold drawer with a tag attached to his big toe somewhere in the bowels of the hospital – or wherever the morgue was located in this dump.

Richard stuck his finger into the collar of his shirt and loosened it slightly, irritably thinking how over hot it always was in these places. No wonder there were constant outbreaks of foot and mouth disease or that Legionwhateveritwasella thing.

As the large red signage of Intensive Care loomed ahead of him he slowed, his eyes wandering to the keypad beside the closed doors. *Damn. He hadn't taken on board there might be restricted access.* They'd never let him in without very good reason and, as far as the hospital would be concerned, he hadn't. Personally, he thought he had a *very* good one.

Hearing people approach, Richard feigned interest in a poster attached to a notice board highlighting the effectiveness of covering the nose when sneezing and the importance of hand washing, while a nurse and a rather scary looking Sister punched in the code for the door. He sighed petulantly. There was no chance of winging his way in with them - they looked far too switched on. After the door closed heavily behind the women, he remained where he was. *All he needed was a quick look. It couldn't be that difficult.*

Hearing another set of footsteps, Richard turned his attention back to the noticeboard; this time staring at a poster about walking frame availability. His eyes swivelled sideways, seeing a slip of a girl dithering by the keycode box. *A-ha! Judging by her uniform and her general demeanour, this one was a trainee.*

As the young nurse clumsily entered the code, Richard confidently strode up behind her and when she pushed the door, he followed. He was halfway through before she went and ruined it.

'Can I help you, Sir?' The young nurse said.

Richard thought it wise to adopt his best haughty, yet irritated attitude. 'With what, young lady? I've been out for some fresh air and now, if you don't mind, I'm returning to sit with my wife!'

Cheeks reddening, the nurse stepped aside. 'I'm very sorry. Please, go ahead.'

Biting back a satisfied smile, Richard walked purposefully ahead. He had no idea where he was going but he had to make out he did otherwise it was only a matter of time before someone with more sense stopped him.

Turning down a quiet corridor, Richard glanced in the windows of each room, hoping to catch a glimpse of *that man*

– the one who had come along to his house, bold as brass with the sole intention of killing him. Rounding another corner, he continued walking and sneaking a fleeting glimpse into the end room, found what he'd been looking for.

'What seems to be the problem, Sir?'

Richard turned to face a doctor eyeing him with suspicion. *Shit*. He wracked his brains to think of an excuse. 'Hello, doctor. I think I must be a bit lost. I'm trying to locate my wife.'

'There are no general visitors to this area, Sir.' The doctor frowned. 'This is Intensive Care. Can you tell me how you got access?'

'A nurse let me in - a young girl, blonde hair – just a slip of a thing. She looked about nine years old!' Richard smiled. *He might as well get the silly bitch in the shit whilst he was at it.*

Seeing no trace of amusement on the doctor's face, he felt it wise to try a different tactic. 'I'm very sorry. I didn't realise where I was.' He made a point of glancing in the window of Hunter's room, hiding his disappointment that the man was still alive. 'I say, that poor chap doesn't look in a good way. Is he going to be ok?' *He may as well ask, being as he was here...*

'I can only discuss patients with their next of kin, Sir. Now, I'm going to have to ask you to leave. There is strictly no admittance to this unit, apart from family and close friends.'

'But, I…'

'This way, Sir.' A security guard appeared from nowhere, stood to the side of the doctor and motioned towards the door.

Accepting defeat, Richard gave the doctor an unpleasant parting look, shrugged away from the guard's outstretched arm and walked back down the corridor towards the exit, knowing security would follow him at a distance to ensure he left. Without a backwards glance he pressed the door release button and moved quickly into the main body of the hospital.

Ok, so what had he got? Well, he now knew the man was still alive but being as he was still in intensive care with strictly no admittance to anyone but family and close friends, he was clearly still in a bad way, which was good.

Also, judging by the glimpse he'd sneaked of the huge body covered with tubes and attached to a ventilator, it didn't look like he was in a rush to go anywhere.

A smile spread across Richard's face. Ashley Hunter wouldn't speak to the police anyway. That sort never did and the chances were, looking at the state of the man, he'd have little memory about what happened that night in the first place. And even if he did, how would he prove it?

Feeling rather pleased, Richard ambled across to the car park. He'd been worrying about nothing and on this one, he was home and dry.

· · · ·

TORI GLANCED IN THE MIRROR and smoothed down her wayward hair. She hadn't washed it for two days and it showed, but that was of no consequence. She'd happily dye her hair pink and wear a bolt through her neck if it meant Hunter would be ok.

She stood motionless, aware she was dithering over going downstairs, still not knowing how to do what was needed. She raised her eyes to the skylights, exhaling slowly.

'What should I do?' Tori gasped aloud in the hope that someone, *anyone*, could give her guidance.

She swallowed dryly. There was no question about it. Not anymore. She *had* to tell Carmen what she knew. It was no longer as cut and dried as hiding the truth about Richard in an effort to save her friend pain. Now it involved Noel and their relationship, she had to speak out and speak out immediately. This wasn't something that could wait, but it would rip holes in *everything*.

Tori's head throbbed. Her hatred for Richard Stevens intensified. This was all his fault – one hundred percent his fault.

Carmen had told her about her unhappy, passionless marriage to Luca and although Tori had initially been horrified when Carmen hooked up with Noel, their unlikely relationship had been a catharsis for both of them. Noel had become a better person – solely, Tori believed, because of his feelings for Carmen and Carmen – well, she was happy - *genuinely* happy, probably, from what she'd said, for the first time in her life. Now it would be ripped from her in the worst way possible.

And, dear God, how would Noel take this news? Tori sighed deeply, her breathing ragged. She hadn't even thought about how Noel would feel. Oh, this was just awful.

She glanced at the bed, wanting to crawl into it, hide under the covers and not come out until all of this had disappeared. But it wasn't going to disappear.

Should she tell Carmen first or tell Noel and Carmen together? Perhaps she should ask Sarah? She was a stalwart and would think of the best way to do this.

Tori stared at her own reflection in the mirror. No. It wasn't right to discuss this with anyone else. Neither was it right to procrastinate any longer.

Without further hesitation and before she lost her nerve, she left the apartment and made her way down to the bar.

TWENTY EIGHT

'I'M SO GLAD YOU'RE HERE,' Carmen smiled, pushing a glass of wine into Tori's hand. 'I thought we'd upset you earlier, by... you know...' She blushed and glanced shyly at the beautiful sparkling diamond on her left hand.

Tori smiled stiffly, watching as Noel traced his fingers along Carmen's collarbone. 'No, you didn't upset me. It's just... it's...'

Noel scraped his chair back noisily. 'I get the hint,' he winked. 'You want to have a girly chat, don't you?' He stuck his tongue roughly in Carmen's ear. 'Make sure you tell Tori my dick's bigger than Hunter's.'

Carmen slapped Noel playfully. 'I wouldn't know, thank you very much! I'm more than happy with yours.'

'And so you should be,' Noel grinned. 'Laters, girls.'

Watching Noel saunter towards the other bikers, Tori fought against the rising nausea of his remarks. *It wasn't their fault – they didn't know.* 'Carmen... I...'

'Listen, I'm glad he's gone.' Carmen leant forward conspiringly. 'I want to tell you something.'

'Let's go somewhere else, shall we?' Tori pushed her chair back, not wanting an audience for what she had to say.

Although they were sat well away from anyone and no one would overhear, it wasn't that which was the problem – it was how Carmen would react. 'Shall we go up to the apartment? We ca...'

Carmen grabbed Tori's hand. 'No, I'm fine here.' She nodded in Noel's direction and giggled fluidly. 'He'll only get possessive if I disappear, you know what he's like. He can't leave me alone.'

'Carmen...'

'Oh Tori, I'm soooo happy! Can you believe it? Me! Getting married, but *wanting* to this time! I'll need to get a divorce first which might prove tricky, but I don't care! Anyway, it doesn't matter if it takes ages. But I want your opinion on something.'

Tori fidgeted nervously, unable to get a word in edgeways through Carmen's overflowing excitement.

'I haven't told anyone this and, to be honest, I never thought I'd want to go down this road. Wait for it... I want a baby! I want one so badly. Is that crazy?' She slugged at her wine. 'I can't believe I'm even saying it out loud!'

Carmen saw Tori blink away forming tears and she raised her hand to her mouth. 'Oh my God! I'm so sorry. I'm not thinking. It's so selfish of me to come out with that. You've not long lost Andrew,' she babbled, 'I'm such a thoughtless cow. I'm so sorry!'

Tori grasped Carmen's hands. 'It's... it's not that...'

Carmen frowned. 'It is! It's because I said about babies. I sho...'

'No, no it's not.' Tori needed to get Carmen to listen. She *had* to listen. 'Please listen to me.'

Carmen studied the strange expression on Tori's face. She'd upset her. She really was an unfeeling cow. First, she dumped her engagement on Tori the minute she returned from hospital where her man lay in a coma and now she'd gone on about wanting a baby when Tori's son hadn't long died. 'It's not Hunter is it?'

'No, it's not. Carmen, please ju...'

Carmen frowned. 'I'm not pregnant if that's what you're going to ask.' She lowered her voice, a small smile creeping across her face. 'Well, I might be I suppose, but not as far as I know.'

'Good,' Tori muttered.

'*Good*? What's that supposed to mean?' Carmen cried, offended.

Tori shook her head. *Shit. She was going about this all wrong.* 'Listen, this is difficult... I've no idea how to do this, except I know I've got to. I wish to God I didn't.'

Carmen quietened, sensing that something bad really had happened. 'Is it my mother? I knew I should have gone to see h...'

Tori shook her head and began to speak.

• • • •

SATISFIED THAT ALL WAS better on the Reapers front than he'd surmised, Richard had treated himself to a nice round of golf, followed by a couple of drinks in the club house. After the stress of the last few weeks he deserved a bit of relaxation, but once in the car his mind had centred back on the issue with the bank.

Turning into his road, his eyes scanned for any cars signifying visitors from head office had arrived and breathed a sigh of relief to see none. Nearing the gates, he pressed the button on his key fob, cranking them into life and pulled up outside his house. Richard pressed the button again, not wanting the gates left open giving anyone the option of wandering in unannounced, like last time...

Getting out of the car he moved to the door with a slight spring in his step and striding inside the house, slung his sports jacket on the coat stand. 'Susan, I'm back!' He might even be nice to her today being as he was in a better mood than he had been for a long time.

Richard's heart sank to his feet when Susan rushed from the

sitting room, her eyes wild. 'Whatever's the matter?'

'You… you've got… see…'

Richard grabbed Susan's shoulders. 'Calm down! Tell me what's wrong.' He couldn't understand a word coming out of her mouth she was hyperventilating so much and anxiety prickled. *Was the bank here after all? Had they telephoned and told her everything?*

Susan wiped her hand across her mouth. 'I… I can't… I-It must be… I-It was in the mailbox…'

Frowning, Richard stalked into the kitchen with Susan close on his heels. *Had she been on the Valium again? It always sent her strange.*

'I-I can't… I can't look at it again… I…' Susan retched into her hands.

Richard scowled in distaste. 'What on earth's going on? I don't understand what this is about!'

Susan gesticulated towards a box on the breakfast table and Richard's eyes narrowed, an unwelcome thought occurring. 'Is this something to do with Lillian? Is she causing problems? What lies has she told this time? If she's upset you, then I'll go str…'

'No, no… It's the package… Look. I-I emptied the mailbox and it was…' Susan gagged again.

Richard moved closer. The box wasn't addressed to anyone, meaning it had been hand delivered. His nerves jangled. Opening the lid and seeing the contents, he immediately recoiled. 'What the…?'

'Oh, Richard. It's awful,' Susan wailed. 'But the note… Read the note.'

With effort, Richard pulled his eyes away from the red lump of meat in the box and spotting a piece of blood-stained paper, snatched it up, his eyes focusing on the words:

You weren't there so she's paid the price

Richard frantically turned the piece of paper over only to

reveal nothing else. *Was that it?*

'What have you done?' Susan wailed.

Richard threw the note down in contempt and slapped the lid of the box closed. 'What do you mean, what have *I* done?' he yelled. 'What the hell has this got to do with me? It's clearly some kind of sick joke.'

'A *joke*? Is this something to do with the man you shot? Has someone found out it was you? Where were you supposed to be?'

'Don't be ridiculous!' Richard barked. 'I wasn't supposed to be anywhere, I…' Stopping mid-sentence, he froze. That letter that Mercer had given him - he *was* supposed to have been at the Corn Exchange last night. He swung around and stared at the box again. *No. No… It couldn't…*

'What?' Susan wailed. 'What is it? You know something, don't you?' She stared at Richard's rapidly fading complexion. 'I can see you know something.'

Richard slumped into the chair, his body beginning to tremor from his toes up to his fingertips. Sweat poured down between his shoulder blades, quickly soaking into his crisp blue shirt. *That was a heart in that box, but it wouldn't be… couldn't be…? No, it was absurd…*

'Richard!' Susan shrieked. 'Tell me what's going on?'

Richard slowly raised his gaze to meet the panicked wide eyes of his wife. 'Where's Carmen?'

'Carmen?' Susan frowned, the immediate thought that Richard had somehow discovered she'd maintained contact with her daughter against his express wishes fleetingly pushed into her mind. 'What's Carmen got to do with it? Surely you can't think she'd do something like *this*?' Her hands pointed accusingly at the box.

'No. No, I don't.' Richard muttered, almost inaudibly.

'Then what are you trying to say? What's going on?' Susan watched Richard put his head in his hands and begin to shake. 'Richard?'

'I don't think Carmen sent it. We need to get hold of her.

I… I-I just want to make sure she's ok…'

'She's…?' Susan stopped mid-flow as the impact of what Richard was saying sank in. Her hands flew to her mouth. *He surely couldn't think what was in that box was…?* 'What have you done?' she screamed.

• • • •

NOEL LEANT HIS HEAD against the wall in the toilets at the Factory, his breathing laboured and his heart crashing in his chest, alternating between seething anger, confusion and desperation.

What the hell was Carmen playing at?

Scraping his hand over his slicked back hair, he tightened his ponytail and stared at his reflection in the cracked mirror, an incessant twitch below his eye irritating him further. Punching the mirror, his knuckles collided into the thick piece of glass, the sight of its shattering fragments showering all around momentarily diverting his focus from knowing the entire clubhouse had witnessed him being publicly binned off.

Had Carmen engineered this all along? Had she made him love her, made him *feel* for the first time in his life, given him the belief they had a future, only to take it all away?

Oh yeah, Noel the psycho, Psycho Noel… He knew what everyone thought – even his Reaper brothers thought him a twisted fuck, but Carmen… Carmen had made him think there was more to him than that and he'd started to believe it.

He fumbled in his pocket, retrieving his packet of half-crushed cigarettes and lit one, his fingers shaking. He'd really thought that after everything they were happy. Carmen had agreed to marry him, for fuck's sake. But had it all been a wind up at his expense? Did everyone find this funny?

Noel's cheeks burned with humiliation. Oh, he'd heard the stunned silence after Carmen had screamed at him and left. He'd been right all along. She'd never taken him seriously, let's face it. He must have had rocks in his head to fall for it, but he had. He'd fallen for it hook, line and sinker.

He rubbed his fist across his face, refusing point blank to acknowledge the burn of tears at the back of his eyes.

His mind replayed Carmen getting up from the table where she'd been busy talking to Tori and his cock had hardened as it always did on the sight of her, but he hadn't noticed her expression. He'd pulled her towards him, his hands on her backside and ground his groin against her, his lips on her neck. Instead of reciprocating like she usually did, she'd brought her knee up hard into his crotch.

'Get the fuck away!' Carmen had screamed. 'You disgust me! Don't you ever, *ever* come near me again!' Tears streamed as she'd run from the room, wild-eyed, leaving him to collapse to his knees.

After what seemed like an age, Noel had pulled himself from the floor, eyes watering, the pain in his stomach and groin rendering him breathless. All focus was on him as he'd flipped a table onto its back in rage, before finding solace in the toilets.

Resting his half-smoked fag on the surround of the sink, Noel turned on the tap and splashed cold water on his face. He had no idea how long he'd been in here; it could have been a few minutes, or an hour but either way it was only a matter of time before someone came in. To avoid that, the only other option was going back out *there* and facing the questioning looks.

No one would actually *ask* anything – they wouldn't dare, but he knew they'd all be thinking Carmen was too good for him. *Fuck, he was a laughing stock.*

Noel closed his eyes in despair. Had Carmen really meant what she'd said? How could he disgust her when his touch melted her, brought her to orgasm every time, made her beg for more? They fitted together perfectly and he *loved* her, so *why*?

His eyes narrowed. What had Tori said? Carmen had been fine before they started talking. Had that woman set him up? Was she jealous of Carmen's happiness because Hunter wasn't here?

But what could she have said to make Carmen turn? Even

if Tori had accused him of cheating or something, Carmen would have had it out with him. Not that he'd even *looked* at another woman since being with her, let alone touched one.

Noel threw his cigarette butt on the floor and straightened the collar of his leather jacket. He wasn't having this. He wouldn't let Carmen just walk out of his life. She'd agreed to become his *wife* and he wanted a fucking explanation.

Almost pulling the toilet door from its hinges, he stormed back into the Factory, the buzz of hushed chatter falling silent once again. Without even glancing at the many pairs of eyes fixed on him, he barged his way over to where Tori sat, her head in her hands.

Sensing his approach, Tori looked up. 'Noel... I...'

'What the fuck did you say?' Noel screamed, his eyes spitting fire. 'Think you can play the "woe is me" do you?'

Tori shakily got to her feet. 'I...'

Noel swiped Tori's hand away as she made to touch his arm. 'Get off me, you bitch!' he growled. 'What lies have you told? You trying to break us up?' He slammed his fist down onto the table, the bottle of wine smashing on the floor.

'I-I haven't told any lies. I need to sp...'

'Shut the fuck up,' Noel roared. 'And to think I'd started to believe you were alright!' He lurched into Tori's face. 'I won't allow you to ruin what we've got, you jealous vindictive bitch!'

'You don't understand,' Tori whimpered. 'I need to talk to you. It's important and I...'

'You think I'll listen to *anything* you have to say now?' Noel shook with rage. 'Get out of my fucking sight!'

Tipping over the table, Noel launched a chair against the wall before turning to the rest of the Reapers. 'The fucking show's over!'

Grabbing his crash helmet, Noel stormed from the room leaving everyone looking after him in stunned silence and no one dared move when Tori sank slowly to her knees, sobbing.

TWENTY NINE

'OH BOLLOCKS!' Colin scraped the razor across his chin, glancing at Sarah's reflection peering over his shoulder in the mirror. 'I knew I'd forgotten something.'

'Finally remembered my warning that if you kept hogging the mirror then I'd do something bad to your dinner?' Sarah quipped, lovingly wrapping her arms around her husband's waist.

Colin turned away from their shared reflection and faced Sarah. 'No, seriously, I was that wound up after those muppets kicked off downstairs last night it slipped my mind.'

'Don't worry, it's hardly surprising. What was it?' Sarah knew exactly what Colin was referring to. Two men, not regulars, were being royal pains in the arse. Bawdy most of the evening, they'd finished the night off by having a drunken fight, smashing a shed load of glasses and wrecking a table, as well as a few chairs - not to mention each other's noses. The Reapers were absent and it had taken a fair effort to offload the pair of scrapping drunkards. In fact, if Jorge hadn't been there it would have taken a lot longer. It had also taken them a good couple of hours after close to clear up the mess and her and Colin had fallen into bed thoroughly exhausted.

'Well, that's just the thing.' Colin continued. 'That woman called again and it sounded important.'

'What woman?'

'The posh one – Carmen's mother.'

'Carmen's mother?' Sarah frowned. 'What did she want? She only called not long ago. The last time I asked, Carmen had said everything was fine.'

'She didn't say what the problem was, but sounded upset.' Colin said, annoyed with himself for forgetting. He rarely forgot anything.

Sarah chuckled despite herself. 'Upset? Maybe she's heard about Carmen's engagement? If my daughter wanted to marry Noel I'd go batshit!'

Colin shook his head. 'I don't know, but she really did sound very upset.'

Sarah pursed her lips. 'Hmm… well, ok. I'd best let Carmen know.' She pulled her hair into a ponytail. 'At least I've got my car back now. I'll go to the Factory; she might have stayed there last night. I've got to pick Tori up to take her to the hospital anyway and if Carmen's not at the Factory, I'll go to Noel's flat and check there.'

• • • •

SUSAN SAT RIGIDLY on the edge of her bed. She'd been sitting next to the phone for hours willing its shrill bell to sound and for it to be Carmen. Both the phone and the doorbell had remained silent all morning, just as they had done all night.

She looked around the bedroom, the thought suddenly crossing her mind as to how many of the material possessions she'd once been so proud of had been gleaned via other ill-gotten gains that she was unaware of.

Susan got to her feet. She could go downstairs? That way she'd be closer to the door if Carmen arrived. But Richard was down there. She couldn't be around him. She could no longer be anywhere *near* the man. If anything had happened to Carmen because of him, then…

Susan's panic escalated further, her eyes boring into the telephone on her dresser. Why wasn't Carmen ringing? She *had* to ring.

She stared at her shaking hands. Richard wasn't as clever as he believed. He'd failed to hide the abject fear shrouding him from head to foot when the unknown connection in his overblown head had sunk in. He may think her stupid and naïve, but she'd seen his terror – however fleetingly.

A shudder wracked her. As much as she didn't want to entertain the thought, she knew she was right. Richard believed, for reasons he wouldn't disclose, that the contents of that box were a piece of their daughter and he didn't even have the decency to explain why. He knew or suspected what was behind this. In fact, he seemed to be responsible for just about *everything*.

Newly burgeoning hatred for her husband increased at an alarming rate. She wouldn't lose *both* of her children.

Susan covered her mouth with her handkerchief to muffle the sobs wrenching their way from her throat and picked up the telephone, holding it to her ear to check there was a dial tone. She'd done the same thing a thousand times and the line was fine, so why hadn't Carmen called? *Come on. Please?*

When she'd called the White Hart last night, she'd made it clear it was urgent. They'd got a message to Carmen quickly enough before, so why not now? Maybe they'd discovered something since and knew where Carmen was but had no means of letting her know?

Susan frowned. She should have left her telephone number. Should she call again?

Richard had no idea she'd called last night. Her initial reaction was to explain that she'd maintained contact with their daughter and had means of getting hold of her, but she'd stopped herself. The bottom line was that she didn't trust him. *Didn't trust him at all.*

Picking up the receiver, Susan quickly placed it back down, light-headedness returning as questions swamped her once again.

She couldn't call the White Hart whilst Richard was downstairs. He was more collected this morning and had a habit of picking up the extension when he heard her talking - his way of keeping tabs on every bloody single thing she did. Probably paranoid she would call the police about the man he shot, or more importantly, *this*.

Susan had wanted to call the police last night. That box was a threat so it was clearly an urgent police matter, but it had been at this point Richard had begun playing it down, saying he'd jumped into panic mode because he'd been doing a lot of thinking. He'd blathered about feeling like it was time to put things right with Carmen and that life was too short to bear a grudge. He just wanted to make sure Carmen was ok, apparently.

Well, she didn't believe it. That wasn't how Richard worked; she'd been married to him long enough to know that. His levels of vitriol and spite were second to none lately and she was now adamant there wasn't a decent bone in his entire body. Susan was more convinced than *ever* that all of the things Carmen had said and Matthew had written were true. Even the one about Richard being paramount to that child's death.

There. She'd said it. Whatever was going on, she knew she could no longer remain married whatever the implications of that were. But before she could think about that, her priority was to make sure Carmen was safe.

And if she wasn't...

Susan shook her head to dislodge the prospect of Carmen *not* being ok. What could Richard have done and to whom to warrant that type of revenge? That was the point - she had no clue and sitting waiting for the telephone to ring wasn't bringing her closer to any answers.

Moving to her dressing table, Susan began making herself look presentable. She'd play it his way – she'd make Richard believe she'd swallowed his waffle and tell him she was going to get her hair done.

A taxi driver would know where the White Hart was, so she'd go there in person.

THIRTY

HUNTER TRIED TO FORCE his eyelids open, but they felt glued down. His throat was agony too – like he'd been gargling with razor blades. To top it all, his mouth felt like the bottom of a bird cage. *Had he got hammered last night because this was one hell of a hangover? And he was still in bed?*

Reaching over to Tori's side of the bed, Hunter winced. Every movement was painful and a glimmer of fear sparked, realising his arms were restrained. *A voice spoke his name. A bloke's voice. What the hell was going on? Where was Tori?*

Finally opening his eyes, blinking rapidly as the bright lights seared his eyeballs, Hunter's attempt to sit up was rendered impossible by the searing agony across his middle. Eyes adjusting, a man came into focus and Hunter yelled, but nothing came out apart from a strange growl, which only hurt his throat more.

'Ashley? My name is Doctor Frost. You need to keep calm and mustn't make any rapid movements. You're in hospital, do you understand? Just relax and let yourself adjust.'

Hunter blinked rapidly, panic getting a hold. *Hospital? Where was Tori? Was Tori hurt?* He tried to vocalise his questions, but his throat disagreed with the concept.

'Don't try to talk,' the doctor said. 'It will take a day or so but don't worry, that's normal.'

Normal? Hunter tried to push himself up again. *He had to get out of here. Had to make sure Tori was ok.*

'Ashley,' the doctor continued, sterner now. 'You *must* relax. We don't want your wound worsening. You've had a lucky escape and we want to keep it that way.'

Hunter stared at the man, his eyes narrowing. *Wound? What fucking wound? Lucky? This was lucky?*

Wait...

Suddenly, his brain put things in order as he became more alert. *He'd been shot! That bastard... That fucking piece of shit.*

Hunter pulled at one of the cannulas in his hand. He couldn't afford to be doing fuck all when Tori was at risk. That lunatic could have hurt her. Could *still* hurt her. Had she been right? Was Richard Stevens behind the rest of it? The threats and the house and...

'*Ashley!* Stop this!' the doctor yelled, fighting to pull Hunter's hands away from the tubes he was so intent on dislodging. He signalled to the nurse who quickly rushed over, a syringe in her hand.

Hunter felt it. He felt the needle going in and within seconds he felt the effect rushing through his veins. They'd injected him with something, but it didn't matter. He continued pulling at the wires, the rush of the tranquiliser increasing. He'd felt drunker than this before, much drunker, so he could still get out of here. It was ok, he could do this and he'd...

Realising he'd lost his coordination and the room was spinning on its axis in a triplicate version of itself, Hunter stopped struggling as the effects intensified, quite enjoying that the pain was now irrelevant and everything felt rather nice. His head sank back into the cloud-like pillow, the room turning blue.

The doctor eyed Hunter and reseated the cannula. 'That's better.' He checked the saline level in one of the drip bags above the bed and nodded to the nurse. 'Keep him at a steady level of sedation for a while. In the meantime, can someone please let Miss Morgan know that she can now come and see Ashley?'

• • • •

STIFF AS A BOARD, Tori readjusted her backside on the uncomfortable plastic chair in the hospital canteen, her stomach in knots. Glancing at the clock she sipped at her lukewarm tea. It wouldn't be long before she could return to Hunter's side and see if there was an update. She was nervous as anything, having no idea what she might find.

She stretched her cramped muscles out as best as she could and wearily pushed her hair off her face. Sitting at Hunter's bedside the entire night was the only thing she could do after what had happened. There was no way she could have remained at the Factory after Noel's outburst, so she'd called a taxi rather than deal with the accusing looks from the other Reapers.

Tori took another sip of her tea, not that she wanted it, but it gave her hands something to do. She desperately needed to speak to Noel and explain. She had to tell him what she'd told Carmen. She knew what it must have looked like, but what he'd said wasn't true. Spoiling their happiness was the *last* thing she wanted, but there was no turning back. She had to find him and tell him the truth before things got worse. And she had to find Carmen, but had no idea where to start.

The look on her friend's face haunted her. She didn't think she'd ever seen anyone look so crushed. Carmen's reaction had morphed from shock, to anger, to disbelief – into bewilderment and disgust and Tori completely understood why.

She'd thought about going to the White Hart, but then thought better of it. She'd have had to explain to Colin and Sarah and although she'd have to tell them sooner rather than later as she'd need their help, it was just too much going through it all again last night.

Tori swallowed dryly. All she'd wanted was to seek solace with Hunter even though he was unable to offer any advice or comfort. Just being in his close proximity had soothed her, but now her nerves were even more on edge. She glanced at the clock again. It was good news that this morning the doctors decided it was time to bring him round, but with that came another load of worry and deep rooted anxiousness.

What happened if Hunter wasn't himself? What happened if he reacted badly and damaged himself? Taking a deep breath, she rose from the table and made her way back. *There was only one way to find out.*

Rounding the corner inside Intensive Care, Tori's pulse upped seeing one of the nurses.

'Ah, Miss Morgan!' the nurse smiled, heading towards Tori. 'I've just been sent to find you.'

Paralysed with nerves, Tori allowed the nurse to pull her to one side.

'Ashley's now conscious,' she smiled, placing her hand on Tori's arm.

Tori exhaled loudly. 'Oh, thank God! Is he alright? Is he…?'

'He's ok, but I must warn you that he's been sedated. He didn't react very well when he first came round, but I'm sure the doctor explained that's a fairly common reaction?'

Tori nodded and couldn't help but smile. *Typical Hunter.* 'But is he ok?'

The nurse nodded. 'He hasn't lost his strength, I can tell you that! He's a little confused, but that's to be expected. And please don't encourage him to speak; his throat will take a little while to recover after the ventilator.'

Tori nodded. 'Can I see him?'

The nurse stepped to one side. 'Of course.'

Smiling her thanks, Tori rushed into the room, her heart in her mouth. Closing the door, she looked at Hunter. Eyes closed, he didn't look much different to how he had earlier, apart from the monstrous tube in his mouth was no longer there.

A rush of love flooded over her as she moved to his side, shakily sitting down on the plastic chair. 'Hunter?' she whispered, taking his hand. For the first time in what seemed like forever, Hunter's eyelids flickered and opened, his eyes, although heavily dilated, displaying the steel grey colour that she'd missed so much.

Tori held her breath watching him focus but when his mouth formed a lazy smile and he reached his hand out to touch hers, she couldn't contain herself any longer. 'Oh, I'm so glad you're back with me,' she sobbed, tears cascading down her cheeks as she leant forward, pressing her lips to his.

Hunter's hand stroked Tori's hair in a heavily, uncoordinated way and opened his mouth to speak, but nothing came out. All she could hear was a throaty gasping sound. 'Don't try and talk. The doctor said you need to let your throat mend.'

She watched his heavy-lidded eyes narrow in frustration and she touched his cheek, now covered with a full beard rather than the neatly trimmed look he usually wore. 'I love you so much,' she gasped, barely able to control her surging emotions. 'It won't be long before you're back to normal.' She squeezed his hand gently, in a way grateful that he could ask no questions. He'd ask what had been happening and whatever she answered, would know straight away that she was lying.

Hunter's hand pulled Tori towards him, his grey eyes beseeching her to listen.

'What?' Tori said, moving closer as he mouthed something. 'What are you saying?' His voice wasn't loud enough to constitute a whisper. She moved closer still, her ear upon his lips and strained to hear his raspy voice over the sound of her breathing.

She frowned. 'Gun? Yes, you got shot, but it's ok, the doctor said th…'

Hunter shook his head and Tori was unsure what to do. The doctor had said not to try and get him to speak and although she was desperate to know what had happened, she couldn't ask him. Not yet. She didn't want to compound his stress and besides, he may not even know. 'Hunter, I…'

Hunter shook his head, pointing to her.

'Me? No, I haven't got shot, I...' Stopping, Tori suddenly realised what he was trying to say. The memory of what he'd asked of her that day at the country pub rushed to the forefront.

Hunter urgently pointed at Tori again and she leant forward. 'You want me to carry the... carry the...' Straining to hear as Hunter mouthed something else, Tori looked into his eyes. 'It's important? Is that what you said?'

Hunter looked at her questioningly and Tori faltered, fear glimmering. She'd promised him she'd carry that gun if he ever asked her to, but she hadn't thought – or rather, hoped, it would ever come to that. She bit back the urge to question it. There must be good reason, she knew that and had to trust him. 'Ok, I'll do what you ask.'

Hunter visibly relaxed, but when Tori remained seated, he gesticulated towards the door.

Tori looked at the door and then back again. 'There's no one there.'

'Now,' Hunter rasped, just about audibly.

Tori blinked. 'You want me to go away and get the... get the gun?' she whispered. 'What? Like now?'

Hunter nodded, his eyes not leaving hers.

Tori stood up resolutely. 'Will it make you feel better if I go and put it in my bag?' She still couldn't believe she was going to do this, but when Hunter nodded, his fingers reaching up to touch her face, she smiled. 'I'll do it, ok?'

Hunter relaxed back into his pillow and closed his eyes just as the nurse entered. Smiling at Tori, she picked up Hunter's observation chart and fiddled with his saline drip. 'He'll be a bit out of it I expect, but will be a lot better tomorrow. He's through the worst now.'

Returning the nurse's smile, Tori took the opportunity to take her leave. Kissing Hunter's sleeping cheek, she slipped from the room and made her way towards the exit, knowing she needed to find the strength to return to the Factory and pick up that... that *thing*...

THIRTY ONE

TORI WAS GLAD when the taxi drew up alongside the kerb and she looked up at the grubby façade of the pub as the driver worked out her fare. It hadn't been comfortable returning to the Factory and facing the questions from the Reapers, but there was no point avoiding them. Without giving anyone the chance to speak, she'd immediately announced that Hunter had regained consciousness and all was looking good. Whilst they were all happy with this news, she took the opportunity to ask of Noel's whereabouts. It hadn't taken long to deduce that neither Noel or Carmen had returned and so she'd left, giving instructions that if either of them came back or were spotted anywhere, it was imperative they came to see her.

Tori opened her handbag to retrieve her purse, flinching as her fingers brushed against the metal of the gun sitting at the bottom. Just the thought of this thing being close, in her own *bag*, made her cold, but she had to honour what she'd promised. Hunter's shooting had been anything but a freak occurrence, so it really did look like they were in grave danger.

What would happen if anyone found out she was carrying around a weapon such as this? Imagine if the police wanted to search her bag? She'd never had cause to have anything to do with them and wanted it to stay that way, but this gun made her feel uncomfortable, automatically adopting the persona of something akin to a rather hapless and nervous drug mule. That's how she felt. *Guilty.*

Paying her fare, she got out of the taxi, Hunter's words resounding in her mind: *You'll know if and when you ever need to use it...*

How? How would she know? Furthermore, how would she use it? Even thinking it was something she'd ever reach for regardless of what occurred was alien. Besides, one lesson had done nothing to improve her genuine ineptitude regarding the damn thing!

Pushing open the rickety door of the White Hart, Tori stepped inside, gratefully for the familiar smell of stale beer and tobacco. She'd love to spot Carmen at the bar talking to Sarah, meaning everything was a bad dream, but unfortunately everything was very much real and there was no Carmen in sight. Thankfully though, Sarah was present in her usual place.

Sarah looked up in surprise as Tori approached the bar. 'Hey! I went over the Factory this morning, but they said you weren't there. Wasn't I supposed to take you to the hospital?'

Tori placed her handbag on the bar, then remembering what was inside, hastily moved it to the floor. 'No need. I've been there all night. Hunter's conscious. He's sedated, but ok.'

Sarah laughed with relief. 'Didn't take things too well? I might have known!' Looking at Tori's face, she paused. 'You don't seem too pleased? Anything wrong?'

'No, I'm pleased, it's just that...' She glanced at her handbag. 'Have you seen Carmen?'

Sarah folded her arms. Just as she suspected, something was amiss. When she arrived at the Factory to deliver Carmen's message and pick Tori up, the Reaper on the door acted oddly. 'What's going on? Carmen's mother called last night asking her to get in contact too, but she's not at the Factory and they're being very cagey over there. She's not at Noel's either.'

'Was Noel there? At the flat, I mean?' Tori asked.

'No,' Sarah said, studying Tori carefully. 'Do you want to tell me what's happened? It's not even midday and I feel like I've missed about three weeks' worth of stuff I should be aware of!'

Tori took a deep breath and glanced around the tap room. There weren't many people in yet, no Reapers, just a handful of regulars, but she knew once it got to midday it would fill up. 'Can we go upstairs?' she whispered. 'I need your help.'

Sarah opened the bar hatch to let Tori through, suspecting she wasn't going to like whatever she was about to learn. 'I'll tell Colin to come and man the bar.'

• • • •

SARAH WAS FLABBERGASTED. Although she'd expected something she wouldn't like from Tori's countenance alone, it wasn't *this*. 'Holy shit!' she muttered. 'Are you *sure*?'

Tori hunched over the coffee table in Sarah's lounge and sipped her tea. 'As sure as I can be.'

Sarah whistled through her teeth, still struggling to get her head around what Tori had said. 'This is heavy duty crap. So, you're telling me Carmen's been sleeping with her own *brother*?'

'Half-brother,' Tori corrected.

'Brother, half-brother, whatever. Jesus Christ!' Sarah gasped. 'No wonder she's disappeared. I'm taking it she didn't take the news very well?'

'What do you think?' Tori snapped. 'How would you feel to learn your father's a rapist and you're marrying your own brother?'

'Fucking hell, this is bad. And you've no idea where she's gone?'

Tori shook her head sadly. 'None whatsoever. I haven't a clue where to start looking either. She just legged it. I'm starting to wish I hadn't said anything. I've made everything worse.'

'How could you *not* have said anything?' Sarah said incredulously. 'It's hardly like you had any choice!'

'I know and especially as she started talking about babies…'

'Babies? Oh, dear God!' Sarah cried. 'How did Noel take it? Jeez, he must be devastated. He loves that woman and Christ knows what he'll do to her father – and *his*.'

'That's the point. Noel doesn't know yet,' Tori said, her eyes wide. 'Oh, it was awful. Carmen went crazy. She said some terrible things to Noel and even kicked him in the, the… you know…'

Sarah raised her hands to her mouth. 'Jesus, Tori, why didn't you tell him?'

'I tried! He was too busy accusing me of sabotaging their relationship. I said I needed to talk to him, but he wasn't having any of it and then took off. I tried, Sarah, I really did.'

Sarah frowned. 'And no one's seen either of them since?'

Tori shook her head. 'No and I don't know what to do.'

'Does Hunter know?'

'I could hardly tell him this morning. He's doped up to the eyeballs. Plus, no doubt he'd insist on discharging himself and that's impossible.'

Sarah nodded. 'I wonder if this is why Carmen's mother wants to get in contact?'

Tori looked startled. 'You think she knows what Richard has done?' It sickened her enough that she'd spent all that time in Richard's company, without Susan being party to everything too.

'You know her better than me. I've never met the woman!'

'She was quite nice the last few months,' Tori mused. 'I can't see her knowing, but then… Do you think we should tell her?'

Sarah sighed heavily. 'We've got to do *something*. You know as well as I do when Noel and Hunter find out they'll kill Richard Stevens. Maybe it would be better if we told Susan and let her go to the police?' She shrugged at Tori's expression. 'It's better than the boys going to nick on account of that wanker, isn't it?'

Tori put her head in her hands. 'I just don't know what to do. Everything's a total nightmare and I feel so alone.'

Sarah pulled Tori in for a hug. 'Well, you're not. You've got me and we'll deal with this the best way we can. That bastard... I could kill him myself!'

Tori clung on to Sarah, her arms giving much needed comfort. 'I can't let Hunter go to jail. Or Noel, come to that.' She reached for her handbag and opened it. She closed her fingers around the cold metal of the gun and pulled it out. 'And there's this...'

Sarah recoiled in shock. 'Shit! Why have you got that?'

'That's just it. I don't know. Hunter told me to carry it. That's about all I could make out from what he said.'

Grabbing Tori's hand, Sarah shoved the gun back into the handbag. 'Don't wave that around in public, whatever you do, otherwise *you'll* be the one going to jail!'

'I don't want it anywhere near me! I hate the things, you know that, but I promised Hunter,' Tori cried.

Sarah remained silent. Hunter must believe Tori was in direct danger otherwise he'd never ask this of her. 'He knows who shot him, doesn't he?'

Tori shrugged, her eyes brimming with tears. 'That's what I thought, but he can barely speak and was so off the planet I'm not sure if he knows what's going on or anything.'

Sarah's eyes narrowed. 'Oh, he knows what's going on, alright.'

'All I know is the day he got shot he went to see some businesses. I first thought it must be one of them, but then I think it's more likely to be connected to whoever threatened him. You know, the ones behind the house break-in?' She shuddered, the image of the balaclava-wearing man still terrifying.

Sarah nodded. 'I agree, but we need to find out.'

'He'd planned to go to Richard's that day too,' Tori added.

'What?' Sarah gasped. 'Why? Are you sure he didn't know Richard was...?'

Tori shook her head. 'No. He believes the rapist is dead. Someone gave a name and, oh... long story... Richard was at the hospital the day Jeanie disappeared and Hunter was planning to ask if he'd seen anyone.'

Sarah felt exhausted with all of this mess. 'Did he see the bastard?'

'Not as far as I know, but I doubt it. He said he was seeing the businesses first and then the next thing he'd been shot and was found in an area close to the businesses he deals with, hence why I presumed it was them,' Tori said, wanting to finish her tea, but her hands were shaking too much.

'But now you think it's related to these threats?'

'I'm not sure of anything, but it makes logical sense. He'd been warned and then...'

Sarah's lips pursed together. 'You need to get Hunter to confirm who did it, because he knows.'

A knock on the door made Tori jump and both her and Sarah turned as the door opened.

'Sorry to interrupt.' Colin stepped into the lounge. 'Carmen's mother is downstairs asking for you, Sarah.'

Sarah and Tori exchanged worried glances, each knowing they hadn't reached a conclusion, but it looked like the time for deciding was out of their hands.

THIRTY TWO

SUSAN WAITED NERVOUSLY and glanced around the bar, paying special attention not to meet eyes with any of the people staring at her with open curiosity like she'd just landed from a different planet.

Refraining from wiping sticky residue off her fingers where she'd rested her hand on the bar top, she looked around. No wonder the taxi driver had questioned if she was sure of her destination - this place was an absolute hovel. The thought of her daughter frequenting establishments such as this made her feel queasy, but reminded herself that she wasn't here to judge, she was here to locate Carmen; nothing more, nothing less.

Her stomach lurched as the rickety door behind the bar opened and a shortish woman, in her early thirties at a guess, stepped out, followed by the man who'd been behind the bar when she arrived. The woman had a lived-in, yet friendly face and it took her off guard. Although unsure what she'd been expecting, she hadn't expected the woman to look, well... so *normal*.

'Mrs Stevens?' Sarah opened the hatch separating the drinking area from the bar. 'I'm Sarah Mathers. Would you like to follow me? It will be easier to talk upstairs.'

Forcing a smile, Susan hesitatingly followed Sarah behind the bar and out of the door up a flight of wooden stairs, her footsteps faltering as she struggled to see in the light given off by the bare twenty-watt bulb hanging limply in the narrow stairwell.

Glad to have made it to the top, she accompanied Sarah into a deceptively spacious open-plan living space decorated in a mish-mash of colours and unmatched furniture. She took the proffered seat – a well-worn armchair covered in a bright crochet throw and gazed about the room, staring at the framed wedding portrait hanging over the open fireplace. The unexpected feeling of homeliness washed over her. It was a stark contrast to the exquisite, yet cold ambience of her own home.

'Would you like a cup of tea, Susan?' Tori stepped into view from the kitchen.

Susan's head jerked in the direction of the voice she immediately recognised. 'Victoria?' Getting up, she rushed over, hugging Tori tightly.

Sarah stared with interest. *Maybe the old girl was half-decent after all?* Can't say the same about the hair though, she thought, staring at the candy-flossed bouffant perching on the top of the older woman's head.

'How are you, my dear?' Susan asked uneasily, thinking of what Carmen had said about Matthew and Richard's treatment of Victoria. Suddenly, what she had or hadn't done by disappearing off with a biker didn't really matter and she only hoped this new man of hers treated her better than Matthew had.

'I'm ok, Susan. And you?' Tori said, not expecting to receive such a warm greeting.

Susan's face fell as the reason for her visit took back priority in her mind. 'I need to find Carmen.'

Tori motioned back to the armchair, taking a seat herself on the sofa opposite.

Susan sat down, her eyes searching Tori's face. 'Victoria, you must tell me if you know where Carmen is. I've been in fairly regular contact with her since... well...' She looked down, embarrassed. 'Richard's unaware of our meetings, but I need to make sure she's ok. I don't care what she's done.' The words flooded from her mouth. Maybe she was saying too much, maybe not enough - she didn't care. All that mattered was locating her daughter.

Tori glanced at Sarah, still unsure what or how much to say, but Sarah responded with a barely visible shrug.

Leaning over, Susan placed her hand on Tori's. 'Don't think for one minute that you'll cause problems by telling me where she is. She told me about her new man. All I want is for her to be happy, but I need to know she's safe. Do you understand?'

Tori paled. *Carmen had told her mother she was with Noel? Oh hell, how would she play this?*

Sensing Tori's unease, Susan realised that unless she acknowledged the situation, this girl would remain guarded and evasive. 'Victoria my dear, Carmen told me what Matthew did to you. Although I was reluctant to believe it at first, I don't begrudge you for finding happiness with another man. I-I also know Andrew wasn't Matthew's child.'

Tori froze. *She hadn't expected that.* The urge to cry for the mother figure she'd never had burnt strongly, but she pulled herself together. Now wasn't the time to be sentimental.

Apprehension slithered its way through Susan. 'I presumed you'd see her regularly, what with you both, you know...' the words stuck in her throat somewhat, 'being involved with those... those biker people.'

Tori inhaled deeply. She'd have to tell Susan - there was no way around it. 'There was an issue and well, I don't want to alarm you, but we don't know where Carmen is.'

'What sort of issue? What about this what's his name... Noel, isn't it? Does he not know where she is?' Susan cried, panic returning.

Tori glanced at Sarah again, unsure where to start. 'Last night Carmen was upset. She ran off and no one has seen her si…'

'Last night, you say?' Susan interrupted, a glimmer of hope returning. 'You last saw her last night? What time?'

Tori frowned. 'I-I'm not exactly sure. 7, or 8 o'clock? Susan, listen, I…'

'Oh, thank God!' Susan threw her hands in the air. 'That means that… oh, it doesn't matter.' *The disgusting contents of that box could be nothing to do with Carmen because it had arrived mid-afternoon yesterday.*

Sarah took a seat. 'Mrs Stevens, we need to speak to you about something that involves Carmen. It's very important.'

Susan wasn't listening, her relief too great. 'I'm sure Richard's losing his mind. He's been so odd lately.' She looked at Tori. 'I don't know what's going on but as long as Carmen's ok, that's all that matters. What does your new man think of it, Victoria? Does he have any idea where Carmen and this Noel person have gone?' Her eyebrows furrowed. 'You don't suppose she'd eloped, do you? She's still married, so she can't just go an…'

'Tori can't ask Hunter's opinion at the moment because he's in hospital,' Sarah interjected, the old girl's flapping making her dizzy. They were either telling this woman the score about her bloody husband, or they weren't.

'Hospital?' Susan cried, 'Oh no! Not a bike accident? I've never liked motorbikes. Death traps those things are.'

'Hunter was shot last week. You might have seen it in the paper?' Sarah continued.

Susan's hand flew to her mouth and her skin turned a ghastly shade of grey. *That was the man Richard shot? The one she'd helped to dump like an animal in the street?*

'Are you alright?' Tori asked, seeing the drastic colour change of Susan's skin.

'Oh my God, oh my God,' Susan muttered, albeit to herself. 'I-I didn't want to be part of it… Richard he…'

Icy tendrils of dread prickled Sarah as she watched Susan cover her face with her hands and sob in earnest. She hoped against anything that she was unfounded in her immediate suspicions. 'Part of *what*, Mrs Stevens?'

Susan slowly moved her hands away from her face and raised her flushed, frightened eyes then hastily averted them. 'I'm so sorry… So terribly sorry...'

Heart pounding, Tori took Susan's hand and forced her voice to remain level. 'Sorry for what?'

'Richard… It was *Richard*. Richard shot him.' The words burnt, escaping from Susan's mouth in a whisper.

'Your husband shot Hunter?' Sarah cried. Her eyes darted to Tori sitting rigid with shock and disbelief. '*Why*?'

Susan shook her head. 'Richard said it was an intruder, but I didn't believe him. I don't believe anything he says any more. He was going to shoot the man again, but I stopped him. I-I tried to call an ambulance, but… but Richard… he made me drag the man into the car.'

Sarah stared at Susan incredulously, her rage burning. 'You mean you *dumped* him in the street rather than get him fucking help?'

Susan sobbed, her stance like that of a rabbit in the headlights. 'I don't blame you for hating me. I didn't have any choice. Richard, he… he…'

Fighting rising nausea, Tori steadied her breathing and pulled Sarah back as she lurched towards Susan. She took a deep breath, a strange sense of calm descending. 'Susan, I think you need to tell us what you know and we will tell you what *we* know.'

· · · ·

EYEING HIS REFLECTION in the mirror, Richard straightened his cufflinks, then his tie. Turning his head from side to side, he was pleased to see he looked good; a lot better than he'd looked or felt last night. He'd been rash, allowing things to get on top of him and making him overreact. In front of Susan too. How remiss of him.

He smoothed his hand over his hair, glad to see it was in

place, but a small frown appeared at the substantial increase of grey. All of this bloody recent stress, no doubt.

It had been stupid to assume someone had attacked Carmen and even *stupider* to give Susan that idea, but he hadn't been thinking clearly. Luckily, his ability to turn things around had not abandoned him and he'd salvaged the situation before she'd gone into meltdown, convincing her that she'd got the wrong end of the stick. He'd insisted he'd *never* insinuated a piece of their daughter was in that box and from there, it had then been relatively simple to convince her she'd read too much into the situation.

He should never have allowed himself to display a visible reaction. Putting people's body parts in boxes was just a film thing – *everyone* knew that.

Regardless of what he thought of his daughter's behaviour he didn't want anything such as *that* to befall her, no matter how much it was perhaps deserved. In reality, he wasn't overly concerned. He didn't doubt Carmen was fine, but he'd casually get the word out in his circles - just to dot the "I's" and cross the "T's", so to speak.

All of this was the bloody Reapers' idea of intimidation, but he wouldn't rise to it. Once their president karked it no one would feel the need to keep this game up any longer. That lot had no loyalty or honour – even less between themselves.

Richard slipped on his blazer deciding he'd go for a drink down at the club, followed by a round of golf if the weather remained decent, happy that he didn't have to listen to Susan. He frowned, half-wondering where she'd got to. It didn't usually take this long to get her hair done, but he wasn't complaining.

Despite her initial angst, last night had somehow flicked a switch in Susan's brain. She'd been so down and on edge lately but this morning she'd been, what he could only describe as "chipper". Having her hair done was a sign she was getting back to normal at last, which was a turn up for the books being as she'd taken little care in her appearance for months. It would be a blessed relief not to have to look at someone who had turned into a bit of a warthog. There really was no excuse to not bother. Women should *always* make an effort – especially at *her* age. Not making the most of nice clothes, hair salons and cosmetics only exposed what she really looked like underneath and these days that wasn't particularly good.

Moving down the hall, Richard spied a letter Susan must have placed on the side and his nerves prickled. Picking up the official looking envelope, Richard's heart sank seeing the London postmark and he dearly hoped it wasn't another one of those threatening letters.

With a sinking feeling, Richard tore open the envelope, his throat constricting spotting the bank's familiar logo at the top of the page.

Dear Mr Stevens,

It is of great reluctance to inform you of serious allegations made against you in relation to the theft of substantial amounts of money from bank portfolios during the extensive time in your position as branch manager.

Due to your long service and previous conduct we chose to begin by investigating this matter internally, however, upon further evidence coming to light in our preliminary investigation, we request your attendance at a formal hearing on Tuesday 18th March, 2pm at headquarters. Failure to attend or bring the required documentation (listed in the attached Appendix), will result in this matter being immediately handed to the police.

We trust you will exercise everything in your power to assist, enabling us to bring this unpleasant situation to a speedy resolution.

Yours faithfully
J Richards

Richard stared at the letter in horror, temporarily paralysed with fear. Peering into the envelope for additional paperwork, he fished out a further piece and scanned the Appendix referred to in the letter, his eye twitching.

His teeth clenched seeing the first item of mandatory paperwork to be supplied was twenty years' worth of personal bank statements from a list of accounts. Sweat trickled under his collar. He'd had several accounts with the bank, but he wasn't stupid – he also had several at *other* banks, but he clearly hadn't been *that* clever because they were all listed too.

Every single account he'd ever had was listed.

Leaning against the wall when his legs struggled to hold him up, Richard concentrated on breathing slowly. *This was not good.*

There was no way he could get out of this. No way at all. He might have scraped through by the skin of his teeth had they focused on his main accounts, but not now they were aware of his other ones...

Not wishing to look at the rest of the list, Richard stuffed it back into the envelope, along with the letter.

He hadn't thought it would ever come to this. Now he knew without any shadow of a doubt what he had to do and he only had a couple of days grace to get it organised.

• • • •

LILLIAN FELT CONSPICUOUS the first evening she'd had dinner alone. It wasn't something she'd ever done before. The way she'd been brought up ladies didn't do that sort of thing unchaperoned, but after another day in the Palm Court Hotel, she realised she wasn't the only lone woman – or man, come to mention it. Some, the men at least, were on business, but the handful of lone women were not those of loose morals. They looked like *her* - women enjoying pampering time. The only difference was there weren't any single women here for the second night in a row.

Relaxing into her wing-backed chair, Lillian fished a book from her handbag and retrieved her leather bookmark. She didn't want it to look like she wanted company.

Shrugging to herself, she took a sip from her wine. She'd enjoyed a lovely evening meal of veal and seasonal vegetables and had been attentively served by the many staff. Now she'd retired to the lounge bar for after-dinner drinks - a pleasant end to a most pleasant day consisting of a manicure and pedicure, followed by a swim and then a period in the sauna. She felt refreshed and relaxed. She'd also come to a few decisions.

She was selling her house. It would fetch a tidy sum. She'd treat herself to a few weeks aboard a cruise whilst waiting for a suitable house to become available. She'd already made a few calls and had settled on finding somewhere in Windsor or close by. She'd need to substantially downsize, but with what she should fetch for her home she could buy something nice in a more upmarket location; one many miles from here, whilst still having plenty of money left over, affording her a good standard of living for the foreseeable future.

She certainly had *nothing* to stay around here for. In Windsor or thereabouts, she could start again and the prospect was exciting; a new life with a completely blank canvas. No attachments or reminders of the past to rear their ugly heads or skew whatever backstory she decided on.

Lillian took another sip of wine, wondering how many children she should have in her story and where they should live, being as they wouldn't be visiting.

Sensing movement to her left, she peered over the mother-of-pearl frames of her glasses and scowled as a man took a seat three tables away. With all the room in this oversized lounge and more empty tables than not, he had to sit nearby? Still, at least he hadn't sat right next to her. That would have been horrible.

She glanced at the man's side profile as the waiter brought

over what looked like a whisky. Another businessman, Lillian thought, judging by his demeanour and expensive suit.

Lillian was about to return to her book because the *last* thing she wanted was for it to look like she was staring, but it was just... She pursed her lips and frowned. There was something about that man. Something she half-recognised, but couldn't for the life of her work out what. Mentally shrugging, she looked away but inexplicably found her eyes drawn back to him and without making it obvious, studied his side profile further.

The man turned, his eyes meeting hers for a fleeting moment and she hastily looked away, pretending to be engrossed in the pages of her book, hoping she hadn't been caught staring. *Now that would have been embarrassing.*

After a couple of minutes, Lillian reached for her drink and at the same time, took the opportunity to sneak a further glance at the man, now entrenched in a newspaper. *That was it! That's who he reminded her of! Luca LeVere – Carmen's husband.*

Although she hadn't attended the wedding, she was sure it was him. Her lips pursed in annoyance. At the time she'd been most put out about not being invited and had taken it as a personal affront. That was until she'd realised that no one, short of family, was in attendance either. It had been odd because that kind of set up wasn't the done thing for the only daughter of someone of the Stevens' calibre, but Richard had made it clear that regardless of what he thought acceptable, the couple had *insisted* on a low-key affair with no pomp or ceremony.

Lillian had found it sad that Carmen – such a flamboyant creature, should have something so far removed from the limelight and miss her chance of being featured in the society pages, but on retrospect, if the choice was down to Luca, then Carmen would have been stupid not to agree with the amount of money the man had.

If she remembered rightly, their wedding had taken place in France, followed by a lavish honeymoon cruise. Even though she was absent, she may as well have been there for the length of time she'd put up with Susan boasting about what a wonderful man Luca was and what a stunning chateau Carmen lived in.

Lillian had smiled graciously as she was subjected to hours of Susan proudly showing her the wedding photographs over and over and *over* again. From this, she knew what Luca LeVere looked like and that man definitely resembled him. The question was, *was* it him? Didn't they say that everyone had a double somewhere?

Lillian sneaked another covert glance. If it *was* Luca LeVere, then why would he be here? Unless of course he'd come to sort things out with Carmen and take her back to her rightful place? Maybe Carmen was also staying here or perhaps he was meeting her for a drink?

Lillian quickly scanning the room. She didn't want anyone who knew her being here. It would defeat the object.

Out of the corner of her eye she watched the waiter return to the man's table and listened intently when the man requested a refill.

That was no Frenchman. He sounded like a Londoner if she had to guess, but then she'd never been much good placing accents.

Lillian shrugged. Mystery solved. Now all she had to decide was what to do tomorrow. Having already utilised many of the pampering treatments, she might break the week up by taking a taxi into the nearest town and treating herself to a new outfit. She'd seen an advert in one of the magazines readily available around the hotel for a local boutique that looked right up her alley.

Pleased with her plans, she returned to her book.

THIRTY THREE

CARMEN STARED BLANKLY at the mildew-stained wall of her room, her head throbbing. Leaning further back against the lumpy pillow, she winced at the noise of the rusty bedsprings groaning loudly from her movement, needing a cup of tea to rid her mouth of the rancid taste from the vast amount of cheap wine she'd consumed last night.

Her eyes tracked across to the dubious looking kettle on the small dressing table, its frayed cable snaking limply across the scratched surface of the dresser. Getting up, she padded over the threadbare carpet and picked up one of the two chipped mugs sitting on a plastic tray, before staring at the mini cartons of UHT milk, their foil lids covered in a liberal helping of dust.

She replaced the mug, giving the idea of tea a miss. The thought of opening one of those milks only to discover a mass of curdled lumps made her already queasy stomach roll further.

It was no use. She'd have to go out to buy something. Some water – *anything*. She couldn't sit here for ever, although it would be tempting if the place wasn't quite so dreadful, but then she knew she'd been lucky to find anywhere to stay the state she was in last night.

The woman, complete with hair curlers and a fag in her

mouth who'd opened the door of the guest house to the dishevelled half-drunk woman with smudged makeup, luckily hadn't asked any questions. Shoving the twenty quid Carmen handed over into the pocket of her button-up pinny, the woman ungraciously handed over a room key before shuffling back into the communal "lounge" to continue her game of Whist with a man wearing stained trousers and an overtight striped pullover.

Dragging the carrier bag full of wine she'd bought from a nearby off licence into her allotted damp bedroom, Carmen had spent what was left of the worst night of her life drowning her sorrows. But what had it achieved short of giving her a headache? *Nothing. She was still no closer to knowing what to do.*

Carmen's eyes welled up thinking of Noel – the man she loved and the man she wanted to marry.

Noel – her brother.

She lurched towards the metal wastepaper bin under the dressing table, retching violently. Her stomach muscles ached from the amount of time last night she'd spent heaving into the shared toilet at the end of the corridor, steadfastly ignoring the intermittent banging on the door from impatient guests.

Wiping her mouth with the back of her hand, Carmen stared at her reflection in the stained mirror. Puffy eyes, lank hair and her face, devoid of all makeup, grey and lifeless. She hardly recognised herself, but that wasn't a bad thing. She didn't *want* to recognise herself. Not now.

Carmen Stevens – the daughter of a rapist and the fiancée of her own brother.

It wasn't Noel's fault. He hadn't known either, but did he know now? Instead of acting the way she had towards him, she should have told him, but the shock and revulsion of Tori's bombshell had been too great.

Her life was over. How could she return and be around Noel without being with him in the way they'd planned? That she still loved him fiercely in the same way as she had yesterday disgusted her further. What did that make her? Some sort of perverted freak?

A vivid series of images of her and Noel – his mouth on hers, pushed unwanted into her mind and she shook her head frantically to remove them. How could she go back there knowing what they'd done? How could she *live* with they'd done?

Carmen dug her fingernails into her scalp, scraping and grasping at her hair, hoping the pain would deflect from this confusion. This *nightmare.*

Further angry tears coursed down her cheeks thinking of her father and what he'd done to Noel's mother…

Grabbing the one remaining bottle of wine from the dressing table she swigged at it. The sickly warm liquid made her gag, but she didn't care. She wanted the thoughts stampeding around her head to go away.

Carmen's shallow breathing quickened. Could Tori be mistaken? She'd seen the despair on her friend's face as she'd told her the news and she hadn't been lying, that was for certain, but could it be a case of mistaken identity? After all, Noel didn't look anything like her or Matt, did he?

Without wanting to, the image of Noel's ruggedly handsome face burnt into her mind's eye once again.

He didn't look anything like her, Matt or her father, but then he didn't have to… *She* didn't look like her father either and besides, they had different mothers…

With shaking hands Carmen reached for the wine again and took another long draft as another horrible thought crept into her brain… If her father was capable of raping a woman, then it was equally likely he was also capable of killing that baby… Maybe what Matt had written was true after all?

And if it was…?

Horror overwhelmed her. She'd left her mother with this man? Carmen knew her mother suspected him of killing the child, whereas she had personally dismissed it. Did her mother know about what he'd done to this woman too? Could she have brushed it under the carpet for the sake of appearances or because she didn't *want* to believe it?

No, her mother wouldn't do that. *Couldn't* do that. *Could she?*

Carmen looked in the mirror again. She had to speak to her mother, but couldn't go there looking like this. Neither could she go when *that man* was there. She'd never be able to refer to Richard Stevens as her father ever again.

Carmen stood up unsteadily. She'd go for a walk; get some fresh air and hopefully sort her head out enough to decide when to go and see her mother. And then she'd have to face Noel.

After that, she hadn't the first clue what she would do or where she would go.

· · · ·

JOHN TURNER WAS expecting the call. Neil had already said Jorge would phone for instructions on where to meet, so the minute the telephone rang he had a pretty good idea who'd be on the other end.

Hearing Jorge's muffled voice, John reached the conclusion that the quality of telephone boxes were no better up north than in London. At least the bad line meant he couldn't talk for long, not that he could give Jorge much of a heads up even though he wanted to.

Earlier, he'd received an irate call from Neil informing him that McFadden had postponed the job. John didn't quite know what he'd expected by only letting the man know of the target's location at the very last knockings. To most people, a target in a hospital would put a completely different slant on the risk. No one would expect a hit to be attempted in that kind of location – *far* too many people. No one would consider it feasible.

Except Neil.

'Hello Jorge,' John kept his voice upbeat. 'How's it going?'

'It's grim up north,' Jorge said in a very bad rendition of a strong northern accent. 'Got an update?'

'The meet's at a hotel tonight. 8pm in the lounge bar. Dress smart.'

'How smart?' Jorge asked tentatively. He'd only got one suit with him and it wasn't his best, plus not having had much use for it in the White Hart it had spent the best part of the last month scrunched up in the bottom of his bag.

'Everything ok?' John asked.

Jorge paused. How he'd love to level with John Turner and explain that he was reticent to be part of this shit anymore, but he couldn't. Even though John seemed a decent bloke, he was still joint head honcho.

'Jorge?' John pressed, aware of the burgeoning silence.

'Sorry. Yes, everything's ok. A few difficult things going on, but nothing overly concerning.'

'But it concerns you?' John could hear something in Jorge's voice. *Reluctance perhaps?*

'No, I'm fine,' Jorge said hastily. 'So, you said I'm meeting Neil at a hotel? I'll need the address?'

'For obvious reasons, I'll let Neil explain the latest news in person, but please be careful of what he might ask of you,' John said cautiously. Now McFadden had postponed he had a sneaking suspicion that Neil might be too impatient to wait. Although John had felt Neil to be genuine in wanting to get to know his son, he hadn't forgotten this was Neil Sparks and Neil Sparks didn't do empathy. People being cannon fodder was not unusual and even his own flesh and blood may not be exempt.

Neil could tell Jorge to carry out the hit and Jorge, desperate to please the father he'd never had, might just be daft enough to humour Neil's madness, dropping himself and the firm in the shit in the process. And that would take an awful lot of digging to get out of – if at all.

'What do you mean, be careful what he might a…'

'Just that if there's anything you're not sure about or uncomfortable with, give me a call,' John said, knowing it was the best he could do or say over the phone.

'Is everything alright?' Jorge said hesitantly.

'Changes to plans sometimes messes things up.' John pulled his usual stance back to the forefront. 'Now, let me grab those hotel details for you.'

. . . .

'SHE'LL HAVE TO STAY HERE.' Sarah pulled the bedroom door closed and moved back into the lounge. 'We haven't a lot of choice.'

'How is she?' Tori asked, her body tense as she perched on the edge of the armchair.

Sarah scowled, having just cleaned up Susan's vomit which had missed the toilet bowl. 'A bit of a state, but that's hardly surprising.'

Tori chewed her lip. 'What about Colin? What wi...'

'Don't worry about Colin.' Sarah rolled her eyes and sighed. 'I'm not sure how I'll explain this whole story in between pouring pints, but I'll manage. The question is, how do *you* feel about it?'

'What do you mean?'

'With Susan? Personally, I'd prefer not to offer shelter to someone who helped cover up almost killing Hunter!'

'You don't know Richard.' Tori wasn't angry with Susan about what had happened. Not really. Disappointed maybe, but Susan wasn't of the same ilk as Richard. 'All I know is she can't return to him.'

Sarah threw her hands in the air. 'Oh, Tori, what do you really think she'll do in a day or a week from now? You really think Susan won't find an excuse to forgive the man? That... that fucking *rapist*.'

Tori sat forward. 'Do you think I've forgotten what that bastard's done? He's been behind or part of most of the bad things that have happened to me for *years* too,' she spat.

Sarah flopped down in a chair. 'I know, I'm sorry. I'm just frustrated.'

Tori smiled thinly. 'I think once Susan's had a lie down and everything's properly sunk in then she'll want to go to the police.'

Sarah frowned. 'Is that what *we* want though? When they

find out about this the Reapers won't want the police involved. Hunter and Noel especially. They'll want to deal themselves.'

'I don't know what the best thing is,' Tori said quietly. 'Is there a best thing?' If Susan went to the police then Noel and Hunter would be robbed of their revenge, but if she *didn't* go to the police and Noel and Hunter dealt with it, *they'd* go to jail.

Sarah folded her arms across her ample chest. 'I think there's only one way we can realistically do this.'

Tori looked up, apprehensively.

'It comprises of two things,' Sarah said. 'Find Noel and tell him the score and bring Hunter up to date. After that, we ask what *they* want to do. But one thing's for certain and that is we need to do it sharpish.'

THIRTY FOUR

JORGE FLASHED HIS BEST SMILE at the prim-looking woman wearing bright magenta lipstick as he made his way towards Neil's table, glad he'd managed to get all but a couple of the creases out of his suit. He admired the collection of tropical ferns and plants grouped to break the big expanse into smaller areas of the large lounge bar thinking it was pretty nice.

Sensing Jorge's arrival, Neil stood up and smiled widely, his hand outstretched. 'Glad you could make it. Find the place alright?'

'Yes, it was straight forward enough,' Jorge said, wondering why Neil was being so formal.

Signalling a bar steward, Neil leant back in his chair and scoured his brain for small talk, finding he could think of none; his mind was far too busy being livid about Liam McFadden.

McFadden called himself a fucking professional? Exactly how long was the man planning on postponing the job? The target could be in hospital for *weeks* yet. He should have just found a bloody way around it. There was *always* a way around things if someone tried hard enough. But where did that leave him?

The hit should have gone ahead tonight he thought,

glancing at his watch. Within the next hour, in fact. Successful completion would have meant he could get on with the other fuckers on his list in this cess pit of a town. Now, because of McFadden pussy-footing about, it meant another one to deal with personally. *Or maybe not?*

The bar steward appeared at the edge of the table and looked between Jorge and Neil expectantly. 'Yes Sir?'

'A refill for me and whatever my colleague's having?' Neil said, his voice pleasant.

'Lager, please.' Jorge smiled, silently wondering how he would broach the subject of, well… *everything.*

Neil waited until the steward had retreated before turning to Jorge. 'So, what do you know?'

Jorge glanced around. *He wanted to discuss things here?*

Reading Jorge's mind, Neil smiled - a smile that didn't reach his eyes. 'I suspect half of these fuckers are senile.'

'Things haven't been going too well,' Jorge said, his voice faltering.

'I expected as much,' Neil muttered. 'How complicated is it?'

'Very,' Jorge muttered.

'In that case we'll finish this drink and then go to my room where there's no one to overhear, senile or not.'

• • • •

'YOU *WHAT*?' Colin searched Sarah's face for a hint of this being a sick joke, but despite her frequent habit of saying things to pull his leg, he knew there was no way she would come out with something like this for a laugh.

'Keep your voice down!' Sarah hissed, glancing at the heavy helping of Reapers who had settled into their usual alcove spot whilst she'd been upstairs.

'And you've said she can stay *here*?' Colin said, still unable to quite believe his wife had given the upper class mother of Matt and Carmen refuge in *their* apartment and, if his ears were functioning properly, *this* was the woman who had helped dump Hunter after her husband had shot him! Oh yes, and also the same bloke who had not only buggered Tori's life up, but was now apparently Noel's father too!

He shook his head, trying to make sense of the avalanche of information.

'We haven't a lot of choice, Col,' Sarah said, resting her hand on his arm. 'She can't go back to that bastard. Who knows what he might do?'

Colin raked his fingers through his hair, suspecting what remained would soon fall out. 'And where's Tori? Dear God, how's she taking this? And Carmen? Fucking hell! She's been unknowingly shagging her own brother all this time?'

'Sshhh!' Sarah hissed, digging Colin in the ribs.

Colin sagged against the wall, realising there were a couple of people waiting impatiently at the bar whilst he and Sarah stood around the back talking. 'I know, I know. It's just… Christ! It's all so…'

'Yep! Tell me about it!' Sarah said. 'Tori's upstairs watching over Susan to make sure she doesn't do anything stupid and as for Carmen – well, God knows! We need to find her, but first of all we need to find Noel.'

'Jesus! I'm surprised he hasn't killed this Richard wanker by now.'

'He would if he knew, but he doesn't yet. All he knows is that Carmen kneed him in the nuts in front of everyone at the Factory last night and then walked out. He took off and no one's seen him since. I should add that Hunter doesn't know either.'

Colin raised his eyebrows and blew noisily through his teeth.

'I'm pretty sure Hunter knows who shot him,' Sarah whispered, 'because he's making Tori carry a gun.'

'*What*?' Colin shrieked.

Sarah nodded. 'I reckon Hunter knows more than all of us and believes Richard is behind all the threats. You know, with Tori and the house? He must think Richard's coming for her next.'

Colin stood back astounded. 'What, so that posh prick – the bank manager – Carmen's father is behind *all* of it?'

'If my suspicions are correct, then Susan, Tori, Hunter – *all* of us are in real danger and I suspect that's the realisation Hunter's reached too.' Sarah squeezed Colin's arm. 'We'll fill him in as soon as we can. By now he should be compos mentis and be able to tell us what he knows.'

'He won't like being unable to act on this,' Colin said, worried exactly how any of this would pan out.

Sarah pursed her lips. 'I agree, but we haven't got time to wait until he's up and about. Either way, we need to locate Noel.' She glanced back to the horde of Reapers. 'Any of them said anything?'

Colin shook his head. 'No, but they were unusually sullen when they came in and now I know why. First Hunter off the scene and now Noel's AWOL.'

Sarah took a deep breath. 'I'll ask them if they have any clue where Noel might have gone.'

'You're going looking for him?' Colin cried.

'What choice do I have? Who else can that knows what going on?'

'Is there any bloody service around here?' A voice shouted.

'Christ,' Colin muttered. 'I'll have to go and serve before people kick off.'

'Sorry love, I must crack on with this for everyone's sake,' Sarah apologised. 'Ask Jorge to give you a hand. He won't mind.'

Colin reluctantly admitted that even having Jorge helping out would be useful, except it wasn't an option. 'He's not in tonight.'

Sarah frowned. 'That's unusual. He's normally in well before now. I hope nothing's happened to him too!' She squeezed Colin's arm once more. 'Right, I'm going to go and speak to that lot.' She nodded towards the Reapers. 'Wish me luck!'

• • • •

BY THE TIME Jorge had followed Neil into his sumptuous suite, the man's demeanour had changed. Gone were the pleasantries and the smiling civil conversation.

Marching ahead, Neil pulled off his suit jacket and tugged at his tie, ripping it from his collar before undoing the top button. 'Shut the fucking door,' he barked, yanking at the handle of the mini-bar. Changing his mind, he slammed it shut, moving over to a glass-topped table to help himself to a large measure from a whisky decanter.

Jorge stood awkwardly in front of the now closed door, aware that Neil had failed to offer him a drink. He was unsure of what to say, or even how to start.

'Well?' Neil swung around, facing Jorge, a vein in his temple throbbing. 'What's going on, then?'

Jorge felt it prudent to firstly outline what the positive things were before listing the negatives. 'I got into the Factory! I also got the access code, 94869. And th…'

'I don't give a fuck about that at the moment!' Neil growled, making a quick mental note of the number Jorge had rattled off. 'Who's the cunt that's really with my wife if it's not Hunter?'

Jorge fidgeted. Now more than ever he was loathe to be part of this any longer, yet still felt indebted to tell Neil what he knew, but didn't feel very good about it. 'His name's Noel.'

'Noel fucking *who*?' Neil spat, pacing in front of the coffee table. 'Sit down will you, for fuck's sake! You're irritating me, standing there like a bloody puppet!'

Jorge hastily sat on one of the leather armchairs in the large sitting area of the suite. 'I don't know his surname.'

'*I don't know his surname*,' Neil mimicked. 'You haven't even managed that? What else do you know then? Anything?' *This kid was useless. Absolutely bloody useless.* He hadn't time for this. Fuck John and his wish for him to get to know this boy - he couldn't be arsed. That twat, McFadden, had put paid to any chance of him being nice to *anyone* right now.

Jorge bristled, realising there was nothing he particularly liked about this man who was his father. 'He's a Reaper and from what I've gathered, used to be the president. Hunter is now - you know the one who got shot and...'

'I'm not interested in their fucking life stories!' Neil snapped. 'I'm sick of this Hunter bloke. He should be dead by now.'

Jorge was secretly relieved that whatever Neil had planned for Hunter hadn't panned out. 'It looks like he's going to be ok. But ha...'

'If *I'd* been the one to do it, he wouldn't be here,' Neil countered.

Jorge swallowed. *So, he was correct.* There *had* been a plan to get at Hunter, but if it wasn't Neil who had organised the recent shooting, who the hell had? 'So, you're not going ahead wi...'

'What else have you discovered?' Neil interrupted, impatiently changing the subject.

Jorge swallowed tightly. 'I delivered the box you wanted, along with the message. Oh and Carmen and Noel are getting married.'

Neil's face contorted with rage, before laughing hollowly. 'And how does the thick bitch believe she'll achieve that, being as she's still married to *me*?'

Jorge shrugged. 'You could divorce her? It might be easier th...'

'You fucking what?' Neil slammed his glass down loudly.

Jorge cringed, waiting for a large crack to appear across the glass tabletop. 'All I meant was th...'

'You don't have a clue, do you, you mindless prick!' Neil yelled. 'After the embarrassment that whore has caused and with what I already owe those bastard Reapers, do you really think I'd let her get out of this so easily?' He shook his head in frustration. *Was this kid trying to wind him up, because if he was, it was working.*

Jorge felt heat creep up his neck. Divorce was the decent thing to do. It was more sensible than *this*.

'That slut has been a bag of shit from the off. And to think I shelled out so much for her in the first place,' Neil muttered.

'You mean she was a…'

Neil scowled. 'Do I look the sort who'd marry a fucking hooker? Don't be stupid! Jeez, did you inherit your mother's brains? From what I remember she was as thick as shit too! Carmen was part of a deal, but that's irrelevant.'

Jorge looked outwardly impassive, but was silently angry and perturbed. Whatever he thought of his mother, she wasn't thick. And Carmen? He'd presumed Neil's upset was down to his love for the woman, but he didn't love her and never had. Carmen and Noel loved each other though – that much was obvious, so if Neil didn't want her, then why not let her get on with her life?

'I'll get rid of that Noel next. Either him or that prick, Stevens or even my bitch of a wife. Can't decide who I'll enjoy offloading first the most,' Neil sneered.

'*You're* doing it?' Jorge said. 'I didn't think that yo…'

'Why the fuck do you think I'm here? For the scenery?' Neil barked. 'And now the plan for that fuckhead in hospital has fallen through, *you've* got that job.'

Jorge nearly choked. *What job? Not taking out Hunter? Neil couldn't be serious?* Wasn't the main reason for his presence here to get to know *him*, not *this*.

'Look at the state of your fucking face!' Neil laughed nastily. 'Who did you work for again? John said you were good, but you've got about as much experience in this line of work as a girl guide!' He continued pacing around the room. 'Tell me – who lied about your experience? You or John?'

'N-No one,' Jorge stuttered, feeling horribly out of his depth. He couldn't admit he'd hugely exaggerated his experience to John Turner, but thinking about it, it seemed like John had exaggerated his ability himself.

He felt even worse as the truth dawned. John Turner must

know he'd got no real experience; he'd just felt sorry for him.

Humiliation burnt. He was a loser. Just like his mother told him and just like his father – now he'd finally met him, also thought. Even John Turner thought him a saddo. *Oh, he'd had enough of this.*

Neil stopped pacing and stared at Jorge, smiling at the quiver tremoring below the surface. 'Oh, so no one exaggerated your credentials? Not you and not John? Well, that's good because now you can prove you're worthy,' he sneered. 'Don't forget you've already screwed things up several times, so you're lucky you're being given any leeway at all, but being as my contact has taken it upon himself to fucking postpone, I'm presuming because you're my *son* it's not possible for you to act so pathetically, so that's why I'm letting *you* take this Hunter bloke out.'

Jorge blinked. He didn't want to kill Hunter or *any* of them. He wasn't doing it. He'd had enough of people telling him how worthless he was and regardless of whether they were right or not, he wasn't having it anymore. Besides, he liked the Reapers and the others.

'This isn't working out for me. I don't think I've got the right kind of experience that you need t...'

Without warning, Neil lurched forward, pulling Jorge from his seat and pinned him against the wall by the throat. 'Listen, you useless piece of shit. *You* don't get the choice to walk away when you fancy it. *I* say if you're walking away or not, do you understand? People like you don't get an opinion.'

Spittle flew from Neil's mouth, landing on the crumpled lapels of Jorge's jacket. 'I've already been shafted by people over this and I'm certainly not letting you be another one, you pointless bastard.'

THIRTY FIVE

NOEL SWIGGED FROM his lager then wiped his mouth with the back of his hand. He glared at a man glancing in his general direction, taking a tiny sliver of satisfaction as he immediately averted his eyes. He was in the mood to smash someone to smithereens, purely because he could. That and the vague hope that it may dilute the pain crushing his heart.

This was why he'd always done his own thing. Developing feelings for someone and giving them the capacity to cause pain was not something he'd ever had to even contemplate before and he didn't appreciate being in this position. He'd always ridiculed those that did, having had no idea how anyone could possibly hold so much sway over the ability to control what someone felt or thought, but now he did.

Carmen had changed that. And now she'd *ruined* it.

Noel's anger spiked again and he ground out his cigarette in the ashtray, noticing he'd smoked it down to the filter. *No wonder his mouth tasted like shit.*

Regardless of being angry over his newfound lack of control over his heart and despite how much he was tempted to use his brute strength and usual reaction of ripping someone to pieces who dared wrong him, he couldn't do that to Carmen.

He ran his hand over his head in agitation. Hurting Carmen was impossible - something he couldn't ever envisage. But he *did* want to know what had changed. What had altered from one day to the next quite so dramatically? It was *that* which was fuelling his search.

He had to find Carmen and hear it from her what he'd done. If she didn't want to be with him anymore and if he "disgusted" her, like she'd said, then he wanted an explanation. And he wouldn't give up until he'd heard it. He *couldn't* give up because he wanted her more than he thought he was capable of. More than *anyone* was capable of.

Noel scanned the pub, his eyes narrowing at a group of men by the pool table. *Were they talking about him?* If they looked at him once more, he'd shove the pool cues up their arses and then see how much they fucking stared.

Raising the bottle, Noel tipped the remains into his mouth and pulling his cigarettes from his pocket, sparked another up with his gold zippo.

He sighed heavily, irritation bubbling below the surface. He'd only come here because he didn't know where else to go or what to do. The Reapers used to have a good crack here once upon a time, but he shouldn't have bothered. There wasn't anyone in here who he recognised. Not *one*. Things had moved on – like everything did.

What was he supposed to do now? Go back to the Factory empty handed? Have everyone in the White Hart whispering behind his back? He didn't doubt that word of being kneed in the bollocks from his wife-to-be would be just about everywhere by now.

But what happened if Carmen had returned? He could be on a wild goose chase when she might already be back, her tail between her legs and waiting to apologise.

The question was, would he forgive her? Would he forgive her for embarrassing him in front of the Reapers and making his heart bleed?

Of course he would.

Noel rubbed his stubbly chin. To his mounting irritation he'd got absolutely nowhere riding around *all* night in his search. He hadn't thought it would be too difficult to find Carmen. She hadn't left long beforehand and hadn't got a car, but he'd been wrong. There had been no sign of her in the maze of back streets in the industrial area around the Factory. He'd cruised around for hours with his eyes peeled, but she'd disappeared without trace. It had only been after an hour that the fear that something bad could have befallen her had crept up on him. He'd kill anyone who touched a hair on her head.

He'd scouted around parks and even graveyards – somewhere no one would think of looking, but she wasn't anywhere to be found. He'd even rushed to a well-known part of the railway track where the line could be crossed, his heart hammering with the sudden notion that she'd taken a leaf out of her bloody tosser of a brother's book and decided to top herself, but there was no sign of her there either.

Not a trace of her anywhere.

Noel frowned. She wouldn't have gone to the White Hart or back to her parents, so he hadn't bothered trying there, but maybe he should have? Maybe she'd *know* he'd presume that so that's where she'd gone? Perhaps he should have ruled those two places out first rather than wasting the entire daylight hours today aimlessly riding around, searching every blonde woman's face on the street in the hope it was Carmen.

He dragged his hand across his face in frustration. By now she could be *anywhere*. She could have boarded a train. She could even have gone back to France…

Sick with the thought of that being a remote possibility, Noel was about to go to the bar for a refill when a familiar voice made him swing around. His eyes narrowed. 'Come to gloat? How the fuck did you know I was here?'

'Somebody told me this used to be one of your favourite drinking holes, so I thought it was worth a punt,' Sarah said, sitting down uninvited. 'Listen, I haven't got time to fuck around whilst you act defensive and snotty. This is *important*, so for once in your bloody life Noel Cooper, you're going to listen to me.'

• • • •

HUNTER COULDN'T MASK HIS RAGE, especially as the increase to his heartrate was resounding loudly through the amplified machine monitoring it for anyone who might enter the room to hear.

'Please calm down,' Tori muttered, glancing at the door. 'If someone comes in, they'll see how stressed you are and make me leave.'

She'd been so relieved on reaching the hospital to learn that Hunter had improved dramatically and was more back to himself than yesterday, but on the same vein she wasn't over the moon with what she had to tell him, which included the additional information that Susan had told her. Information that she hadn't even been able to tell Sarah as yet.

She also hadn't been happy leaving Susan in the White Hart, half-expecting the woman to do a flit, but she'd promised to stay put and Tori had no choice but to take the woman's word. She had to speak to Hunter; it couldn't be left any longer and she just hoped it wouldn't be too long before Sarah joined her. She'd left a message with Colin to let Sarah know she'd gone to the hospital to do what they'd discussed, but she desperately needed some help in keeping Hunter calm, although that was an extremely tall order under the circumstances.

Tori grasped his hand. 'Hunter, *please*!' she begged. 'You're no use to yourself or anyone if you relapse. 'I need you to step back from this and tell me what's the best thing to do. What *you* want to do.'

Hunter clenched his jaw, a vein pulsating in his neck. He struggled to push himself into a raised position against the pillow, scowling as pain shot through him. 'How else am I supposed to react?' he growled. Although his throat was still sore, at least now his voice afforded him the ability of having a conversation.

Tori nodded. She herself, had been floored when Susan came out of the bedroom saying there was something else she should know. 'We don't know whether what Susan said is true. It's only based on her suspicions and what Matt wrote.'

'Don't mention that wanker's name!' Hunter spat. 'Why did Carmen not tell us this?'

Tori shrugged. 'She probably still believes, like we did, that it was Matt.'

'Well, she should have told us regardless, even if she didn't know if it was true or not,' Hunter said. 'In my opinion both of those bastards are capable of it.'

'Perhaps,' Tori agreed, 'but maybe she didn't want to bring it all up again for something that Ma… someone wrote. Susan said Carmen believes his letter was insurance because we suspected him.'

Hunter gingerly stretched to grab his cup of water and gulped at the tepid liquid. 'I'll kill Stevens anyway,' he muttered.

Tori looked away. *Where was Sarah?* She needed her help on this one. The way Hunter's anger was ramping up, she wouldn't put it past him to pull himself out of bed and up sticks. 'Why didn't you tell me it was Richard who shot you?'

'Jesus Christ, Tori,' Hunter cried. 'Don't you think I would have done had I been able to string the words together? The most I could manage was to make sure you protected yourself and that took me long enough.'

'So, you think Richard's behind all of this?' Tori asked. 'Are you saying we're all in danger?'

Hunter nodded. 'He must have been behind the break-in and now with what you're saying about Andrew.'

'But why would he want to hurt me?'

Hunter narrowed his eyes, picturing the smug face of Richard Stevens. 'I can only presume he thought I'd discovered he'd killed my son,' he spat. 'Or he hates me for fucking up his son's marriage? Blames me for that wanker topping himself?'

'That's another thing. If Matt didn't kill himself out of guilt, then why did he?'

Hunter shrugged, before wincing at his own sudden movement. 'Are you sure Stevens didn't kill him?'

Tori raised her eyebrows. 'Now you're being crazy!'

'Am I?' Hunter's voice was sharp. 'Am I really?'

Tori swallowed nervously. Maybe it wasn't such a ludicrous thought? This time a week or so ago, she wouldn't have believed any of this to be possible and look what had happened.

'And don't forget, *you've* embarrassed the family,' Hunter continued. 'He'll want to make you pay for that, no doubt.'

'What, so all of this is *my* fault?' Tori shrieked. *Even Hunter blamed her? Blamed her for being the curse on everything around her?*

'That's not what I said,' Hunter snapped.

'You might as well have done.' Tears welled in Tori's eyes. 'And how do you think Carmen's feeling about all of this?'

Hunter closed his eyes, anger churning. He could kick himself; still barely able to comprehend the person he was after was under his nose all along. It all just beggared belief and the anger that he'd missed it grated like broken glass. Why had he not recognised that tosser from the photo? He must have seen the guy in the local papers or on Tori's wedding picture in that magazine, so how had he missed the bloody obvious? *How stupid was he?* There was *no way* he could sit here and let the bastard get away with it. He'd got away with far too much for far too long.

Tori jumped back in shock, her eyes widening in horror when Hunter pulled his sheet back, ripping the sticky pads of the monitor from his chest, making the machine let out a steady tone as it lost its connection. 'What are you doing?'

Hunter's jaw set resolutely as he braced himself against the pain and moved to the edge of the bed, his long legs dropping down so his feet touched the floor. 'What I should have done a long time ago.'

Moving forward, Tori grabbed Hunter's arm. 'No! You

can't! Please, Hunter – you'll make yourself ill, you can't n...'

'I'm doing exactly what I need to do to protect you, avenge Andrew and take the bastard out who should have died at the time, instead of your father!' Hunter's steely eyes bored into Tori's. 'I'm doing this, Tori, whether you like it or not!'

'Actually, you're not... *I* am!' Noel growled, pushing into Hunter's room with Sarah on his tail.

• • • •

SARAH DIDN'T THINK she'd ever been as grateful for Noel's timing as she had been today. It had taken resources she didn't realise she possessed to stabilise him enough to listen to reason, even if under the circumstances, once she'd told him the truth why Carmen had left, she'd believed he'd been about to blow a gasket. And she couldn't say she'd blamed him. Not this time, but she'd made him listen. *Somehow.*

Sarah smiled sadly. Her heart had gone out to Noel as he'd fought to mask the pain hearing for definite who had attacked his mother. And then seeing the abject desolation replace the anger as the penny slowly dropped *exactly* who Carmen was in all of this was gut-wrenching.

Noel hadn't even pulled away when Sarah had squeezed his hand, pretending not to notice the tear in his eye that he'd rapidly blinked away.

Sarah let out a long breath. She'd thought Noel had more right than anyone else to be the one to make the decision about what to do over Richard-Bastard-Stevens. That was until at Hunter's bedside she'd learnt of Susan's suspicions over Andrew's death.

Sarah glanced at Tori ashen-faced, before moving her sights back to Hunter, rigid with anger. The room had been silent for over a minute whilst everyone sat locked within their own minds, their brains a mass of swirling turmoil. She wanted to ask the obvious question, but vocalising it would make it real. It was only a matter of time, but she still wanted to clutch on a bit longer before learning the inevitable. She, like everyone else in this room, would be party to deciding Richard's fate. Although his fate was pretty much determined, it was a case of *when*.

After all, it was *her* who had to return to the White Hart, talk to Susan and pretend to be unaware of what was going on behind the scenes. *And she wasn't looking forward to it.*

Hunter broke the silence. 'Noel, I know you'll go ahead regardless, but I appreciate you coming here first.'

Noel shrugged and glared at Sarah, his eyes burning. 'I very nearly didn't come here at all.'

Hunter nodded, unable to meet Tori's eyes knowing as well as she did that despite his condition he'd been about to up and leave to do the job if Noel hadn't arrived when he had.

His teeth clenched. Whether he liked it or not, he wasn't fit enough to make a *proper* job of finishing the bastard. Oh, he'd do it alright, but he wasn't well enough to deliver all of the things that he wanted to painfully inflict on Richard Stevens, so at the end of the day it had to be Noel who got the honours. The only definite fact in this long chain of events was that Stevens raped Noel's mother – there was no doubt about that one.

Hunter locked eyes with Noel. 'The job's yours if you want it.'

'Of course I want it. I'm going to rip the bastard to pieces,' Noel spat.

Sarah glanced at Tori sitting almost trance-like and before she could help herself, she spoke. 'When?'

Noel's head swung in Sarah's direction. 'As soon as fucking possible.'

Hunter's eyes remained fully-focused on Noel. 'I know I don't need to say this, but do this for Andrew too. And possibly Jeanie…'

Tori's head snapped up. *So, Hunter did have suspicions about Richard being involved in Jeanie's disappearance?*

Noel smiled grimly. 'Oh, don't you worry. I intend to get a full confession about everything before the job is completed.'

'Pick who you want with you,' Hunter said. 'I'm thinking

Grin and perhaps also how ab…'

'No need. This one's mine and mine alone,' Noel interrupted, his voice icy. 'I'm having this one all to myself.'

Hunter nodded in acceptance. *If that was what Noel wanted, that was fine.*

'I'll need the van,' Noel continued. 'I'll collect it from the Factory and won't let the rest know anything until it's done.' He glanced at Tori, then at Sarah. 'That goes for you two as well. No mention of this to Colin either. Not a word to *anyone* until you hear otherwise, understand?'

Tori nodded nervously, but Sarah pursed her lips. 'What about Susan? Shouldn't we tell her? It's her husband after all.'

Hunter looked up startled. 'I don't give a fuck! She's lucky she's not being removed along with him!'

'Susan didn't know, Hunter. She didn't know about any of the things Richard's done, I'm sure of it. I know her well enough to see she's devastated,' Tori whispered.

'Not as devastated as *some* people and certainly not devastated enough not to help him dump me!' Hunter snapped, his bitterness evident.

'She was talking about going to the police,' Sarah added. 'In fact, *we*,' she glanced at Tori, 'wondered if that was feasible? At least that way it would keep any of you out of jail.'

'Don't be fucking stupid,' Noel barked. 'This will be done by the Reapers. By *me*, not the fucking police! *No one* will go to jail for this, trust me!'

Sarah chewed her bottom lip. 'Ok, so what about Carmen? Should we not at least warn her? He is her father.'

Tori shifted uncomfortably, glaringly aware that whichever way they looked at it, Richard Stevens was also Noel's father. She risked an intrepid glance at him, seeing his face crimson with rage.

'Carmen will learn afterwards,' Hunter jumped in. 'That's if we ever see her again.'

Noel stood up. 'That's it then. Nothing else to say. I'll get on to it.' He leant over, shaking hands with Hunter vigorously.

'I'll be back in touch once it's done.'

THIRTY SIX

RICHARD EYED THE CREASES of his blue slacks as he pulled them from the wardrobe. Where the hell was Susan when he needed her? He didn't have time to work out where the bloody hell she kept the iron. Furthermore, he doubted whether he'd even remember how to use the damn thing. *Besides, that was woman's stuff.*

He glanced at the clock as he dragged some weekend bags out from underneath the bed. Opening one, he folded the trousers as best as he could and placed them into the holdall.

Richard wiped his hand across his brow. It was too hot in here – something *else* Susan insisted on that drove him up the wall. Always insisting she was cold and putting the central heating on, setting the thermostat to silly levels. It was like a bloody sauna! *Damn woman!*

By dinner time last night, he'd become so irritated by Susan's lack of presence that he'd been tempted to book himself a table at that nice Italian restaurant in town. Even if she showed up it had been far too late to begin cooking and she hadn't even bothered telephoning to say she'd be that late.

Eventually he'd settled with a jar of olives, some cheese and biscuits and his whisky. It had only been when bedtime approached with still no sign of his wife that he'd begun to wonder.

For a split second it had passed through his mind that perhaps her disappearance might be another message, but he'd quickly dismissed that concept. What the hell would the Reapers want with a wizened, moaning old cow? It was hardly good leverage.

Susan had clearly decided for once in her life to do her own thing, probably to spite him. No doubt she'd taken it upon herself to swan off with some of those self-important witches in her ladies' group on some kind of retreat for women. She used to frequently go on that kind of rubbish not so long ago. Bloody stupid stuff, like "art weekends" to draw a bowl of fucking fruit.

Richard rolled his eyes. *A weekend to draw a bloody banana? Ludicrous.*

Well, it was alright for Susan. When did she have anything to really mither about? When did *any* bloody women have anything to worry about? They had it easy – all of them. The men did everything whilst they fannied around getting their bloody hair done. Pointless, the fucking lot of them.

Richard yanked open the middle drawer of the large oak chest and pulled out a selection of neatly pressed socks and underpants, placing them into the holdall along with more clothes from the walk-in wardrobe.

Well, he'd got his answer now, that was certain. Having still no word from Susan this morning, his decision had been made a lot simpler.

Most of the night he'd been planning. He had to be out of the country by Monday, which meant the latest he could leave was Sunday, so if she wasn't back by tomorrow, then he'd be going without her.

He'd assumed he'd have to take her. She wouldn't appreciate being left to face the music on her own, but quite frankly he'd prefer it if she remained. He could do without her around his neck any longer than she already had been. How many years was it now? It had to be coming up to thirty. *Jesus!*

And if she did return, then she'd better have a bloody good explanation as to why she'd felt it acceptable to disappear without a word.

Richard swallowed down a smirk. Well, it was all sorted now. *He* knew exactly what he would do, having toyed with a few different ideas during the long night before settling on what was a good decision all round.

Glancing at the small pile of paperwork on his bedside table he took his passport from the top, smiling bashfully at the non-too complementary photograph of him on the inside back cover.

'A dreadful likeness,' he muttered. Despite having had the photograph taken professionally, they had still managed to make him look fat and old. He glanced sideways into Susan's oval mirror on the dressing table and smoothed down his hair. *He looked a lot better in real life.*

Putting his passport down he picked up Susan's, his nose wrinkling. Her photograph was much worse than his, but then it was more of real likeness. He could have done with getting some fake passports sorted, but there just wasn't time.

He threw Susan's passport down the back of the bedside table. If she ever bothered to show up, then she could damn well search for it herself. First thing tomorrow he'd be heading down to Dover and jumping on the ferry, meaning he'd be in France by lunchtime. From there, he'd head south and either stay there or continue into Spain. He hadn't decided yet, but as long as he was out of England that was half the battle.

Richard scowled. He should have foreseen this a long time ago, but he hadn't ever thought anything would escalate to this level. This sort of thing happened to *criminals* – people who lived in council flats and went around robbing blind disabled folk, not to successful well-bred people like *him*.

Still, he wasn't sitting here waiting to explain himself whilst the bank went through his business with a fine-toothed comb, only to become the latest piece of gossip around town. *No thanks.*

Harrumphing loudly, Richard continued packing. He still

had lots to do. There was paperwork, as well as other things to sort out which would enable him to build a new life somewhere else for a fair amount of time.

· · · ·

FOR THE FIRST TIME since he'd arrived in town, Jorge had felt unable to sit in the White Hart last night, acting like everything was normal. The meeting with Neil had left an unsavoury taste and despite spending longer than he cared to admit dressing down the conversation, whichever way he looked at it didn't change that his father was a Grade A tosser.

Neil Sparks didn't give a flying fuck about him – or come to mention it, *anyone.*

He wanted to pretend that it didn't hurt, but it did and he didn't like it. He'd stupidly believed Neil actually wanted to get to know him.

Slamming his fist down on the dashboard, Jorge glared at the overflowing bin in the layby, having no clue why he'd parked up or more to the point, where he'd been going in the first place. All he knew was that his so-called father was using him.

Jorge was swamped with indignation, anger and a crushing sense of betrayal. He'd been enthralled by the supposed "glamour" of being part of and perhaps eventually inheriting the Sparks' empire, but the truth was he wasn't cut out for this shit and furthermore, he didn't *want* to be.

He took a swig from a slightly warm bottle of coke lying on the passenger seat and frowned so hard his eyebrows almost touched his nose. People around here had shown him more kindness than he'd ever experienced and he wouldn't pay them back by doing what Neil Sparks dictated.

It was feasible to make a life for himself here – not this pretence of one, but one for *real*. He got on with the White Hart crowd and even the Reapers had now half-accepted him. Well, sort of. Between them these people exhibited a loyalty and care for each other that he'd always craved, so why not?

Looking down at his hands, Jorge picked at his fingernails. He wouldn't be part of Neil's plans. Not anymore. It was bad enough that he'd done *any* of those things for Neil and for that, he didn't have much respect left for himself. *It stopped here.*

He'd left Neil believing that his heavy-handed threats had gleaned the desired effect and that, as instructed, he would indeed be removing Hunter from the planet tomorrow night. It was almost laughable. The hitman had had the sense to pull out, yet it was expected for *him* to walk into a busy hospital, shoot a man dead and hey presto, go straight to jail.

Mission accomplished at *his* expense. *Wonderful.*

Jorge's mouth tightened into a resigned half-smile. That wasn't the reason he wouldn't be going ahead though. The reason was because he *liked* Hunter. He liked Sarah, Tori and Carmen. Even *Noel.* He liked all of them, but Neil Sparks didn't need to know that. He'd let him believe what he wanted.

Jorge's slight elation at having made a decision evaporated. After tomorrow when Neil realised the job had not been done, he wouldn't be allowed to walk away. It also scuppered the chances of him staying among the people he'd grown so attached to.

Unless he told them…

Jorge frowned. It was unlikely he'd be well-received after admitting he'd been the one to break into Hunter's house, hit Tori, sent animal parts to Carmen's parents and then given Noel up to the man who wanted to kill him. Oh yes, and not forgetting agreeing to murder Hunter…

Jorge raked his hands through his hair. He wasn't going to be able to stay here after this, but what he *could* do was let them know who their enemy was and then subtly disappear somewhere that neither they, nor Neil could find him.

Starting the car engine, Jorge drove away. He'd head back to the flat, have a shower and then go down the White Hart, but first he could do with something to eat because there wouldn't be time later.

Driving through a small town and spying a bakery, Jorge

parked and got out of the car. Crossing the road, he smiled wryly at the quintessential feel of the street with its selection of independent shops. No chain stores here he thought, glancing at a butchers with braces of pheasants hanging from hooks on a striped canopy and a boutique sporting mannequins in the window decked in clothes akin to Ladies' Day at Ascot.

Walking past the boutique and coming level with a café surrounded by the strong aroma of freshly ground coffee, he glanced absentmindedly at a woman sitting in the window.

Jorge frowned. That woman looked a lot like Carmen, although a markedly different version. He covertly studied her, not wanting to come over as a weirdo on top of everything else.

If it *was* Carmen, then he had no idea what could have befallen her. Nursing a cup of tea with downcast eyes, the woman looked exhausted, whereas Carmen was always so glamourous. *This* woman, without being rude, looked anything but! And if it *was* Carmen, why would she be over this neck of the woods anyway? *But then, the same could be said about him.*

Oh, it was no use. He had to find out. His curiosity was just too much. Furthermore, it was a welcome diversion from the thousand and one unanswerable questions rattling around his brain.

Pulling open the door of the café, Jorge went inside.

· · · ·

CARMEN STARED BLANKLY at the table. She wasn't expecting an epiphany; she wasn't expecting anything – she just didn't know what to do other than pass the time until she either did have an epiphany or had settled her mind enough to make the move to visit her mother.

Yesterday, she'd only managed a short walk from the guest house before the warning signs of an impending panic attack forced her to backtrack as quickly as physically possible, even though her speeding mind and the crushing pain in her heart had given her genuine concern that she wouldn't make it. But she *had* made it back to her damp room and had then proceeded to spend the rest of the day and evening alone with her thoughts. Nothing had brought her any solace. The only positive thing she had accomplished was not drinking copious amounts of cheap wine for the second night running, instead sticking to finishing the rest of the one bottle left from the night before and moving on to disturbingly musty-tasting water from the washbasin in the corner of her room.

At least today she'd successfully made it far enough to have a change of scenery and step back into the land of the living, even though she felt like an imposter.

Carmen glanced around the café, not wishing to meet eyes with anyone. She'd been here a good part of the afternoon and thankfully no one minded her long term presence. The problem was, if the last few hours were anything to go by, she was still no closer to seeing how *any* of this could be resolved or how to feel any less panicked about seeing her mother to confirm the truth on what she'd learnt. Neither was she feeling able to risk going to the house only to bump into *him* – her father, but she'd have to at some point. And that point had to be soon.

At least she'd stopped crying, but she still didn't look good. Not that she cared anymore, but she could feel someone staring at her - the nagging knowledge of someone's eyes fixed on her burnt brightly.

Carmen glanced to her right and her mouth almost in slow-motion, formed into an "O" of surprise. 'Jorge?'

Even if Carmen hadn't spoken, Jorge had the confirmation needed the woman *was* who he'd thought purely from her expression alone. 'I thought it was you,' he smiled, approaching her table. 'Are you alright?'

Carmen felt the overpowering urge to cry. It felt like a year since she'd not felt utterly alone in an anonymous sea of faces. Although her need to get away from everyone had been immense, Jorge was a welcome sight. But did he know? Did *everyone* know what had happened? Did they all know the dreadful truth about her and Noel? About her father?

Putting his hand lightly on Carmen's arm, Jorge bit back his guilt as she flinched, betting whatever had happened was probably linked to something he'd engineered. Anger balled silently inside him. 'Can I join you?' He nodded tentatively towards the empty chair at Carmen's table. 'Another cup of tea? Coffee?'

Carmen gestured towards the chair, but brushed away the offer of a drink. She'd already had four cups of tea and might be sick if she forced herself to drink yet another one.

'What's happened?' Jorge asked quietly, sitting down on the opposite chair.

Carmen shrugged. 'Surprised you haven't heard,' she said, the bitterness in her voice, strong.

Jorge raised his eyebrows. 'I wasn't around last night. I was meeting a friend.' *Friend? Friend my arse. Neil was the very opposite of that.*

Carmen knew she shouldn't say anything. Didn't *want* to utter out loud *any* of the things she was now aware of, but the knot of built-up angst festering deep in the pit of her being weighed so heavily she had to loosen it, even if only slightly.

Jorge wasn't involved enough to be biased, so could he offer a subjective opinion? Not that it was plausible for any of this to warrant anything realistically subjective, so what exactly was she expecting him to say? What *could* he say to make any of this better?

Nothing.

Jorge watched Carmen struggling. 'I know you hardly know me, but you guys have been good to me, so if there's anything I can do...' he smiled. 'Even a friendly ear? You never know? It can't be that bad, surely?'

Carmen laughed. Not a proper laugh, but more of a strangulated sound. 'Can't be that bad?' she muttered. 'You have no idea...'

THIRTY SEVEN

LILLIAN WAS RATHER PLEASED. The boutique she'd spotted in that magazine had stocked just the right sort of clothes and she'd spent a very pleasant couple of hours drinking cups of tea and chatting, in-between trying on a whole host of lovely two-piece skirt-suits, blouses and dresses that the attentive shop assistant suggested.

Smiling, Lilian patted down her hair smugly. The girl had been most complimentary too. She glanced at the powder-blue bag in her hand and smiled. Even the boutique's bag was pretty – none of that plastic rubbish – a lovely holdall-style bag, complete with plaited handles. *Classy - just like herself.*

There had been lots to choose from in that boutique and she could have quite happily purchased every single thing; it wasn't like she couldn't afford it, but she hadn't. Only because it gave her the excuse to go back, maybe in a couple of days and have another nice afternoon.

Lillian continued slowly walking down the road, glancing in all of the shops. *This* is the sort of place she'd like to move to, but unfortunately it was out of the question. The town was *far* too close, so the Windsor location would be the one she'd stick to.

The estate agent called only this morning suggesting some houses that sounded exactly what she was after. And even better, the person showing interest in her property was pushing for a viewing. She was in no rush to get back to sort that out though, so she'd arranged for a spare set of keys to be delivered to the estate agents. That way they could sort it out, leaving her to sit back and relax.

Now she'd got a choice of two lovely new suits to wear, along with three nice blouses and wearing them in the pleasant surroundings of the Palm Court was a fine choice.

Spotting a newsagents, Lillian thought about buying a copy of the local paper. With any luck Richard Stevens' face would be on the front page with the headline: *"Theft. Fraud..."*

Her face cracked into a wide smile. That would round off a good day perfectly. Or should she treat herself to a cream tea first?

Stopping outside a café she glanced at the menu, pleased to see they did scones. Deciding to go in, Lillian paused when a man came out of the door and headed off down the road. *That was the man she'd seen last night with Luca LeVere's double!* Shaking her head in disbelief of what a small world it was she stepped into the café, looking for an empty table. Being busy was a good sign in an eating establishment and there were no spare tables at all, but there *was* a spare seat.

She walked over to the table in the window. 'Excuse me, do y...' Lillian stopped as the woman sitting at the table glanced up. 'Carmen?' Without waiting for an answer, she sat down. 'What are you doing here?'

Lillian eyed Carmen's bedraggled appearance and fought to suppress the smug smile itching to creep across her face. The girl looked awful. Did her general appearance mean her father had been arrested? 'I barely recognised you, dear. You look, well, shall we say... not yourself... Is everything alright?'

Carmen forced a smile. The *last* person she wanted to see was Lillian. There was no way she wanted to give her any inclination just *how* horrendous her life was right now. 'I'm ok, thank you. How are you?'

Lillian's beady eyes scrutinised Carmen. The girl was hiding something; she could see it as clear as day. 'How are your parents? I expect you've heard that there's been some, let's say, *animosity*, at least from your father's side.' She waved her hand dismissively. 'It's a horrible misunderstanding, of course, but what with everything your family has gone through of late, it's fully understandable that he isn't thinking straight. I just want you to know there's no ill-will from me. Your parents and I go back a long time, so I'm sure it can be rectified once things are back to normal.'

Lillian smiled sweetly. Richard would *never* think straight once what he'd done become available for the world to see. Furthermore, there was no chance on earth she would ever forgive him for spreading her business around. '*Please* don't feel awkward because of your parents or because of what my daughter did to your brother. I couldn't bear it.' She made the sign of the cross over her chest. 'God rest his soul.'

Carmen swallowed the steadily rising bile. She knew what Lillian was doing and she wouldn't be sucked in. And she *really* didn't want to discuss her father. Whatever that man had done to offend Lillian was of no consequence.

'So,' Lillian pressed. 'Have you been in contact with your parents?'

'No, I haven't,' Carmen snapped, struggling with her patience.

Lillian raised her hands to her mouth in mock worry. 'Don't tell me you've fallen out with them too? That would be such a shame if...'

'No one's fallen out with anyone. I've just been... been really busy,' Carmen interrupted. *Shut up, Lillian. Stop talking.*

Lillian's eyes narrowed, a sickly smile spreading over her face. 'Are you *sure*, dear? You don't look... well... your usual glamourous self.'

'I haven't been feeling well,' Carmen muttered, bending down for her bag. She had to get out of here and away from this woman.

Lillian placed her bony hand on Carmen's arm, her grip surprisingly strong. 'Nothing catching, I hope?'

Carmen shook her head. 'No, nothing like that. Listen, I…'

'Oh, that reminds me,' Lillian said loudly. 'For a minute when I wasn't sure it was you, I was beginning to think that something must be in the water around here for doubles of people! I was convinced I saw your husband last night too.'

Carmen tried to stop herself from reacting, but it was too late. 'My husband?'

Lillian smirked, pleased to see she'd garnered a reaction. 'Yes, you know – your husband? I presume you can remember him?' She tittered loudly. 'He was in the hotel I'm staying at.'

Luca was here? 'You're staying in a hotel? Where?' Carmen blathered.

'Oh, not far from here,' Lillian said vaguely. 'I needed some time away from all the stress and have a bit of a relaxing break.'

'Yes, but what abo…'

'Even though I wasn't invited to your wedding, your mother was obsessed with showing off a never-ending stream of your wedding photographs.' Lillian eyed Carmen pointedly. 'But the man I saw wasn't Luca, although I must say the likeness was uncanny.'

Carmen blinked, unsure of how to react. *Why was Lillian so sure it wasn't him? What if it was? What if he was looking for her?*

Lillian tittered again and Carmen glanced at the wooden napkin holder on the table, imagining shoving it, along with all of the floral napkins it contained, into Lillian's mouth. 'Why are you so sure it wasn't him? For all you know he could be here visiting me.'

Lillian smiled, the snide grin not lost. 'Because of the expression on your face when I said I thought I'd seen him.'

Carmen's need to retaliate deflated. *The nasty old trout was right. It was obvious.*

'Look,' Lillian said, the pseudo-sereneness firmly back in place. 'I don't know what's happened between you two, although rumours have circulated…' She ran her eyes over Carmen pointedly. 'Don't get your hopes up. It definitely wasn't him. The man I saw was English with a strong southern accent.'

Carmen was halfway through an internal sigh of relief when she reminded herself that Luca wasn't Luca. And whoever Luca *really* was, he was English… From London…

'The man's voice was the *only* thing that convinced me it couldn't be your husband,' Lillian said. *Judging by the state of her, the silly girl obviously regretted throwing what she had away – all that money and lifestyle, but she'd made her bed… A bit like her father…*

Making sure she masked the increasing mounting dread, Carmen smiled. 'They say everyone's got a double somewhere in the world, so Luca must have one.'

Lillian frowned. 'You're right. In fact, a man I saw last night, sitting with that double of a husband of yours, left this very café just before I came in! How's that for coincidence?'

Turning, Carmen quickly scanned the customers; the majority being women and the only men, much older and grey-haired.

Amusement danced in Lillian's eyes. 'Like I said, he left just before I came in. I'm surprised you didn't notice him. A young man. Much younger than your husband. More of your age…' she continued, making sure she got that twist of the knife in. 'Dark hair – a bit foreign-looking. Attractive.'

Carmen's heart raced. *Dark haired man? Young? Foreign-looking? Jorge? It wasn't Jorge, was it?* He'd said he'd met a friend last night? Someone who was a dead ringer for her husband? *Oh God. It was Jorge and it must be Luca. Jorge was involved with Luca?*

'Are you alright?' Lillian frowned at Carmen's sudden paling complexion. 'You look like you've seen a ghost!'

Carmen nodded absentmindedly. She'd told Jorge all that

stuff and he was in cahoots with Luca... Panic overwhelmed her. Was *he* behind the things that had happened? Was he behind the break-in? Hunter's shooting? Could it possibly be...

'Carmen?' Lillian pressed.

Carmen grabbed her bag and pushed her chair back, the loud scraping of the wooden legs on the parquet floor causing heads to turn in her direction. 'Sorry, Lillian, I have to go. I've come over unwell again,' she lied.

Forcing a weak smile, she unsteadily got to her feet and hurried from the café before Lillian could say any more. She had to go and tell the others that it looked like her husband was behind all of this. She also had to let them know Jorge could not be trusted.

• • • •

NEIL TAPPED HIS FINGERS impatiently against the steering wheel; his manicured fingernails horribly at odds with the hideous set up of the manky tracksuit and baseball cap ensemble he was wearing again.

From where he had parked and through the wrought iron bars of the tall gates at the end of the driveway of Richard Stevens' property, he could see the pompous old fool going in and out of the house.

Neil scowled. Three times now Stevens had come out to load things into the Aston Martin. Knowing the jumped-up prick, he was probably off on a golf weekend, but he needed the bloody idiot to stay inside. He didn't want Stevens suddenly appearing whilst he was making his way up the drive. He'd be recognised immediately and that would ruin the element of surprise that he was counting on. Getting through the locked gates was simple enough; he had an easy way of overriding an electronic system like that - he just didn't want any interruption.

Sighing, he leant back against the uncomfortable headrest and pondered how this nasty hire car had continued running despite its less than salubrious start. Thank God for small mercies, he thought, giving the dusty plastic of the dashboard a

THE TARGET OF LIES

disparaging glance.

A deep frown creased Neil's forehead. Stevens didn't seem perturbed to have received a heart in the mail. Jorge couldn't have got the message across properly, but no surprises there. In fact, he probably hadn't even bothered sending it at all, but he'd be damn well doing this next job. Who exactly did the idiotic little shit think he was? Neil thought, remembering Jorge's words. He hadn't been insulted in such a way for as long as he could remember.

No one, aside from himself called the shots and if that muppet thought their shared genes gave him special leverage, then he was very much mistaken.

His mouth formed a tight line. Despite the boy's clear inexperience in just about *everything*, he was the ideal candidate for undertaking the Hunter job. Due to the busyness of hospitals it was all but a dead cert Jorge would get a tug, but that was ok. He had no worries of Jorge opening his mouth and dropping anyone in it; not because of the boy's loyalty, but because he wasn't planning giving him the option to prove himself one way or the other.

The minute the job was done, Jorge would be surplus to requirements and would be removed as quickly as he'd appeared. The firm wouldn't miss Jorge's "wide range of skills" and his absence would have no detrimental effect on the business.

Neil smiled slowly. Tonight, as per instructions Jorge would carry out the required task and as soon as he'd received proof the Reapers' president was no more, the boy would follow suit. John Turner wouldn't be happy, but it was easy enough to explain that. Perhaps something like Jorge was exhibiting suspicious behaviour which could put the firm at risk?

Acting suitably heartbroken would be more difficult, but he'd manage.

Neil shrugged. *Whatever.* Either way, once Jorge had been dispatched, John couldn't change it so he'd gladly put up with the cold shoulder for a couple of weeks before John came round and carried on as normal, like he usually did. In the meantime, he should make the effort to do a bit of digging over that crap about with Jorge, saying he wasn't cut out for this.

Suspicion formed. Had his son ever had the intention of doing what was asked or was he instead hellbent on fucking everything up on purpose?

Neil's eyes narrowed. Jorge could have an axe to grind if he had a hang-up about "missing fathers" and that psycho-babble stuff. It would explain why he'd got everything so bloody wrong. The kid might just be stupid enough to try and set him up and he was playing a very dangerous game if that was the case.

Neil fixed his gaze back on the driveway. That was a good sign. Stevens had settled back into the house, so he'd give it five minutes and then get started, but diverted by the sudden approach of a white van pulling over the end of the driveway, he scowled. *Oh, that was just typical! A bloody delivery, now of all times? Really?*

What had Stevens ordered now? A replacement fondue set? It certainly wasn't more body parts, but he'd have a few of his own to choose from soon enough, the fucking idiot.

Huffing, Neil focused on the van, watching closer as the driver leant forward in his seat and spotted several things which caused his heart to pound. *That's a bloody Reaper! What the fuck was he doing here?* They must have beef with the man too, but there was no way on God's earth they were getting in first. Over his dead body. *And his body wouldn't be the dead one.*

Retrieving his gun from under his seat, Neil glanced around, glad to see there wasn't a soul about. Flicking on the ignition, he fumbled with the button to open the passenger window. This was hardly ideal, being in full view of the house and road in broad daylight, but what choice did he have? Any Reaper was a viable target, so regardless of who this greaser was, it was all good.

Raising his gun, Neil aimed at the head of the man. 'Stay still, damn you,' he muttered. Steadying his arm, he applied pressure to the trigger then froze as someone else approached Steven's drive. *Who the bloody hell was this now?*

Quickly lowering the gun, Neil trembled with rage as an overweight man bumbled up to the gatepost and pressed the intercom button, then peered inquisitively into the white van. Even from his position opposite he heard Stevens' nasally voice amplified through the small speaker.

The engine of the white van started and moved off and in fury, Neil knew he had no choice but to do likewise.

That was it then. Jorge must have tipped the fucking Reapers off! Why else would they be there? It was a good job he hadn't taken a pot-shot at the driver because if he was right and this was a set up then it would play straight into their hands. They could have a sniper waiting and he might be in their sights this very second.

Glancing uncomfortably in the rear view mirror, Neil fired the engine. He knew exactly where he was heading next. His good-for-nothing son would, without a doubt, be at the White Hart so he'd head over there and watch from a distance and see if anything might prove his theory one way or the other. Thanks to this balls-up it wasn't like he had anything else to do.

• • • •

NOEL COULD HARDLY BELIEVE IT. He'd been up all night planning this and now having the van, he'd been ready and all set to go. *More* than ready, but there was always something to scupper things, wasn't there? And now his finely-tuned plan was ruined.

It had taken all of his power not to steam ahead and get it done last night, when after leaving Hunter, he'd gone to the address to spec out exactly how to achieve his goal. He could have easily done it, apart from he hadn't got the van and he needed that for definite. But he *had* worked out how to get into the seemingly impenetrable fortress where this bastard – this rapist – this *wanker* who had forcibly fathered him, lived.

He raked his fingers through his hair as he accelerated

harder. The last time he'd been at that address it had been to see that dickhead, Matt. All that business now seemed like a thousand years ago and he wished he'd never bothered getting involved with that stupid bastard in the first place.

Noel punched the steering wheel, his stress levels off the scale. His face screwed up into a ferocious scowl. *Matt – that idiotic twat. That piece of shit who turned out to be his brother? Unbelieve. Just un-bloody-believable.*

Speeding down the road, Noel wound the window down and spat out a ball of phlegm, his eyes burning with rage.

When he'd arrived at the house he'd clocked the car opposite straight away, so had acted like he was looking at a map giving whoever it was time to move on, but after a minute or so it looked unlikely to happen.

He'd had to make a decision quickly and had been busy working out if it was worth doing a circuit and come back again, but it wasn't like he could keep doing drive-bys. If he kept swinging past it would only be a matter of time before someone noticed the long-wheel based Transit and he couldn't cause any overt suspicion.

The choice had been taken out of his hands when some fat balding twat peered in his van window, so he'd had absolutely no choice but to disappear.

What the hell were the chances of that? He had no idea who the fat bastard was, but he was obviously a cunt because he knew Richard Stevens - that much was obvious because he'd seen the gates opening in his rear view mirror as he'd driven off.

Noel gnashed his teeth. *Fucking hell. What a balls up.*

Against his better judgement he found his mind wandering back to Carmen. He'd done little else but think about her and what he'd been told since he'd been smashed in between the eyes with it last night.

Noel glared angrily at a bunch of kids he'd had to stop for at a zebra crossing and itched to move forward. Staying still allowed thoughts to enter his mind at a breakneck speed and all that was keeping him even slightly together at this precise second was not thinking. He found the whole thing almost impossible to take in.

His brain hurt; the pounding of the headache assaulting his temples was proof of that and his whole body pulsed with adrenalin. How would he ever come to terms with any of this? That the woman he loved – correction, the *only* woman he'd *ever* loved, was the one he could no longer have?

He hadn't known, though. He *hadn't*, but even that made him feel no better or less sick. Or less devastated.

Noel's eyes narrowed almost to a close as he focused on his trembling hands. Gripping the steering wheel harder, his mind span on an endless circle of hate.

Relieved to see the crossing was now clear, he stamped his foot on the accelerator and with a loud screech of tyres, took off down the road.

And Richard Stevens. The bank manager. The rapist. The epitome of who he hated. *His father.*

Noel swallowed the lump forming in his throat, his long-standing guilt that his birth had been the cause of his mother's death intensifying. He'd been feeling a lot more at peace recently. Carmen had given him faith to believe in himself and had made him feel he was worth more than anything. But then she would, wouldn't she? Being as she was his fucking sister!

It didn't matter now because anything he had with her was dead and buried. *Over.*

Noel roared in anguish, the rawness of his own pain ripping at his throat. And now he couldn't even take the bastard who'd caused all of this pain out when he wanted to? He'd have to completely rethink the plan because of that nosy fat cunt. What if he told Stevens someone was outside? He glanced down at himself as he took a corner at speed. *He'd been stupid to wear the leather. Why hadn't he thought about that? Stupid, STUPID!*

Stevens would do a bunk if he believed the Reapers were on to him. *Bollocks.* He'd miss his chance and there was no way he was going to do that.

Fuck it.

'I'm not postponing this, you bastard!' Noel screeched into a left hand turn and swung the van around. He wasn't losing the opportunity of taking the bastard out who'd ruined his mother's life, as well as countless others.

Speeding back towards the house, Noel's eyes focused on the road in front of him. Anger churned and a vein throbbed wildly in his temple.

Come hell or high water, he was doing this right *now*. And he'd take the fat visitor too if he so happened to still be there.

THIRTY EIGHT

RICHARD STEVENS KEPT HIS SMILE in place as Andrew Mercer trailed him into the kitchen. 'What a nice surprise,' he lied, hoping his voice didn't reveal that it was passing through tightly gritted teeth. His jaw was so clenched he thought he'd developed tetanus.

Did he not have enough on his plate without Mercer descending unannounced? For Christ's sake – it was bad enough that there was still no sign of Susan and the stuff hanging around his neck with the bank, without Mercer sticking his bloody bulbous nose into everything.

A sudden wash of fear ran over him. Had Mercer found out that he was under investigation for fraud? An investigation that was fast gaining pace and one he couldn't get out of? Had that ponce from the bank bandied it around the Conservative Club over drinks? His reputation would be in tatters if that was the case. But once this got out his reputation would be in tatters anyway. It hardly mattered as he wasn't sticking around waiting for that time to come.

Richard watched Mercer waddle across the kitchen, his beady eyes darting around and coming to rest on the one remaining bag left to be loaded into the car.

'Off somewhere?' Mercer eyed the bag inquisitively.

Richard glanced dismissively at where Mercer's eyes were focused and shook his head. 'Me? No. Just having a tidy up.'

Bending down, Mercer poked the contents of the open holdall and frowned. 'Tidy up?'

Richard scowled. *Trust that bag to be the one containing all of his nice shirts.* 'Well, I was tidying at the same time. We were toying with the idea of having the weekend away.'

'But it's only Friday!' Mercer exclaimed, his eyes scouting around the rest of the kitchen.

'Oh, so it is,' Richard laughed, eying one of Susan's carving knives in a wooden block on the work surface. *That would look lovely embedded deep in Mercer's eye.* 'I find I lose track of the days,' he continued. 'I haven't got used to this retirement lark yet.'

Andrew Mercer hovered near to the kettle, wondering whether Richard would bother offering him a drink. 'Susan not around?'

'Erm, no. She's gone to get her hair done,' Richard said. Well, she had... *Yesterday.* God knows where she was now but just because he had no idea where she'd been for the last twenty-four hours he wasn't lowering himself to ask Mercer if he had happened to see his wife on his travels. Neither would he ask about Carmen. The nosy bastard would ensure *that* went round quicker that a sandstorm.

Richard Stevens – the bank manager – the one about to be exposed for fraud. The man with no idea of the whereabouts of his wife or daughter...

'Sandra only remarked over dinner last night that she hadn't seen Susan at any of the ladies' lunches recently. In fact, we haven't seen either of you out together for some time...' Mercer raised his eyebrow suggestively. 'Divorced you has she, Stevens? Is that it?' He laughed loudly, his puce-coloured jowls wobbling. 'Or have you murdered her?'

Richard joined in with Mercer's grating laughter, wishing the man would go away before he had no choice but to cave his head in with the heavy pestle and mortar he'd spotted on the side. 'No, no… Nothing that exciting.' He moved across the kitchen and stood by the doorway, hoping Mercer would take the hint. 'Anyway, thanks for popping over. It's been nice to see you. I might come down the club later and we'll arrange an evening with you and Sandra. I'll talk to Susan when she returns and see what dates she has free.'

'Super! Sandra will love that.'

Richard's heart sank when Mercer made no effort to move towards the door. He'd just have to come out with it and tell the overweight turd to bugger off, but he didn't want to alert the man, giving him any reason to think him on edge. But he was on edge. *Very*. He had to be out of here by tomorrow morning at the latest and still had loads to do yet. Facing facts, he wouldn't be able to come back for some time. *If ever*.

'By the way, you had a right odd looking chap hanging around outside,' Mercer said, finally moving his bulk towards the hallway.

Richard's senses prickled. 'Odd-looking? What do you mean?'

Mercer shrugged. 'I don't know really. He pulled across the end of your gateway in a white van.'

'Must have been a delivery,' Richard muttered.

Mercer shook his head dismissively. 'Funny kind of delivery without delivering anything… He was there a good half a minute before I reached the gates. I thought it a bit strange for someone to just be sitting there. I mean, wouldn't a delivery man actually get out of his damn van?' He raised his arms melodramatically, large sweat stains visible under the armpits of his blue shirt.

'Anyway,' Mercer continued, his voice taking on a dramatic tone. 'Because I thought it so weird, I peered through his window.' He shook his head in disbelief. 'The man immediately pretended to look at a map. Can you believe the cheek? He only did that because I looked in. Right savage-looking fella too. One of those with a stubbly face - you know the sort – the type who can't be bothered to shave, or more importantly, don't know how to!'

He tutted loudly. 'I mean, it doesn't take much effort to look presentable and urgh, that sort never bother! Long hair in a ponytail. I ask you, what sort of a man has long hair? It's not the 60s and even back then, I wouldn't have been seen *dead* looking so bloody scruffy! It's not a great advert for whatever firm he works for either. Fancy wearing a leather jacket! Ruffian.'

Richard felt sick. *Leather jacket? Long hair? Was it a bloody Reaper? There was a Reaper outside his house again? Oh no, no, NO!*

'I say, are you alright?' Mercer asked, concerned by the grey pallor spreading across Richard's face. 'Are you thinking it could have been one of those people, who – what do they call it, *case* houses? There's been a spate of that going on around here lately, so it could well have been an opportunistic thief! Don't worry – I scared him off. The minute he saw me looking he took off like a tornado.'

Richard finally dared to breathe. 'So, he's gone?'

Mercer nodded. 'Absolutely. He started the engine the minute he saw me, but gave me a horrible glare for good measure first. Very fierce-looking, sinister man that he was. But no, he wasn't risking hanging around once he knew I was on to him,' he added, puffing his chest out in self-righteousness.

'Good, good.' Richard's mind whirred rapidly. So, the man had gone, but if it was a Reaper – which sounded plausible, then he'd *definitely* be back. They must have discovered it was *him* who'd shot their president.

His breathing quickened. There was no time to waste. He had to get out of here today and Susan, whether she bothered coming back or not, would have to sort things out for herself. He wasn't wasting any more time waiting for her. Not now. *Sod her.*

Richard grabbed his holdall, leaving Mercer staring at him pointedly.

'What are you doing?' Mercer asked. 'Surely you're not letting some half-wit drongo scare you? Call the police if you're worried, but those scum won't dare come back now they know they've been spotted.'

Richard flushed crimson. 'I'm not *scared*, Mercer. I just don't particularly want to hang around wi...'

Richard froze mid-sentence as the top of Mercer's head exploded, the unmentionable contents of the inside of his skull splattering in slow-motion over the apple-white satin paint of his kitchen wall.

Ears ringing from the gunshot, Richard's eyes, despite not wanting to, involuntarily moved and he found himself staring down the double barrel of the shotgun now aimed at him.

· · · ·

WALKING INTO THE WHITE HART, Jorge was first struck by the subdued atmosphere. There was a marked difference to normal, but nothing that he could state as a blatant reason. Self-consciously moving to the bar, despite no one paying him more attention than usual, his internal guilt and the pressure of being involved in this whole situation pressed heavily at the base of his skull.

Sarah smiled warmly, adding to Jorge's suffocating guilt, but despite her usual friendliness, the spark usually present behind her hazel eyes was nowhere near as bright as normal and Jorge's heart accelerated in pace with the burgeoning dread of warning her of the impeding problems without completely dropping himself in it.

Even though there was a slight chance of explaining why he'd become involved in the first place, once he'd said what was needed to make sure the people he'd become so fond of did not fall foul of Neil's plans, he wouldn't get that chance. The sadness of leaving this area without being able to even *attempt* to half-justify his reasoning, with the general consensus of everyone believing he was a lying, snake-in-the-grass bastard, was something he'd just have to live with. If that meant no one else suffered from Neil Sparks' psycho plans, then it was the best outcome he could hope for.

What Carmen had confided had chilled him to the bone, but he suspected the small amount she'd disclosed why she was no longer at the Factory, the White Hart or with Noel, was merely the tip of the iceberg.

Shame burnt deeply. All he'd done was make matters worse, but the only one part of Neil Sparks' plan that Jorge wholeheartedly agreed with was his intentions towards Richard Stevens. That man deserved *everything* he had coming – plus more, but he had to warn them of everything and it had to be done *now*. He had to tell them before anyone else did. Or before anything else happened.

'And where were *you* last night?' Sarah asked, her voice stern.

Jorge flushed. *They knew. He was too late… He wouldn't even get to explain.* 'Listen… I…'

'Hey, chill out!' Sarah eyed Jorge strangely. 'I'm only joking. You don't have to explain yourself to me!'

Jorge smiled sadly, his internal panic lifting slightly. 'Sorry. A lot on my mind.'

'Your usual?' Sarah asked, holding up an empty pint glass. Jorge was usually so upbeat, but tonight he was acting oddly. *Defeated.* 'Are you alright?'

'I'd love a drink, but I can't,' Jorge said, his face serious. He glanced around, grateful for once there was no one breathing down his neck at the bar. 'Look, I need to speak to you urgently. Tori, too.'

Sarah frowned, worry glimmering. 'This sounds dubious. You'd best come out the back. I'll give Tori a shout - she's upstairs with Carmen's mother.'

'Carmen's mother?' Jorge yelped, walking through the bar hatch Sarah lifted up for him.

Sarah walked through the door leading to upstairs, gesturing for Jorge to follow. 'Tori!" she shouted up the staircase. 'Can I borrow you for a minute, please?' She turned to Jorge, her voice a whisper. 'Carmen's mother is staying for a while. She's got some problems with her husband and she's looking for Carmen as she's gone AWOL too - big problems with Noel.' Sarah tried to smile. 'You'd be surprised just how much can happen in a day and you've missed lots. It's all very complicated.'

'I saw Carmen earlier,' Jorge said as Tori made her way down the steep staircase. He could barely bring himself to meet her eyes with what he was supposed to be doing tonight. 'She told me what's happened – well, some of it.'

Tori's eyes widened. 'You've seen her? Where? Oh, I must tell Susan.'

'Wait, *please*!' Jorge raised his hand. 'I need to talk to you first. Do either of you know where Noel is?'

Sarah and Tori exchanged glances. They didn't know at this specific moment in time exactly where Noel was, but they knew where he'd been planning on going. Being as they hadn't heard anything to the contrary last night to suggest the job had already been done, then the presumption was it was happening today. He could even be doing it this very *minute*.

Sarah had been finding it difficult, almost impossible, seeing how scared Susan was about what Richard's reaction may be to her absence not to tell her she needn't worry and that he wouldn't be hurting her or *anyone* ever again, but she couldn't. She'd given Noel and Hunter her word and regardless of how painful it was watching Susan struggle with her well-founded fear, she had to get on with it. It also begged the question, whether they *ever* told Susan once the job was done? Could any of them *really* be sure she wouldn't react in a way to endanger them? Freak out and go to the police? Get Hunter and Noel – and probably all of them, sent to jail.

Sarah leant towards erring on the safe side; never letting Susan know who was behind Richard's sudden disappearance or what had happened, but that was something they'd discuss later. *One thing at a time.*

'Noel's out of town,' Tori said, stepping into the

conversation. 'We don't know when he'll be back.'

'Is he searching for Carmen?' Jorge asked, knowing they weren't levelling with him.

'What is it exactly you want him for? Is there something we can do?' Sarah added.

Jorge sighed. 'I was counting on Noel being around for the physical side of things. Hunter's a big bloke.'

Sarah frowned and looked at Tori, seeing a similar level of confusion. 'I'm not sure I underst…'

Sweat ran between Jorge's shoulder blades. 'We need to get Hunter out of the hospital.'

Tori nearly fell down the last couple of remaining steps. '*What? What do you mean? He's not well enough to leave the hospital. The doctors will never let him le…'

'We have no choice. We need him out of there. Like *now*!' Jorge said, his voice insistent. There wasn't time to analyse, deal with suspicion or Tori's panic. Pushing his snagging guilt to one side, he met Sarah's eyes. 'I need you to trust me on this. I know it sounds bizarre and not the best thing health-wise, but you've got to believe me when I say it's both necessary and urgent.'

'What's going on?' Tori cried, her eyes pleading.

Placing her hand on Tori's arm to try and keep the situation calm, Sarah could see by Jorge's face that now was not the time to push for details. 'Tell me this – how important is it?'

'Very,' Jorge answered quickly, wanting to shout at Sarah and Tori for their inability to understand the severity of the situation. Ok, so he hadn't given many details, but did he really have to spell it out?

'Is Hunter in danger?'

Jorge nodded. 'Yes. Grave danger.'

Tori clutched at Jorge's arm. 'What's going to happen? How do y…'

'Enough, Tori! Go and tell Susan we'll be back later. I'll tell Colin.' She glanced at Jorge. 'I can't ask him to help because he can't leave the pub, but I'll get one of the other

Reapers, shall I?'

'No,' Jorge said hastily. 'There'll be too many questions and we haven't got time. We'll manage. Please hurry. I'll be waiting in the car outside.'

Tori and Sarah exchanged worried glances as Jorge rushed back out into the bar.

THIRTY NINE

RICHARD'S HEAD SLAMMED REPEATEDLY against the wheel arch of the van as the vehicle careered around yet another corner. Bound at the ankles and the wrists, he could do little but roll around inside the cavernous interior whilst the savage driver took every corner as fast as possible and relished driving over every speed hump or pothole.

He longed to wipe the freely running blood streaming from his nose away from where it was soaking into the greasy rag stuffed half down his throat, but he couldn't. The strong metallic taste combining with the foul musty smell of whatever was on the gag made him feel even sicker and whatever the residue was covering the floor of the van was sticking to his face and stinging his eyes, making everything just that little bit worse.

Richard found himself absentmindedly wondering how Susan would deal with finding the body of Andrew Mercer on her kitchen floor when she returned. *That's if she ever did.*

The thought that she had left him took hold. Why else would she not have returned? Unless these people had her too? And if they did, then there was no way she could raise the alarm.

But what would the police do even if she could? Choosing

to inform Susan about nothing of what had been going on, she had little to tell them. Besides, telling the police would bring its own set of problems. Susan always talked too much and that would spell problems.

Richard refused to let the rising panic overwhelm him, but it was difficult because each time he stabilised his speeding mind with wisps of logic the suffocating panic returned with a vengeance. Whichever way he looked at it, his chances of successfully walking away from this didn't look too optimistic, but he couldn't think like that. He *refused* to think like that. Someone would sort this. They *had* to.

A tiny spark of resentment ignited. He'd been *so* close to getting away. *So close.* If Mercer hadn't slowed him up, then he might have disappeared before this ape had attacked him in his own home. Fighting against the hot tears threatening to spill down his bloodied face in a fit of self-pity, Richard's mind replayed the moment when the top of Mercer's head shattered like an eggshell; a glutinous mass of brains splattering against the wall as if the top of a food mixer had come loose mid-cycle.

Would the same befall him?

Tears finally escaped, running grooves down Richard's dusty cheeks.

The van abruptly came to a standstill and Richard struggled to get upright rather than give this sadist further satisfaction, but he couldn't, instead remaining face-down on the van's floor. *Like a bloody animal*, he thought angrily.

Blinking as the daylight seared his eyes after the darkness of the back of the van, Richard forced his eyes to adjust and focused on the man pulling him by his collar towards the gaping double doors. It was definitely the same man he'd seen in his very own kitchen all that time ago. For Christ's sake, if he hadn't put Matthew in charge of that bloody stupid property portfolio, then his son wouldn't have got mixed up with this bunch of cretins in the first place. This was all Matthew's fault.

He took in the swarthy features of his attacker and committed as many details to memory as possible for when he got out of this. Because he *would* get out of this one way or another. He *refused* to be beaten by someone of this ilk. It just wasn't feasible.

Wracking his brains back through the annals of time, Richard replayed the conversation he'd had with his son. *The man's name, what was it? Come on, think, THINK!*

Recollection dawning, Richard would have smiled, had it not been for the rag stuffed in his mouth. *Noel. This savage's name was Noel.* He remembered Matthew telling him who the ruffian was in his kitchen. *Yes, it was Noel.*

Well Noel, you won't beat me, Richard thought, resentment simmering.

His newly resurfaced confidence abruptly shattered when he was unceremoniously dragged from the back of the van by his hair and his eyes darted around seeing a large warehouse door directly in front of him.

He tried raising his hands to pull the filthy rag from his mouth, but with nerves getting the better of him, succumbed to the pure power of the man bending him double whilst effortlessly opening the lock of the warehouse door with one hand.

As the large metal doors noisily opened, Richard retched pointlessly, exhausted – fear rendering him weak. His stinging eyes looked around the hangar-like area that was all but empty, save a few chairs and workbenches covered with tools and boxes. *Was this where these filthy Reapers stored their ill-gotten gains?*

He wanted to laugh. It didn't look like they'd been doing too well, judging by their lack of stock… Most likely the police weren't aware of this secret Reaper location which could be a useful bargaining chip if he was arrested over the bank investigation.

The man quickly moved inside and Richard's thoughts were diverted by his hair being yanked once again, his bound legs causing him to fall to his knees to be dragged across the concrete floor.

Grateful when his hair was released he lay still, overriding the burning pain of his torn kneecaps, now rid of most of their skin and hearing the metal door clang shut and the buzz of a fluorescent overhead strip light fizzing into life, he waited apprehensively when the heavy echoing footsteps of the lunatic headed back towards him.

This man, this *Noel*, hadn't uttered a word. Even after Mercer had been shot and Richard was faced with the double barrel of a shotgun, the man had remained silent. Despite demanding to know what was going on, the man's only reaction was to club him with the butt of the rifle. The next thing he knew he'd been trussed up like a turkey and bundled into the van.

Richard's heart beat faster. He hadn't even locked the house. Anyone could be stealing his possessions as this very minute! This worry was rudely cut short when he was lifted from the floor and slammed into a plastic chair, unable to stop his already bound ankles being tied to a chair leg, forcing him into a painful, twisted angle.

With sweat pouring freely down his face, he made a muffled squawking sound as his arms were wrenched over his head and bent back almost double to be secured behind the chair, dislocating his shoulders.

Waves of nausea rose, realising whatever his theory was about getting out of here would be nowhere near quick enough. He'd never been good with pain and the smirk on the man's face made him suspect the cycle of agony had only just begun.

The material was tugged from Richard's mouth and although he gagged, he was glad to be free of the suffocating cloth. 'Why are you doing this?' he sobbed, the pain in his shoulders setting his entire body on fire. 'Don't you realise I know who you are?'

Noel's eyes narrowed into slits. 'I doubt that,' he growled, eyeing the shivering man with contempt. His hands shook with the overwhelming urge to remove the world of this miserable sick fuck immediately, but there was far too much he wanted to do first, plus a lot he needed to find out.

Richard's defiance overrode the pain. 'I recognise you. You might have forgotten, but *I* haven't. Your name's Noel, I know it is.' *Oh yes, this moron might think he had the upper hand, but he wouldn't soon – not once the police had hold of him.*

'Is that so?' Noel smirked at Richard's pointless attempt to assert his authority, coming to the conclusion that the man was more deluded that he'd first assumed. 'Who's in the better position here? You or me?'

'Look,' Richard reasoned. 'You'll get into a lot of trouble for this. Is it money you want? You were blackmailing my son, Matthew, if you remember? If you want more then that can be arranged, but you'll need to let me go.' *This ape would not be getting one more penny, but the greedy money-grabbing bastard hadn't the brains to work that out.*

Noel laughed, the throaty noise echoing around the cavernous space. 'You think that's what this is about?' He leant closer, his eyes scrutinising Richard for any resemblance, hoping against all odds to find none. *Thankfully he was right.* 'You owe me a *lot* more than money, you cunt,' he spat.

Richard flinched at Noel's face close-up. This creature really was a heathen; feral eyes like a wild animal – green and cat-like. *Revolting.* 'And why would that be?' What am I being blackmailed for this time?'

Noel fought the urge to rip this prick's nose off with his bared teeth. 'I'm not blackmailing you. I want answers.' His arm shot out, his hand closing tightly around Richard's throat. *Keep it calm, Noel. This is a long way from over.*

Gurgling, Richard rocked the chair in panic and fought to dislodge the man's vice like grip. 'Can't breathe... Can't...'

Dropping his grip, Noel inched closer. 'I've found something out that's upset me somewhat.'

Richard spluttered, gasping for breath as air forced its way down his half-flattened windpipe.

'Yeah,' Noel grinned, waiting until Richard's eyes, now holding no sense of defiance, met his. 'Much to my disappointment, I've just discovered that you're *my* father, which if you think back to how that could be possible, you'll know why I'm going to have to fucking kill you.'

AS HE WAITED, Neil could barely stop himself from scraping his nails down to the quick against the nasty plastic dashboard. He'd been here almost an hour and was in a good position to see anyone coming in or out without being in full view himself.

They wouldn't be too much longer and if he was right about what he expected to see, then he'd got his answers. And those answers were all he needed to know.

His breathing quickened as his rage grew. He'd never been double-crossed. Well, he had - by the fucking Reapers, but *never* by one of his own. Not that Jorge counted as that. He should never have been so stupid to allow him into the fold, son or no son and *regardless* of what John had organised.

Neil moved to rake his fingers through his hair, further angered to find he couldn't, courtesy of the hideous chavvy baseball cap still on his head. *Christ. If he was correct on his suspicions, then Jorge would be so dead.*

Neil had travelled to the White Hart as planned. Obviously, not inside but waited outside down the road, close enough to see the pub's front door.

His lip curled in derision. The place and general area was as grotty as he'd imagined. A shudder ran through him remembering his bitch of a wife frequented the shithole and he'd been glad he hadn't set eyes on *her* otherwise he couldn't honestly say he'd have been able to resist taking a well-aimed shot at her plastic fucking face. Thankfully he hadn't spotted her, but he *had* seen Jorge.

Watching carefully, he'd begun to think he'd been wrong with his theory. It was right for Jorge to put in an appearance at the pub before going off to do the job at the hospital. He'd have done the same thing himself, but when Jorge left the White Hart and got into his car, he hadn't moved. He'd just sat there with the engine running - waiting.

Waiting for what?

Neil's teeth clenched. His fucking lying shit of a son had been waiting for two tarts. At least that's what he'd presumed watching both women hurry from the pub and clamber in the back. Jorge was supposed to be taking out the target, not taking a couple of slags back to the flat – the flat that *he* paid for.

He'd successfully swallowed the urge to shoot Jorge in the back of the head there and then, but when the motor started moving, he'd followed.

It was worse than he'd expected. *Much* worse.

Following Jorge to the hospital, Neil had watched him *and* the women enter the building. He ground his teeth harder, the rasping noise making him even more stressed, his head pounding.

And now he was waiting...

Sensing sudden activity, he trained his eyes back on the hospital's double doors and seeing a group exit, his eyes squinted in the darkening twilight. *That fucker! That piece of shit, lying son of a bitch!*

He slammed his fist against the steering wheel. *He knew it. The stupid, stupid bastard.*

Neil focused on Jorge, the two women and then onto the fourth person; the man whose size dwarfed the well-built silhouette of his lying scumbag of a son. There he was, that fucker. The target - *Hunter.* Jorge was removing him from the hospital…

A sneer twisted Neil's mouth. Jorge Castello had just signed his own death warrant.

• • • •

HUNTER DIDN'T HAVE A PROBLEM being asked to leave the hospital; he'd been there far too long as it was, but what he did have a problem with was why it was needed and why Jorge was involved?

To take his leave, all he'd had to do was firmly tell the doctors he was going against their advice. He knew as well as they did they could not force him to remain, but the doctors made it *very* clear his decision was a big risk and not condoned. They'd also stated any complications arising from his self-discharge were *completely* his own responsibility.

Hearing this, Tori had panicked and Hunter admitted he'd been a bit harsh the way he'd spoken to her, but he'd had little choice. From Sarah's urgency and Jorge's body language he had to act, rather than worry whether it would cause problems later.

He glanced at Tori next to him in the back seat of Jorge's car, staring dully out of the window and guilt prickled. The last thing he'd wanted was to upset her, but there had been no time for discussion. Wincing, he reached over, gently touching her face, saddened at her slight flinch. Everybody was on edge, including himself and it was horrible. Whatever was going on had to stop. If discharging himself helped achieve that, then so be it.

Taking Tori's hand, Hunter squeezed it, gladdened to see a small smile as she turned towards him. How he'd love to wrap her up in his arms and kiss her. Take her to bed. *God, he'd missed her.*

He watched the houses and streetlamps rush by as the car sped towards the White Hart, much preferring to go to their own place where he and Tori could have some peace and much needed privacy, but that out of the question, at least until they got to the bottom of everything. Even the Factory wasn't an option until he knew what was going on. And he didn't because no one had spoken a word since getting into the car.

'Is anyone going to tell me what the fuck's happening?' Hunter growled.

'Something was due to happen at the hospital…' Jorge muttered, his jaw clenching. He glanced in his rear view mirror, his eyes momentarily meeting the cold grey of Hunter's. 'I'll tell you everything but only once we're back. Just let me drive.'

Tori turned her face back to the window so no one would see the tears escaping from her eyes. *Was this ever going to stop?*

• • • •

THE TAXI HAD barely stopped before Carmen shoved the fare into the driver's hand and clambered out of the back seat. 'If I'm not back in five minutes, then go, but please wait until then. This extra should cover your waiting time.'

She'd already wasted enough time waiting to get a taxi from the little town where she was staying and she could ill afford to waste more. If her mother wasn't in, then she couldn't afford to wait possibly for *hours* for another taxi. She needed to get her mother away from her father and also needed to let the others know that Luca was the one behind everything and his spy, Jorge had wormed his way into everyone's confidence – including *hers*.

Carmen ran up the long driveway, her feet slipping on the deep gravel and her heart sunk seeing the Aston Martin parked by the house. *Did that mean her father was at home?* The Jag was missing though.

Nerves jangling, she hammered on the door, surprised when it swung open.

She paused, her heart hammering and faltered on the threshold, straining her ears for any sound coming from within.

'Mum?' Carmen's voice echoed up the long hallway as she slowly made her way inside.

Trepidation raced as her calls went unanswered, the sound of her footsteps on the wooden floor, loud in the silence. 'Mum?' she repeated, this time a little quieter. *Something was wrong. Why was the door open?* The door was *never* left open. Her mother was one of those people who constantly checked it was locked.

She was being ridiculous. It could be as simple as her father had pulled the door on their way out and forgotten to check it. But what if her parents were out and someone had broken in? What if a burglar was still in here?

She glanced through the door into the lounge, relieved to see nothing had been disturbed and everything looked as it should. But then sickness washed over her. What if Luca was the one who'd broken in looking for her and was hiding upstairs?

Carmen stopped at the far end of the hall. Her mother wasn't here and she didn't want to hang around. The taxi should still be waiting – she'd only been a couple of minutes.

About to retrace her steps she was overwhelmed by the sudden urge to have a quick look in the kitchen before she left just to be sure everything was fine.

Carmen stuck her head around the door and when the bloody mess on the walls and the twisted body of an overweight man lying face down on the tiled kitchen floor came into view, a silent scream lodged in her throat like a fish bone and she staggered back against the doorframe in terror.

FORTY ONE

'WHAT ARE YOU TALKING ABOUT?' Richard blathered. 'How on earth could I possibly be your father?'

'Don't insult me any more than you already have done, you cunt,' Noel spat. Squatting to his haunches, he rested level with Richard, not appreciating the ill-concealed contempt visible on the man's blood-stained face. He tapped hard on the side of Richard's left temple. 'Have a think about it and try again… Go on…'

Richard stared at Noel incredulously. *What on earth was this idiot thinking?* Regardless of the unfavourable position he was in he would not tell this moronic freak he was his father purely to please him. 'Look lad, I don't know your circumstances, but I can assure you th…'

'You're not fucking listening.' Noel slammed his fist into Richard's chest, knocking him backwards still attached to the chair. He then landed one of his steel toe-capped boots hard into Richard's stomach. 'You killed my mother with what you did to her!' he screamed.

Richard heaved, the side of his face pressed into the dusty concrete of the warehouse floor. This person was insane. How could he reason with someone clearly mentally ill? Possibly even a paranoid schizophrenic? They were really dangerous that lot were. He'd read about in a *Readers Digest* a year or so ago. Incapable of normal thought processes; hearing voices and everything. Unusually violent too…

Fear churned. He had to get through to this man. It must be possible he had occasional lucidity? 'I haven't killed your mother! I don't even know who sh…'

'I said, what you *did* killed her… Try and think… Does the name Leila Cooper ring a bell in your fucking head?' As much as it pained Noel uttering his mother's name out loud, it was time for answers.

The blood drained from Richard as sure as if a plug had been wrenched from an overflowing bathtub. *Leila Cooper? The gypsy girl? Oh shit… That time in the woods? She'd got pregnant? Oh shit, shit, fucking shit.*

Noel smiled ferociously watching the truth dawn in Richard's mind. 'Now do you want to talk sensibly?' he growled.

Richard's mouth flapped open and shut soundlessly. *Fuck. What should he do? Deny it? Say it was someone else? What? Quickly!* If he could convince this ape it wasn't as it seemed then he could turn all of this around, couldn't he?

Interrupted from his crashing thoughts when Noel's large hand crushed back around his throat once more and pulled him back into a sitting position, Richard's eyes bulged in pure terror.

'Are you going to explain yourself wanker, or am I assuming you have nothing to say?' Noel spat, his eyes burning black holes into Richard's skull.

'Urgh,' Richard mumbled, desperate to get the point across that he was willing to talk and hoped his beseeching expression would resonate somewhere in the man's mind. 'URRRGHH!' he squawked more urgently.

Dropping his grasp around Richard's windpipe, Noel smiled thinly. 'Go on then, let's hear it!'

'W-Why you think it's me?' Richard gabbled. He'd have held his hands out in a pleading gesture if they weren't securely attached to the chair. 'I know you must be angry and I cannot blame you, but you've got it all wrong.'

Noel's eyes narrowed. As predicted, the prick was trying to wheedle his way out of it, but it wouldn't work. He'd let him think he was prepared to listen though. This tosspot's excuses would only rile him further and that was just fine.

Noel's silence gave Richard a small morsel of hope. He'd tell this man whatever he wanted to hear if it meant he could get out of here.

'Please, you've got to believe me,' Richard begged, forcing himself to meet Noel's rabid eyes. *The man who was his son.* Dear God. Fancy that! How could it be possible his decent genes helped create such scourge of the earth? It showed how dominant filthy gypsy blood was in securing their tainted line if it overruled decent traits that fifty percent of his DNA should have contributed. Christ, imagine if *this* got out? Imagine if people discovered he'd fathered this... this *thing*?

'I'm waiting, dickhead, but won't stand here all day!' Noel prodded Richard hard in the chest.

Flinching, Richard dared a slight apologetic smile. 'I'm sorry. It's a horrible thing for you, but you've got the wrong information.' *How he hated apologising to a low-life such as this.* 'I believe that many years ago, your people – the Reapers, I mean, disposed of the person you're looking for. Maybe they didn't tell you, I don't know?' Richard tried to shrug, wincing as he attempted to force his dislocated shoulders to rise. 'I'm ashamed to admit that I was aware of what happened to your mother and I should have reported Jack Jacobs to the police, but I... I was scared...' he lied.

Feeling confident he'd got Noel's attention, Richard continued. 'Your mother was a lovely woman. I remember her from our college days, but I had no idea that anything had happened to her after... after than terrible incident... Did she have an accident or did sh...'

Richard's head snapped back as Noel backhanded him. 'Don't you *dare* spout how lovely my mother was. I never knew her. She killed herself after I was born.'

Richard ran his tongue around the inside of his mouth, tasting blood. *Hardly surprising she'd killed herself, giving birth to you,* he thought viciously, wisely not voicing his opinion. 'I'm so sorry to hear that. Maybe if I'd reported Jack then your mother wouldn't ha…'

Before he knew what had happened, Richard was on his back on the floor, searing pain in his jaw where Noel had just driven his fist. Yowling in pain, he knew without checking that he'd lost some teeth. Blinding flashes of pain and light ricocheted through his skull as the back of his head was slammed repeatedly on the floor. 'STOP!' he shouted, panic rising like a cloud of dust.

With one knee on Richard's chest, Noel poised himself over the prone man and looked down with pure hatred. 'You fucking coward! It wasn't Jack Jacobs because the guy who ordered the hit admitted a mistake had been made.'

The crushing weight on his chest lifted as Noel got to his feet and slowly walked to a cupboard and Richard strained to hear what was being said over the banging noise in his head.

'Yeah, it was known Jack Jacobs was the wrong target pretty early on.'

Richard blinked when Noel span around, a baseball bat in his hand. *That bat… It was… It was covered in something.*

Noel moved closer, a maniacal grin on his face and Richard began shaking. He didn't want to shake. He didn't want to show this lunatic his fear, but he wasn't in control. He couldn't stop the trembling. 'But, wait… I…'

'And you shot Hunter. Getting away with raping my mother wasn't enough for you, so you decided to shoot him as well? Scared he would expose you for what you are, were you?'

'No! I…'

'You see, Hunter did the hit on Jacobs and spent a very long time trying to locate who he *should* have taken out. Eventually he got it on good authority that it was you…'

'I-I didn't mean to shoot him. I was merely defending

myself. He was trying to kill me. I know that you're angry, but you've got the wrong person.'

'No, I fucking haven't!'

Richard feared he would projectile vomit. This wasn't going anywhere near the way he'd hoped.

Noel raised the baseball bat and smiled. 'As you seem reticent to speak the truth, maybe you need a bit of help?'

Richard's eyes widened as Noel advanced, now able to see what the wooden object in his hand was wrapped with. 'NO!' he yelled, fear raging. *Barbed wire. It was covered with barbed wire!* 'Don't be crazy! Are you trying to kill me?'

'That's the general idea,' Noel laughed, bringing the bat down hard on Richard's right dislocated shoulder, smiling as the sharp barbs cut into his flesh. 'But not just yet...'

'Aaargh!' Richard wailed, the pain intense, blood seeping through his shirt sleeve. 'Don't. *Don't!*' he gibbered, seeing Noel raise the bat again.

Noel grinned in satisfaction. How he'd missed this. There was little better than smashing an utter bastard to ribbons. He'd play the game though and let this perverted fuckhead think there was a chance he could walk away if he played his cards right.

'Ok, well... let's have a think...' Noel pulled a pair of pliers from his pocket and held them up inches from Richard's bright red sweaty face. 'How about these? Fancy a pedicure?'

'W-What?' Richard babbled, unsure whether he wanted to focus on what else this lunatic had in his hand.

Noel squatted down and expertly untied the shoelaces of Richard's right shoe. 'Hmm, this is never a very pleasant part of the activity.'

'W-What are you doing?' Richard cried indignantly, failing to move his foot away from Noel's grip. *What was this maniac doing?*

Everything became clear when Noel ripped off Richard's sock and without warning, removed the nail from his big toe. Pain rolled in waves and Richard screamed, the noise echoing loudly through the warehouse.

Smashing Richard in the face with the barbed wire-covered bat, this time against the cheek, blood cascaded from the jagged tears. 'Shut up dickhead, you're putting me off... Teeth next...'

Richard heaved with fear and pain as his terror gained pace like a giant snowball. 'Aight, ceez aight!' he gabbled as Noel loomed closer, pliers raised and grabbed his face with one hand. He was unable to form the words thanks to nicotine-tasting fingers in his mouth forcing his already painful jaw apart. Raw pain shot down the side of his mouth from exposed nerves of his newly missing teeth.

He would be tortured and die slowly. He'd have preferred to be shot like Mercer - at least that was over quickly. *Not like this...*

To his horror, Richard felt a warm sensation as his ability to control his bladder abandoned him and a mixture of desperation and abject humiliation engulfed him. Even that was nowhere near enough to divert his spiralling panic.

Noel paused. 'Of course, if you tell me the truth and I *mean* the truth, then things might not be as bad for you.'

Making a yowling noise, Richard tried to nod his head, but couldn't move it under Noel's powerful grip.

'No? Oh, ok then!' Noel rammed the pliers into Richard's mouth, enjoying smashing them against a tooth. He knew Richard was trying to nod, but would pretend he hadn't noticed. The trick was how to keep his cool until he'd got all the answers if this mug admitted doing what he was suspected of.

Bloody hard, but he'd do it.

Noel spotted the spreading wet patch on Richard's crotch and scowled. 'You dirty bastard! You've pissed yourself. It had best not have gone on my shoes!'

'Nnnh, NNNHHHH!!' Richard garbled. *The pliers were in his mouth. They were in his fucking mouth! Oh God. He couldn't stand it!* His tongue pushed pointlessly against the cold metal, whilst the pliers rooted around, cracking and scraping and grasping for his teeth. 'Nnnnn, NNNNNNH!'

Stopping, Noel raised an eyebrow and peered down into

Richard's face. 'Are you saying something?'

'Nnngh, NNNNGH!' Richard repeated, hoping his eyes conveyed to the lunatic that *yes*, he was trying to say something.

Noel removed the pliers. 'Go on then.'

'W-What do you want to know?' Richard stuttered.

Noel gritted his teeth. He wanted this cunt to tell him the *real* truth about Leila – his mother. He wanted him to admit what he'd done. He wanted to hear the words coming from between this bastard's lying lips with his own ears. And then he wanted to smash what teeth the prick had left down his gullet and laugh as he choked. But he hadn't forgotten what he'd promised.

He brought the barbed wire-covered baseball bat down on Richard's other cheek – hard enough to shatter the bone and tear another gaping wound.

'AAARGH!' Richard screamed, his eyes bulging. 'You said you'd…'

'I'm waiting, but you're taking too fucking long!' Noel snarled.

'Ok, ok!' Richard garbled. The very act of speaking was difficult. He felt like crying. This man would rip him to pieces, but if he kept his cool and didn't panic, if he overrode the agony of what this monster had done, then *he'd* be the one in control, not this idiot and he felt slightly calmer with the realisation.

Noel sensed Richard's whirring brain. *The cheeky bastard still believed he'd got something to bargain with?* Folding his arms across his wide chest, he paced slowly over to the workbench and leant against it. 'What do you know about Matt's kid?'

Richard blinked. *He hadn't expected that.* 'What do you mean?'

Noel smirked. 'Ok, come now. You can't tell me you've forgotten your grandson died, surely?'

'Of course not, it's hardly likely that I wo…'

'Cut the crap!' Noel barked. 'I wouldn't have been best pleased either if I found out it weren't *my* son's kid!'

Richard eyed Noel suspiciously. *Was this a set up?* This man was clearly unhinged and it was difficult to gauge which way he would go, although he must believe he was innocent where Leila was concerned, otherwise surely he'd be pressing for more? If he really thought it *was* him, then he had no doubt he wouldn't still be sitting here.

'And then there was Tori.' Noel continued. 'What do you know about that? She said you tried to force yourself on her.'

'I most certainly did *not*!' Richard spluttered. 'I never once touched the girl, the nasty little bitch.' *So, he was right. Victoria had put this bunch of heathens up to this.* 'I suppose it was *her* spouting this clap trap about Jack Jacobs too?'

Noel shrugged, his face neutral. *The twat was playing right into his hands - Tori had never said anything like that.* 'I personally don't give a fuck about the silly cow. She's not my type. I've always despised her and would rather cut my own cock off than put it anywhere near *her*!'

'I swear, I did not touch the stupid girl!' Richard insisted, his anger resurfacing. 'She's a manipulative liar –like her mother!'

Noel lounged lazily against the workbench, his knuckles clenching behind his back in suppressed rage. *Come on, cock-end, spill it out.* 'That's one thing we agree on then.'

Richard paused, feeling relief that this moron hated Victoria as much as he did. 'I suppose you lot have to put up with her now?'

'Nothing to do with me. Besides, no one's seen hide nor hair of her since you shot our president. Hunter didn't want Tori around anyhow. She was only a shag!' Noel lied, guilt stabbing, but if his lies gleaned the truth, then he'd done his job.

Richard felt familiar stirrings of resentment over Victoria and the trouble she'd caused Matthew. The grief her whole *family* had brought was immeasurable. 'It might have helped if your mate hadn't got her pregnant,' he snapped.

'Hunter wanted Tori to get rid when he learnt she was pregnant. He didn't want a fucking kid. Especially not with her!

Everyone would have been better off if she'd stayed in that loony bin. By the way, she said you were behind that,' Noel growled.

Richard laughed, despite himself. *Maybe this boy had certain traits of his after all?* 'I wish I had, but it was Matthew. I must say I was very impressed by how well he engineered it. I couldn't have done it better myself.'

Noel faked a grin, when really he wanted to slice the fucker's face off, but he thought he was on side, which was good. 'That must have been well thought out. Probably why it was more believable that *you* were the one behind it.'

Richard bristled. 'It was probably the only useful thing Matthew did,' he muttered bitterly.

'Oh, I don't know…' Noel drawled. *This might work. The prat was so pompous it could just play in his favour.* Even though he wasn't remotely superstitious, he found himself crossing his fingers behind his back as he prepared to say things that even thinking of made him feel horrible. 'He offloaded the bloody kid alright though? Bet that was a relief? I know it was for the rest of us. That little bitch would have attached herself to Hunter for ever because of the fucking brat otherwise and now she can't.'

Richard's chin jutted out in indignation. '*That* wasn't Matthew. You should have seen him. He was unhappy discovering he wasn't the father. Ridiculous! I *told* him it made little difference. No one would know unless he told anyone.'

Noel waited with bated breath, forcing himself to act like he was actually having a normal conversation with this bastard. He needed to hear it from his mouth. He needed to hear Stevens admit *he'd* killed the child.

Richard's mind replayed the disappointment of realising Matthew was losing his ability to play the game and act upon what was needed. The fact that his own son would let something so damn trivial get to him and risk affecting the family and his career still stuck in his throat. 'It was pathetic!' he spat, his eyes dark. 'All those years and then he lets me down over something like that? Victoria was always a little whore masquerading as butter wouldn't melt, but she didn't fool me. That slag was destroying our family and Matthew was close to allowing her to, so I had no choice but to solve the problem.'

Noel pretended to act surprised and was unsure how he'd not already wrung the paunchy bastard's neck. 'So, *you* killed the kid?'

Richard sneered. 'I could hardly let it continue living under my roof, not with Matthew being so weak, could I?'

Noel shrugged, getting off the subject before his will to remain together broke. 'I guess not. Tori wasn't happy though.'

Richard scowled. 'Well, she wouldn't be. That kid was her bargaining chip! Not any more though. Besides, she was never all the ticket, that girl. Susan, that's my wife – she's just as bloody bad; wailing left, right and goddamn centre. The kid wasn't even a relation, the stupid cow! I tell you, don't bother with women. They're more trouble than they're worth.'

Noel bit against his cheek. Because of what this piece of shit had done, he could not have the woman he wanted. His rage spiked further. There was only to so long he could keep up the pretence of reaching common ground with this grade A wanker. 'Did you not feel bad? I mean, killing someone is one thing, but a kid?'

'*No one* ruins what I've worked for,' Richard scowled, his eyes hard. He was on a roll and had almost forgotten the bizarre situation he was in. It felt good getting all of this shit off his chest. 'People just want, want, *want*! You don't understand the pressure all the bloody time. Susan's bleating of, *I want this, I want that*. Family... keeping up appearances... The list is endless.'

Noel smiled calmly. 'I don't hesitate removing anyone who's in my way either.'

'Well, maybe you do take after me after all?' Richard said, more relaxed than he thought possible. It was only when Noel lurched forward that he realised the grave error he'd made.

The bat connected against Richard, the barbs tearing deeply

into his flesh. 'That's what I wanted to hear - you finally admitting it, you son of a bitch!' Noel growled, pushing Richard off his chair onto the floor, his head hitting the concrete with a sickening thud whilst the barbed wire covered bat continued to rain agonising blows to his face and body.

Richard howled, his head splitting with roaring pain.

Grabbing the back of the chair, Noel dragged Richard towards the side door. 'You raped my mother!' he roared, spittle spraying from his mouth.

Richard was too incensed to think rationally any longer. 'So fucking what? Acting virtuous she was, the gypsy bitch. Well, fuck that! I only gave her what Jack Jacobs was thick enough to wait for, the silly bastard. Who did she think she was, the stupid cow?'

Noel's anger flashed white. He wanted to crush the life out of this piece of shit, but there was still one more question. 'And what about Jeanie? Know anything about that, do you? Offloaded her because she knew your secrets?'

'She was another silly bitch, turning up out of the woodwork and trying to blackmail me. I've had enough of people using things against me,' Richard spat.

'And Matt? Did you top him too?' Noel asked. This twat was haemorrhaging information, so he might as well find out all he could.

'I wish I bloody well had, the useless boy. I did everything for him! He was set up for life, yet I still had to wipe his arse. I should have strangled him at birth!'

Noel frowned and stared at Richard with ill-hidden contempt. This prick was more demented than he'd thought.

'I've answered your questions, so now let me go,' Richard said, folding his arms petulantly.

'Yep, you're right.' Noel kicked the side door of the warehouse open.

Richard gasped with relief as bright daylight scorched his face and even the wracking pain of his body didn't dampen his enthusiasm. He knew it. He knew he'd get out of here, although for a short amount of time he'd worried that his plan wouldn't pull off after all. 'You need to assure me there will be no more of this rubbish. You've got the information you wanted, but don't think you're owed anything else because you won't get it,' he continued. He wasn't having this eejit sniffing round for handouts or playing his mouth.

Noel smiled despite his burning rage. This ponce was almost funny. Releasing his grip from the back of the chair, he yanked open the top of an industrial skip at the side of the building.

The crash of the metal lid ricocheted through Richard's throbbing brain. 'Are you getting me off this stupid chair? You said th…'

Spinning around, Noel effortlessly sliced through the restraints, sneering as Richard shook his hands to get his circulation flowing.

'By rights I should demand compensation for what you've put me through,' Richard said, his nose wrinkling up with revulsion as he eyed the state of his missing toenails.

Noel shook his head in disbelief. *This guy was something else.* 'What are you thinking of? Calling the police? That would go down well, considering what you've just admitted.'

Richard's mouth twisted into a sneer. 'It's only *your* word on that.'

Noel ignored the comment. The quicker he finished this, the better. He'd kept his rag for a record length of time. Bending down, he grabbed Richard by the shirt and yanked him to his feet.

Richard stumbled, his stiff legs struggling to take the sudden weight of his own body. 'Aaargh! What are y…'

'Shut up, fuck ya!' Noel roared, pulling Richard towards the skip. 'You *really* think you get to walk away from this, you piece of shit?'

A ball of panic reignited in Richard's gut. 'But we agreed th…'

Noel laughed, this time heartily. 'You should have had

more sense than to trust someone like *me*, shouldn't you?'

An all over tremor started as Richard saw Noel's naked hatred burning brightly and the truth seeped into his brain, his bravado evaporating as quickly as his shakes had begun. 'But… No… Wait… I'm your father…'

'Don't *ever* insult me like that!' Noel hissed. 'You may have forced me into my mother and caused her death, but you'll *never* be my father. Do you understand?'

Richard nodded hastily. 'Ok, ok, whatever you say. I…' Before he could finish, Noel's large fist smashed his nose. Reeling, he stumbled backwards and fell heavily, landing painfully onto his shoulder. 'Wait! WAIT!' he bleated, his eyes streaming.

Yanking Richard to his feet by his throat, in addition to the smashed bones and blood, Noel enjoyed the look of pure terror now ingrained heavily on this hated man's face. 'I'm done with waiting,' he spat, dragging Richard up the three metal steps to the large skip.

Richard's arms flailed wildly in all directions. He was being dumped in a skip? No, he couldn't be? He might be stuck in there for days, or perhaps for ever?

He could do nothing as Noel lifted him by the waistband of his torn and urine-soaked trousers and threw him headfirst into the large metal container.

Richard blinked painfully, finding himself surrounded by blackness. *Was he dead? Was this what it was like?*

He touched his head; his dislocated shoulder making the movement painful beyond words and gingerly pressed a new lump on the back of his head. *Where was he?*

Confused and disorientated, he adjusted his eyes to the darkness, heartened to see thin strips of light in a rectangular shape several feet above him. *The skip. The lunatic had dumped him headfirst into the skip.*

He must have lost consciousness for a moment there, but how long had he been here for? The slivers of light signified daylight, but was it the same day or had he been stuck in here for longer?

Straining his ears, he listened for outside noise but could hear nothing, so felt around where he lay. Just a few bits; maybe some wood and something metal too? Could he get up and push the lid of the skip open and haul himself out? It would be difficult and damned painful with his shoulders in this state, but he wasn't rotting away in here.

Sweat beaded on Richard's brow, his face tight from the thick covering of crusted dried blood. If it was locked, he'd bang on the side wall until someone heard. There were other industrial units around here so someone would hear and rescue him.

It was going to be alright.

. . . .

NOEL LEANT AGAINST the outside wall of the warehouse and slowly smoked a cigarette. He tuned his hearing into the muffled sounds coming from within the skip and a smile spread across his face. The prat was moving around, so it would only be a matter of time before banging on the skip started. He could bang all he liked. No one would help him.

All the neighbouring firms knew who owned this unit and knew better than to question anything. They'd happily turn a blind eye to any unusual noises coming from within the Reapers' compound, so Richard-arsehole-Stevens would be in for a very long and fruitless wait if he played that game. *Not that he'd get the option.*

Noel sneered. He'd love to leave the cunt to sweat it out for a day or so and then return to slowly beat the bastard to the most painful death imaginable, but alas - current timeframes did not allow for that extension of enjoyment. There were far too many people waiting on him wrapping this up sooner rather than later, so he'd have to settle with the next best thing.

This method would not be anywhere near as drawn out and fitting of Stevens' crimes, but it *would* be excruciatingly painful for the short amount of time it lasted.

Grinding the remains of his cigarette on the floor, Noel grabbed a jerry can he'd placed by the warehouse door and in long confident strides, made his way back to the skip. As predicted, banging on the metal roof started and his irritation prickled. Pulling the heavy bolt back, he yanked up the metal lid and peered down into the blackness.

'Enough's enough!' Richard barked from somewhere in the gloom. 'Let me out!'

Noel chuckled. He could see Richard below, his eyes screwed up against the bright daylight foisted on him. 'You still don't get it, do you?' Unscrewing the jerry can, he sluiced it over the figure below.

'What the...' Richard wailed, his indignation of being soaked quickly changing to pure terror as the pungent and unmistakeable fumes of petrol assailed his nostrils. 'AAARGH! NO! NO! You wouldn't! You wou...'

'Shut the fuck up!' Noel roared unperturbed, watching the cowering man in the darkness scrabble out of the direct line of the descending petrol.

He shook the can, making sure every single drop was emptied. The bastard was soaked more than enough to do the job, so he reached for the box of matches from his pocket. He wasn't wasting his zippo on a turd like this.

'Don't do this. Come on, *please*!' Richard screamed, his voice hoarse as he fought against the overpowering fumes surrounding him. 'My eyes! It's gone in my eyes! What have you done, you stupid bastard? You've got to help me, *please*. I'm sorry... I'm...'

'You've got to be kidding, right? Burn in hell, you piece of shit!' Noel roared. Lighting a match, he wasted no time flicking it into the skip, staying where he was long enough to see the petrol ignite with a loud whooshing noise.

Stepping back, Noel pulled down the lid of the skip and shot the bolt home, leaving the pleading man alone with the flames.

Holding the empty can, he walked to the side door of the warehouse, choosing to spend a few more minutes listening to the panicked banging and the animal-like wailing now coming from inside the skip, signifying the flames had found their host.

FORTY TWO

IT HAD TAKEN A fair bit of effort to get Hunter up the back entrance of the White Hart. She'd always disliked the separate doorway accessible via the narrow alleyway at the side of the pub, giving access directly to upstairs. It was an easy option to anyone trying their luck with breaking into the pub in the middle of the night, but now she was grateful for it. Had they only had the choice of entering through the bar, then everyone would know of Hunter's return and they needed to keep that under wraps for the time being.

This old staircase hadn't been used for years and Sarah only hoped the old floorboards hadn't been attacked by woodworm and would withhold everyone's weight as they slowly inched up the steps.

'I can manage,' Hunter grumbled, trying to shake off the many pairs of hands.

As they climbed higher, Sarah rolled her eyes at Hunter's stubbornness. A good sign he was returning to normal.

Brushing a cobweb from her hair she was glad to finally make it to the top and into the lounge, doubly glad to see Colin had done what she'd asked and kept Susan out of the way. Hell knows how she was faring being downstairs in the tap room with everyone else, but that was the least of her worries right now.

Sarah glanced at an ashen-faced Tori. 'Get settled and put the kettle on. I'll just tell Colin we're back.' She looked at Jorge. 'And then you're going to fill us in with what you know.'

Turning on her heels, Sarah ran down the other staircase that led into the bar. 'We're back!'

Colin looked up, a beer towel in his hand as he replenished the shelves with clean glasses. 'Everything ok?'

Sarah moved closer, putting her arms around Colin. 'Not really. I've yet to discover the latest, but I just wanted to let you know that we're here.' To say she was uncomfortable with what Jorge had said was an understatement and the prospect of hearing the rest was not sitting well in her mind.

Colin kissed the top of his wife's head, then nodded in the direction of Susan perched on top of a bar stool, her eyes fixed on a beer mat and her hands clasped tightly around the stem of one of the few wine glasses they had left. 'Not much to report here. As you can see, Susan's having a *wonderful* time…'

Sarah couldn't help but grin. Susan certainly didn't look very relaxed. 'How many has she had?'

Colin grimaced. 'Not enough to stop her looking so freaked out, that's for sure!'

Sarah laughed despite herself. 'I'd better go back up and listen to the latest.'

'Wait for me, then!' Noel barked, approaching the bar, his eyes cold.

'Noel!' Sarah exclaimed, unsure from his expression whether things had been dealt with or not. 'You're back! Come on up.'

'N-Noel?' Leaping from her bar stool, Susan rushed over, her bony fingers clawing at Noel's arm. 'Are you my Carmen's Noel? Please tell me you know where she is? I'm terrified something's happened to her. My husband, he…'

'Now's not a good time, Susan,' Sarah interrupted. Susan's wraith-like presence had made her all but invisible until now.

317

She'd been stupid yelling Noel's name - she should have known Susan would overhear and react. She looked at Colin for support and then at Noel, a nerve twitching below his eye.

'What do you mean it's not a good time?' Susan wailed. 'If this young man knows where my daughter is, then I…'

'Come and sit back down.' Colin took Susan's arm whilst Sarah quickly ferried Noel through the door to upstairs. 'Something really important is going on at the moment and th…'

Something more important than my daughter being missing? That was *him* wasn't it? That's the man Carmen's involved with? Why won't anyo…'

'Let me get you another drink.' Colin all but forced Susan back on her bar stool, already sensing the surrounding atmosphere had quietened. The last thing anyone needed was bringing attention to what was going on, not that he knew half of it – or even a *quarter* of it, but something was definitely not right. Whatever it was appeared to have complicated fourfold in the last couple of hours.

'I'm sure Tori and Sarah will explain everything as soon as they can.' *That was a lie.* Colin wasn't sure about anything. All he knew was that Hunter had been sneaked upstairs when he should still be in hospital, Jorge had something of utter importance to explain and Carmen had disappeared after discovering she'd been sleeping with her own brother. He really didn't want to have to explain to Susan about *that* and asking Noel about his relationship with her daughter was not great timing either. In fact, there would never be a good time to ask him about that.

Colin raked his hand over his thinning hair and topped up Susan's wine glass, hoping he could get her to drink more in record speed. With any luck then she'd be incapable of asking questions that he didn't have the answer to. And he certainly didn't want to answer the ones that he *did*.

FORTY THREE

'IT'S DONE,' Noel said, grinding out his cigarette in Sarah's ashtray. He locked eyes with Hunter. 'You were right about your suspicions.' He felt oddly deflated, expecting to feel relief or achievement now Stevens was dead; a closure to all the years of need for retribution for his mother, but he felt numb. For once retaliation hadn't brought any closing of doors.

'So, he's dead?' Hunter growled, his fist clenching as it always did when Richard Stevens was the topic of conversation.

Noel nodded, his eyes flashing. 'He raped my mother, he killed your kid and he killed Jeanie, so yes, he's dead.' He glanced at Tori. 'And he fucking hated you.'

Tori flinched. She knew Richard Stevens hated her, but had underestimated quite how much. He'd hated her so much he'd killed her baby. She'd half-expected that to be the truth, but it didn't stop pain from surging once again from deep within her soul.

Sarah expelled a deep breath, the relief rolling off her in waves. 'Thank God,' she cried cheerfully. 'It's over. All this shit and game playing is done.'

Standing up, she smiled brightly. She never thought she'd feel quite so exhilarated hearing of someone's death, but this was definitely an exception and one she wanted to celebrate. She wouldn't taint the moment by thinking about how or when the subject should be broached with Susan. *Not now.* 'What's saying I go and grab a couple of bottles of bubbly? I think this calls for a bit of a toast, don't you? We can now all finally relax.'

Jorge fidgeted. He'd worked up the courage knowing he'd got to tell everyone what he knew but Noel's sudden arrival had deflected it. He glanced at the faces surrounding him, well aware he was about to spoil their relief and wished he could think of a reason not to utter a word.

Taking a deep breath, Jorge spoke. 'Before you celebrate, I need to explain some things.'

Hunter focused his hard stare on Jorge. 'You think I'd forgotten that? I've been waiting to find out what was so urgent to ask me to discharge myself from hospital, so get on with it!' He glanced at Tori, seeing her nervousness and adjusted himself to a more comfortable position to give her hand a reassuring squeeze.

'I'm intrigued too,' Noel muttered, glaring at Jorge. 'I was surprised to find Hunter here. No one told me of this change of plan.'

'We didn't know ourselves until a couple of hours ago,' Sarah said, her eyes also fixing on Jorge.

Jorge shuffled uncomfortably under the scrutiny of so many pairs of eyes. *No pressure...*

'We're waiting...' Hunter said, popping two painkillers from a blister packet into his mouth and swallowing them dry.

Jorge hesitated, then met Hunter's eyes. 'Ok, here goes... Someone put a hit on you. The original hitman postponed. I'm not exactly sure why, but I'm guessing it was because you were in hospital, but he...'

'Wait! A hit on *me*. In the hospital?' Hunter exclaimed, leaving Tori to gasp in shock. 'What fucking bloke is this?'

'Oh my God! Richard Stevens put a hit out being as he failed to do it properly himself? The fucking wanker! I'm so glad he's dead!' Sarah spat, her voice loaded with venom.

Hunter leant forward, tense and ignored the pain, his knuckles whitening as he clenched his fists tighter. 'That fucking man? *Again.*'

Jorge shook his head. 'This is nothing to do with Richard Stevens.'

'Hang on, you're saying it's someone completely different?' Sarah yelled, shocked.

Tori stared at the ceiling, her relief from a few minutes ago evaporating. There was someone else out there who wanted to hurt Hunter? She bit down on her bottom lip hard to deflect from the forming burning tears of panic. She'd thought this was over, but…

'How many other people are trying to kill me?' Hunter raged. 'This is getting ridiculous!'

Noel eyed Jorge, seeing the panic of a trapped animal. 'Wait a minute… How do *you* know this?'

Jorge swallowed drily. 'Because he's my father and…'

'*What*?' Sarah screeched, jumping to her feet. 'You mean to tell me that you're sitting in *my* living room, in *my* pub and telling us that your *father* has been plotting to kill Hunter?'

She looked between Noel and Hunter, wild anger building rapidly. 'Oh my God! I get it now!' She rubbed her hands across her face in agitation. 'You turned up here out of the blue with some blag about needing a new life, but it was all about *this*, wasn't it? I bet you have no dead sister at all! You've been acting as a fucking insider for your father!'

Tori stared aghast at the man who had been so kind and helpful when she'd most needed it, when all the time he'd been using her to get information to help get the man she loved killed.

Noel lurched to his feet and grabbed Jorge around the throat, pulling him from the armchair. 'You low-life scum! I'll kill you!'

'Wait!' Jorge squeaked. 'I know it sounds bad but please let me try to explain. I…'

'Let him talk, Noel,' Hunter growled. 'I want to hear this.'

Noel reluctantly let go of Jorge's windpipe, dropping him unceremoniously back into the chair. 'Ok, but when he's finished talking, I'm wringing his fucking neck.'

'You and me both!' Sarah spat, glaring at the man she'd begun to really like. She'd even cooked him dinner, for God's sake! Christ, this wasn't the first time she'd been a bad judge of character! No wonder Colin had never liked him.

Jorge rubbed and stretched his neck, limbering it up before stiffness set in. He cleared his throat and smiled sadly. 'I only met my father for the first time a couple of months ago. I-I wanted a father...'

Hunter sighed, his irritation building past a level where he had any chance of remaining calm. 'Quit the fucking bleeding heart. Just get on with it.'

Jorge nodded frantically. 'I know, I know... it's no excuse. Sarah's right, my sister wasn't killed. I was sent here to get information on you.' He nodded to Hunter. 'It was also me who broke into your house...'

Tori emitted a high squeal. Springing forward, she slapped Jorge around the face, her timid persona replaced with fury. '*You*? You *hit* me?' Her eyes filled with tears. 'You threw my dead son's booties on the fire! They were the only thing I had left of him.' Her arm dropped to her side, her anger replaced by hurt and desolation.

Jorge put his head in his hands. 'I'm sorry,' he said quietly. 'I'm so sorry for all of it. I had no idea about your son either. I didn't realise what they were or I'd have nev...'

'I'd advise telling us the rest of what you need to say very quickly before I rip your throat out here and now,' Hunter roared, his jaw clenched as Sarah steered Tori away and sat her back down on the sofa.

'I was told the other night to carry out the hit. I refused. He then threatened me, so I said I'd do it. I had no intention of doing it, I might add. I-I've already done enough shit I'm not proud of.'

Hunter frowned. 'Why didn't you just do as he asked?'

'Because I realised what he was like. I saw the fucking light!' Jorge's voice became small, embarrassed. 'And I like all of you, that's why... No one's ever been nice to me before and...'

'And we're supposed to be grateful for that and feel *sorry* for you now, are we?' Noel yelled. 'Grateful that you've been conning us for weeks and...'

'Who the fuck is this joker?' Hunter barked.

'Neil. Neil Sparks,' Jorge said. 'He runs a London firm. He'll kill me when he discovers I haven't carried out the hit tonight, that's why I had to get you out of the hospital. When he discovers I haven't done it, after killing me, he'll be coming for you himself.'

'Neil Sparks?' Hunter muttered, frowning.

'He wanted Richard Stevens killed too. I was watching him. Watching all of you, but I didn't really understand Neil's motives apart from it was something to do with a grudge with the Reapers and his wife.'

'I don't know any Neil-fucking-Sparks!' Noel growled. 'And who the hell is his wife?'

Jorge swallowed dryly. 'C-Carmen...'

'*Carmen*?' Sarah screeched, flinching as Noel bolted from his seat straight for Jorge.

'Sit down, Noel,' Hunter yelled. 'I've been wracking my brain to think of where I've heard the name and now I know... Neil Sparks is a guy Rafe exiled years ago after he encroached on our turf. I remember it.'

Jorge nodded. 'I don't know the details, but I do know Neil's just returned from France and...'

Hunter's eyes narrowed. 'He'll have beef with all of the Reapers, but especially me as the President'

Jorge stared at the floor, then glanced at Tori uncomfortably. 'He originally thought Hunter was sleeping with Carmen.'

Tori's mouth dropped open. 'That's what was said during the break in. *You* said that! You wore the balaclava and you said you'd se…'

'I got it wrong… I'm sorry. I shouldn't have ev…'

'And now I suppose you've corrected your "mistake" and told your lovely father that it was Noel?' Sarah snapped.

Noel bristled, needing no reminders over the relationship he could no longer have.

Jorge nodded shamefully. 'I-I've been trying to stop everything. I've been trying to h…'

'Is he planning on taking Carmen?' Noel barked, her name burning the back of his throat. No matter what couldn't be between them ever again, he would not let anyone touch her.

Jorge shook his head. 'Taking her, no. He's planning to kill her too. I said he…'

Hunter banged his fist down on the table. 'Shut the fuck up!' he raged. 'Sparks has to be disposed of and disposed of *now*!' He glared at Jorge. 'And *you* will help us.'

Noel stood up. 'What? You're actually trusting this cunt after what he's done? How the hell do you know this isn't a set up? That's he's not purposefully leading us into a trap with this Sparks bastard?'

Jorge looked around him, panicked. 'It's not! I wouldn't d…'

'I *said*, shut the fuck up!' Hunter roared. He turned to Noel. 'You think I haven't thought about that? Besides, he should be more scared of what we'll do to him than what his daddy might do!'

'So, you *are* letting him get away with this?' Noel yelled, his rage incessant.

Hunter's eyes narrowed. 'No, I'm fucking not! I'll deal with him when we've finished.'

Jorge nodded resolutely. 'I'll do whatever you ne...'

'Phone him!' Hunter interrupted. 'Phone your cunt of a father and tell him that you went to do your "hit" on me, only to find that I'd disappeared. You'll phone him in front of all of us so that we can hear every single fucking word you say. We'll soon know if you're trying to warn him.'

He frowned, well aware that everyone hinged on his every word. He had to get this right the first time to enable his quickly thought out plan to work. 'Make him believe that you reckon the Reapers are on to him.'

'But then he'll know I've told you and t...'

'Why would he think that? Tell him you were surprised to get to the pub and find me there. Tell him you get on with us so well that we trust you. You'll bring me to him under the guise of taking me somewhere else.'

'That's ironic! We *did* fucking trust him! Well, *I* did – stupid cow that I am,' Sarah sniped.

Hunter shot Sarah a warning glare. He needed to concentrate. 'Make him believe that you'll lead me to him and that will give him the opportunity to kill me as desired.'

Tori's eyes widened. 'What? You can't be serious? You're going to willingly le...'

'Hunter will take Neil out before he gets chance to do anything,' Sarah interrupted.

'But what if he can't?' Tori wailed. 'Hunter's not in a great state at the moment. This Neil person will be quicker than him.'

'She's got a point,' Noel acknowledged. '*I'll* go. Besides, it's probably more me that he's after now...'

Hunter scowled. *Was he going to be useless for ever more?*

'A Reaper's a Reaper in his head,' Noel added, sensing Hunter's annoyance. 'Does it matter, providing the job gets done?'

Nodding begrudgingly, Hunter turned to Jorge. 'What are you waiting for? Call him now. Arrange to meet him at your flat in half an hour or as quickly as he can get there. And in the meantime, Noel, get yourself tooled up.'

• • • •

CARMEN CLUMSILY KNOCKED the gear stick into second and the Aston Martin jerked, the engine screaming. Taking the roundabout at speed, her heart lurched as she narrowly missed the edge of a kerbstone and she grappled with the stiff steering wheel, scowling at the heavy steering of the old classic.

Squinting against the sun's glare she accelerated harder, having already wasted far too much time. She'd had no choice but to take the Aston Martin if she stood any chance of getting to the pub in good time to tell everyone what she'd discovered. If she damaged the car it wasn't like she cared if it pissed her father off. She didn't much care *what* happened to him anymore, but she *did* care about what happened to her mother.

She involuntarily shuddered as the vivid image of the man on the kitchen floor flashed back into her mind and doubted whether she'd ever be able to erase it. *All that mess... All that brains and goo...*

Nausea rose and Carmen found herself swerving again. *Calm down. Calm the fuck down*, she told herself on a repeating mantra. She'd recognised the dead man. She couldn't remember his name, but knew he was an acquaintance of her parents; an irritating bastard who had been at several garden parties her mother had insisted on throwing to encourage networking. Bloody ridiculous. How could her life have been like that? And why was it now even worse, just in completely different ways?

Her heart raced in line with the speedometer, its needle trembling precariously on seventy mph within its glass dial in the walnut dashboard, Carmen prayed she didn't get pulled over. She was driving much too fast and would probably lose her licence if she was stopped. And how would she begin to explain her rush to the police? Furthermore, how would she explain not calling 999 the minute she'd walked into a murder scene?

She'd spent far too long paralysed against the kitchen wall, unable to drag her focus away from the wide-eyed staring corpse, the top of his skull blown to smithereens. The situation was down to Luca. It *had* to be.

Familiar panic flowed through her veins. Luca must have come to the house looking for her, but instead found her parents and one of her father's cronies and look what had happened. Was Luca using her parents as a means of getting revenge on her?

Carmen wiped sweat off her forehead and quickly replaced her hand back on the juddering steering wheel. She had to find her mother and get her away. Luca had already killed that fat man, so God knows what he might do... She may already be too late.

She also had to warn Noel.

Sickness and apprehension washed over Carmen, sweat trickling between her breasts with the thought of how she would cope seeing him, but she couldn't dwell on it. She owed it to him to warn him that her husband would be gunning for him too. Furthermore, she had to warn *everybody* that Jorge was the one leading them all straight to Luca. He was reporting everyone's whereabouts, what was being said, what everyone was doing and she had to tell them. *NOW*. There was no time to waste.

FORTY FOUR

'YES?' Neil said tersely as he answered the phone in his suite.

'Neil?' Jorge asked, his voice breathless.

'Hello Jorge.' Neil ensured his voice remained level, when really all he wanted to do was roar at the pointless bastard on the other end of the line – the pointless bastard that he now knew was turning him over and working for the other side. A snake in the grass of the highest order.

Oh, but he'd keep it cool. In fact, the thought of lulling Jorge into a false sense of security and making him think he believed every single thing coming out of his lying mouth was the only thing that had stopped him from blowing the treacherous fucker's head clean off his shoulders the second he'd seen him helping that bastard out of the hospital earlier. Now he couldn't wait to hear what bullshit this little scrote had to say. 'Did everything go to plan?'

'No, it didn't...' Jorge muttered, glancing at Hunter whose eyes, unwavering from their steely concentration honed directly on him. He knew what to say; they'd been through it several times, but blatantly lying to Neil made him nervous. Not as nervous as Hunter did though.

Neil waited for Jorge to elaborate, but nothing else was

forthcoming. Did the prick think he was a mind-reader? Actually, he didn't need to be a mind reader because he'd warrant a guess that at this very second Jorge was surrounded by at least some of the Reapers and if they had one brain cell between them they'd have a trained ear on every single thing Jorge said. He knew that's what *he'd* be doing. Once a double-crosser, *always* a double-crosser. And that was Jorge all over. Still, he'd play the game – make Jorge and the idiotic bikers believe they had the upper hand. For the time being, at least.

Neil swallowed the urge to laugh. 'Jorge, are you going to tell me what's gone wrong or shall I fucking guess?'

'He… he's gone!' Jorge stuttered. *Remember what you need to say, Jorge. Remember! It's vital you get this right.*

'Who's gone?' Neil said, bored with waiting for Jorge to get to the point.

'Hunter!' Jorge gabbled. 'I got to the hospital. I specced it all out. Everything looked more straight forward than I'd expected. I had a clear run, but then I reached the room to find he'd disappeared. Completely gone!'

'Gone?' Neil made his voice sound incredulous. The boy was trying too hard. He wouldn't have believed this to be kosher even if he didn't already know it was utter lies.

'Yes,' Jorge gasped. 'He's found out a hit's been put on him.'

'What do you mean "found out"?' Neil exclaimed. 'Where are you calling from?'

'A call box up the road from the pub.'

Neil smiled to himself. *Another lie.* It was hard to believe the boy was so stupid he didn't know posh hotel phones displayed the caller ID on a small screen. The number showing clearly on the telephone in front of him was the number of the White Hart itself. As suspected, the joker was with the Reapers on loudspeaker. 'Where is he now?'

Jorge looked at Noel, unnerved to see him shaking his head in frustration. 'W-Where is…?'

'Hunter, you fool. *Hunter.* Where is he?'

'He's in the White Hart. That's where I've just come from and how I know he's found out. You don't understand. They trust me and I hear a lot.' Jorge fidgeted and glanced at Hunter nervously, aware he'd done a good job of using his knowledge against the Reapers. *Not anymore though.*

'And so how did he find out? *You* by any chance?' Neil spat.

'Me?' Jorge squeaked. 'I haven't said anything! I know I said this wasn't for me and all that, but that doesn't mean I told them. I've said jack shit!' Glad to see Hunter's nod of approval, he continued. 'I've told them nothing. I mean, you're my father so I'm not going to go against you, am I? I said I'd do what you wanted regardless. I want t…'

'If it wasn't you, then how?' Neil casually poured a tot of whisky from the decanter into his tumbler. *Wouldn't go against him indeed? Yeah right.* At least the boy sounded half-convincing now, not that it made any difference…

'Hunter heard something from a friend of a friend. Don't ask me who because I don't know, but whoever it was gave your name up. Something to do with an old score with Raff… or Rafe? Dunno – something like that.' Jorge looked at Hunter again, hoping against hope that he'd remembered that part of the story correctly.

Neil raised his eyebrows. The Reapers had briefed Jorge well. If he had not seen with his own eyes what Jorge had previously done, he'd be tempted to believe what he was hearing. 'Did they mention Carmen or Stevens?'

Jorge saw Noel give him a clear shake of the head. 'No, they didn't mention them at all. They were talking about getting in contact with you to come to a new arrangement.'

Neil laughed. 'Like what? Shooting me?' *He'd meet them alright. That's exactly what he wanted.* 'And this is from Hunter? Hunter wants to meet me?'

'No, Noel. Noel's been put to deal with you. Hunter's not well enough,' Jorge continued.

'Noel? That's the one fucking my wife? Oh well, that'll be

good.'

Jorge felt hatred rising from Noel like a miasma. 'They don't know about the link between you and Carmen. As far as they're concerned, Carmen's married to a Frenchman.'

'I'll come to the White Hart,' Neil said, playing his hand. 'Where are the rest of the Reapers?'

'At the Factory, I guess. Only Noel and Hunter are in the White Hart tonight.'

'I'm wondering whether the White Hart is the best place to meet this prick. I'll be shooting Noel before he shoots me and I won't be able to do that if there a ton of them suddenly turn up.' He paused. 'We'll have to think of somewhere else. Don't forget after I've dealt with Noel, you're finishing Hunter like planned, ok?'

Jorge's eyes darted to Noel who nodded casually. 'Ok, but how will I get Noel to meet you? And where?' *He had to make this sound good.* 'If I say I've spoken to you and that you want to meet them they'll know I'm connected to you, so that isn't going to work.'

Neil scowled. 'That's why you don't tell them, you idiot!' he snapped. 'Ask Noel to give you a hand with something at the flat.'

'You want me to take Noel to the *flat*?'

'Yes, Jorge. I'll come there. Ask him to help you. I don't know with what, just think of something. Or offer to give him a lift somewhere, then tell him you need to stop off at the flat on the way an…'

'But what if he won't? Why would he need a lift anywhere?'

Neil growled under his breath, losing patience. 'Just do it! You're friendly with them and they trust you, so think of something.' He glared at his watch. He wanted this wrapped up tonight. And by wrapped up – he meant completely, but the timing had to be perfect because there was one more thing he needed to do before dealing with Noel.

Receiving Hunter's nod, Jorge sighed. 'Ok, I'll try my best.

Give me half an hour.'

'Try your best? You *will* do it! And make it an hour. The minute I've taken Noel out, you're removing Hunter at the White Hart whilst I catch up with that errant bitch of a wife of mine.'

Noel stiffened in his chair at the mention of Carmen's name, his jaw setting resolutely.

'No one knows where she is,' Jorge added quickly.

'I'll find her, don't you worry about that. Just sort Hunter and then get yourself on the road back to London. I won't be long behind you,' Neil said. 'An hour. At the flat. Make sure you're there with Noel; just you and him.' He abruptly put the phone down before Jorge could say anything else. He didn't want to hear one more grating word out of the slimy twat's mouth.

Leaning against the cool wall, Neil let out a long breath before a smile spread slowly across his face. Jorge wouldn't be getting on the road to London at all. Neither would he be doing the job on Hunter. He'd have the pleasure of taking that loser out himself. Jorge's dead body would be left on the deck next to the greasy bastard who had fucked his wife and as for her – she'd be next. Last but not least, he'd take Carmen's body to dump on Richard-fucking-Stevens before finishing him too.

Then and only *then*, would he make his way back down south.

Pushing himself away from the wall, Neil walked into the suite's bedroom and slid open the right hand door of the large wardrobe. He punched in the code on the safe and retrieved the holdall safely placed there after he'd first checked in.

He'd change into his chavvy get-up for the last time and then check out of the hotel. He wouldn't need to stay here anymore after tonight.

Neil grinned savagely. Almost done, but he needed to get a move on. He didn't want to be late.

· · · ·

'JESUS CHRIST!' Colin cried when Carmen burst through the heavy wooden door of the pub.

Carmen stumbled towards the bar, her eyes wild. 'Colin, you need to help me! Where's Sarah?' she shrieked.

Colin grasped Carmen's arm over the bar. 'Holy God, calm down! Sarah's upstairs. Are you alright? Where have you been?' She clearly wasn't alright – that much was obvious. Apart from looking dishevelled and ill, she also looked scared. More scared than he'd seen anyone look for some time.

Colin glanced at Susan's empty stool, saying a silent prayer that she was in the toilets rather than witnessing this. The woman was in a bad enough state as it was, without seeing her daughter mid-meltdown and without another word, Carmen pushed past him and disappeared through the door to upstairs.

Bursting into Sarah's sitting room, Carmen stumbled against the door jamb.

'Carmen?' Sarah cried, jumping to her feet.

'He's got my mother,' Carmen cried, her breath coming in rapid pants, her eyes darting between Sarah and Hunter.

Tori moved to Carmen's side and guided her to a seat. 'Where have you been? Are you ok?'

'Luca!' Carmen panted. 'It's *him*. Everything is to do with him,' she babbled, struggling to vocalise what she needed to say fast enough. 'You need to stop him. The Reapers have to stop him. There's a dead man at my parent's house.' Her hands shook violently. 'My parents are missing. My mother... she...'

'Whoa! Slow down!' Hunter said. 'Your mother's fine. She's here.'

Carmen's eyes widened. 'Here? My mother's *here*?' Her head turned from side to side rapidly searching.

'Downstairs,' Sarah said. 'She's in the bar... Your father... he...'

'Who the fuck is Luca?' Hunter interrupted.

'My husband! He'll go for Noel next. Matt told him that I was slee...' *She didn't want to say it. Not now.* 'I should have told you before now. I didn't think he'd do this, but it's him. It *must* be and he's behind everything.' Her eyes widened further. 'And Jorge. He's a spy. He's been telling Luca everything everybody does.'

Hunter sighed, quickly putting two and two together. 'Just stop, Carmen. We know about this. Jorge told us, but your husband isn't Luca. His real name is Neil. Neil Sparks.'

'I don't much care what his name is,' Carmen cried, her eyes panicked. 'Where's Noel? You've got to warn him.'

'Noel's just left. He's on his way with Jorge to meet Neil,' Sarah said.

Carmen's eyes widened. 'But he can't. I've just told you that Jorge *works* for Neil an…'

'Jorge is Neil's *son*,' Sarah interrupted.

'Luca… Neil… he has a *son*? Jorge is his *son*? Wait… I…'

Susan burst into Sarah's living room closely followed by Colin, who looked around apologetically. 'I tried to stop her, I…'

'Carmen!' Susan screeched, almost falling over herself in her haste to reach her daughter. 'I was sure I could hear your voice from downstairs and I was right!' Grabbing Carmen, she pulled her into a tight hug, tears streaming down her face.

'Oh Mum!' Carmen wailed. 'I thought you were dead! I thought Luca had kidnapped you an…'

'Luca? Why would you think that? Where have you been?' Susan cried. 'Oh my God, I've been so worried about you.'

Carmen suddenly looked petrified. 'Dad! Oh no! He's not here too is he? Oh Mum, it's dreadful.' She burst into a round of heavy sobs. 'You've no idea what he's done. You can't *ever* go back to him, you can't! He's a vile, murdering ba…'

'I think you both need to sit down,' Tori interrupted, stealing a glance at Hunter whose brows were knitted together in deep thought. She didn't care if anyone disagreed with her or not. Both Carmen and Susan had to be informed of what had happened to Richard and as much as it pained her to speak of what he'd admitted to, she knew she had to tell them.

FORTY FIVE

HUNTER SAT DEEP IN THOUGHT despite the constant buzz around him. The main source of the noise was Sarah's talking in her effort to keep the spirits up of the others, all locked within their own minds thinking about what they'd learnt. He commended her resilience, but also wished she'd button it and shut up. He needed to think.

Although not surprised Noel had confirmed his suspicions regarding Richard Stevens, his anger continued to burn brightly that the person who had inflicted so much damage on him had been under his nose all along. Noel had done his job and done it well – Stevens was out of the picture, but Hunter would be lying if he hadn't wished he could have been the one to wipe the man off the planet.

Hunter shook out his shaggy hair, well aware it was long overdue for a decent wash and stretched his torso, his teeth clenching with the incessant throbbing pain clamouring for attention in his side. It would take *weeks* before he was back to normal and that was providing he hadn't caused more problems by leaving the safety of the hospital prematurely. His eyebrow twitched at the irony. The hospital *should* have been safe, but it wasn't.

Neil Sparks eh? Who would have thought it? He hadn't expected him to turn up out of the woodwork and certainly wouldn't have guessed the man was married to Carmen!

Hunter glanced at Carmen sitting with her mother, both in a state of shock. It was hardly surprising. What a bloody mess. Out of the two of them, Susan had taken the news about Richard the worst and he wished Tori hadn't made the decision to tell them what had happened, along with everything the man had done. It wasn't a good time and Susan's ensuing hysteria made the situation worse.

He glanced at the clock impatiently. Twenty minutes before Sparks met with Noel. He was on edge. Something was prickling at him. Not because Noel wasn't capable of dealing with the man, it was just… something…

Hunter scowled. He should be alongside Noel. This wasn't something that one alone should deal with.

'What's up?' Sarah asked studying Hunter's serious face, his expression like stone. 'Noel will deal with everything,' she said reassuringly.

'I don't doubt it,' Hunter mumbled, but something wasn't sitting right. It was just… just *something… Had he made the right call letting Noel deal with this?*

'Jorge did a decent job. We all heard him on the phone. Sparks believes he'll be catching Noel unawares and won't expect him to be tooled up. He thinks he's got it sussed and that Jorge is setting Noel up,' Sarah continued.

Hunter nodded, although he was far from convinced.

'I cannot quite believe that man… Noel… the man I saw… the man you were…' Susan glanced at Carmen, her face bewildered. 'He's Richard's *son*? Oh, how could he have done that? She put her hands over her face, wiping at her puffy red eyes. 'What he did to that poor woman…'

'Susan,' Tori said quietly, capturing the older woman's attention and when Susan raised her eyes, she nodded towards Carmen. 'I don't think that… you know… Carmen… I don't think she needs to…'

'Oh and that makes it even *worse*, doesn't it?' Susan carried on blindly, oblivious to intensifying her daughter's pain.

Carmen picked at her chipped nail varnish to tune out her mother's constant talking. Being reminded over and over who she'd been having a relationship with wasn't helping. And her father was dead? She didn't quite know how she felt. Relieved? Sad? Angry? *Anything?*

The man she'd loved had killed her father and she was glad about that. But she was also sad. Although was "sad" the right word? She didn't know. Now, as well as her father, her *husband* was out to cause her and people she cared about even more grief. Now Noel would kill him too.

She couldn't get her head around it. Nothing seemed real, but alarm bells were jangling. Jangling really loudly.

They didn't know Luca, or whatever he called himself. They didn't know him like *she* did. Aside from her father, Luca was the coldest, most manipulative person she knew — and there was just something was wrong with what had been arranged. It seemed far too easy.

· · · ·

EVERYONE LOOKED UP as Colin burst into the sitting room with an ashen-faced Reaper in tow.

'Shaky?' Hunter sat forward quickly, immediately knowing this was bad. The kid was a prospect, not having been in the club long, but he had potential and had worked hard over the last year, but by the look on the kid's face something bad had happened. Being as he'd been on compassionate leave helping to care for his terminally ill father, he could only presume the worst. 'You're not supposed to be back for another two weeks, are you? Your father?'

'He died two days ago, but th…'

'Oh hell! I'm so sorry, mate!' Hunter went to stand, but pain forced him to stop halfway.

'Come and sit down, love.' Sarah cleared a space on the sofa. 'That's dreadful news. I'll get you a drink and…'

'Let the boy speak,' Colin interrupted, his voice stern.

It was only hearing Colin's voice that Sarah properly looked at her husband, his face haunted. 'W-What's going on?'

Hunter watched the young prospect shaking and a horrible creeping fear travelled the length of his spine. *Was this about Noel?*

He glanced at the clock again. Sparks wouldn't have arrived yet - still ten minutes to go. Unless he's been early... A trap? Had Noel been ambushed? 'Come on, speak!' he growled.

'I needed to come back and see the boys. It was getting me down sitting there after my dad...' Shaky's voice trembled as much as his hands. 'They're fucked...'

'What are you talking about?' Hunter barked.

'The Factory!' Shaky cried. 'I got back... The door... They're all gone...' His voice trailed off.

Icy tendrils crept up Hunter's neck. 'What? They've disappeared? I don't understand?'

Shaky shook his head frantically. 'No, they're all still there... they... they...'

Hunter scowled. *Was this kid talking in riddles? Had he been on some kind of gear?* He didn't appreciate Reapers being incoherent and certainly wouldn't tolerate that from a prospect. 'Shaky, what the fu...'

'Someone's attacked the Factory,' Colin interjected. The young biker was a mess and in no fit state to be questioned like this. He'd crashed into the bar jabbering wildly about what he'd seen and Hunter needed to know about this fast. Judging by the expression on his face, he'd lamp the kid if he didn't start talking sense.

'Someone has shot up the club,' Colin continued.

'WHAT?' Hunter jumped to his feet despite the wrenching pain in his gut. 'You fucking *what*?' His eyes darted to the young prospect.

'They're all dead, Hunter,' Shaky said. '*All* of them.'

Hunter was rendered speechless for a few seconds unable to comprehend what he was hearing.

'Oh my God!' Susan wailed at the top of her voice. 'This is madness! You people, you go around wi…'

'Shut the fuck up, Susan!' Sarah screamed, her face white. Turning back to the young biker, she grabbed his hand. 'When was this? When did this happen?'

Shaky dragged his fist across his eyes welling with tears. 'I-I don't know. I've just come from there. It must have been recent because… because the ones I checked were… they were still warm…'

'Jesus fucking Christ!' Hunter muttered, his mind racing at nine to the dozen. 'They're all dead? *Everyone?*'

'I-I think so. Everyone I saw was. Loads of the old ladies too. Some kind of automatic, judging by the casings on the floor. I-I didn't know what to do. I just came straight here… I didn't know where to…'

'Could any of them still be alive?' Sarah pressed.

Hunter sat rigid as the boy blinked nervously at Sarah's question, clear he had no idea.

'What should I do, Hunter? What sh…'

'Wait!' Hunter growled. His whole club had been gunned down? His brothers? Grin? Billy? All the women folk? They were all gone? *This was Sparks. This was him.* The ultimate retaliation. He'd said he had something to do before meeting Noel and Jorge.

His eyes narrowed. That's what his instincts had been telling him. Noel was walking into a trap. Sparks knew. He knew it was a set up. He fucking *knew*! 'Shit! SHIT!' he muttered under his breath.

'I'll get over there now and see if anyone's alive,' Colin said. 'Sarah, man the bar downstairs. We need to act normally.'

'What do you mean?' Sarah shrieked. 'I can hardly go downstairs and serve pints when this has happened and wh…'

'Just fucking do it!' Colin snapped. He didn't know the ins and outs of what was going on here, but knew enough to see that something had to be done and he wasn't about to let his wife, Carmen or Tori be the ones to walk into a room of shot-up bodies with the additional risk of the gunman possibly still being about.

Carmen sat forward sharply, her eyes on Hunter. 'This is Luca isn't it? You know it and I know it. You've got to stop Noel. You've got to listen to me. You've got to stop him from going there. Stop him, Hunter, *please*!'

Hunter agreed. He'd been wrong. It was *them* who'd fallen into the trap. He struggled to his feet. 'I need to get over there. I need to intercept them.'

'I'm coming with you,' Carmen said resolutely.

'As will I,' Tori added.

'Don't be ridiculous!' Susan screeched. 'Carmen you cannot possibly think to put yourself in a position such as this. Or you, Victoria.'

Carmen swung around to face her mother. 'I'm going and that is all there is to it. Regardless of what has happened, Noel is important to me!'

Hunter glanced at Shaky. There was no point in taking him – the kid's head was mashed, but he was in no way happy or comfortable with two women accompanying him on something like this. Especially with Tori being one of them, but it didn't change the fact that he needed someone to drive.

'You can come but *neither* of you are to get out of the fucking car,' Hunter growled, staring at the clock once more, his face fierce.

By the looks of it, whatever he did, he was too late.

FORTY SIX

'STOP TWITCHING, WILL YOU? You're getting on my fucking tits!' Noel hissed, glaring as Jorge hovered restlessly near the window.

'Sorry,' Jorge said, still unable to stop himself from peering through the dirty panes down onto the deserted street below.

When he'd given Noel the flat's address, he'd mentioned something about it being in an area part of a property thing a while ago. Noel hadn't elaborated and Jorge hadn't dared ask for details, but Neil was correct on one thing – the place was perfect for no interference. The inhabitants of these flats above the shops in this once busy area had long since departed, along with the owners of the shops. Some were boarded up; others, the windows clouded with white chalk signifying their emptiness. *It was a ghost town.*

Pulling his eyes away from the empty road he turned to Noel. 'I'm not sure about this… I can't help but think that Neil wi…'

'Oh, shut up!' Noel barked, inspecting his shotgun. He couldn't say he was happy about his selection of weapon, but given the circumstances, this was the only gun he'd got to hand in the van. There hadn't been time to collect any of the better ones from the Factory.

He shrugged aimlessly. It wasn't a problem. He'd easily blow the fucker's head off with this beauty, he thought eyeing his trusted double-barrelled shotgun. It was a bit loud and messy, but it would have to do nicely.

Noel looked at his watch. Any time now the fucker should show, providing he had the balls, of course. He'd better show anyway. He glared at Jorge, the two-faced bastard. Why had any of them given him the time of day in the first place? 'Where is he?' he growled. 'The cunt had better show up!'

'He'll be here.' Jorge kept his attention fixed on the street. *Anything* was preferable to meeting the eyes of the man he was stuck with in this small lounge. It was clear Noel despised him. The hatred rising from him was so thick it could be cut with a knife.

He shuffled nervously, aware the forced civility from Noel wouldn't continue and it was only down to him being a necessity right now, but after…

Jorge shuddered. In all fairness, he was surprised that he was still breathing and knew once this was over, he most likely wouldn't be, but he'd done the right thing. Stopping Neil in his tracks was good, even if he didn't see the rewards of it. He had to placate himself that helping rid the world of an evil bastard was good enough. It was his only option anyway, but despite everything, alarm bells rang loudly in the back of his mind. Something was off, he could sense it.

Sensing Noel moving behind him, Jorge stiffened.

'This prick best get a move on. I'm getting impatient,' Noel muttered.

'I've got a really bad feeling. I don't trust Neil. He's a nasty piece of work and I…'

'Quit whining. Sparks doesn't have a bloody clue. You heard him on the phone. He thinks he's got the upper hand, but it's obvious he doesn't realise I know what he's planning.'

'But he's going to kill you!' Jorge exclaimed.

Noel laughed loudly. 'He *thinks* he is, you mean. Trust me, he won't. Listen, you worry far too much. As far as Sparks is concerned, *we* have no idea you're working for him.'

'*Was* working for him,' Jorge corrected, immediately wishing he hadn't when Noel's eyes narrowed menacingly, penetrating him with a fierce glare.

'As I was saying, he believes you're working for him, therefore doesn't suspect you've grassed him up. He thinks I'm here only because you've tricked me. He thinks he'll walk into here and catch me off guard.' Noel raised his shotgun and smiled nastily. 'For a start, he won't expect me to be tooled up.'

Flinching as the double barrels passed precariously close to his face, Jorge attempted to rationalise the rising level of bad feeling. 'I still can't shake off the feeling that something... Oh, I don't know... How will you play it? Will you shoot him as soon as he walks in? What happens if he shoots you an...'

'He won't walk in and immediately gun me down!' Noel snarled. 'He'll want to *tell* me what he's going to do and why. He'll try to wind me up, but it won't work. As long as I focus, I'll let him say his piece and *then* I'll fucking take him.'

Jorge swallowed uncomfortably. 'But what if...'

'Just shut the fuck up now, eh?' Noel placed the shotgun out of sight down the side of the grubby two-seater sofa. Flopping onto the saggy cushions, he lounged back and crossed his ankles. 'Get yourself back to keeping an eye out. The one thing we don't want is him sneaking up unannounced.'

· · · ·

NEIL SPED TOWARDS the flat, his adrenalin pumping from the episode at the Factory. It had gone superbly well. It had been so bloody easy. In fact, he'd been surprised just how bloody easy it was.

The greasy slob he'd found in the hallway the second he'd entered the code Jorge had given him for their stupid reinforced metal door hadn't had a second to think before he'd been permanently removed by a single shot to the face. The silencer on his pistol ensured an unobtrusive and unnoticed entrance into the main room where a whole host of the skanky Reapers had been present.

Swapping his pistol for his semi-automatic, it had been almost orgasmic showering them with a steady rain of metal. No one had time to apprehend him; a textbook example of meticulous orchestration. The whole operation took less than three minutes.

Turning into the deserted street where the flat was situated, Neil glanced in the rear view mirror and smiled. He was only five minutes late and there was no chance of Noel and Jorge having not bothered hanging around. Noel would be eagerly awaiting his chance to kill him, but the man wouldn't be going anywhere he may have planned. *He'd* be the only one moving on tonight.

Only three more to do after this and they wouldn't take long. They were all nicely in place, making things straight forward and quick. He couldn't wait to see Hunter's face learning he no longer had a vice president – or come to think of it, no club to govern over at all.

A wide smile passed over his face. Neither Hunter or Noel had the faintest clue their beloved club was reduced to piles of mangled bodies. In fact, he might inform Noel of that before he finished the greasy fuck off.

Noel, Jorge, Hunter, Carmen and finally, Richard Stevens. *Easy.*

Pulling up outside the flat, Neil turned off the ignition. Having no need to keep things quiet, he removed the silencer, then placed the pistol in his waistband, stifling the urge to glance up at the window, knowing that one of them would be watching for his arrival.

His shithead of a son's face would be a picture when it sunk in that he'd been aware of his double-crossing stunt and at that moment in time the thick fuck would realise it was all over. Neil grinned. He was looking forward to seeing the Venezuelan colour drain from his snake in the grass son's face as the penny dropped.

Neil's pulse pumped hard and he struggled to contain his rising excitement. It was time to remove the greasy wanker who felt it his right to shag Carmen... *Bye, bye Noel, you gypwack fuckturd.*

Taking a deep breath, Neil stepped from the car and casually walked towards the flat's entrance.

Life was good.

FORTY SEVEN

HEARING THE BUZZER, Jorge rushed to the intercom, his body tense. Receiving a nod from Noel, he pressed the door release button with shaking fingers.

He'd been expecting the buzzer to sound after seeing Neil pull up in a dodgy looking motor, then confidently stride towards the flat's entrance door off the pavement, but expecting it didn't make him feel less on edge.

'Calm the fuck down, would you?' Noel hissed, still lounging on the crummy-looking sofa.

Jorge swallowed uncomfortably. How could Noel be so relaxed? It was abnormal. At this precise second a man was making his way up here with the sole intention of killing him, yet he was acting like he didn't have a care in the world?

And *he* would watch someone get murdered in the next few minutes. He couldn't say he was looking forward to it. Neil Sparks was his father and the large part he'd played in setting up his death brought about a conflicting mix of emotions. He wanted to rid the world of someone who, in a normal situation, he should want to protect.

The footsteps got louder and Jorge hovered nervously, yanking the door open on the first rap. 'Hello,' he garbled.

Smiling pleasantly, Neil pushed past Jorge without a second glance and strode directly into the lounge.

Jorge followed, panic rising. 'Can I get you a drink or h…'

'*You* must be Noel,' Neil said, his voice calm. He brushed his fingers over the pistol in his waistband concealed under his jacket. 'How nice to finally meet you…'

Noel eyed the man in the doorway. He was acting just as expected. *Ok, game on.* He forced a look of bemusement and glanced at Jorge. 'Who's this?'

Jorge looked from Noel to his father and then back again, unsure what to do or how to react. What was he supposed to say? 'Oh, erm… this is…'

'Cut the shit.' Neil glared at Jorge, then turned to Noel. 'How's my wife?'

Noel bristled. He'd expected this, but it didn't mean he wanted to talk about it. The situation was far too raw and he certainly didn't want to discuss it with this prick – the guy who had treated Carmen like an ornament. The guy who had *paid* for her.

Noel's eyes travelled slowly over Neil Sparks. Confident-looking, self-assured and well-built. Arrogant. All of those things. Not difficult to remove, but he'd bide his time. He had to play things carefully. His gaze flicked across the man's jacket. Unnoticeable to the untrained eye, the unmistakeable hint of a gun present at his waist level was clear. Again, not surprising, but he'd be keeping one eye on this tosser's hand. Any slight movement in that direction and he'd be grabbing his shotgun quicker than this fucker could say "boo".

Neil remained still, a vein in his neck pulsing. 'I asked you how my wife is?' he snarled, an edge to his voice betraying his inner anger.

'Who's your wife? And who are you?' Noel countered. *If this prat wanted to play games, then he'd got it.*

Neil smirked, a half-smile forming. 'I presume you know the name of who you've been shagging? You remember Carmen, my wife? You also know who I am, so let's not waste time.'

Jorge listened, fear racing up his spine. *Neil knew. He knew that Noel knew. Oh, shit!* He glanced at Noel, hoping his eyes conveyed his worry. Surely Noel had reached the same conclusion, but judging by his casual stance, it didn't appear so.

His heart rate accelerated, along with his anxiety. *Come on, Noel. You heard what he said, didn't you?* He glanced back to Neil.

Noel chuckled, the sound rumbling deep in his throat and a lazy grin spread across his face even though smiling was the last thing he felt like doing. The prick was trying to wind him up, but he wouldn't fall for it. 'I don't know where Carmen is,' he said, his voice level. *That was true, but two could play at this game.* 'And yes, I do know who you are. You're Neil Sparks - the one who's, for some unbeknown reason, trying to kill our president.'

It was taking all of Noel's control not to gun the man down right here, right now, but he'd play the game. Just when this twat felt it time to move, he'd get in first. He prided himself on his lightening reactions and, if he was honest, enjoyed the risk of leaving playing his hand right up until the last minute. Loved the extra rush that sailing so close to the wind brought.

To prove his ability further, Noel folded his arms across his chest, his hand well out of range of the shotgun concealed to the side of him, should he need it and ignored Jorge's fidgeting. He wouldn't waste time even looking at that ponce. If Hunter thought he'd been joking when he said he'd rip the toe-rag to pieces once this crap was finished, then he was very much mistaken. *No one* crossed the Reapers and lived to tell the tale and that wasn't changing now – for *anyone*.

Noel's eyes slowly moved back over Neil, knowing the man would take his overt scrutiny as an expression of outward contempt and smiled to himself once more. That's exactly what he hoped to achieve. Each added insult that he could pile on only made each second more gratifying. He sighed heavily. 'Not willing to embellish why you have a weird penchant for wanting to off our president, no?'

Neil raised an eyebrow. 'Big words for someone of your intellect. Well done.'

Ignoring Neil's barb, Noel continued, 'Have you noticed the president your deal was with isn't the same bloke, or did that escape your notice? Oh, wait… it doesn't matter, right? A Reaper's a Reaper… I get it. I guess if I'd been forced into exile because of my greed and inability to do a job competently, then I'd find it easier to blame the other party too, rather than admitting I was a useless cunt!'

He laughed sarcastically, watching Neil twitch with suppressed rage, his face flushing a deep shade of crimson. 'Must be humiliating? Especially when everyone knows about it.' Noel shook his head, still chuckling. 'You must have some decent hands in your firm to scrape back your business' reputation, but they must be gutted you're back. Neil Sparks… returns to fuck things up…. Again…'

Clenching his teeth, Neil's fingers itched to reach for his pistol but stopped himself. Losing his temper would make him weak. It would make him take his eyes off the ball. Make him lose his concentration and he'd come too far to do that.

Watching the stand-off, Jorge felt sick. He was balancing precariously on a tight rope; one half of the rope would snap, but he had no idea *which* half until it did.

Bringing Noel here was a mistake. A *big* mistake. Neil was planning to do something they hadn't factored into their plans. The air sat heavily around his shoulders like a succubus and before he could stop himself, his mouth started moving. 'Neil, I do…'

'Shut the fuck up, Jorge!' Neil hissed, not moving his glare from Noel. He could and *would* not allow his idiot son to interrupt his concentration. There could be no diversions, however slight. 'I'll deal with *you* later.'

Jorge blinked, now more convinced than ever they had made a very bad decision.

. . . .

HUNTER'S TEETH CLENCHED as they sped along the road. He watched the stream of houses and shops blurring into one as Carmen drove through the town. They were going fast but nowhere near fast enough. 'Get a move on,' he growled, his fists clenching and unclenching in his lap.

'I'm going as fast as I can,' Carmen muttered, grappling with the heavy steering wheel.

Hunter looked at Tori next to him in the back, her face white with fear. 'I need the gun. We're almost there.'

And there was no time to waste. He just hoped that with a tiny smidgen of luck he'd be in time. The handgun he'd given Tori was hardly the best, but it was the only one he'd got access to. There certainly wasn't the time to go to the Factory or warehouse to pick up a different one and, funnily enough, he hadn't a range of firearms stashed in his hospital bag.

Besides, going to the Factory and having to see his brothers lying all over the floor shot to ribbons, wasn't a sight he wanted to see. Not until the man responsible lay in pieces. His skin prickled with rage, unable to comprehend how this had happened. He could just not take on board that all the Reapers may be dead.

That fucking prospect hadn't even checked all of them. There must be fatalities but not all of them, surely? But even *one* was too many and this bastard would pay.

Hunter's jaw tightened. He couldn't change what had already been done and had to concentrate on what was needed now. He should never have allowed Noel to meet Sparks on his own. Had being shot scrambled his fucking brain? Why had he not foreseen something like this?

Turning into the street where Jorge's flat was, Hunter's frown caused deep furrows across his forehead. This was the area that held the majority of the properties that had been sold to that ponce, Matt, during all that set up with the bank. Anger swirled further. Neil Sparks must have been consistently watching the area all the years he'd been exiled in France and bought a property whilst they were going for a song after Matt and Noel's plan went down the toilet.

Slight resentment for Noel's part in those unsavoury dealings surfaced before Hunter squashed them back where they belonged – in the past. His main concern now was not that – it was Noel's safety and he berated himself once more about making the rushed and severely foolhardy decision over not seeing through what Sparks' plan actually was. *How could he have been so blind?*

Trembling with a mix of dread and rage over exactly how many of his loyal Reapers had been lost, Hunter ground his teeth.; the inflicted pain barely touching the sides of his incessant anger. Being rendered impotent over not being properly able to deal with this situation himself only made matters worse.

Hunter bypassed the incessant throbbing in his side. Right now, he didn't care if his insides fell out. Whatever happened he was dealing with this one way or the other and had to make sure Noel was unharmed and Sparks was removed.

And he'd never thought in his wildest dreams he would be rendered so physically bereft to enlist the help of two women to drive him to a situation such as this. Involving *them* in something so dangerous and possibly putting their lives in the firing line was not something that should ever be an option and he despised himself for being in this position.

With a start, Hunter suddenly realised that they had pulled up to a stop. He glanced around. 'Is this it?' he asked. 'Which one is the flat?'

Carmen fumbled with a scrap of paper. 'No idea, but it's "30a".' She peered out of the window into the gloom. 'That shop there is 30, so it must be the flat above.'

'Right,' Hunter said, aware Tori still had possession of the gun in her handbag. 'Tori, give me the gun. I need to go and do this.'

Tori turned to Hunter with wide frightened eyes. 'I don't

want you to go in. You can barely walk. You'll be a sitting duck and y…'

'We haven't got time for this! Noel's in danger. I might already be too late, but I've got to at least try, so give me the fucking gun.' Hunter spat. 'You two are not to move or leave the car under *any* circumstances. If I don't come back out and you see someone else come out of there, drive away. *Fast*. Do you understand?'

• • • •

SARAH POURED HERSELF ANOTHER DRINK. By Christ, she needed it. For the first time ever she'd made the decision to close the White Hart early. She'd never *ever* done that despite all the things that had previously happened, but her head was mashed. Things had gone one step beyond.

The punters had taken the early closure well. They weren't daft. They knew something major was going down. They didn't know what, but they knew Sarah well enough that if she said she needed to close, then she *did*.

She glanced at the clock and grimaced. Every minute passed like treacle and time felt like it was going backwards. She pulled tighter at her ponytail, random strands of hair sticking out of it in all directions. God, what a night and it was nowhere near over yet.

She flipped the tap of the lager as it reached the top of her pint glass, then gulped at it greedily. *Hurry up, Colin*, she thought, deep worry nagging. Whoever had trumped over the Reapers could still be hanging about. Could they really all be dead like that prospect had said?

She glanced at Shaky's empty stool and pint glass, a third still remaining. She'd tried to get him to stay – he was in no fit state to wander around. Plus, she was worried what he might do or say. She'd pleaded with him to stay put until Hunter returned, or at the very least, Colin. He'd been intent on going and she could hardly force him not to. She had, however, made him promise not to breathe a word about anything until it was known exactly what the state of play was.

Shaky had agreed of course, but Sarah doubted he hadn't been anywhere near coherent enough to take on board anything she'd said. He'd muttered something about needing to get back to make sure his mother was alright and that he shouldn't have left her in the first place and then he'd left.

Sarah took another massive gulp of her lager and wiped her hand across her brow before turning her attention back to Susan. She had, in all fairness, taken things a hell of a lot better than expected, but her constant mithering wasn't helping. Aside from Sarah's worry about Colin's safety, the dread of what was, or could be unfolding where Tori, Carmen, Hunter and Noel were, was very much forefront in her mind too. She hadn't quite decided how she felt about Jorge yet. What he'd done was totally unexpected. *Completely* unexpected and it had knocked her for six.

'What possessed her?' Susan asked suddenly, making Sarah jump with the abrupt infringement on the silence. 'What on *earth* made her go? In this situation?' She dabbed at her clammy face with a lace-edged handkerchief. 'I-I just don't know what to think of any of this.'

'You and me both,' Sarah muttered, finishing her pint, then immediately refilling it. She nodded at Susan's empty wine glass. 'Top up?'

'I might as well,' Susan said. 'I've drank more tonight than I have in my entire life!'

Sarah forced a smile. Personally, she needed a lot more to drink before it took the edge off the swirling thoughts racing in her mind. Reaching for the wine, Sarah all but dropped it as the pub door opened. Her body stiffened and her heart lurched.

Colin walked in, his face tinged with grey and the slight shake of his head confirmed to Sarah what she'd most dreaded. The prospect was correct. *The Reapers were dead.*

A wave of cold rushed over her and she bit down on her bottom lip.

Shit, this was bad.

FORTY EIGHT

'YOU CAN INSULT ME whichever way you like, but you're the one who committed the cardinal sin. Sleeping with another man's wife is out of order.' Neil smiled, seeing a slight twitch behind the maniacal grin plastered across Noel's swarthy face. *So, Carmen was his Achilles heel? Was the greasy bastard in love with the whore? Oh, that was even funnier.*

'Personally, I don't know why you bothered,' Neil continued. 'You know as well as I do that she's as shit in bed as she is out of it - a cunt like an old haystack, but maybe your gyppo types get off on shit like that?'

Bolstered by the building rage visibly increasing at a rate of knots inside Noel, Neil smiled. He'd been right. Despite his steely countenance, insulting the Reapers wasn't what would blow Noel's control. It was *Carmen*. This was easier that he'd thought. Noel was going to lose - he just hadn't quite realised it yet. A few more digs and it would be time to strike.

'How did it feel fucking my wife?' Neil asked. 'Did you enjoy shoving your mouldy cock in her? Make her scream, did you? Didn't you notice that she was pretending? Or perhaps she really does get off on half-bred imbeciles?'

Noel's knuckles whitened as he clenched his fists, his nails digging into his palms. *Concentrate, Noel. Don't let the wanker make you lose concentration.* Despite his intentions, Neil *was* getting to him. His brain conjured up vivid images of Carmen, her legs wrapped around his neck, her mouth forming a distinct "O" as she'd gasped in pleasure, shouted his name…

And he couldn't have her. He shouldn't have ever had her because she was… she was his…. He uncrossed his arms, his fingers twitching.

'Neil,' Jorge said, watching Noel struggle to keep his cool in check. He had to divert this. He hadn't mentioned a word to Neil about what Carmen had disclosed in the café, but Neil was speaking as though he knew exactly what to say to rub the salt in the wound. He stepped forward. 'Listen, I…'

'Fuck off out of this, Jorge,' Neil spat. He was wearing Noel down. He could see it. His slag of a wife had finally come in handy and he wouldn't let this unexpected opportunity go to waste.

'Her running off with you pissed me off, I admit it. She couldn't have insulted me more than by fucking a Reaper!' Neil's eyes gleamed at the raw hatred on Noel's face. 'But it's funny really, because you fell for her lies! You fucking fell for it, you loser!' he laughed. 'I can see it! She's fucked you off as well, hasn't she?'

Noel's jaw clenched, the nerve in his face picking up its familiar angry twitch and a low growl emanated from the back of his throat.

'Don't worry…' Neil grinned. 'Replace her with one of those sluts you lot keep at, what do you call it – the Factory…? My wife's probably already got your replacement between her legs as we speak!'

Neil grinned gleefully as Noel bared his teeth, his green eyes feral. 'Always a slag – nothing changes.' He glanced at the ceiling momentarily. A risk taking his eyes from the target, but Noel was his now. *The job was all but done.* 'Oh, wait…' he said, returning his cold stare back to Noel. 'That can't happen.' He smiled icily. 'Want to know why? Because the Reapers are finished. They're no more. They're all done. They're all fucking *dead*.'

'You're lying,' Noel growled, the knot in his stomach telling him regardless of what he wanted to believe, this wanker was telling the truth. They'd been done over. *Fuck. They'd been set up.*

'Yep. Just now... Well, on my way to see you, that is. None of them saw it coming, bless 'em. They looked ever so disappointed as they hit the deck... Especially the women...'

Jorge stumbled backwards in horror. He'd made things worse. They'd walked into a trap. *He'd* told Neil all of the other Reapers were at the Factory tonight rather than the White Hart. He'd asked of their whereabouts during the phone call and *he'd* supplied it. And he'd given him the door code that night at the hotel... *Oh fuck. Shit. FUCK!*

'I'll be finding my wife shortly and I'll do what she always pestered me for. Not that I often bothered. Whores aren't my type, but *this* time I'll enjoy fucking her brains out purely to rid her of every trace of your gyppo cock. And then after that, I'll kill her.'

Blinding white rage finally descending, Noel lunged towards his shotgun, his eyes on fire. 'You piece of shit!' he roared.

'Noel!' Jorge screamed, far too late. Neil had already pulled his pistol from his waistband.

· · · ·

'I'M NOT LEAVING YOU, HUNTER,' Tori gasped. 'We'll wait here, but we won't be driving away under any circumstances, whatever happens.' She reached for her handbag to retrieve the gun.

'Hurry up, Tori,' Carmen said from the front of the car. 'Give him the gun. He needs to g...' Hearing a loud crack echoing around them, she yelped. 'That was a gun! Oh my God!' She yanked at the door, her fumbling fingers desperately reaching for the door mechanism.

EDIE BAYLIS

Hunter lurched forward, gasping as pain twisted his insides when he grabbed hold of Carmen's arm. 'Stay where you are! I'm going in!'

Twisting her body away, made a lot easier by the seat between them, Carmen broke free of Hunter's grip and shoving the door open, she jumped from the car.

'Carmen!' Tori screamed. 'Stop! *Carmen!*'

Seeing Carmen disappear through the flat's entrance, Tori grappled with the catch of the back door. 'I must stop her,' she gasped, 'I've got to stop her bef...'

'You're going *nowhere*!' Hunter roared, grasping Tori around the waist, hoping to God that the shot which had rang out had been Noel's and that Neil Sparks was the one lying face down in a pool of his own blood. 'Give me the gun,' he roared. 'You stay here.'

His heart raced. What was Carmen thinking of, the stupid woman. Now Tori was trying to do the same thing. He didn't want either of their deaths on his hands.

Heart pounding, fear and desperation overtook Tori's common sense and she struggled with Hunter. Thanks to his injuries, she found it not too difficult to twist herself from his grasp and fling herself out of the door. She had to stop Carmen. Hunter wouldn't be quick enough, but she might be. She could still reach her in time. *Just.*

• • • •

CARMEN RACED UP the rickety, smelly stairwell to what she hoped was the correct flat, her heart banging loudly in her chest. *Please let Noel be alright, please...*

Whatever had happened between them, whatever *couldn't* happen between them now, was irrelevant. She'd hoped not to have to face him ever again, but she didn't in her wildest dreams want this. She'd never wanted this to be the reason not to see him again.

Reaching the top of the stairs, she moved as quickly and as quietly as possible towards the ajar door of the flat. She could

357

hear voices and with a sickening start, recognised the voice of Luca. Luca, Neil – whoever – her husband...

It wasn't the voice he'd used to speak to her, but a very different voice. The one she'd heard just that once when overhearing the phone call between him and her father. That conversation where Luca's strong southern twang was obvious. The phone call that had made her realise she'd been one of Luca's purchased commodities arranged by her own father and which had given her the impetus to leave. It had exposed her husband as the phony he was, but the one thing that she'd had no idea of until recently was that he was such an evil psycho. If she'd realised that before, then things might have been a lot different. She'd have had some warning of *this* for a start.

She swallowed, her dry mouth making it difficult. If she could hear Luca's voice, *Neil's* voice, then did that mean...? The shot... did that mean that...

Oh no, please no...

Creeping up to the door not wanting to look, but knowing she must, Carmen forced herself to peer through the gap.

There was Jorge... He was standing frozen. And Luca...

Her stomach lurched seeing her hated husband pointing the gun at Jorge.

But where was...

Tears burning, Carmen's eyes darted feverishly around the room, focusing on Noel's motionless body on the floor to the side of a small sofa, a large pool of dark red blood spreading out around his head like a flower in bloom.

In that instant she knew they were too late. *Noel was dead. That bastard had killed him.*

An ear-splitting scream enveloped Carmen and it took a good few seconds before she realised the noise was coming from her own mouth.

· · · ·

NEIL'S EYES DARTED TOWARDS the sudden and very unpleasant noise, unwilling to admit that it had actually startled him, but his face broke into a wide sneer when he realised where it was coming from. 'Ah, how nice of you to join us.'

Jorge's head swung around, initially relieved that the barrel of the gun had been momentarily diverted from him, but his relief was short lived seeing Carmen was the source of the unholy sound, her body sagging against the door jamb. *Hell, what was she doing here? She wasn't supposed to be here.*

Crossing the room in two large strides, Neil effortlessly dragged Carmen into the centre of the room, forcing her head down to within inches of Noel's inert body. 'Look what you've caused, you bitch! Because of you, your greasy fuckwit lover is dead! Have a good look, go on! See what you've made me do.'

Carmen retched at the sight of Noel's eyes staring sightlessly, his head twisted at a strange angle and she whimpered, her chest heaving.

'Yeah, shame isn't it? One shot to the heart is all it took. Not as infallible as he liked to believe.' Still keeping hold of Carmen, Neil swung around, aiming the gun back to Jorge just in case he was stupid enough to try and move. 'And as for *you*, you're a pointless worthless piece of shit, just like your mother.' He laughed loudly. 'Too thick to notice that you'd set your new "mates" up good and proper. Well, fat load of good you are. You've got every one of them killed, or you will have very soon.'

A sinister grin crawled across his face as he stared into Jorge's eyes, wishing his hatred for the boy could melt his skin off his body. 'Did you *really* think I wouldn't spot your double-cross? Did you presume I hadn't the nous to follow you? Yeah, that's right, I know exactly what you did, rescuing your mate from the hospital.' Clearing his throat, Neil spat a ball of thick phlegm into Jorge's face. 'You're no son of mine.'

Neil clubbed Jorge around the face with the butt of the pistol and smiled as he fell to his knees, blood gushing from his nose. 'I can't be too long playing with you two. I've got a few more to finish off before the night is out.'

He turned back to Carmen, satisfied Jorge wasn't going

anywhere in a hurry. 'Hunter will be next and his pretty little wifey, or whatever she is too. Why not eh? Might as well add her to the list. Oh and of course, *him* – my plastic, pointless son...' He jerked his head at Jorge. 'But I don't want to leave you out, do now I Carmen? How rude would that be? And then finally, I'll go and see your daddy.'

'You're too late for that,' Carmen spat, rage replacing her terror. She jutted out her chin in defiance rather that than let the bastard she'd married see her devastation. 'Noel beat you to it. Richard's dead.'

Neil masked his flinch before it became visible, but her words had got to him. *He'd wanted Stevens. He'd wanted to be the one to shaft that pompous fool.*

Walking over, Neil slowly traced his finger along Carmen's face, down her cheekbone and across her jaw. 'Now now, my beautiful wife... Do you think that matters to me now?' He forced himself to plunge his hand inside her top, squeezing her breast hard. 'Now then, whore. Let's see what you're going to do for me.'

Carmen stiffened, nausea enveloping her. To think that once she'd wanted his attention, but not now. *Certainly not now.* 'Get your hands off me,' she spat.

Chuckling, Neil grabbed a handful of Carmen's long blonde hair and yanked her forwards. 'I paid your ponce of a father *thousands* for you, so I'll do what I damn well want!'

Yelping in pain, scalp burning, Carmen found herself dragged to the centre of the room and flung forward to land heavily on Jorge who grunted as her elbow smashed into his already broken nose.

Jorge looked up, his panicked eyes portraying more than his voice. 'Don't worry... I'll think of som...'

'Get the fuck up. *Both* of you!' Neil roared. 'Get on your feet NOW!' He pressed the barrel of his gun hard into the back of Carmen's neck.

'Just get up,' Jorge muttered to Carmen under his breath. He had to think of something. Anything to stop Neil in his tracks. Now Noel was dead he was at a distinct disadvantage where manpower to assist was concerned, meaning it was down to him and him alone. He could *not* let this maniac shoot Carmen. He'd been party to getting everyone into this mess, so it was down to him to try and get them out of it.

Carmen gingerly moved into a kneeling position, acutely aware of the cold metal pressed firmly into her. One slight wrong move would be all it took. Her heart raced. Could she swing around and kick the gun out of his hand? Would Jorge be able to overpower him?

She risked another glance at the half-visible crumpled body of Noel to the side of the sofa and felt a choking sob rise.

'I said, get up' Neil roared. Stepping back, he allowed enough room for Carmen and Jorge to struggle to their feet, ensuring the barrel of the gun did not divert from keeping one or other of them in its sights.

Once they had staggered upright, Neil eyed Jorge scornfully. 'The question is, which one of you should I kill first?' He swung the gun in Jorge's direction. '*You* to start with, I think. As I said, there's things I want from Carmen first.'

Abruptly changing direction, Neil pointed the barrel between Carmen's eyes. 'Although perhaps my errant scrubber of a wife deserves to die first? In actuality, I'm not sure I want to go anywhere that's been with *that*.' He kicked Noel's body as an afterthought. 'Hmm, it's a difficult call... you've both betrayed me.' A slow smile passed across his face. 'And that was a very silly thing to do...'

'Shoot me!' Jorge exclaimed, stepping closer to Neil. If he could divert Neil enough, Carmen may be able to make a run for it. There was a small chance it might work. 'Go on! You would have anyway, regardless. You're a fucking nutter, so go on. DO IT!'

FORTY NINE

BREAKING FREE FROM HUNTER, Tori raced towards the entrance to the flat.

'Tori!' Hunter yelled, knowing he wouldn't catch up with her in time. Heart beating ten to the dozen, he placed his hand over the throbbing wound in his mid-section and limped slowly after her. 'Tori! Use it! Use the damn gun!' he shouted. 'Do what I showed you! Use the fucking gun!'

Tori had already disappeared into the flat's stairwell, but she'd heard Hunter's words. *Jesus Christ.* Her heart in her mouth, she slipped up the stairs, her shaking fingers scrabbling in the bottom of her bag as she went.

Closing her hand around the cold metal of the gun, she pulled it from her bag. *Was she really doing this? Could she really do it?*

Tori swallowed the rising bile. She had to. She had to at least attempt to stop this nightmare. It went against everything she'd ever stood for, but Carmen, Noel and Jorge were up there and they were in danger. Or maybe it was just Carmen and Jorge? Or Carmen and Noel? Someone had been shot already and being as Carmen hadn't come out, she didn't think Neil Sparks was the casualty.

Please let them be alright, she chanted silently as she moved further up the stairwell, wishing beyond anything that she wasn't in this hideous situation. Hunter was following, but it would take him an age to get up these steps. He could barely walk as it was. This was down to her.

She would have to do it. She would have to shoot Neil Sparks.

Desperately recalling what Hunter had shown her, she fumbled with the pistol's safety catch. *Was that it?* Oh, dear God, she had no idea, her mind a complete blank. Her heart banged noisily in her ears.

She could hear voices. *That was Jorge talking.*

Tori edged towards the open door, spotting Noel on the ground at once. She bit down on the inside of her cheek to stop the sob from escaping her mouth.

There was Carmen too, standing behind Jorge. Jorge was to the front, his face covered in blood, contorting with rage as he shouted at the man. That man… That must be Neil Sparks.

Creeping down the hallway praying for no squeaky floorboards, Tori neared the room. What if the man spotted her? He'd got a gun; it was pointing at Jorge and she guessed he was much better at using one of those things than she was.

Unsure how she mustered the strength to lift the pistol, Tori took aim, her arms and fingers shaking violently. *Calm down and concentrate. Remember what you need to do.*

Jorge was close to the other man and the man kept moving as he toyed with Carmen and Jorge. She had to do it. She *had* to do it…

If she aimed for the man's arm or leg Would it be enough to make the man helpless? Would that be enough to stop him and enable Carmen and Jorge to escape?

Tori willed her arms to stop shaking and she focused her mind on what Hunter had said when attempting to teach her to shoot. Her finger closed around the trigger, the barrel wobbling. She wasn't aiming this correctly, she was sure of it.

Come on. Think… THINK!

Squinting one eye, she lined the barrel up with Neil's arm. If she shot his arm, he'd drop the gun. He'd drop the gun and wouldn't be able to shoot anyone. *Just do it. Come on, Tori.*

Applying more pressure, she squeezed the trigger.

Jerking from the recoil, Tori's ears buzzed when the shot rang out deafeningly as the bullet released.

She watched in slow motion as Neil Sparks turned in her direction in surprise, whilst Carmen's head snapped around to face her, her mouth hanging open. Jorge's eyes widened, his expression one of being stunned, the bullet making a clean round hole through the centre of his forehead before he soundlessly collapsed to the ground.

· · · ·

RAPIDLY REGAINING HIS COMPOSURE from the interruption, Neil laughed loudly, the nasal cackle echoing loudly around the sparsely furnished room. He grinned watching the gun the woman held fall from her hand and clatter to the floor.

'Wonderful shot,' he said, enjoying how the woman remained exactly where she was, paralysed in complete shock. 'I couldn't have taken a better shot myself, although I'm presuming that bullet was meant for me?'

Lurching forward, he kicked the gun away from Tori, sending it skittering down the hallway and grabbing her arm, yanked her into the lounge. 'Well, well,' Neil said, eyeing her curiously. 'That's two women now coming to the aid of men. What's the world coming to? How times have changed.'

Carmen touched Tori's arm gently for no real purpose, other than to perhaps reassure herself that Tori was real and what had just happened wasn't a figment of her imagination, then forced her eyes to look down at Jorge lying on his back, devoid of life. *Christ, how could all of this be happening?*

Tori stumbled slightly. 'I-I didn't mean to shoot him... I...'

'Shut it!' Neil barked, cuffing Carmen's hand off Tori. 'And you can stop moving about as well. This is why women should be exterminated. Another classic example of how they consistently fuck everything up.' Raising his arm, he pointed the gun at the women. 'No men about to do their job? The only one left is recuperating somewhere from a half-healed bullet wound. What a shame that will all be in vain.'

He shook his head patronisingly. 'Oh well. Never mind, girls. You,' he glared at Carmen, 'shouldn't have turned me over and insulted me and *you*,' he turned to Tori, 'should have stayed home and not stuck your nose into other's business.'

A strangled sob emerged from Tori. She'd killed Jorge. *She'd killed him.* Oh God. How had that happened? She knew she couldn't be trusted to use one of those things properly and now she'd killed someone. Sweat poured down her neck and her legs felt like they might fold on her. Her ears were making a humming noise and the walls felt like they were closing in. *She'd killed Jorge… No, oh NO…*

Neil glanced at his watch, sighing in boredom. 'Do you know what, I'm sick to death of this. I'm fed up of wasting time. You two aren't worth the fucking hassle. I want to wrap this up now. You've saved me a bit of time, so thanks for that, but I need to get on the road.'

Raising the gun, he pressed it against Tori's temple, satisfied she hadn't the energy to move and he was right.

• • • •

WITH SWEAT POURING down his face, Hunter's breath caught in shallow gasps as he pushed through the excruciating pain. Overriding the overwhelming nausea smothering him, he edged closer to the room where he could hear the man's voice. A man's voice he didn't recognise – *Neil Sparks' voice.*

Strands of damp hair clung to his face as he reached the top of the stairs and began to move along the narrow hallway. He'd been two steps up when he heard the unmistakeable sound of a gun once more and despite his physical limitations, he'd have gladly disembowelled himself to find the reserve to run up the remaining steps and into the flat if it meant he could keep Tori safe. But despite the urge and need to race to her aid, he kept his head, knowing well enough that if he had any chance of turning this around, then he couldn't afford to burst in.

If Neil Sparks was still breathing and judging by the voice he could hear, he was, then he would be shot on sight and that would not help anyone. That's if there was anyone left to help?

There must be. Sparks wouldn't be having a conversation with himself would he, Hunter reasoned? The question that was ransacking his mind was *who* he was having the conversation with?

Hunter's stomach twisted into a knot as he inched closer to the open door. He couldn't hear anyone else's voice and his instinct told him that the overall news wasn't good. A congealing mix of anger and raw pain engulfed him. *Was Tori dead? Noel? Carmen?*

A bead of sweat dripped from the tip of his nose onto his top lip, it's salty taste strong. How would he do this? He had no gun. Tori had the gun and Noel had the other one. And they were both in the room with Sparks. *Somewhere.*

Christ, if anything happened to Tori...

Nearing the door, Hunter spotted the edge of a pair of boots. Noel's. Noel was down.

Clenching his jaw, Hunter flattened himself against the wall, the coolness of the damp hallway soothing his burning skin through the T-shirt clinging clammily to his back.

There he was. Sparks, the bastard. And he'd got his hands on Tori...

Sparks' left arm was wrapped tightly around Tori's slender neck, her head twisted at an angle, her eyes wide, yet dull – almost trance-like. In shock...

Get the fuck off her, Hunter raged silently, his inner fury building higher.

It was then he saw the gun pressed against her temple.

'Luca, let her go!' Carmen's voice sounded clearly from inside the room. 'It's me you have the issue with, not her. Let her go, I beg you.'

Hunter's breath was ragged. He couldn't see Carmen, only Tori and that bastard, Sparks, but her could *hear* her. No sound from anyone else.

Adrenalin coursed furiously through Hunter's veins. *If he shot her… If he fucking shot her…*

He had to act quickly, but how? Sparks was facing in his direction. Any detection of sudden movement and he'd be dust – or worse, Tori would be shot.

Hunter's eyes darted around the dark hallway in the hope of finding something, *anything*, he could use as a makeshift weapon. A chair? An ornament? But there was nothing. Nothing at all.

Wait! He squinted in the gloom, spying the slight glint of metal in the corner this side of the door, almost hidden in the shadows and his heart raced. *Tori's gun. It was Tori's gun… If he could reach it without being spotted…*

Staying flattened against the wall, Hunter twisted his hips, his right leg inching painfully slowly towards the gun. If he could just reach the edge of it…

He willed the toe of his boot to catch the edge. Anywhere that he could begin to pull it towards him. *Don't make sudden movement, he'll spot you*, Hunter repeated to himself silently. *Slowly, slowly does it…*

'Luca!' Carmen yelped from inside the room. 'Let her go!'

'I am *not* Luca and never have been as you now know, you stupid bitch, so stop calling me that!' Neil growled. 'And I heard you the first time. Beg all you want, but it won't make a bit of difference.'

Anger pulsing, Hunter stretched his foot further, his leg at full capacity. *Come on, come on!* He was running out of time and he knew it.

'And shut up with the whining,' Neil barked. 'Nothing's going to help any of you now.' He laughed caustically. 'It's too late for them and too late for you!'

'NO!' Carmen screamed.

Hunter heard the unmistakeable sound of the gun being

cocked and knew he was almost out of time. Sparks was going to shoot and he had nothing to lose by going for it now. *Come on!*

Lurching forward, Hunter bypassed the aim of avoiding detection and swiped the gun off the floor with his hand, hoping it was still loaded and praying that Tori hadn't done something ridiculous like bothering to put the safety catch back on.

It would be tight getting the shot right with only a few inches to spare between the woman he loved and the man he wanted to kill and he had to somehow factor in that the man would move the second he was aware of his presence.

And he didn't know which way that move would be. It would make all the difference.

Without a moment to lose, he swung his body into the doorway in full view, knowing he had less than a second to take aim before pulling the trigger.

Hunter could only say a silent prayer as he unloaded the gun whilst Neil Sparks, seeing him suddenly appear in the doorway, changed direction and swung his gun.

· · · ·

THE ROOM WAS DEATHLY SILENT for a few seconds that felt like hours before Tori began screaming. Screaming a gut-wrenching animalistic sound as the body of Neil Sparks weighed heavily on top of her, blood and gore dripping steadily onto her from the missing piece of his temple.

The weight of the man was crushing her, suffocating her. What had happened? She couldn't stay here like this! The noise of her own screaming barely registered through the ringing in her ears from the gunshot. The gunshot that had come from nowhere.

Suddenly, the crushing weight lifted and Tori gasped feverishly, air flooding into her crushed lungs. Still screaming with unbridled panic, she scraped at her face to rid her eyes and skin of whatever had spilled out of the man's skull. It was horrible. *Horrible.*

'It's ok, it's ok.' Hunter scooped Tori into her arms as he knelt next to her, her blind panic making her fight against him. 'It's me, Tori. It's *me*!'

Tori blinked. *The voice...* 'Hunter?' she gasped, focusing as his familiar face came into view. 'Is that you? Is it really you?'

Pulling her tighter against his chest, Hunter held Tori close, feeling every single fibre in her body trembling. He'd done it. His gamble had paid off. *Thank Christ!* 'It's me and you're alright. It's over. It's all over.'

'But Carmen?' Tori cried. 'Carmen? Is she...?'

'I'm ok, I'm here too. We're ok,' Carmen said, her shaking legs somehow propelling her forwards from where she'd been paralysed in terror, still not quite able to fathom that the situation had been turned around. *She'd really thought that... thought that it was the end... That both she and Tori would die.*

Suddenly, a horrible thought bulldozed into her brain. 'Is he dead, Hunter? Is the bastard dead?' Carmen crouched on the floor next to Tori, putting her arms around her friend, whilst Hunter, grimacing with pain, pushed himself to his feet.

With narrowed eyes he stared with abject hatred at the man who had very nearly taken the life of the woman he loved from him as well as everything else he'd already taken. He cocked the gun once more. 'He is, but just to make doubly sure...'

Carmen and Tori screamed again as he unloaded the gun twice more into Neil Sparks' face sending more fragments of bone and flesh flying.

Hunter stepped back and lowered the gun, wiping his hands down his jeans. He shoved the pistol in his waistband, angrily glancing at the bodies of Noel and also Jorge that he could now clearly see. 'The bastard...' he muttered.

Tori dissolved into further sobs, along with Carmen finally giving way to her tears. 'Jorge was trying to save Carmen and... and I ruined it. It was me... I killed him... I...'

Hunter glanced around the room and pulled both women to their feet. 'It's over. We need to leave.'

FIFTY

SARAH WALKED SLOWLY UP THE ROAD. Raising her head, she looked up at the clear blue sky, not a cloud in sight and exhaled deeply, releasing some of the pent up stress she'd been holding in the whole night.

She'd been unable to truly let go how she felt, but by the end of last night she'd let more go than she had for a long while. Still, no matter how much she worked on her deep breathing techniques today, it was unlikely that she'd reconcile this anytime soon. God only knew how the rest were feeling.

Sarah shuddered. It had been bad enough when Colin had returned from the Factory, confirming all the Reapers were dead, along with the women present too. It was too horrible for words. All those people – most of which she'd had a lot of time for, gone. Grin, Billy – *all* of them.

She shook her head in disbelief, unable to imagine what it must have been like for Colin picking his way through the pile of mangled bodies, but she'd hazard a guess the experience wouldn't be leaving his brain any time soon – if ever.

Sarah paused, tempted to wander off to find a nice park well off the beaten track where she could chill out unmolested for the rest of the day. Somewhere that she wouldn't have to deal with this. But whether she, or any of them wanted to take it on board, even though the main part of this nightmare was thankfully finally over, there was still more that had to be done. She sighed, knowing what was needed, but no one had yet broached it.

She looked up the road towards the newsagents where she was heading. She had to get what she'd come out for and return to the White Hart pronto. Although it was still early, they needed to face this, talk and decide exactly how to handle the aftermath before the aftermath handled *them*.

When Hunter, Tori and Carmen had appeared about an hour after Colin, the mixture of emotions she'd experienced last night were a combination of relief and shock, but within seconds her relief became bittersweet, quickly realising with a heavy heart, from their combined expressions alone, that Noel wouldn't be appearing. Not then, not ever.

Nor Jorge. Although she'd been previously angry about his part in things, from what Carmen had said, he'd been trying to protect her until the end.

Sarah cringed. Of course, she'd put her foot in it by ranting about Neil Sparks again, only to discover that it was *Tori* to inadvertently put a bullet in Jorge. She still couldn't quite believe it. There was a lot of questions she'd wanted to ask – that she *still* wanted to ask, but last night that had been impossible. Everyone was far too punch drunk. Hunter had been in his own angry world, Carmen was numb and Tori, well, Tori hadn't stopped sobbing.

Sarah sighed sadly. Tori would find it near impossible to forgive herself. She would have had a problem hurting *anyone* – even Neil Sparks, but to accidentally kill Jorge would never sit well with her psyche. The girl would have to pull herself together fast if she wanted to get through this. In fact, she didn't know if *any* of them would, but she had to hope they could.

Susan had surprised her though. Maybe it was the vast amount of wine she'd consumed during the long evening or down to finally letting loose some inner strength she'd previously been unaware of, but whatever the reason, she'd taken control of the situation and ordered, yes, *ordered* everyone to get some sleep.

It was the best thing that could have happened under the circumstances and Sarah was glad because for once in her life her self-control had begun slipping away. It could have been a delayed reaction, or the culmination of too many things, but for the first time in a very long time, she'd felt completely helpless and at a loss at what to do. She'd surrendered to the tears and had all but crumbled, her bones reducing to jelly as she'd folded into a chair, sobbing.

Sarah made her mouth form into a smile as a couple she recognised waved from the opposite side of the road and hoped they didn't walk over to strike up a conversation. Despite feeling a lot better in herself after a few hours sleep, she wasn't anywhere near up to answering questions just yet.

Quickening her pace, Sarah neared the shop. She must hurry and get back. It was only a matter of time, if it hadn't already happened, before the bodies at the Factory and elsewhere were discovered, so they had to expect questions sooner rather than not.

Reaching the shop, Sarah took a deep breath before forcing herself to look at the sandwich board outside displaying the latest local headlines and her heart sank. *At least it wasn't about the Factory.*

Stepping inside and grabbing a bottle of milk, Sarah picked up a copy of the morning edition of the paper.

The newsagent smiled. 'Morning, Sarah.'

'Hi, Kev,' Sarah replied, happy to sound no different to any other time she'd been in here over the past few years and hoped she'd ventured out early enough before punters from the pub put it on the grapevine that she'd made the previously unheard of decision to close the White Hart early.

Kev nodded at the newspaper Sarah laid on the counter with the milk. 'Crazy business that,' he said. 'I wonder where they've buggered off to?'

Sarah shrugged nonchalantly. 'God knows…'

Kev snorted in derision as Sarah handed over the money. 'I'm just glad I never banked there! Jeez, all that hard earned cash probably paying for a villa in the Maldives for the pair of them, by the looks of it. Cheeky bastards!' He frowned. 'Hey, are you alright?'

Sarah nodded and made a point of rubbing her temples. 'I woke up with a stinking headache,' she lied. 'I'll be alright once I get a decent cup of tea down my neck.'

Keeping her smile firmly plastered in place until she left the shop, she walked until reaching a low wall further down the road. Sitting down, she eyed the photograph of Richard and Susan on the front page and scanned the accompanying article:

Bank Manager Shock

A body has been found at the home of local bank manager, Richard Stevens.

Sixty-two year old Andrew Mercer, a friend of the Stevens' family, was discovered at Richard Stevens' home late yesterday afternoon by the family's horrified gardener, Darren Davies.

Mr Davies, worried when arriving for his weekly gardening job at the property, spotting the front door of Mr Stevens' palatial home open. Receiving no response to his knocking, he attempted to investigate, only to be met with the most gruesome scene.

The police, who arrived following Mr Davies' 999 call, found Mr Mercer's body in the kitchen. Cause of death - a single shotgun wound to the head. Several shotguns were discovered at the house and a source confirmed that initial forensic tests showed one of these guns was recently fired.

Although the police are yet to formerly confirm matters,

this was clearly not an accident.

Concern was raised for the safety of Mr and Mrs Stevens, who appeared absent from the property. Mr Stevens' Aston Martin, as well as his Jaguar is missing, although paperwork found in the house shows the Jaguar has recently and unexpectedly been sold.

Tracing possibilities of Mr and Mrs Stevens' whereabouts revealed a further worrying development: shockingly, Mr Stevens is under investigation by the bank for fraud and theft. Popular and renowned in his circles, this will surely come as a shock that Mr Stevens, recently retired from his long-standing position of branch manager, is suspected by the bank of stealing millions of pounds over the last twenty-five years.

The bank's headquarters in London confirmed that Mr Stevens is due to attend a formal hearing this coming Tuesday, but now he and his wife – Susan, are nowhere to be seen. Speculation is that Mr and Mrs Stevens, aware that they were about to be exposed for fraud, have disappeared, possibly fleeing the country to evade imprisonment.

As well as committing fraud and stealing from many trusting people and companies over the years, is Richard Stevens also responsible for the murder of his friend, Andrew Mercer?

The police are appealing for anyone with any information on the possible whereabouts of Mr and Mrs Stevens to get in immediate contact using the telephone number at the bottom of the page. They have also stated that under no circumstances should anyone approach or attempt to apprehend the couple as they may be armed.

We will, as always keep you up to date as more news comes in surrounding these shocking events.

Sarah swallowed down a giggle surfacing with the thought of Susan brandishing a shotgun when she could barely bring herself to use a can opener.

It wasn't funny though, *certainly* not funny. The police had found one body and Susan was in the frame for fraud. She couldn't say she was surprised at Richard's theft from what she knew personally of his business dealings, but it was only a matter of time before someone from the pub put two and two together and recognised Susan from the photograph in this paper. They needed to make sure they got in with things before that happened otherwise it would open a whole can of worms.

Quickly getting up, Sarah increased her pace back to the White Hart, hoping that by now everyone had surfaced. Whether they liked it or not, decisions had to be made. And it didn't look like they had much time.

FIFTY ONE

'IT'S THE ONLY THING WE CAN DO,' Sarah said, glancing at everyone crammed around her kitchen table, her common sense managing to hold everyone in check.

'I-I still can't believe they think *I'm* involved in what Richard's done... or rather what he *did*,' Susan corrected herself, staring obsessively at the paper's front page.

Sarah raised an eyebrow. 'You've got to see how it looks from an outside perspective. It certainly does look like you were involved or at the very least, aware of what was going on. I mean, a dead guy on the floor and "pair disappears amidst fraud investigation", doesn't look great.'

'B-But I had no idea he'd been stealing money. I never knew, I swear!' Susan wailed. 'I don't know what happened with Mercer either! It horrifies me. I'd never have carried on wi...'

'No one's saying you did, Mum,' Carmen reasoned. 'We believe you but...'

'All of these things... these things Richard has done, he...'

'Listen,' Hunter barked. 'Sarah's right. We've got to move on this quickly.' Although quiet when Sarah had returned, demanding they discuss what to do, he had been thinking and thinking hard.

Figuratively speaking, his head was split in several places. Although he hadn't slept much, in the end he'd got an hour or so, but had woken equally as angry as he'd been last night. His concern for Tori was high and he'd found it difficult to console her to any great effect. No matter what he'd said, she was beside herself; absolutely destitute over what she'd done.

He should never have asked her to carry that gun. He knew what a dreadful shot she was. Telling her that the outcome would most likely have been Jorge's fate anyway hadn't helped much, but it was true. Whichever way anyone looked at it, Jorge had double-crossed everyone. Tori had just saved him the trouble of doing it, but that hadn't made her feel better.

Hunter took a slug of his now lukewarm tea, the increasing pain around his wound worsening. He winced, feeling physically sick. He hadn't helped himself by leaving hospital, but what was he supposed to do? No matter, he'd deal with that later. First of all, he had to deal with *this*.

Despite zoning out Susan's self-righteous and panicky bleating as much as possible, it was still infiltrating his brain and he wished she'd just give it a rest. However, the paper Sarah had brought back with her had, despite horrifying Susan, given him food for thought and a decent amount of info to work with.

'Like I said.' Sarah took the paper out of Susan's hands. 'For once it will be *us* who go to the police before they come for us.' She glanced at Hunter. 'I know you don't like that idea, but they'll discover… discover what happened at the Factory before long, plus everything else and…'

'We'll all go to prison!' Carmen said, her tone matter of fact.

'Actually, it will be *me* who goes to prison,' Tori said sharply. The only words she'd uttered all morning. 'I-I killed Jorge, so I deserve it. I'll phone them myself.'

Hunter banged his fist on the table, making everybody jump. 'Stop right there, all of you! Over my dead body will you be going to prison, Tori. Sparks and Stevens will take the rap for this.'

'But they're dead, how can th…'

'I'll be the only one serving time from this, so hear me out,' Hunter said, looking at each of them in turn, glad to see that he now had everyone's undivided attention.

'This.' He snatched the paper from Sarah's hands. 'Has helped us immensely.'

'Helped us?' Susan shrieked. 'How can that possibly have helped? I'm a wanted person. The police are looking for me an…'

'Mum!' Carmen said sternly. She wanted to hear Hunter's thoughts. As much as she didn't want her mother arrested for what her bloody father had done, neither did she want Hunter going to prison for shooting her husband. And she certainly didn't want Tori being locked up for that dreadful accident either. Because that's what happened to Jorge had been. An *accident*. Going to prison would kill Tori and it would kill her mother. It wouldn't kill Hunter, but why should he suffer for shooting the man who had done… done all of those things?

Luca, Neil or whoever the bloody hell he really was, had caused this – along with her father, not Hunter, not Tori and not her mother.

Satisfied Susan was staying quiet, Hunter continued. 'Look, none of us are in a good state. I'll hold my hands up to that.' He stared around the table, his eyes wild with anger. 'I have personally lost virtually everyone that matters to me and I also very nearly lost *you*.' He looked at Tori, his eyes softening for a split second before hardening again. 'We've *all* lost and we're all gutted, right?'

Receiving small nods, he continued. 'So, if anyone's going down, it will be *me*,' he growled. 'It will not be *you*.' He squeezed Tori's hand and then glanced at Susan and Carmen, 'or anyone else.'

He took a deep breath. 'We all know who the real offenders were here and so, despite not wanting to involve the police, Sarah's right. We'll let them come to their own conclusions, but we'll be putting our side first. They'll be coming for me and all of us soon.' A slight smile spread across his face. 'So, we're going to get in first and,' he stabbed his finger at the paper, 'we'll let the others take the rap for the rest of this too. Noel is dead.' Hunter's voice faltered slightly. 'But he won't be posthumously carrying the fucking can for Stevens' demise, I can tell you that much. Sparks will be taking the rap for that.'

Carmen frowned. 'But how wi...'

'Think about it.' Hunter folded his arms across his chest. 'Between them, Sparks and Stevens can take all of this, short of Sparks' own end of course. I'll take that one.'

Hunter spread the paper out on the table. 'All it needs is us all sticking to the story – most of which, I might add, is true, so it won't be hard.' His attention focused on Carmen and Susan. 'And I'm afraid ladies, it does mean things will be brought up that that you would rather weren't.'

Carmen and Susan nodded numbly.

Hunter pulled his full attention to Susan. 'Susan, you need to corroborate that you made the decision to leave your husband the day before this happened.'

'Which you did,' Carmen agreed, squeezing her mother's hand.

'Witnesses – not any of us, but people from the pub can truthfully state that you were downstairs in the bar of the White Hart, because you *were*. You did not disappear with your husband. You had no knowledge of his fraud, but you had recently found out that he... that he may have killed a child... You have the letter from your son as evidence of this.'

Tori sobbed quietly behind her hand watching Susan nod.

'That's the reason you left. Stevens can take the flack for shooting Mercer. His shotgun had been fired – they already know that. *We* know he used it to shoot me, but *they* don't. I said I had no idea who shot me and quite frankly, I don't think they care.'

'But why would my father kill Mercer?' Carmen asked. 'How do we explain that?'

379

Hunter shrugged. 'Who knows? I need to think about that one.'

'Actually, Richard hated Andrew Mercer, even though he outwardly pretended not to. I-I can tell them that and suggest that perhaps Andrew Mercer found out about the fraud and could have been blackmailing him?' Susan said, her voice small, yet growing in confidence.

Sarah smiled at Susan's newly found attitude. 'That's the spirit. But where does Sparks come into it?'

'That one's easy. He was after Stevens,' Hunter said before looking over to Carmen apologetically. 'That's where I'm afraid it'll come out about your arranged marriage.'

Carmen nodded. 'That's ok. Say what's needed. It's not like it wasn't true – just embarrassing.' Her face fell. 'I-I don't want it to come out about... about Noel being my... my brot...'

'That won't be mentioned,' Hunter said resolutely. 'There's no reason why they will dig that up. I wouldn't want to do that to you or Noel. Any of you, in fact. All the police will be told is that Sparks had an issue with Stevens. It was Sparks who killed Stevens.'

'But you said Noel did that in the Reapers warehouse?' Carmen cried. 'What can we do about that?'

Hunter thought for a moment. 'Hmm... perhaps Sparks was attempting to set Noel up for Richard's murder when he discovered he was having an affair with Carmen?'

Carmen flushed red, her hands shaking. 'But that will mean...'

'It will be easy for them to find out you were with Noel, but it doesn't mean your genetics will be revealed. Why would they be? Whatever happens, Neil will get the blame for Stevens' murder. It will then follow suit why he killed Noel and why he killed Jorge.'

Tori's eyes opened wide. 'I killed Jorge!'

Hunter frowned. 'Concentrate, Tori. *Sparks* killed Jorge because he discovered his son was trying to save *me* from what was planned after trying to set us up first,' he corrected, a smile forming across his face. 'You've got to get over this guilt. It happened, but that's it.' *It was all coming together and providing Tori got a grip, it would work.*

'When we speak to the police, Carmen will say Sparks said that he killed Stevens and set the Reapers up to take the flack. You'll also state you heard Sparks tell Noel that he'd gunned down the Factory.' Hunter raised his hands. 'It's all true and Sparks was planning to kill you all, so no one would have known what he'd done. Listen, before you get on your high horse, the only bit we're twisting is Stevens and Jorge. It's not a problem.'

'But what about *you*?' Sarah interjected. 'Who killed Sparks?'

Hunter cocked an eyebrow. 'Me of course. What else could I have done when he had a gun to the head of the woman I love and was also planning to kill Carmen as well as me? No court in the land will see that wasn't self-defence and provocation.' He shrugged. 'Besides, I have a good brief, who I'll call as soon as we're finished here. Then we'll call the cops. I'll probably get a couple of years, but I can live with that.'

Tori looked up. 'I-I don't want you to go to prison... I...'

'This is the only realistic way any of us will be able to do anything without looking over our shoulder for the rest of our lives,' Hunter said dismissively. 'We can't wait for them to come for us, agreed?'

Receiving a stunned silence, Hunter grimaced as he rose to his feet and clutched the table for support.

'You need to get that checked out again, Hunter,' Sarah said, eying his pain-ravaged face.

'Probably, but that can wait,' he said. 'Let's get this over with first.'

ONE YEAR LATER - 1993

'IT'S SO GREAT TO SEE YOU BOTH!' Sarah exclaimed, possibly for the fourteenth time since she'd arrived. Swigging from her pint of lager she smiled widely at Tori. 'You look absolutely fantastic, Tori, doesn't she Col?'

Colin grinned seeing Tori smile self-consciously. 'Definitely! And how's things with you now, Hunter?' he asked. 'Everything fixed?'

Hunter nodded and patted his midriff. 'As much as it can be, mate, yes.'

Tori smiled at Hunter. Yes, he was physically much better, although she'd wondered how things would go after being readmitted to hospital shortly after that fateful night…

Her face fell. She didn't really want to have to think about that, but seeing Sarah and Colin properly for the first time since would invariably mean some things being mentioned – at least to some extent.

By the hint of uncomfortableness on Hunter's face, Tori knew this was difficult for him too. Physically he was much better, but it couldn't quite be said the same mentally. On the whole he was gradually settling down, although there were still many days when she worried incessantly about him, but she accepted there would always be a part of him trapped in what had happened, as there would be for her too. For *all* of them.

It had taken a long time and she was getting there slowly, but it had been a long road.

But they had new things to look forward to now. Somehow, after everything they'd been through, they'd been given a second chance. Although they both had their difficult days, keeping busy and concentrating on the here and now was the key to move forward and before too much longer they'd be even *more* busy than they were at the moment.

Trying to keep herself upbeat, Tori smiled. 'I'm just so glad you could make it,' she said. 'I don't know what we'd have done if you couldn't get cover for the pub.'

Sarah grinned. 'Wouldn't have missed this weekend for the world! Hopefully the place won't burn down in our absence!' Seeing Tori's face, she laughed. 'I'm only joking! We gave up trying to find a punter sober enough to cope, so got a temp couple in from the brewery. They'll be absolutely fine.'

'I can now actually say for once that I know how you feel,' Tori said. 'We were lucky enough to get the previous tenant here to stand in for us. They're well averse to the ropes as well as the locals.'

'We didn't get chance to look around much on our way in, but it seems a lovely place you've got here,' Colin said, admiringly.

Coupled with Hunter's support, having this pub to run had made a huge difference to both of them. Initially sceptical and worried as to how she'd cope with it, or even if she *wanted* to do it, Tori was now more than grateful that Hunter had pushed her to accept his decision on what to do with the money from the sale of the Factory.

The Black Dog; the sixteenth century coaching house in the village was good for her. Popular with the locals and tourists alike, the Dog had a well-established trade and they'd been very lucky in securing it. The previous owners were only selling as they'd wanted to retire and spend their time the other side of the bar, rather than behind it. In fact, they were organising the spread for tomorrow and all the regulars were invited.

Tori and Hunter had been accepted into the close knit community with open arms and for the first time in a very long time, if not *ever*, she felt contented.

She watched a bird land on the feeder she'd placed in the small private garden at the back of the pub and smiled. 'It's fantastic. Do you know, this time last year I didn't think I'd ever have anything to smile about again.' *And now she had lots.*

'I think we all felt like that,' Sarah agreed. 'But it couldn't have turned out better for any of us really, given the circumstances.'

Tori nodded. That was true but she still had nightmares. She still had days when she felt consumed with guilt about Jorge. As always, Hunter had been her rock and kept her focused, despite his own demons. And she was more grateful than words could say to have been spared him being sent to jail.

Hunter had been correct when he'd said his brief was good. He'd got Hunter off the charges against Neil Sparks with self-defence and extreme provocation. The judge had agreed the circumstances were extenuating and that a custodial sentence was not relevant, given the situation, so he'd walked. He'd actually *walked* free.

For all of them, half of the last year had been consumed with lawyers, courts and police and she'd been living on a tightrope dreading what might happen, but it was all over now. Well, that side of it was. What remained inside would never really go away.

'So why here? Why so far away?' Colin asked.

Hunter shrugged. 'Obvious isn't it? We didn't want to embarrass you by being too close and nicking all of your punters!'

Tori laughed, but everyone knew that wasn't the real reason. Hunter more than most needed to start afresh. How could he remain somewhere and attempt to pick up the pieces whilst being constantly reminded of what had happened to Noel and the other Reapers? The answer was, he couldn't. And she hadn't minded either. It was the best thing for her too. That town had only ever held bad memories – apart from one: *Hunter*. Wherever he went, she would follow. He was her life and she'd have never got through this without him.

Despite promising herself she wouldn't let anything get to her this weekend, overwhelming emotions flooded her and her eyes filled up with tears.

'And you can stop that right now!' Sarah nudged Tori gently. 'We don't want any unhappiness. Not *this* weekend,'

Tori smiled through the brimming tears. 'I'm just overwhelmed. I feel so blessed. It's so nice to see you and things… things are so good. They're so good, I'm afraid I'm dreaming.'

'She on her monthlies?' Colin whispered to Hunter with a wink.

Sarah elbowed Colin good-naturedly. 'You can shut up as well. You chauvinistic pig! What the hell would you know?'

Tori laughed, before her face fell slightly. 'I wish Carmen was here though.'

Sarah pulled a face. 'I know. I'd love to see her too, but it's just bad timing, what with her planned opening. She'll make it up to you, I'm sure.'

Tori nodded. 'She was as gutted for this to fall on the same weekend. Do you know she even said she'd delay the opening, but I wouldn't hear of it.'

'I wonder how she's coping with Susan?' Colin laughed. 'I can just imagine Susan mithering all the customers. I bet she'll be flapping, pulling faces and making unhelpful comments over every single thing in there!'

Tori giggled. It was true. Trying to imagine Susan not being aghast with some of the couture creations inspired by the Paris catwalk was difficult, but from what Carmen had said, her mother wasn't doing too badly. 'Carmen's got a full house for the official opening of the boutique tomorrow, including some well-known designers, so she's very pleased. It's so exciting and I'm over the moon that she's finally doing something she's always wanted.'

Tori smiled. Carmen had always had a love for fashion and now, not having to play the dutiful wife, she could follow her dreams. There was no way she could blame Carmen for wanting to go back to France. It would be horrible having to remain somewhere where it was common knowledge exactly what her father had done in addition to the theft and fraud from the bank.

The same for Susan, but Carmen also had the additional need to remove herself from the haunting memory of Noel. Tori shuddered, not thinking that would ever go away, but at least this way she had something else. Something she loved to concentrate on and that was good.

Personally, she'd have loved Carmen to remain in England so they could still see each other regularly, but it was the right thing to do. She hadn't moved back to the chateau that she'd lived in with that awful man, but she knew France and she'd always liked it. The money she'd received from the sale of the chateau had enabled her to purchase a beautiful boutique on one of the best and most eclectic streets in Paris' shopping district outright and the money Susan got from her house sale ensured the purchase of a magnificent vinery along with a beautiful home – not in Paris, but in a lovely little village several miles away from the capital. Close enough to enable easy access into Paris for the boutique, but enabling country life without the bustle of the city.

Tori had pored over the photos Carmen had posted. It looked just wonderful and hoped maybe one day they'd be able to go and visit her there.

'Unfortunately, Lillian can't make it tomorrow,' Hunter said suddenly, his eyes sparkling with mischief.

Tori's mouth dropped open. 'I can't believe you've just mentioned that woman!'

'Please tell me you didn't invite *her*?' Sarah gasped.

'Of course not!' Tori cried. 'I don't want her near me or any of us ever again!'

Hunter wrapped his arm around Tori and pulled her sideways, kissing her on the top of the head. 'Sorry, babe. I couldn't resist that one. I wanted to see their faces.'

'It's hardly like she'd be able to come anyway!' Colin grinned. 'Not unless she's added escaping prison to her repertoire!'

Relaxing, Tori laughed. She really must remember not to take things too seriously. These days, most of the time she could manage it, but sometimes and on certain subjects, she still struggled. Her mother being one of them.

'I know it's wrong, but I really did laugh when I saw in the paper that she'd been arrested,' Sarah added, a twinkle in her eye. 'I can just imagine her glee finding Richard up for fraud and then dead, then her abject horror when she got arrested – her blackmail exploits plastered over the paper for all to see.'

She chuckled, then stopped, belatedly realising mentioning Richard Stevens wasn't the best idea. There were some things that could never be anything but raw. 'Sorry,' she muttered. 'I shouldn't have mentioned him, I…'

'It doesn't matter,' Tori interrupted. 'You're right. She'd have been horrified, but it serves her bloody right. She'd been blackmailing that bastard for years and thought she'd won, obviously.' She also had been secretly more than pleased seeing the statement in the paper that it had been her mother who had instigated the events leading to the bank investigation on Richard in the first place, but she clearly hadn't counted on him safeguarding a document which the police found whilst turning over his house for evidence, logging every single time and instance that she'd blackmailed him and exactly how much money she'd been paid for her troubles.

'She's far from won now. Tell us how long she got in the end again?' Hunter asked, still pleased that the spiteful old bitch had finally received her comeuppance. 'I like hearing this!'

'I didn't take too much notice of following the story at the time,' Tori lied, having followed it intensely. She wanted to know how long she could relax without the risk of her poisonous mother ever descending on her. 'She got two years.'

'Shame…' Sarah said sarcastically, a smile twitching at the corner of her mouth.

Wishing to get off the subject, Tori rose to her feet. 'Shall we go down to the bar? We can have another drink and you can have a proper look around.'

'I'd love to,' Colin said. 'No getting drunk for you tonight though, Hunter.'

'Nope, not for me. I don't want to be hungover when I marry this gorgeous woman of mine tomorrow,' Hunter said, getting up and wrapping his big arms around Tori.

'*None* of us will be getting drunk!' Sarah laughed. 'I've waited *far* too long to see this to risk any memories being dulled by headache tablets!' She raised her eyebrows at Tori. 'Are you *sure* you won't give me a sneak preview of your dress?'

'As you know it's at registry office, so the dress isn't fancy, but no – you're not seeing it until tomorrow.'

'You'll look stunning in whatever you wear - even a bin bag,' Hunter muttered, his lips grazing down Tori's neck.

Tori gazed up at Hunter, her love for him crushing. Everything was working out and she even felt she'd been able to finally put the chapter on her father to rest by Richard Stevens' exposure and demise giving her the comfort. The unfairness of her father's situation had finally been somewhat absolved.

Hunter gently traced his finger down her cheek and brushed his lips on hers and Tori melted into him. She still frightened about the future and the burgeoning next big milestone not too far ahead in their lives, especially after what had happened to Andrew, but she was excited and happy. *Very* happy.

'Oh, give it a rest you two lovebirds, for Christ's sake!' Sarah cried. 'Thought we were supposed to be having a tour of your pub!'

Unable to help himself, even though they'd agreed to wait until dinner before breaking the news, Hunter's large hand moved to Tori's stomach, his fingers splaying over the small, yet now visible bump under her dress and his eyes sparkled.

'Wait a minute...' Sarah cried, her eyes honing in on the shape she could see outlined. 'Are you telling me...? You're not...? Are you...?' Seeing Tori beam widely, Sarah squealed, rushing forwards to hug both her and Hunter. 'Oh my God! This is the best news *ever*!'

'Congratulations!' Colin said, his smile wide.

Sarah hopped from foot to foot. 'How far... When's it due? Oh, I can't believe it! This is *fantastic*!'

Hunter's hands smoothed the fabric down further over Tori's bump. Although not yet big, his baby was growing steadily and every day he cherished the sight of his wife-to-be's slowly expanding waistline more and more. 'Four months along now. And I've never been happier!' he said, his grey eyes shining with love.

He could look at Tori for hours. He wasn't missing a *second* this time around. He could look at her for the rest of his life and he intended to do just that.

THANK YOU!

Thank you for reading *The Target of Lies*. I hope you enjoyed reading it as much as I did writing it!

If so, would you please consider leaving a review on Amazon and/or Goodreads.

Reviews from readers are SOOOO helpful and especially important to us authors and without you we would have nobody to write for!

Thank you once again and hope you enjoy the rest of my books.

Edie xx

MORE FROM THIS SERIES

HUNTED SERIES:

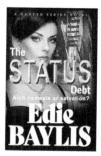

#1: THE STATUS DEBT

Lillian Morgan would do anything to regain the status she lost by marrying beneath her and to cover the sordid details of her husband's death. This includes blackmail and the hand of marriage of her own daughter.

Tori thought her life couldn't get much worse, but someone is not being honest and secrets have the power to rip everyone to shreds.

Especially when life is built on lies.

#2: THE FAMILY LEGACY

Unsure of whether Matt or Hunter has fathered the child growing inside her, Tori's unwanted wedding to Matt grows closer, but is there light at the end of the tunnel? Unfortunately, Tori hasn't counted on another man present in her life. One who is more instrumental in her misery than she realises.

Sometimes the truth is too late in coming and makes bad things happen and sometimes a hidden legacy can cause the most horrific thing of all…

MORE FROM THIS AUTHOR

RETRIBUTION SERIES:

#1: AN OLD SCORE

Three families... One prize...
Teagan Fraser had no idea what she was getting herself into when she took on an assignment as a live-in carer for Dulcie Adams – a retired dancer from a Soho club. Dulcie has waited forty years for a time that never came and left looking after something important, which Jonah Powell and his firm want back.

A lot can happen in the space of two weeks and Teagan might wish she'd never become involved.

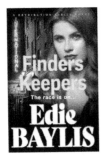

#2: FINDERS KEEPERS

The race is on...
When Saul Powell is released early from prison, it causes mayhem for the family firm. His brother, Jonah, has enough problems trying to keep semblance amidst the chaos, not to mention his fast approaching unwanted marriage.

Teagan Fraser is also facing a dilemma – one which could ruin her life completely. Can anyone come out of this nightmare unscathed?

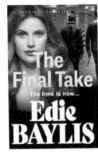

#3: THE FINAL TAKE

The time is now...
Even knowing Ron O'Hara is somewhere in the vicinity, Jonah Powell feels it's time to finally get rid of the diamonds which have haunted his family for decades and caused so much trouble.

However, other problems start to arrive from unexpected and additional sources, some of which Jonah didn't expect.

But what does it all mean? It may be apt to call time on the curse plaguing his family and of those around him, but how can this be achieved while so many other things are at stake?

MORE FROM THIS AUTHOR

ALLEGIANCE SERIES:

#1: TAKEOVER

Samantha Reynold hadn't bargained on unexpectedly needing to step into her father's shoes and take over the family casino business and known nothing about the rules of this glamorous but deadly new world. But she won't let her family down, especially when it looks like they could lose everything to their biggest rivals – the Stoker family.

Eldest son Sebastian hasn't got time to pander to pretty girl Samantha as she plays at being boss. Rumours are swirling around the streets of Birmingham that have the power to rip the Stoker family apart and destroy everything they've built.

#2: FALLOUT

With the odds stacked against her, Samantha Reynold is determined to prove she's tough enough to be the boss. But when a secret from the past threatens to ruin Sam's reputation, she suddenly feels very alone in this dark new world. There's only one man she can turn to – rival club owner, Sebastian Stoker.

Seb knows first-hand how secrets and lies can tear a family apart. He wants to protect Sam at all costs, but siding with her could threaten his own position as head of the Stoker family and risk accusations of betrayal.

With loyalties divided and two families at war – the fallout could be deadly.

#3: VENDETTA

Once bitter enemies, Samantha Reynold and Seb Stoker's powerful alliance enables their firms and casinos to go from strength to strength. With the families no longer in opposition, it seems that Sam and Seb are untouchable…

But not everyone is happy with the new power couple of the club world.

Unbeknownst to everyone, someone new wants to see Sam's perfect life ruined. And they will stop at nothing to seek their revenge – even if it means destroying everything - and everyone - in their path.

MORE FROM THIS AUTHOR

DOWNFALL SERIES:

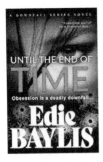

#1 - UNTIL THE END OF TIME

Dive into Seth and Jane's train wreck of a life, where drugs, alcohol and obsessional love means this downright dangerous pair will do *anything* to ensure nothing gets in their way.

They do bad things. *Very* bad things and their promise to love each until the end of time turns into a war against each other.

A war neither of them can win.

#2 - ESCAPING THE PAST

Things have changed and Jane has got on with her life.

Well, not *entirely*…

Embroiled in a bitter feud between two rival firms, it is clear that not everyone is who they proclaim to be.

The net is closing in and some things just can't be changed.

#3 - VENGEFUL PAYBACK

There is something missing. Something *very* important and no one is above suspicion.

Past vendettas are gaining pace and it is vital that whoever is behind this never-ending stream of cleverly engineered payback is discovered before it is too late and everything held dear is ripped apart.

** This series contains written depictions of graphic violence, sex and strong language. It also contains some themes that may be uncomfortable for certain readers. **

ABOUT THE AUTHOR

Over the years Edie has worked all over the UK as well as in several other countries and has met a lot of interesting people - several of whom have supplied ideas for some of the characters in her books! She has now settled back in central England with her partner and children, where she is pursuing writing her gritty gangland and urban fiction novels.

Edie is currently signed to Boldwood Books for a 5-book gangland fiction series set in Birmingham. The first three in the *Allegiance* series, *Takeover*, *Fallout* and *Vendetta* have been released and the fourth in the series, *Payback*, is due to be released in January 2023. She is also concurrently writing the *Scarred* series - the first titled, *Mirrors Never Lie*.

Edie's other series are the *Retribution* series, the *Hunted* series and the *Downfall* series - all trilogies.

When she isn't writing, Edie enjoys reading and is a self-confessed book hoarder. She also enjoys crochet and music as well as loving anything quirky or unusual.

Visit www.ediebaylis.co.uk for the latest news, information about new releases, giveaways and to subscribe to her mailing list.

CWA MEMBER

CONNECT WITH EDIE

https://fb.me/downfallseries

https://www.goodreads.com/author/show/17153586.Edie_Baylis

https://twitter.com/ediebaylis

https://www.amazon.co.uk/Edie-Baylis/e/B075FQHWCZ/

https://www.bookbub.com/authors/edie-baylis

https://ediebaylis.co.uk/

info@ediebaylis.co.uk

https://www.fantasticfiction.com/b/edie-baylis/

https://www.instagram.com/ediebaylis/

https://www.tiktok.com/@edie747

https://www.pinterest.co.uk/ediebaylis/

JOIN EDIE'S MAILING LIST

Subscribe to Edie's mailing list for the latest news on her books, special offers, new releases and competitions.

https://ediebaylis.co.uk/signup.html

Edie Baylis

gangland | crime | urban

THRILLER AUTHOR

ACKNOWLEDGEMENTS

Thanks to the people that kindly read my drafts of *The Target of Lies* – you know who you are and I appreciate your time and feedback.

Printed in Great Britain
by Amazon

24468144R00229